OUT FOR REVENGE!

In the rearview mirror Scorch saw the guard draw his revolver as streaming mourners scattered, giving him a clear shot.

He aimed and she accelerated, taking the corner on two wheels, tires screeching, as she tensed for that terminal flash from a brain-shattering bullet. When it didn't come, she fought the car as it fish-tailed, slowing until she got a feel for its steering. Minutes later, satisfied she was clear, she pulled over until her hands stopped shaking enough to clip on her seat belt. Never let it be said Scorch Amerce wasn't law-abiding.

Free! She smacked the steering wheel. *Yes!*

Keeping to side streets, ones less likely to be patrolled once they reported the car stolen, Scorch considered her future.

It wasn't as if she had a home or family to return to.

So, time for payback. She headed for the White Plains bus to root out Marie before she heard Scorch was hunting again. . . .

JOEL ROSS

EYE FOR AN EYE

LEISURE BOOKS NEW YORK CITY

LEISURE BOOKS ®

May 2004

Published by

Dorchester Publishing Co., Inc.
200 Madison Avenue
New York, NY 10016

ISBN 0-8439-5338-1

The name "Leisure Books" and the stylized "L" with design are trademarks of Dorchester Publishing Co., Inc.

Printed in the United States of America.

Visit us on the web at www.dorchesterpub.com.

Thanks isn't a strong enough word, but I'll try anyway.

First, this novel is dedicated to the memory of:

My father, though he's been dead nearly forty years, his lessons as a photographer and an observer of the human condition taught me to find the beauty in almost anything.

Greg Hines and O'Sensei Antonio Pereria, who both used the dojo to instill and reinforce the lesson: "Never give up! Ever!"

Of course, there's editor Don D'Auria, who may have overheard my father and saw merit in a story it took five years to pour forth.

I also appreciate the efforts of various Capital Region writers who listened patiently week after week as I wove a tale of a world as harsh and alien as the dark side of the moon, but which existed for millennia and will continue to do so.

I am grateful to those horror and suspense writers I met over the years who encouraged me or, conversely, told me to give up, which only made me madder and more determined. They know who they are. Keep it up.

DISCLAIMER

Note: The corrections systems of this country are continually evolving, especially New York State's, whose avowed goal is to be the best in the world. When this book was written no one resembling any of its characters was working for the department or was incarcerated in any of its seventy-one facilities. Thus any similarity or resemblance to anyone currently in one of its penitentiaries is purely coincidental.

In the interest of security some details or procedures have been omitted or left vague. Rest assured not everything is as presented on television or in the movies. It certainly isn't as glamorous. The people who are there are there because for the most part they want to be. If it were an easy job, anyone could do it.

EYE FOR AN EYE

"A wounded rescuer saves no one."
　　　　　　　　　　—Old Yiddish saying

"Living well is the best revenge."
　　　　　　　　　　—Spanish proverb

Prologue

June 20
Eight Years Ago

How long can a petrified fifteen-year-old kneel at her murdered sister's grave after her funeral? You stay until you run out of tears and the cemetery staff locks up for the night.

Trudging home, you think of Nancy writhing on the filthy concrete, clutching at you as if to hold on to life itself, as you clamp small palms over her gaping wounds, unable to stanch the flow even for an instant. Who knew a person could bleed so much?

What hellhole will the social worker dump you into? Will you have the strength to get the cops to renew their half-hearted efforts to find Nancy's killers? Arriving home, you find the door bashed in, your apartment trashed, everything shattered into the same state of ruin as the rest of your life.

When you race to the precinct, the sergeant sighs. "Back again, Suzanne? No witnesses this time either, no leads for us to go on? Sounds like just a burglary, so we can't give you any protection. Ask Social Services to place you. Have a nice day."

You slink out into the muggy night, flinching at shadows, knowing if the Tigresses don't find you today, they'll get you tomorrow, or the next day. Then you spot an empty wine bottle in the gutter and siphon off a quart of high-octane into it. Later you steal a bat from a bike, pound rusty nails into it with a bent tire iron, bum some matches, then grab the youngest Tigress, a kid your age, and wring enough information from her to get the others.

You wait until three A.M., that unholy hour when no good can happen. Then, the sweat dripping off you, you dial 911 so innocents don't die along with the Tigresses. "Fire! Basement of 1972 Morris Avenue!" you shout before sprinting to the gang's lair, your Point of No Return. You hesitate, but it's them or you, and they've already made the choice. So you scratch match against striker and with a stink of sulfur light the rag stuffed in the firebomb's mouth and heave it through the open window. The humid stillness is broken by the tinkle of shattered glass, then by their screams as you wait at their door, spiked bat on your shoulder.

The first one stumbles out naked, coughing, groping.

You give a home-run swing to her legs, like the Romans did to Jesus on Calvary. She shrieks and falls, another girl topples onto her, and you flail at them both, yelling, "That's for Nancy! That's for Nancy! And that's for Nancy!" until your throat is raw.

A third girl staggers out, choking, and you smash her, too, until your arms ache, but you keep pounding until the bat splits, then you pull the tire iron from your belt and hit and hit until the next thing you recall is dashing from the wail of sirens.

Only three down. Seven Tigresses had butchered Nancy.

You race all night, knowing the next four will be harder to get. So what? Your life is over, just like Nancy's, because in that moment of terror and rage you crossed the line, so you might as well finish the job and leave the world a better place.

So you run and hide for the few hours or days you have left.

Chapter One

Saturday, June 1
The Present

Enough already. Twenty-three-year-old Suzanne "Scorch" Amerce was doing it to herself again, replaying the psychic tape of that torrid Bronx night when she flushed her life. She did it whenever she lay on her lumpy bed and blew smoke rings at the smudged spot on the puke-yellow ceiling of her cell.

How could she help doing it, still hearing those girls' screams, night after night for eight years?

At least it took her mind off attending her mother's funeral. Due to be released today, after serving two months in solitary for promoting contraband, Scorch trudged to the rec room to kill time with Karen and the others until the memorial service. Two steps inside and she realized the politics of the prison had changed while she had been "keeplocked."

Time might not be the only thing killed this afternoon.

Fewer inmates clustered around Karen as she lounged by the stereo dispensing cigarettes. Meanwhile, Barb and Iris roosted in the corner, surrounded by lots of fellow leeches eager for drugs or protection. The shift in the balance of power suggested her next dozen years here would be more hellish than the past eight.

Everyone stared first at her, then at Barb and Iris, who drew fingers across their throats when Scorch made eye contact with them. To compound the problem, one of today's officers was a trainee from upstate New York, unaware that covering this group was like being shoved into a sackful of cats. Yeah, the rookie didn't have the niceties down yet, the swagger, the callousness from a decade's worth of burnout. If one dared close their eyes and judge only by the clack of mah-jongg tiles and the pop of Ping-Pong balls, one might think this was just like home—if home meant stale cigarettes, wasted lives, and chronic fear.

Scorch bound her hair into a long ponytail as conversations around her died a little at a time.

"Look, gang," Karen said as she slipped Scorch a pack of Camels and matches. "Little Scorch is back." Karen leaned closer. "Watch yourself, college girl. Barb told everyone she'll kick your butt today, and those aren't dancing shoes she got on. Plus, she brought Iris along, just to make sure."

Scorch lit up before her hands trembled too much. "Fight or flight," Dr. Glass called it, and her legs were much too short for running. Yes, they knew how to light her fuse, and she always accommodated by supplying the spark. Barb and Iris ambled toward Scorch as the others backed away, leaving her alone to pick through dog-eared magazines. Barb's toadies moved between Scorch and the officers, distracting them with chatter.

This was it, predator and prey, comparing dinner plans.

"If she don't leave now," Barb rasped in her three-pack-a-day voice as she pointed to Scorch, "we'll just dice her up."

Really. As if any of Barb's plans ever worked. So the first

problem on today's pop quiz was how to subtract two lifers from general population and still have Scorch Amerce left over. The trouble was, Barb and Iris had been abused spouses on the outside, their brain chemistries jumbled by too many shots to their craniums, making them unpredictable and doubly dangerous.

"Hey, Scorch, you got a problem?" Barb asked.

"Me? Never," said Scorch, her cigarette dangling from her mouth as she strained to roll the thickest magazine into a tight tube. Would Karen watch her back?

"You want one? If not, take a hike and don't come back."

"I'm hoping you'll cut me some slack," Scorch said.

"Only thing cut will be your wrists again," said Iris as she shuffled to Scorch's right.

"Yes, ma'am," Scorch said. She curtsied, then blew smoke into Iris's face. As the larger woman blinked and coughed, Scorch rammed the end of the magazine into her solar plexus.

Iris doubled up and slid down the wall as Barb ran up, arms flailing, long nails aimed at Scorch's eyes.

Scorch feinted at Barb's stomach, then shot the magazine into Barb's jaw, her teeth clicking together, ensuring a real problem for the prison dentist come Monday.

Barb's buddies moved in, surrounding Scorch.

Whistles blew, gates clanged open, and keys jingled as more officers charged in, inmates parting for them like tender flesh under a butcher's knife. "What happened?" asked the sergeant.

"Slipped," said Barb as she clawed herself upright.

"Right," said Scorch. "Slipped while dancing."

The sarge rolled her eyes. "Right. So how come she's got a fat lip?"

Scorch grinned. "It matches the rest of her face, or is that her butt?"

The sarge turned to the rookie. "See anything?" she asked.

The rookie shook her head.

"Why aren't I surprised?" the sarge said. She tapped her watch crystal. "Four o'clock, Amerce. You ready?"

"All set," Scorch said.

"You going to your mother's funeral dressed like that?"

Scorch looked at the scarlet T-shirt worn over her green prison pants. "What? I'm naked? Sorry, but my furs are in cold storage and my gowns are at the cleaners."

As they escorted Scorch away, Karen reached out so Scorch could caress her fingertips. Barb spat at her, and Iris gave her the finger. Imagine, holding grudges all these years. Yes, Scorch understood that all too well. She blew them kisses.

Fielder, tonight's escort officer, slouched at the front gate with a portable metal detector and smirked as he passed it over Scorch's body. "You going out dressed like that?" he said.

"We've been through that already," she said. "You looking to do a cavity search, or will a strip frisk satisfy you?"

"You just did two months for smuggling," Fielder said, and pointed to the pack in her pocket. "Hand it over and say 'ah.'"

"I was set up," said Scorch as she surrendered her Camels and matches, stuck out her tongue, and rolled it around her lips.

"That's enough," the sarge said. "Chain her up, move her out."

They snapped their smallest cuffs onto her wrists, then shackled her ankles.

Things weren't all bleak. "Flatline" Fielder, lover of junk food, pro wrestling, and mooched cigarettes, was working a double shift, and neither stamina nor brains was his strong suit. As a bonus on this long Memorial Day weekend, the shorthanded watch commander needed to pair him with a woman officer, and the only one to spare was that upstate trainee. Fielder had already handed her the keys to Scorch's restraints. As they hustled Scorch to the prison station wagon, she recalled Dr. Glass saying that the Chinese words for crisis and opportunity were the same.

The vehicle, out in the sun all day, was comfortable as a blast furnace and reeked of discarded Chinese takeout, hamburgers, and fries. That, coupled with Fielder's company, should make this a delightful forty-minute trip. As they drove off, Scorch twisted around in the caged-in rear for her first glimpse of the outside of Midland Knolls Correctional in eight years. As the sun glinted off the razor wire, she wondered if she would be a withered, silver-haired crone the next time she saw these walls from this side, if indeed she ever got out again.

She might not get another chance this good until her first parole hearing, twelve years from now.

They should have written "Abandon Hope, All Who Enter Here," or "Arbeit Mach Frei"—Work Makes Freedom—what Dr. Glass said was inscribed over the entrance to the Auschwitz concentration camp.

The rookie, so new her shoes still shone, drove as Fielder sprawled in the passenger seat, two weak links comprising the chain holding her. "Why do they call her Scorch?" she asked.

Fielder's laugh was liquid and guttural. He leaned out and coughed up something resembling an undercooked egg. "Most jailhouse names don't mean anything, but with her, it's perfect."

Scorch needed to derail his train of thought, fast, before the trainee learned the sort of person she was escorting. "It's hot," she said as sweat trickled down her back. "I need a drink."

"Sure. You want Scotch?" asked Fielder. "Champagne? Coke?"

"Anything cool," Scorch said. "We don't want the warden

to hear you let a prisoner dehydrate, do we?"

He sighed as he poured ice water from a thermos and passed a paper cup back through the cage's window. She sipped and smacked her lips. "Thanks," she said. "Just what I needed."

Fielder looked at the thermos and poured himself a drink.

"Have more," Scorch said. "Muscular men need a lot."

A sign read "White Plains, 10 miles." The number 20 bus ran from there to the Bronx, and then a simple subway ride got you to Manhattan. The word was Marie had woven a new web down there and hatched out a kid. If so, payback could be doubly sweet.

Scorch studied how the rookie handled the car as Fielder drained the thermos. Glancing down, Scorch saw mustard packets on the floor. A godsend, or a gift from the opposite end of the spiritual spectrum? When the guards weren't looking, Scorch lifted the packets with her sneakers, palmed them, and slipped them into her pocket as they pulled into the funeral home's parking lot.

They ushered her into a cool, dim lobby scented with perfume and Glade as muted organ music piped in. As sweat cooled on her, Scorch's mind raced. Across the hall, another memorial service was about to begin. Whoever lay in that casket was as well-liked as Scorch's mother had been unpopular, with a spill-over of red-eyed friends and family in the hall. Most looked away as Scorch shuffled in with the six-inch chain rattling between her ankles.

Too bad she hadn't been born into that family.

The rest rooms were discreetly placed down the hall. Good.

Her mother's coffin, a cheap job supplied by her latest alcohol-rehab clinic, was open and it was obvious her morticians were artists. The witch looked far better in death than in life, a drunken sot who delighted in tormenting her younger daughter.

Scorch hobbled to a water cooler to pour herself another round, then handed cups to the officers. "Ah!" she said, wiping her mouth. "Refreshing." They all had another drink.

Through the open door Scorch saw those other mourners file into the larger room. After sniffling a while, Scorch went to her mother's casket to commune with the ripe corpse inside. In the other room, the murmur of conversation died and only one voice was speaking. Good, eulogies last maybe ten minutes. Just enough.

Scorch crossed herself, her cuffs clinking, before laying her hands and forehead on the pine casket. "Mama dearest," she whispered as she glared at that hateful face. "I'm the last Amerce. Remember that as you broil in hell." Behind her she imagined Fielder snickering while the rookie stared at those shiny new shoes, uncertain whether to be solemn or embarrassed.

Scorch's fingertips tingled as she visualized her moves and calculated the distance from the hall bathroom to the parking lot. How great a head start would she need to outrace a forty-year-old man with a belly deserving of its own zip code and an upstate girl who had probably attended a one-room schoolhouse?

"C'mon, Scorch," said Fielder. "Say your good-byes and let's get going."

"Just a moment more, please," she said. The people next door were still listening to the praises of their lately departed and wouldn't be milling around for another few minutes.

"Whatever," said Fielder. "We're earning time and a half baby-sitting you here." An armchair creaked as he plopped down and settled in, content as long as he could get back in time to watch the Yankees or Hulk Hogan.

A louder voice spoke in the next room. Preacher perhaps. Good, they'd be wrapping up soon.

"Let's go, Scorch," Fielder said. "She never visited you, so

I doubt you got much more to say. Actually, you had no visitors in eight years. Right, Scorch?"

"Yes, boss." She stood. "Got to go to the bathroom first."

"Christ," said Fielder. "What next?"

"It's a long trip back," Scorch said, bouncing from foot to foot.

"All right." He nodded toward the ladies' room, and the rookie led Scorch in as Fielder took up his position outside.

"Wanna go first?" she asked the rookie.

"Later."

"Lots of us get urinary-tract infections from few bathroom breaks. Rumor is the prison doctor did his internship at Devil's Island. Uh . . ." She gave her most sheepish look while pointing to the fetter chafing her ankles. "Can't go with these on."

The young officer looked at the steel links, then to the door where her partner waited outside.

"C'mon," said Scorch, accelerating her hopping dance as if her bladder were seconds away from bursting. "Please!"

As the chain jangled the rookie glanced around, as if the solution were scrawled on a wall. "I don't think . . ."

"You want me to tinkle on this chain? If it rusts out they'll deduct it from your pay, plus you'll go through your career known as somebody who let an inmate wet her shackles."

The young woman looked pained.

"You know how cruel people can be," Scorch said. "C'mon."

The rookie bent over, exposing the back of her neck, proving she hadn't been interviewed and hired by Dr. Glass. The locks popped open. Ah, freed of five pounds of clanking hardware.

Scorch sat in the farthest stall and relieved herself. "It sure is hot for late spring, isn't it?" she said to cover the sound of her tearing open the mustard packets.

11

Joel Ross

"Uh-huh," said the rookie. "Let's go."

Scorch came out with the mustard back in her pocket as she went to the sink to wash up.

"Let's go," said the officer.

"Just a little more. It's torrid out there. Too bad they don't think enough of you to provide air-conditioned cars." Scorch patted more cold water on her face to wash the sweat bubbling from her as she anticipated her next move.

Fielder rapped on the door and opened it a few inches, letting in the sound of the other mourners stirring. "Not done yet?" he asked. "Got to go myself now. Cuff her to the handicapped toilet's railing meantime." He shambled to the men's room as Scorch prepared to go to plan B and get physical, but could she hurt somebody who hadn't tried to hurt her first?

"Don't feel so good," Scorch said. "Dizzy."

The rookie led her to the handicapped stall. "Sit on the john for few minutes and you'll be okay."

"Gonna faint," said Scorch as the rookie unlocked one cuff.

"Wait," said the rookie.

Wait to faint? What idiots were they hiring these days?

As the rookie turned to clamp the open cuff to the rail Scorch collapsed onto the cool tile floor, the sudden shift of her hundred pounds wrenching the cuff from the officer.

Scorch rolled away, retched, and pulled out the mustard.

Outside, the mourners began leaving for the cemetery.

When the rookie bent over her, Scorch aimed the packets at the woman's face and squeezed a yellow glob into her eyes.

As she yelped Scorch kicked her in the stomach, then sprang up, snatched the keys, and elbowed the rookie in the solar plexus once, twice, again. Again. Make sure. Stop! Enough!

Scorch slammed the doubled-up rookie against the toilet,

12

unlocked her other cuff, and hooked the trainee's arms behind her, cuffing her to the rail. Then she stuffed a wad of toilet paper into the woman's mouth as she gasped for air. "Don't swallow." Scorch said as she yanked off the rookie's skirt.

The woman spit out the toilet paper, but before she could scream an alarm Scorch pushed more into her mouth. Scorch skinned off her green prison pants, pulled on the rookie's navy skirt, and found the car keys and her wallet in her bag.

All set. "Don't be a hero, lady. Just sit quietly."

The other mourners milled about in the hall, preparing to go to the cemetery. Scorch zipped between them, elbowing her way to the head of the pack as Fielder waddled from the men's room, buckling his belt as he headed for the other bathroom. Damn!

Scorch burst into the muggy air, back out into the world.

As she got to the car, she heard Fielder yell, "Stop!"

Yeah, right. And if she didn't . . . ? They had already done their worst, all of them. She rolled up the windows and locked the doors. She hadn't been behind a wheel since Nancy's boyfriend had given her lessons when she was fifteen, but she had watched the rookie. She started up, slammed the gearshift into Drive, and hit the gas. The car lurched and stalled. She twisted the key again and an idiot light flashed: PARKING BRAKE ON.

Fielder ran up, using his cuffs like brass knuckles to smack the window, creating a spider's web of cracks as Scorch released the brake and the car shot forward, tires squealing.

In the rearview mirror she saw him draw his revolver as streaming mourners scattered, giving him a clear shot.

He aimed and she accelerated, taking the corner on two wheels, tires screeching, as she tensed for that terminal flash from a brain-shattering bullet. When it didn't come, she fought the car as it fishtailed, slowing until she got a feel for its steering. Minutes later, satisfied she was clear, she pulled over until her hands stopped shaking enough to clip on her seat belt. Let it never be said Scorch Amerce wasn't law-abiding. It would be so dumb to get pulled over on a routine traffic stop, and while she had been accused—and convicted—of many things, stupidity wasn't among them. She rolled down the window, its cracks another reason to be asked for license and registration.

Free! She smacked the steering wheel. YES!

The rookie's wallet held ninety bucks and a credit card. Keeping to side streets, ones less likely to be patrolled once they reported the car stolen, Scorch considered her future. She could cruise until the money and gas ran out or the cops did a routine check on a corrections vehicle with out-of-state plates, discovered it stolen, and dragged her back.

It wasn't as if she had a home or family to return to.

So, time for payback. She headed for the White Plains bus, to root out Marie before she heard Scorch was hunting again.

This time she wouldn't let mercy or decency get in her way.

Chapter Two

Dr. Eric Glass paused inside the front gate as it clanged shut. Something was out of sync today, even more than usual for a Monday morning, like slightly altered lyrics to a favorite old song. When he saw those two men in polyester suits handing over their side arms to the arsenal officer, he knew what was wrong.

"Inspector General's boys, huh?" he said to the key room officer. She nodded as she slid his prison keys out to him from beneath the bulletproof glass.

Uh-oh, a "UI." Somebody was in for it today, big time. When Eric stopped by the watch commander's office to peek into the Unusual Incidents log, a sergeant glared at him, displaced anger at its most primitive. Eric checked the latest entries.

There, for this past Saturday night:

Amerce, Suzanne Rene, 88 G 1666: Escaped while on "out-count" from Eastman's Funeral Home.

Suzanne escaped! And it was too late to call in sick.

He dropped into a chair and reread the entry, as if it might change if he stared long enough.

Then voices came from the corridor, growing louder. "What were you thinking, sending a jerk out with a rookie? You considering a career change?" The new deputy superintendent for security tromped in, the captain and a lieutenant in tow. The lieutenant, her face red as a Santa Claus suit, must have been watch commander Saturday night and was paying for it now. The dep snatched the UI log from Eric and waved it. "The first escape New York Corrections had in five years, the first ever from this facility. And not just any inmate. Scorch!"

Here a month and already the dep knew Suzanne's moniker.

The sergeant slipped away and Eric stood, ready to follow. The captain drifted to the corner, out of the line of fire as the lieutenant pointed to Eric. "Scorch was his patient," she said. "Why didn't he know something?"

"Ah," said Eric. "Breakfast time at the Donner Pass."

The captain noticed Eric. "Yeah, Glass. You're supposed to be the 'answer man.' She give any clue she was plotting this?"

"Hardly," Eric said. "She'd just learned her mother died after a drinking binge while taking a carload of medications." Would he be spared from the microscope the IG's people were sure to train on this incident? The room became too small, too warm. They stood looking at each other like a bridge foursome without a deck. Then walkie-talkies squawked codes with the clarity of a fast-food restaurant's drive-in window speaker, breaking the spell.

The captain pointed to the door. "See you later, Dr. Glass."

All too soon, probably. The captain, also new and insecure as one of the highest-ranking men in a women's prison, might—like a fine wine—improve with age.

Stranger things happened. Trudging to his office, Eric almost cut in front of a column of inmates. Not only would that interfere with the hall officer's head count, it was unhealthy to disappear in a sea of inmate green and tick off someone with a sliver of plastic in her hand and angry voices in her head.

The inmates were noisier than usual, probably savoring the news of the escape. One winked at him. The faded name on her shirt read "Rainey." Sure, Karen Rainey, Suzanne's "big sister."

Unlike male convicts, women prisoners clustered for support and encouragement in pseudofamilies. Karen Rainey had adopted Suzanne through blood oath and looked after her, for a price. Rainey knew lots of things, none of which she'd divulge to him or any other man, nor to any woman not in prison green. She gave him the creeps, reminding him of the evil queen in "Snow White."

Eric nodded to her, in no hurry to get to his office since his nine A.M. appointment would be a no-show. He always scheduled Suzanne for a Monday-morning session. Locked in her eight-by-ten tomb for forty-eight hours, she was desperate to ventilate to the first person who would listen, and this was no place to be free with thoughts or feelings.

The air was already sultry. The passageways reeked of discount detergent as apathetic inmate porters pushed dirt around with sour mops that were old when he'd come here ten years ago. Despite lighting which allowed no shadows, these halls were dismal, as if a half-century of despair had permeated its walls. The only energy exhibited here anymore came on payday, or when younger inmates visited their newborn in the nursery.

Everyone was checked out by COs and inmates alike, with everything noticed and usually resented. "Trust no one and you'll never be disappointed" should be the motto here.

The hall officer nodded hello. "Doc, sure I can't persuade you to play right field for us? We need your throwing arm."

"Sorry," Eric said. "My baseball days are history." Yet another of life's simple pleasures wrenched from him. Eric plopped into his office chair, wondering what he could do for Suzanne now. Pray for her? Millions died daily with prayers on their lips, and none of his had been heard in recent years. She had made her choice and taken the plunge, preferring to risk dying quickly rather than rot in this dungeon a day at a time.

He recalled the first time he'd seen her, eight years ago, the prison buzzing with the news that a sixteen-year-old had come straight from Riker's Island, a girl too scary even for a Division for Youth secure facility. He'd ambled down to see for himself and there she was in the corner, a petite brunette whose dark smoldering eyes took in everything but revealed nothing. Then those eyes, large as a doe's, locked onto his like a heat-seeking missile, and in that instant he felt her rage and pain.

The pendulum clock on his wall sounded twice as loud in the unaccustomed quiet as he kindled enough energy to paw through her records. Removing it required two hands; no other folder was more than half an inch thick. He recalled a session years ago with her doing chin-ups on his office window's bars, straining to glimpse the expensive homes beyond the prison. "Jesus was wrong," she'd said. "The meek won't inherit the earth. I'll bet Darwin believed passivity dooms you to extinction. It's got to be better to drown in the ocean than float in the sewer."

So she'd swum for it, leaving him behind.

The Talmud said, "Even in Paradise it was bad to be alone."

He imagined the scene Saturday, her excitement when she sensed the opening, the adrenaline surge as she went for it, heart thumping. Finally, the terror of pursuit, followed by the exhilaration of successful evasion, that rush of danger.

Now she was gone, just like his Debbie.

Whatever turn he took these days left him positive his love of life was unrequited. He was in danger of becoming a paranoid agnostic, no longer certain of the existence of God but sure that some cosmic force out there had it in for him.

Suzanne's file fell apart on his desk. As he reassembled it he reviewed her life, her abortive suicide attempt her first month in general population after being molested by a bunch of sadists, her fights, her depressions every holiday knowing she had no reason to go to the visiting room.

It took a half hour to reread her evolution from raw teen to veteran con as she mastered things one could never learn in books. Then he found the yellowed *New York Post* headline:

HONOR STUDENT EXECUTES SIXTH IN WEST BRONX VENDETTA

Her rap sheet was nearly as long as Michael Jordan's leg. Six counts, murder two. One count, assault with intent. Arson. Enough capital crime for an entire cell block, all from a five-foot, one-hundred-pound teen, one of the first fifteen-year-old girls sentenced as an adult by a society grown terrified of its emotionally mutated offspring. In addition to her GED and bachelor's degree, she had earned a postgraduate education in survival here from Karen Rainey and others with poisoned souls.

Suzanne had been doomed from day one, her jailhouse name already chosen for her, her reputation and crimes preceding her. As he wedged her folder into the Inactive drawer, he wondered what her odds were of surviving the week. With her looks and brain, she might make it if she forgot about revenge.

So many things left unsaid, unlearned . . . Once again wrong in his belief that he had enough time for both of them to heal.

It was three P.M. when Eric got the call from his supervisor, the deputy superintendent for programs. "Glass," the dep said. "I just got a call from 'people in Albany' so high up I get a nosebleed just thinking about them. They expect your assistance regarding the recapture of inmate Amerce, and they don't want to know from therapist–client confidentiality. Counsel's Office wants you to spill your guts."

Great. "Somebody in the corridor might do it for me."

"You worried one of the girls is going to shank you because you're a snitch? I thought you were a jujitsu guy."

"Years ago. It's Tai Chi now." Since five years ago, when he realized he needed self-defense for his soul more than for his body. "What's told to me in private is supposed . . ." Then Eric remembered a landmark case of a quarter-century ago, *Tarasoff vs. the University of California,* which imposed on therapists the "duty to warn" if their patient threatened to harm another.

"Eric, she's an escaped murderess who committed assault, robbery, and grand-theft auto for Saturday-night entertainment, so expect a call from the state police or NYPD soon."

New York? Would she head back there? She had no family or friends left in the city, certainly nobody she would have anything to do with, or vice versa. Unless she was going for Marie? After all this time . . . ? Was Suzanne's hate that strong?

"Eric, you still there? This comes from the top. Cooperate. The commissioner doesn't need any more calls from the attorney general's office this week. Oh, and have a good night."

Maybe Eric could still do something for Suzanne: He could save her life. He stared at the chair, the one she had come to think of as hers. He recalled the first time she'd sat in it, at age sixteen, in pigtails, huddled in the farthest corner with her bandaged wrists across her chest. Over the years she had moved it closer, like a feral beast learning to trust.

Four months ago she had lounged alongside his desk in a miniskirt, legs crossed, just as millimeter by millimeter she had lowered her shields to expose her demons—and show him her soul.

Chapter Three

Monday, June 3

Detective Sergeant Lucy Moreno peeled off the note taped to the mug holding the congealed remnants of Friday evening's coffee. Something about state police in Westchester . . . ? That demanded attention before her first shot of caffeine? Would she need a new excuse to give Tony for not being home by midnight?

The best part of this note was that she could still read it without glasses. Something about somebody escaping prison. Somebody sent up nearly a decade ago. *This* demanded immediate action? It must have been scrawled by someone demonstrating warped humor, or no humor at all.

Then the hard drive inside her skull booted up, the name conjuring up a file—a life. Suzanne Amerce? Amerce . . . Wow, "Scorch," back from the living dead. With a long evening ahead Lucy called Tony, gave him the standard ten-second apology, and endured the usual two-minute ribbing before signing off.

Then she rummaged in a rusting file cabinet to fish out the case that helped her make detective second grade after weeks of prowling alleys in the West Bronx. Scorch, architect of the "Morris Avenue Massacre." That had been before "conservation of energy" became Lucy's theme, when she was still fueled by self-righteousness, still thinking she could make deputy inspector. This was long before the Girl Scout became Wonder Woman, who was fast becoming eligible for early retirement.

Lucy remembered getting the call that night, standing in the drenching humidity of Morris Avenue to glance down at Scorch's first victims, each resembling raw hamburger.

The Scorch child . . . Lucy's ancient chair screeched as she leaned back to recall that olive-skinned, undernourished, underloved waif with large, dark, bloodshot eyes and long, stringy hair. Obsessed little Scorch was twenty-three now, having somehow survived eight years in max.

Lucy glanced at the note again. Scorch hadn't escaped from the prison but instead had outwitted two witless corrections officers in a funeral home Saturday, stealing clothes, a wallet . . . their car! Where had she learned to drive? Well, she had shown her genius on more than one occasion. Where would Scorch go? Where *could* she go? Escapees returned to their roots, but Scorch had none anymore, not since her family of one had been butchered on a filthy sidewalk near Grand Concourse Boulevard.

What was she like after eight years? Lucy swiveled to the computer terminal, her chipped fingernails dancing on the keyboard as she retraced Scorch's steps from Saturday back to her first day in Midland Knolls.

After five minutes she laughed and hollered for her boss, Lieutenant DiGiorio, to okay her strategy. DiGiorio approached and shrugged, his favorite form of exercise these days, as he heard Lucy's plan. "Even if she had a prison shrink, do they have to cooperate with us?"

"That's where you come in, Lieutenant," Lucy said.

"Oh, no." DiGiorio waved his hands as if shooing away

flies. "I'm not getting sucked into one of your holy crusades. I remember the last time."

"Lieutenant." Lucy rose and clapped a tanned hand on her boss's shoulder. "Can't you just see the *Daily News* with this: 'TEEN MASS MURDERER AND FIRE BUG AT LARGE! ARE WE SAFE?' Don't you want NYPD to get the credit for allowing New Yorkers to sleep soundly again?"

DiGiorio twitched Lucy's paw off his arm. "The only way New Yorkers sleep soundly is when they're dead." He took two steps, then did an about-face. "What do you want?"

"A simple call to the Bronx district attorney," she said. "And then maybe one to the attorney general."

"I knew it. A few years before retirement and my puss gets plastered all over the six-o'clock news." He stormed off.

Lucy checked her watch. Five minutes for DiGiorio to see the light and talk to the captain. Five minutes later, after the Cap blew his top, DiGiorio would pick it up, put it back on, and get the Cap to call the D.A. Giving those anal-retentive lawyers a couple hours to agonize over it and the same amount for those people up in Albany . . .

She didn't have much time. . . .

Figuring the logistics, Lucy made sure all paperwork was completed minutes before DiGiorio whistled to her. Kickoff time.

DeSantis waved a piece of paper. "You win, Moreno. Dr. Eric Glass at Midland Knolls was Amerce's psychologist. The attorney general's office called his boss, who assured us Glass will be thrilled to tell you what you need to know. This is his home address and phone number. He should be in this evening."

"You won't regret this, Lieutenant."

"I regret it already. Just keep us off the front page of the *Post,* huh?" He gave her a faxed letter. "Here's something from the D.A. to encourage Glass to pour his heart out to you."

Lucy dialed the psychologist's number, and the answering machine kicked in.

"Hi, you've reached the elusive Dr. Glass. If you're an obsessive-compulsive, hit one, then one again, and again . . ."

A live voice took over. "Hello?"

"Dr. Glass, I'm Detective Moreno of NYPD. I need to—"

"I know. We eat at six. Can we meet before or after?"

"I can be there in a half hour if—"

"Perfect, Detective. I'll talk with you then."

Whatever. Lucy thanked him and skipped to her car, happy as a tyke on Christmas Eve. Why not? Eight years ago, promoted after less than five years in uniform, she was in the Five-Two in the Northwest Bronx, a precinct coveted by veterans marking time until they filed retirement papers. Then the neighborhood deteriorated at a record clip and being assigned up here became more stressful than leaving the Four-One, "Fort Apache." To compound the problem, she had been without a partner for months since her last one had been killed.

Now Scorch had returned, maybe as an omen. Nabbing her back then had jump-started Lucy's career. Perhaps recapturing her would restore the magic.

It took half an hour to drive to Glass's home, a Yonkers loft by the Hudson River, one of those favored by artists in the seventies, then renovated further by the hip set in the eighties and nineties.

Lucy checked herself in the car's mirror. Her makeup hid the fact that she was thirty-five with a rocky home life and a fifty-hour workweek. She unbound her shoulder-length hair, shook it free, and opened the top buttons of her blouse. Glass was a shrink, but he was also a man and might be put off guard by a more feminine and less threatening interrogator. Over the years, she had found that men lost a bit of their reserve when she did this, and that might be all the edge she'd need, or get. Tomorrow he'd be more prone to remember how she looked than what he'd told her.

As she thumbed the bell, a black woman with skin the color of weak tea burst out the door. She wore a Caribbean-style outfit, the dress and kerchief splashed with vivid colors so far beyond loud they were deafening. She glanced at Lucy's ID and shield, clucked her tongue, and called upstairs. "Oh boy, Rick, you in trouble now. Da fuzz here. Run fast and far." She curtsied. "I'm Madam Cassandra. Pleased to meet you. Now go give Dr. Glass what he deserve."

Lucy nodded, smiled, and chugged up to the second floor, smelling garlic and oregano. She walked through the open front door as a man ambled from the kitchen like a jaguar cruising its jungle.

"Eric Glass at your service," he said. "Ready for action."

Behind him a girl worked at the stove, banging pots to the beat of whatever poured from her headphones. The oak dinner table had three chairs but only two places set.

Glass checked Lucy out, as if calculating how hard a time she might give him. Most people she questioned were scared, resentful, or stoned, but this man seemed like he'd relish a contest of wits. In his late thirties and muscular, he looked like an aging athlete with lots of mileage, struggling to hang on. His hazel eyes were red-rimmed, and his wavy hair was graying at the temples. At first Lucy thought Glass had a perpetually furrowed brow, but then realized he had a wide, deep scar running across his forehead. Maybe he *was* an ex-athlete, or just a man who lived dangerously.

A pair of cats sauntered ahead of him, the black one reaching up to dig front claws into Lucy's leg in order to stretch. Lucy avoided it before it shredded her panty hose.

"Achilles, Athena," Glass said. "Come here."

The white one did figure eights against Lucy's legs, shedding. Then, their mischief done, they strutted off.

"They say 'dogs come when you call,' " said Glass. " 'But cats take a message and get back to you.' "

The room was solemn as a buddhist temple, a dozen scented candles competing with cones of incense whose smoke wafted to the high ceiling. Were these rich smells to mask the stink of pot?

No, Glass seemed too focused to be stoned.

"Thanks for seeing me on short notice, Dr. Glass. I'm Detective Lucy Moreno, and I'll keep this short." If not sweet. She hoped not to step on the cats in a room lit only by those flickering red candles. The oak coffee table was covered with fortune-telling cards. Had she come in the middle of a séance, perhaps? "Am I interrupting anything?" she asked.

"No, we just finished," he said as he gathered up the tarot cards and slotted them together before assuming the pose of a therapist privy to almost as many secrets as the CIA. Lucy settled into an armchair with carved frame and legs, one comfy enough to relax even her wired captain. "What you tell me may help us recapture her quickly and save us all some grief."

"I'm in a bad spot with this," Glass said. "Even though I have a 'duty to inform,' I'd be in hot water if word got back to the prison that I aided the police."

Lucy nodded. "I know. 'Snitches get stitches,' but this is real important. And we won't tell them."

"I heard my superintendent received a call from the commissioner, who had gotten one, they say, from the attorney general. I'll need something . . ."

She produced the faxed memo from one higher-up to another.

Glass went to a curtain and drew it, letting the evening sun shine into Lucy's face, his version of tilting the playing field in his favor. He read the fax, shrugged, folded it, and tossed it onto a side table. "For my files," he said. "CYA. 'Cover your assets.' The Bronx D.A. got enough publicity from this case to get elected attorney general three years later. I guess he got nostalgic for past glories. So what happened?"

Lucy stretched her long legs. "She made it at least as far as White Plains, where we recovered the stolen vehicle."

"Oh?" Glass sat forward and grew pale now that he had learned his ex-patient might be only a few miles away.

Lucy knew the bait had been swallowed, the hook embedded. Even guys like Glass, with nearly as many degrees as a thermometer, became eager to cooperate once self-interest or fear took over. "Yes," she said. "Not far from here. Why?"

"Our therapeutic relationship extends almost a decade, with sessions at least twice a week. I watched her evolve from child victim to woman predator, one who chose to be feared rather than pitied. She survived by psyching herself into berserk rages when threatened, making all but the most dense or masochistic inmates leery of setting her off. At five feet and one hundred pounds, that was her only way to survive."

"You think she might come here?" asked Lucy.

"I don't know." He grimaced. "She doesn't know my address, but she's one of the most resourceful people I know."

He looked back to the kitchen, the furrow on his brow even deeper than before, as the girl, her headphones off now, bounded out and headed right for Lucy. "Hi." She clutched Lucy's hand and looked her up and down, as if appraising her to see if she was worth the purchase price. "I'm Veronica. My parents were into fancy names when I was born." She smiled, showing dimples and looking cute as only one entering adolescence could.

"Look on the bright side," said Glass as he tousled her long auburn hair. "We could have named you Crystal."

"Dad, you didn't say we were having company for dinner."

"We're not," he said. "This is Detective Moreno, come to get your father's brilliant insights."

"Oh." She released Lucy's hand and looked as if she'd just learned there was no Santa Claus. "What happened?"

"One of your father's patients escaped," said Lucy.

"Wow. How long was she locked up for?" asked Veronica.

"Forever," said Glass. "They call it 'football numbers.' Twenty-five to ninety-nine, six concurrent sentences."

"So what do you think she'll do?" asked Lucy, cutting to the chase, eager to be home for dinner with Tony.

Glass looked at his daughter and shrugged. "Don't you have homework to finish?"

Veronica grinned. "All done and supper will be ready soon." She looked at Lucy. "Dad never talks about work."

"And with good reason. This inmate got into terrible trouble when she was fifteen, not much older than you are now."

"I want to stay." She looked to Lucy as if she was the arbiter of good sense. "Maybe I can learn something. So what did she do to earn such a long sentence?" she asked.

Glass sighed, surrendered, and patted the couch beside him. Veronica scooped up the black cat and settled in as her father spoke. "A girl gang, the Tigresses, stabbed Suzanne's sister Nancy to death, then intimidated the witnesses so there were no arrests. When Suzanne tried to get the case reopened, they invaded her apartment to silence her."

"I remember," said Lucy. "I investigated the break-in." She recalled the smashed door, the slashed furniture, broken dishes, mirrors and glassware crushed into a multicolored pile on the living-room floor. As with the sister's murder, without witnesses Lucy doubted there would have been arrests made.

"That night," said Glass, "Suzanne staged a preemptive

strike on their basement hideout to get them before they killed her. She was fifteen, tiny, and without a gun, so she lobbed a firebomb through the window and waited with a nail-studded bat and sharpened crowbar as they stumbled out single-file, smoke-blinded, and choking." Glass closed his eyes, his knuckles whitening as he gripped the sofa. "She tracked down the rest of them, getting all except the youngest and their leader, Marie."

His fingers clawed deeper into the sofa cushion, and the cat jumped away.

"That's so gross," Veronica said. "How did a small girl inflict such damage?"

Glass opened his eyes. "Don't underestimate the maniacal energy of suppressed rage. At flash point it's capable of anything for a few moments. Sort of like a summer storm—brief but violent." He laid his hand on her shoulder.

"She sounds wacky," Veronica said, snuggling closer.

"No, it's normal for abused children," he said. "They bank their rage, like money, letting it fester until a stressor ignites it. Then comes the explosion, followed by the cooling-off period, until the next time." Glass took a breath and turned to Lucy. "Did you know she let herself get caught?"

"Huh?" Lucy leaned forward, off balance, her throat turning dry. She had long suspected she'd nabbed Scorch too easily. Lucy had rationalized that like a cougar run ragged by hounds, treed and awaiting the coup de grâce from hunters, Scorch had run out of steam and given up, rather than fall victim to the rest of the gang. Old beliefs die hard, but they die.

"Yes," Glass said. "Suzanne tortured the youngest gang member and learned it was Marie who ordered her sister's death after they had robbed her. When Suzanne heard Marie had been arrested on an unrelated charge, she let herself get captured." He shook his head. "She hoped to kill a cornered Marie on Riker's Island, but Marie beat the rap on a technicality and was released the day Suzanne arrived. Since then Suzanne spent most of her time and energy scheming to earn cigarettes, curry favors, collect obligations, all the prison media of exchange so she could learn where Marie was and if she ever got sentenced."

"And did she?" asked Lucy.

Glass shook his head. "If she did, it was under a different name and sentenced not to Midland Knolls, which at that time housed all women inmates, but to one of the new medium-security female facilities. The joke was on Suzanne."

"And on me." Lucy sighed. "Here, all these years, I thought I was a genius."

Glass's eyes narrowed. "You? You arrested her? Jesus, you were as obsessed as she."

"Thanks. And I thought I was so great." Lucy shook her head. And so did everyone else all these years. There's no fool like an old fool. Time to salvage what she could. "This Marie," she asked. "You have a last name or address? Anything?"

"No, and I doubt Suzanne does either, but my money is on her to find out."

"She's that bright?" asked Lucy, knowing only a skinny, maddened fifteen-year-old who refused to cry in public.

"One hundred forty-seven IQ. Considering her upbringing, it might have been even higher with a better family life."

"It sounds like extenuating circumstances with her case. Why not the usual sentence, manslaughter, five-to-fifteen?" Lucy asked. "Did she 'blow trial'?"

Glass grimaced. "Ironically, she 'pled out' on the advice of a rookie Legal Aid lawyer. Otherwise, the judge threatened to make the separate twenty-five-to-ninety-nine-year sentences for murder and arson each run consecutively, not concurrently, if she went to trial and was convicted. If that had happened, she might not have been eligible for parole

31

until she was sixty-five. As it is, when I first met her she figured her parole officer hadn't even been born yet." He shook his head. "The D.A. said because she'd called the fire department before lobbing that Molotov cocktail, to minimize the danger to other tenants, it showed premeditation on her part. Murder one. It panicked her lawyer into copping to a very harsh sentence."

Lucy suspected Glass knew more about Scorch than he wanted to. "The criminal injustice system seldom makes sense," Lucy said to Veronica. "A kid upstate steals a car, gets five years. A kid in Harlem shoots somebody, he gets one to three. Who knows? I catch them, your father watches them, but the courts sentence them. Maybe the judge was constipated that day, or was trying to send a message to teenage killers. So instead of manslaughter two she almost got murder one. If they had been as lenient with her as they are with most kids, she could have been paroled already." She turned to Glass again. "You have no other ideas about Marie?"

Glass shook his head. "Can't you check the names of twenty-year-old women who were arrested between the time of Suzanne's initial rampage and when she gave herself up?"

Lucy chuckled at the blind faith people had in the police. The Unabomber terrorized for over a decade until his brother turned him in. "Know how many girls in the Bronx get busted in a month? Besides, Marie could have been her street name, or she could have used an alias when booked. She may have changed her name since then. A girl that wild dies of AIDS, drug overdose, gets killed fighting over a man, or another woman." She shook her head. "She might not live in the same neighborhood."

"Well . . ." Glass looked like a man perched on barbed wire. "She spoke of revenge the first few years, but less and less as time went on. Mostly she talked of what she might do in the unlikely event she made her first parole board at age forty." He looked at Lucy, as if hoping she was reasonable, or pitying, and would let him off the hook.

No such luck.

"If Marie's still alive, Suzanne can find her," he said.

Veronica Glass stood and nodded to Lucy. "Nice meeting you." She slipped her headphones back on and returned to the kitchen, the novelty of this meeting already over.

Lucy stood too, ready for the sixty-four-dollar question. "What's the verdict? Gut feeling, not psychoanalytical stuff."

Glass sighed. "If you find her, you'll take her alive?"

Here it came, the psychobabble. She'd wasted a half hour with this guy. "Yes, Doc, it's my duty to. You have my word. Now, does Scorch still want revenge after all this time?"

Glass's voice was a hoarse whisper. "Of course. It's all she's lived for."

Chapter Four

A white Mustang cut Scorch off as its bucktoothed driver flipped her the finger. Was that his IQ? She stomped on the brake and slammed forward, then parked far from the mall, careful not to bump fenders. To have driven so far, only to get sideswiped in this lot . . .

Using the car's dome light, she practiced the signature on the rookie's stolen credit card. Satisfied that it was passable—"close enough for government work," as Dr. Glass would say—she checked the glove compartment but found only a tarnished chrome Cross pen.

Where should she go? What should she do? Any place or anything she wanted. The past third of her life had been strictly regimented, but for the next few moments she was on her own, for better or for worse.

Once inside the mall, it became hard for her to breathe. All these people milling, wandering, jostling into or gliding around each other. In prison such contact was a "dis"—disrespect punishable by delayed payback, usually with interest.

34

Scorch had never been to a "megamall," and the White Plains Galleria rivaled Madison Square Garden, its huge vaulted ceiling reminding her of a cathedral. A "church of capitalism," Dr. Glass would have called it. He also might have diagnosed her as agoraphobic, to be upset by this crowd. Her flesh tingled from so much random contact, forcing her to sit, to let the throngs flow past, so many people, different clothes, ages . . .

So big, crushing her. Her chest tightened as if an invisible python were wrapping around her. A coronary from stress? If she hadn't had one by now she never would, but she followed Dr. Glass's advice and relaxed each muscle until she was ready to continue her mission. After eight years of intensive therapy, she sure clung to more than her share of neuroses.

Young guys stared at her. Was the word already out that a convicted killer was stalking their mall? No, they were admiring her legs and butt. She paused to ogle back, unused to such attention from men. Where were they when she was fourteen and needed the ego boost? Resisting to urge to flirt back, she zeroed in on the most crowded shops, buying nothing over fifty dollars so the clerks, overwhelmed on a Saturday night, wouldn't call to confirm if the credit card was valid. Finally, something worthwhile from listening to larcenous conversations in the rec room.

One cashier stared as Scorch began to sign the credit slip, then paused, trying to recall the signature on the card. Scorch had to distract her, quick. "What time is it?" she asked. The cashier peeled back her sleeve to glance at her watch, giving Scorch the respite needed to complete the forgery. The clerk took it without missing a chew of her gum. Close. Scorch was more careful when getting the rest of her new wardrobe.

Buying piecemeal took forever, but she got decent skirts, tops, jeans, and sneakers to go with the flats and red "screw me" shoes bought at young-miss shops. Ready for the road, except for purchases she had to make in cash to avoid clues: hair dye, peroxide, curlers, and—most important—good barber shears. Her years in the prison beauty salon were about to pay off, and these scissors could cut a lot more than hair. She next got makeup, bold shades of lipstick to draw attention from her large, dark eyes. Last came transition sunglasses to camouflage her most prominent facial feature.

Closing time. The officer's skirt now stuffed in a garbage bin, a bright silk scarf on her head, she headed for an exit when she glimpsed a navy uniform out of the corner of her eye. Guard or cop, it didn't matter. She turned on her heel and bumped her head into the chest of a mall rat with tight jeans and loose morals. He grinned down at her. "Hi," he said. "If I said you have a dynamite body, would you hold it against me?"

Oh boy, where was the nearest exit?

Scorch maintained eye contact an instant too long and the guy, encouraged, leaned closer, clutching the railing for balance. "Want to go for a beer?" he asked. Even downwind he smelled as if he had already completed a brewery tour.

"Uh . . ." She tried to ease around him.

He must have misinterpreted her hesitation as playing hard to get, because he grinned at his buddies, neither of whom looked to be in better shape. They were all under twenty-five, full of testosterone fantasies and little else. Could she play this to her advantage? Her experience with guys was limited to four boys when she was fifteen, so long ago it might have been more myth than memory. If she misread cues now or blundered, she'd wish she were back with those officers. Her heart again pumped harder through the silk blouse she'd bought.

This guy *was* cute, though, with firm pecs. It had been so long since she had touched a hard, warm male. He'd do;

she needed fresh wheels. Driving a stolen Corrections vehicle was like standing under a neon light flashing "Escaped Con." She leaned closer, breathing from her mouth to avoid smelling vapors of Bud Ice. "Got your own place?" she asked.

"Uh-huh."

"Share it with anybody?"

"Uh . . . no." He needed more time to answer that than Scorch had taken to plead guilty eight years ago. He grinned at his buddies again and dug a hand into his jeans for keys. Behind him came that uniformed guy. No time to lose. Scorch snatched his keys. "I'll drive," she said, figuring her twenty minutes behind the wheel made her a better bet to get them to his place alive. She pulled him through the line for the late show.

"Got beer at my place, but we can always use more," he said.

"Condoms?"

"Condoms?" His forehead furrowed from unaccustomed thought.

"Rubbers." Dr. Glass called them "Coney Island whitefish."

"Oh yeah." He brightened. "Plenty." She had made his day.

Plenty? She doubted he'd be able to use them after another six-pack. She dragged him as fast as she dared without making him pitch forward, but she had to lose his friends in case they figured an orgy was in the making. His smile widened as if he hoped she was as horny as he was. "What's your name?" he asked.

"Helen. Helen Troy. What's yours?"

"John."

John? Yeah, sure. Lucky he hadn't read Homer in high school, assuming he'd gone to high school or even learned to read.

"What happened to your wrists?" he asked, pointing to the chafe marks left by the handcuffs.

"My bracelets were too tight." She got him out into the muggy night air. "Okay, John, where's your car?"

"Truck. There."

Truck? Something huge with ten gears? No, only a pickup with blinding chrome and useless accessories, probably used for hauling groceries and little else. Thankfully it was an automatic. "Mount up, Romeo," she said, boosting him into the cab by the seat of his pants. Nice butt. She gave him a final pat on the rump and wondered, as she slid behind the wheel, if this should be the night she'd finally lose it officially. No way. She had to attend to business. "Where to, Romeo?"

"First we get more beer. What brand you like?"

She had never drunk beer. Her sister had let her taste wine twice and fruit brandy once. That might be nice. "Peach brandy," she said. "You old enough to buy?"

"Me?" He cocked his head, reminding her of pictures of old hound dogs listening to their masters. "Sure. There's Rolando's Liquors. Here." He peeled off a twenty from a roll of bills thick enough to gag a pig. Payday.

The clerk stared at her as John struggled to fit the bottle into a bag. "When were you born?" the clerk asked before taking the cash.

"Seventy-two," she said, not missing a beat as she swept up John's change and tugged him back to the truck. It was the second time in eight years she'd told the truth to anyone except Dr. Glass. "You remember where you live?" she asked John.

"Yeah. Three blocks down and a left." Unable to wait, he popped open a can and ran a callused hand up her thigh. "Boy, I thought we was going to have to cruise all night. Who would have thought I'd get so lucky?"

Yeah, who? She just hoped he stayed conscious until they

got to his door, on the top floor of a four-story walk-up.

They were hardly inside when he started to paw her. A foot taller, sturdy, and powered by the uninhibited strength of the inebriated, she couldn't fend him off.

"Stop!" she said before he muffled her mouth with his own, one hand sliding up her skirt while the other roamed frontward to squeeze her breasts. He was giving her a thrill all right, but of fear, not pleasure. The story of her life.

She tried to push him away, but he had her in a bear hug, muttering gibberish as he sucked the air from her lungs.

Headlines flashed through her brain:

SMOTHERED GIRL FOUND IN DUMPSTER BELIEVED
TO BE ESCAPED CON

or

MECHANIC'S HELPER SLICED UP BY MASS MURDERER/ARSONIST

The scissors lay in the canvas carryall she'd bought, just beyond arm's length. Might as well be on the moon, for all the good it did her. His breath was toxic, his mouth hot against her neck. If she couldn't slow him down, she was in big trouble. She lunged for the carryall, but he pulled her toward the bedroom.

She considered jabbing him with the tapered pen, but his sweaty arms wrapped her tight.

She couldn't tear away and fight back unless she hurt him badly—and too many witnesses had seen him leave with her.

She wriggled until her mouth was free and she could breathe.

"Relax! You'll get some," she said, and moved with him, shifting her weight until the back of his knees hit the edge of the bed and he plopped onto the mattress. "Here." She handed him a beer, like a mother giving her petulant infant a pacifier.

"Thanks," he said as he popped it open. "Don't worry, Helen. You're gonna have the night of your life."

As if she already hadn't. She checked the place out. It was a sty, confirming that John lived alone. She dumped her stuff on the floor and circled him, wondering how to avoid braining him with the brandy bottle to keep from getting mauled.

Just ply him with beer. She took a sip of brandy and her neck and shoulders relaxed. This could work without bloodshed.

His eyes roamed over her body as beer dribbled down his chin. "You're the prettiest thing I've seen today."

High praise indeed. "Drink up and I'll show you something nice." She lifted her skirt three quarters of the way up to keep him interested. Only nature—or plastic surgeons—gave you great breasts, but you can keep your legs solid. Unlike male prisoners, most women inmates let themselves slide until they resembled the title character in *Throw Momma From the Train*. Dr. Glass believed they grew apathetic about their appearance without men around or were subconsciously adopting the look of pregnant women without the hassle of carrying a fetus.

John finished his beer with a burp and reached for another.

"Where are your rubbers?" she asked. Worse come to worst, it paid to be ready if she went through with this tonight.

"Toilet," he muttered.

"Don't go 'way." She took her peroxide, hair dye, and scissors to a bathroom stocked with condoms, Vaseline, and aspirin in the medicine cabinet and penicillin growing on the shower curtain. Everything she needed.

When she returned with the Vaseline, three spent beer cans stood alongside the bed. Perfect. He should be out soon, right? She tugged down his pants and up it popped to attention, like a thick pink rod. Not bad, she guessed, although except for *Cosmo*, she hadn't a clue as to what constituted "good." So that's what they looked like when they were primed for action.

"Want a little warm-up?" she asked. Unable to recollect the AIDS-prevention classes in prison, Scorch wondered if she was taking a chance even by handling him. In the aftermath of what had happened today, her brain was shutting down. What to do? "Lie back and enjoy it," she said, "while I butter your cob."

She pulled pillowcases free. They were just the right length, if he cooperated. "You like kinky?" she asked, tempted to cross her fingers.

"Love it."

Good answer. "How 'bout some bondage?" she asked as she tied one end of the cloth around each wrist, then looped the other around the bedposts.

"Excellent," he said.

"We aim to please." She coated his hard-on with Vaseline and started stroking.

"Ah, this is great," he said.

Was it? She couldn't tell from her end.

"Yeah, baby, more," he said, arching his back.

Whoa—down, boy. She had no idea what she was doing, but she had once served a stint in the prison bakery. Kneading one thing should be like manipulating another.

"Go, baby," he gurgled.

She tried to remember what the other inmates had said about this stuff, but like most jail talk, it was probably all lies.

She started moving it like a gearshift. First, second, reverse. Might as well practice now. "You're getting every man's fantasy," she said. "All parts in mint condition." She recalled the pottery scene from the movie *Ghost* and started singing "Unchained Melody."

"You got a nice voice," he said.

More compliments. "Yeah, I sing in the shower." Whenever Karen Rainey wasn't all over her, lathering her, sliding her hands across Scorch's body, lapping her tongue in every orifice. That got her even more excited. She refocused by thinking again about rolling dough in the bakery and burst out laughing.

"Huh?" he asked, eyes closed, hands gripping cloth.

"Nothing. Just having a ball." That did it. She laughed so hard the tears came, and then he did.

Ugh. Squirting all over her hands . . . And women liked this?

He grunted, sighed, and snored. Out for the count. Suzanne "Scorch" Amerce had done it all today—cursed out Mom, beat up officers, stolen a car, and brought a guy to orgasm—in just a few hours. After all those beers, she figured he'd sleep until she finished her makeover. She hurried to the bathroom and scrubbed his sticky white mess off her hands and down the drain.

Speaking of scum, she recalled her fight this afternoon. Damn bitch Barb! Scorch grabbed the scissors, examining its edge in the bathroom light, imagining it plunging and ripping into Barb's soft, fat stomach, Barb's steaming viscera spilling out . . .

Whoa, get a grip. Recalling Dr. Glass's advice, she counted to ten and took deep breaths. Then she opened the scissors, but hesitated, staring in the mirror for one last look at hair it had taken years to grow. Sighing, she snipped before she chickened out and changed her mind. She had no choice. They'd be looking for a brunette with waist-length hair, not a perky blonde with shortened locks. She had done this for plenty of others in the prison barbershop, but never to herself. If necessity was the mother of invention, desperation must be the father.

It could always grow back, and they say blondes have

more fun. One misstep, though, and she'd wind up with green hair.

An hour later, it was done. The face peering back at her was recognizable only to someone already familiar with it. To a casual observer in the local post office, she was a new woman.

John was snoring softer, pants still around his ankles. She took the vehicle registration from his wallet, along with most of his cash. A cheap lesson, teaching him not to pick up desperate women when he was so drunk his eyes couldn't work as a team.

"Lost your chance to sleep with me," she whispered as she stuffed a sock into his mouth.

When she was fifteen, it had almost happened in the darkness of her room, as if they needed to hide from the light. Too fast was what it had been, the boy—she could barely remember his face, couldn't recall his name—all over her, breathing hard, slobbering as their mouths met. Then he was lifting, tugging, squeezing, hands groping, cool air washing over her as he stripped her. Then, back on her, stroking and sucking nipples, thighs, pussy . . .

At the last moment she'd panicked and pushed him away, promising they would do it next time.

Only, next time never came. Three days later, her sister lay on the steamy pavement, spurting her life away through severed arteries, Scorch holding her, screaming for help, unable to keep her from dying. Passersby turning away, afraid of the Tigresses, intimidated into not testifying against them.

After that it was a blur—the raid on her apartment, the fire, the tire iron, the alleys, the cops, the judge—everything consumed in a firestorm of fury.

Stop! Don't cry! She smacked the scissors handle on the bathroom sink, chipping a quarter-sized chunk from the porcelain.

Everything grew red and hazy as she visualized Marie before her, the knife-wielding Tigress pinned to the wall. Scorch lunged, ripped, slashed, and tore, hearing Marie screams grow higher, shriller as her putrid blood splattered in a red mist through the muggy air.

Cut faster, deeper, harder until there's nothing left. Nothing.

Chapter Five

Scorch peeled open a sleep-crusted eye to find herself huddled on the seat of John's pickup. Her scrunched limbs protested as she stretched, the increased blood flow reminding her of the need for the bus stop—and a bathroom. For once she wished she were a boy and could use any convenient tree or wall.

Five A.M.! Overslept! Dawn came early in June. She had to be on her way before John awoke, noticed both her and his keys gone, gnawed free, and called the cops.

After a quick trip to the rest room of the all-night diner down the street, she'd visit Cathy Webster in the Bronx. Two years after her parole, Cat had passed on the rumor of Marie living in Manhattan. Anemic, but her only lead.

The diner had a few customers when she pulled up, either insomniacs, early risers, or party people not yet ready to come home. None looked like they were heading for early Mass.

In the bathroom's peeling mirror Scorch saw a blond stranger with short, pert hair. Not bad for an amateur. On the way out she stopped for donuts and coffee that looked and smelled as if it had been brewing since midnight and was probably strong enough by now to jump-start a corpse. Two guys studied her. Was her hair remake that bad? Were they plainclothes or off-duty cops responding to an all points bulletin? If she left without her coffee it might arouse suspicion, so she fished change from her new bag while casting glances at the morning paper.

No mention of her escape, with a California quake and a Mideast peace treaty hogging the headlines. She'd be showering about now if she were still locked up, and the thought of Karen Rainey's soapy hands on her made Scorch feel tingly. Enough. There was a new life to live and an enemy to kill, so she ambled for the door, as if eager to enjoy the late-spring morning.

The guys at the counter were more bewitched by her butt and legs than her face. Most women would be miffed, but she exhaled with relief. Hopefully, John was still out for the count after last night's hand job and twelve-pack. With his truck parked under a leafy roof of blooming maples and oaks, he might find it before lunch and chalk it up to lessons in living.

She dunked the bag with her shorn hair into a trash can and hiked a quarter mile to Central Avenue, sunglasses, silk scarf, and shortened locks her only disguise. The streets were empty, like the jungle with a predator nearby, as the soft light of dawn gave way to a bright June sun casting long shadows. The air filled with the smell of sizzling breakfast, the sounds of birds, bees, dogs. Church bells pealed, summoning the hopeful and the guilty to pray for a better week to come.

Forgive her, Fodder, for she sinned. She robbed, beat, stole, and stripped last night. She also drank liquor and touched a boy's wiener, a lifetime's worth of forbidden pleasures crammed into a four-hour period. Not to mention the shopping spree.

Eyes closed, leaning against the bus stop pole to relish the scent of honeysuckle, she heard the crunch of rubber on gravel. A White Plains police car cruised her way, the cop old enough to be her dad—if only he had lived. The bus was coming, a long block away. Out of the corner of her eye she saw the cop talk into his radio. Where could she run to? Nowhere.

Her hand caressed the smooth steel of the scissors. Should she pull a "Pearl Harbor" and pin his gun hand to the dashboard? She had little to lose, already doing six concurrent life sentences. She pretended to check her shopping bags while waiting for the telltale shout or squeal of tires announcing his attack. She felt his eyes on her.

The bus pulled up, finally, maybe too late. Boarding, Scorch saw again it was not her face that held interest, but her rear end. Good investment—those tight jeans and her twice-a-day workouts with the stationary bike were reaping dividends. She relaxed in the back with a Clive Barker novel, wondering what the reactions of fellow passengers would be if they knew real horror sat inches away.

Five minutes later, she dared glance out the rear window to find that cop cruising behind her bus. Play it cool; wait for a stop where there was lots of traffic before bolting for the door.

She fished out her new compact and in its mirror watched the cop watch her bus. If he'd called for backup there would be patrol cars all along Central Avenue, ready to gun her down if she sprinted from the bus. Would that be worse than getting hauled back to Midland? How would it feel, hot lead ripping through her body? She might find out all too soon.

At the Yonkers line the cop car turned around. Free.

Back into a world that had changed lots in eight years.

Yonkers . . . Like most staff, Dr. Glass was mum about his personal life, but Karen said he lived there.

Scorch spied a young couple walking hand-in-hand. It prompted her to hum "Unchained Melody" again, a smile coming as she recalled John, stewed on beer, complimenting her singing.

The smile vanished when she recalled the ending of *Ghost*. When she died, would dark wraiths drag *her* off? Was that all she had to look forward to? That and killing Marie?

Not much of a life, but then Dr. Glass said God didn't sign a contract with us, offering only pleasure. Judging by how serious Dr. Glass was most of the time, *he* believed it. He used to be so cheerful, with a smile and joke for every occasion, like a human greeting card. Then, five years ago, something happened.

He missed weeks of work, returned with yellowed bruises and a gashed forehead, and never laughed or smiled again.

Finally, the last stop, the Northwest Bronx at Bedford Park Boulevard. After a ten-minute search, Scorch found a working phone booth that wasn't a toxic nightmare and called directory assistance for Cathy Webster. Bingo. Cat was back on Valentine Avenue near the Concourse and Scorch's old neighborhood. Scorch decided on a surprise attack with the ten-block walk letting her unwind after the forty-minute bus ride.

A block from Fordham Road came the blare of horns and the stink of exhaust as hordes of people got an early start to the zoo, the Botanical Gardens, or Orchard Beach.

Hearing a siren wail, Scorch dashed into Cat's building. Could she escape through the basement? Cops pulled up and dashed into a grocery, guns drawn, and it didn't look like donut withdrawal. She waited behind the door, heart thumping double time. Avoid the street. Was the basement door locked? Where did it lead? How had they found her so soon?

The cops emerged seconds later, a cuffed kid in tow.

Close. Scorch trudged up five flights to Cat, the hall smelling of bacon and roach spray as she thumbed the buzzer, then rapped on the door. After a moment, she heard shuffling feet and a mumbled "Who's there?"

"Census Bureau," Scorch said.

A chain slid into place before the door cracked open to let a bleary eye peek out. "Scorch? Scorch!" The chain slid off and the door swung wide. Cat stood in a bubble-gum-pink robe, half open to reveal her substantial breasts. "Scorch, what the hell you doing here?" She ran a hand through hair that looked like it had been in the wash of a jet engine.

"Paroled. Who's your barber, Helen Keller? Stevie Wonder?"

"Huh?" Cat rubbed her head, as if to get her brain up to speed. "Parole? Girlfriend, you doing life. Ain't no early parole for that." Her grogginess faded. "Girl, you didn't escape?" Cat looked down the hall, as if expecting an audience. "Why you here? Listen"—she leaned close—"I got me a good man who don't care I done time at Midland Knolls. Don't screw it up for me by making me a fugitive harborer, huh?"

Scorch planted her foot against the door in case Cat got the urge to slam it. "I need money and the whereabouts of Marie."

"Marie? I don't know no Marie." Sure enough, Cat reached behind her for the doorknob. Eight inches shorter and eighty pounds lighter, Scorch glided past Cat into her apartment.

"Sure you do. Marie, leader of the Morris Avenue Tigresses."

"There ain't no more Tigresses. You seen to that. Damn, Scorch, you gonna screw me up. Why you want to do that?"

Scorch needed to stand on tiptoe to place her hand over Cat's mouth. "Shush. Nobody will know I'm here unless you blab it. You wrote Karen a while ago, saying Marie was on the West Side. You're going to tell me, aren't you?"

Cat nodded. Karen had taught Scorch the hand-on-mouth trick, how it took the initiative from the dumb and docile, not giving them a chance to argue or protest. It was even more effective if you held something sharp in your other hand.

"Good. Now, how about an address for Marie, plus a loan of, say, forty or fifty bucks?" That would give her more than two hundred, enough for a couple days' worth of freedom and movement.

She released Cat's mouth but remained toe-to-toe with her.

Cat shook her head. "I don't want trouble."

"And you won't get any. Get real. Where in Manhattan?"

"Told you, don't know. Might find out from Tanya Smith."

Tanya! The youngest, the Tigress cub, a murderess-in-training. She was Scorch's age and the weak one who broke easiest under torture, telling Scorch enough about Marie and the others to make the Morris Avenue Massacre possible.

"Where's Tanya now?" Scorch asked.

"Five-oh-two Forty-ninth, corner of Eleventh, last I heard, but that was a year or so ago."

"It's a place to start. Now, how about some cash?"

"Scorch, what I look like to you, First National Bank?"

"Give what you can. Pretend it's Christmas."

"Damn, I should have known nothing knocks on Sunday at seven A.M. except trouble." She shuffled off, and Scorch heard a deep voice—Cat's man, probably—muttering. Cat returned with thirty-three dollars in crumpled bills. "That's all I can spare."

"And it's appreciated. I'll return it someday."

"Hell no, Scorch. I don't want to see you no more. We had a few laughs in jail, but I'm free now and want to stay that way. If I were you I'd buy a bus ticket, head someplace they don't know you, and start over."

Scorch stashed the bills in her fancy new brassiere. "Yeah." She patted Cathy's flabby arm. "If you were me."

Chapter Six

Tuesday, June 4

". . . report of shots fired, corner of Morris Avenue and One Hundred Ninetieth Street." Lucy Moreno knew the block and hated it, with its graffiti-streaked walls, the corner bus shelter with its sides shot out, its burned-out tenements.

She acknowledged the call. "Detective Moreno on the way."

As she hit the gas, she wondered if she was going in as backup or if she might need some herself, this being the second shooting there this week, the local pushers engaged in the drug version of a price war. With the epidemic of a lethal new heroin from the Caribbean, "Dark Paradise," they were fighting over the right to kill their clientele.

She parked behind a patrol car as two uniformed cops scoured the block. One approached her. "Skinny teenage boy ran down that alley," he said. "Don't know if he was involved."

She nodded. "I'll go in. You head around the corner in case he tries to slip out through the basement." She thought about her Kevlar vest, stored at home, its cotton shell at the dry cleaners as the weather turned sticky and uncomfortable. Fellow detectives accused her of leaving it behind because it ruined her figure. Her late partner, Ray, always kept his safely locked in the trunk. Lucy tiptoed in, hand on the nine-millimeter Glock the department made her use after a dozen years with the thirty-eight she'd never fired on the job.

The dim, rubbish-filled alley, between crumbling tenements, split into a T, the perfect place to earn a posthumous medal if she got careless. Maybe the kid wouldn't put up a fight and it would be her easiest collar of the year.

Then again, a week from now, after a departmental funeral, Tony might be staring down at her coffin, shaking his head, wondering yet again why she hadn't quit last year, as they'd talked about.

Inching down the alley as the stink of garbage too long in the sun made her eyes water and her nose wrinkle, Lucy heard only the repetitive beat of salsa music floating from open windows.

A crash and clang of sheet metal—trash cans overturning. A man yelling, "Police! FREEZE!" The clop of sneakers, louder, closer. A kid streaked by in a blur of white and red. She couldn't get her legs going. Move it! She stepped into bright sunlight and watched the kid leap onto a fire-escape ladder.

Moreno, c'mon, in this lifetime! She came to life and dashed after him, the belated rush of adrenaline like a booster rocket. He clambered up, turned, and spit on her before continuing his impersonation of Spider-Man.

She whipped out her cuffs and took a gulp of overripe city air. He was almost to the second floor when there was a snap and the rusted ladder broke, sending the kid sprawling onto the hot concrete. He squawked, clambered to his feet, and hobbled away.

Lucy chugged after him. The old saying was right. Old

age and experience beat youth and strength, occasionally.

The kid whirled, revolver in hand.

Christ! She reached for her own weapon, her thumb fumbling with the holster snap.

The kid pivoted as if on a lazy Susan as his ankle buckled. He squawked and fell, his revolver clattering at his feet. Lucy whipped out her pistol, aimed at his torso, and brandished cuffs with her other hand. "You have the right to remain a jackass!" she said. "You have the right to be gunned down like a rabid dog and fed to rats. Or you can be smart, forget the gun, roll over, and let me have the rest of the day to recover."

The kid's eyes bulged.

"I'm not nuts, and I'm not fooling. Give up before I show you what police brutality was like in the bad old days before the liberals took over. I'm counting to five, starting with four."

The kid nodded and turned onto his stomach, wrists behind his back. "You crazy, lady."

"Yes, that's me, mad Mama, but it pays the rent." She clicked on the cuffs as the uniformed cop finally showed up. "You want to kick him, buddy, this is a good time."

"Maybe later," the patrolman said, looking down at the kid. "You have the right to remain—"

"Yeah, we did that already. Up, cretin, your cage awaits."

The cop hauled the kid to his feet. "We'll take him in, Sarge."

"Yeah, but you try to beat me in and get credit for the 'collar,' I'll see you pounding a beat midnights in Harlem. And don't lose my cuffs. They were my uncle's, from when he was an MP in Saigon."

This cop looked young enough for Vietnam to mean nothing more to him than an answer on a history test. As he carted the kid off, Lucy noticed her hands shaking. First armed arrest in a while and she was coming apart. Not good. Ray Castile once told her, "Stick with me and you'll have hundreds of busts."

Only, Ray was dead now.

Lucy took the scenic route back to the precinct, driving to a vacant lot between abandoned tenements near St. James Park. In that dark, narrow alleyway Scorch had set up her lair after her first set of killings, once she realized the police knew her identity and were watching her apartment house.

At first Lucy thought Scorch lived like a rat, but after the arrest Lucy checked the nest out, realizing that Scorch had existed like a fox, stealing food, getting water from hydrants, living like kids in Beirut or Sarajevo. Who would have thought to search for her there? Not the best way to spend your last weeks of freedom, but that's where Lucy finally found her.

Scorch had just marched out, with Lucy thinking, I'm so smart, hounding a scrawny little teen into surrender.

Until Eric Glass set her straight last night.

Lucy recalled that moment as if it had happened last week, that skinny, disheveled girl emerging, arms outstretched, hands clasped together.

"Hey, cop," she'd said, marching out. "I'm Suzanne Amerce. I killed six Tigresses and tortured another. Ready to take me in?"

Lucy had watched, incredulous, uncertain whether to reach for her revolver or her cuffs. "Don't say any more," Lucy had told her, praying a flawed Miranda warning wouldn't mess up her arrest. "You have the right to an attorney."

"Yeah, like who? Earl Warren? Perry Mason? Just do it."

"If you cannot afford an attorney, one will—"

"Yeah, whatever. I killed them," Scorch said, strutting right up to Lucy, clad in ragged cutoffs and a dirty T-shirt, her long hair bound in pigtails with torn scraps of ribbon.

"Take me in already, for Christ's sake. What took you so long?"

"Don't say anything to anybody until you talk to a lawyer," Lucy said as she snapped the cuffs onto Scorch's bony wrists. For an instant she felt pity for this tiny killer. "Trust me. I've been in this business longer than you."

Then came the tears, finally, leaving clean streaks across Scorch's grimy cheeks. Then Lucy's partner Bryan Acinar came up, yelling, sneering, chuckling. Scorch had sniffled, blinked, and stopped crying, like shutting off a faucet, but Lucy sensed the incredible effort that had taken.

Scorch Amerce was barely fifteen and looked twelve that day, but she strode into the station house like a lady, head up, shoulders back. Throughout the fingerprinting, the mug shots, everything, she kept that composure until the gate clanged shut, locking her in the holding cell until she'd be carted off to Central Booking. Then she lay alone on a cot, knees drawn up to her chest, her back to the bars, but Lucy could see her shoulders shake. Scorch had hardly made a sound, both her hands clamped over her mouth to smother her sobs.

That image stayed with Lucy longer than the photos of Scorch's victims—or should she say the objects of her justice.

Then came Eric Glass's revelation, with Lucy now wondering if she ever would have caught her on her own.

Truth isn't always beauty. Too bad. She had liked being a genius. At the precinct, DiGiorio was waiting. "Busted a kid, Moreno? Listen, the chief's getting pressure from the mayor's office. Stopping this Dark Paradise is priority one, okay? Oh, you got e-mail. Westchester County Sheriff."

She ripped the paper from the printer. Her first lead on Scorch Amerce and it was cold. Scorch had used the stolen credit card Saturday night at the mall where they'd found the car, purchasing nothing over fifty dollars, either through dumb luck or a sharp battle plan. A canvas bag, nice skirts, good jeans, stuff you'd expect from a gal who never had much until Saturday. Victoria's Secret—32B and size 2. Neiman Marcus. Macy's. The Gap. Even a Zippo lighter and Swiss Army knife.

Lucy sat with tepid coffee as she wondered if this was to throw the police off. Was she giving Scorch too much credit, assuming she left red herrings? Why else the paper trail? What next? Unless Scorch did something stupid, unlikely from what she had seen so far, there were no leads, with her boss demanding she spend her time keeping the lid on the deadly heroin epidemic. Tomorrow she'd talk to the one who knew Scorch best, even though Glass had just found out about her escape yesterday. It was like stew: Once the ingredients were added and you set the heat, it took on a life of its own. Glass couldn't help thinking about Scorch. It was his big challenge, figuring out what she was thinking, what she'd do next. He wanted to help Lucy catch Scorch, even if he didn't know it yet.

Lucy made a paper plane of the printout and sailed it onto her cluttered desk. For one thing, Glass was afraid Scorch would be killed if found by any other cop, with all his invested time and energy wasted. Those guys were like that, thinking they were going to cure the world and not wanting to stop until they had. For another, Lucy had a hunch there was a deeper link between them. Not sexual, no, but deep inside Glass needed to prove something. As she did the paperwork on today's arrest, she caught herself thinking back to Glass's candlelit home, with the melancholy daughter and Caribbean buddy.

Strange, as strange as Scorch herself, but Lucy would have to let things simmer. Glass had a point about finding this Marie, so Lucy left her arrest report stillborn to run a list of girls in their late teens who were busted just before Scorch's arrest and released on a technicality the next day.

She came up with eleven names, none beginning with *M*. Four girls were dead, another incarcerated out of state. Of the remaining six, after so many years, there were no current addresses, nothing more recent than four years ago.

Marie must have used an alias and phony ID when busted, making her trail as cold as the bones of Scorch's sister. Scorch's father's death when she was six had sent her mother over the edge. Mrs. Amerce spent the rest of her life in and out of alcohol-treatment centers. Big sister, a secretary, looked after the younger one, determined she finish high school and go to college before she got knocked up and spent the rest of her life changing diapers and watching daytime soaps. But "Life is what gets in the way while you're making other plans," and "life" was what Scorch was to do, to live from sixteen to sixty with scummy crooks, until she took matters into her own hands and busted out.

Instinct and logic said Scorch head for New York. North or east there were few buses or trains. From the city she could find Marie, then flee anywhere. With no remaining family or any friends who would acknowledge her as such, Scorch's world withered, leaving few options. Lucy played with her printout of possible Maries, all she had to go on until or unless Scorch made a blunder. Would it be so terrible, Scorch killing a killer? A hundred years ago, it was called frontier justice. We'd come far since then, releasing murderers like Marie on technicalities. Kids were afraid on the streets and in their schools, while old people were prisoners in their homes. This was progress?

Lucy, sworn to uphold the law, couldn't pass judgment, although those from before Miranda had other ideas of justice.

She grinned when she thought of those dinosaurs who charged ahead, trampling the rights of the unrighteous. She grabbed her jacket, ready to go check out the ladies on that list of Maries.

DiGiorio loomed over her. "Going somewhere? First finish all your reports, Moreno. C'mon, the D.A.'s office awaits." He leaned over her cluttered desk. "That's why we pay you, remember? And how your fitness rating will be judged."

She waved the printout. "I've got potential—"

"Potential headaches if you don't work on current cases!"

She nodded, pretending to listen, wondering how to get around him on this case. That evening at home, Tony Moreno poked his head out of the refrigerator. "Got beer?" he asked Lucy.

"If you bought, you got, so don't look at me," she said.

He shrugged. "Didn't see the point in buying if I'm off to Boston tomorrow. What happened? You're home on time, a cause for celebration. It's not every night we don't eat reheated meat loaf or burnt pot roast. You've got that look again."

"Made a good collar today, got hot leads on two others."

"Still loving danger, attracting it like a magnet?" he said.

"Some find working with me an adventure, a learning experience. Two of my partners made lieutenant." And two others made early graves. Fifty percent wasn't a passing grade last time she looked.

"Found that teenage serial killer yet?" her husband asked.

"She's twenty-three now, a mass murderer, and no, Di-Giorio is giving me hell about working on it."

Tony touched her hand. "I got a bad feeling about this. I remember you saying how cold-blooded she was in hunting those girls. Join Acinar as a P.I. After you collared her, he quit."

"He enjoys it, but I think peeking through motel keyholes to prove infidelity is a torture worthy of hell. Besides, I'm looking to nab Scorch again, and without any help from her this time."

Chapter Seven

Eric Glass sighed as he gazed out his window, his usual pastime these days. Detective Moreno hadn't called for help or to update him. She probably thought the evaluation he'd faxed her was too technical or just plain useless. If she only knew what he'd gone through to get it, testing Suzanne a week after she'd been discharged from the hospital after slitting her wrists.

Suzanne had zipped through the verbal half of the Wechsler Intelligence Scales, obtaining an IQ of 151. Her performance score, despite emotional agony and bandaged wrists, was still 142 for a Full Scale IQ of 147.

The Rorschach inkblots, though, were another story. She started well, then fidgeted, falling prey to "color shock," overwhelmed by the sudden rush of color on cards II and III. On card IV she squirmed, tossed the card back, and said, "It looks like a giant, about to jump on and squash me." It went downhill from there, with card V seen as "a bat, swooping to snatch me up." At this point, he knew what was coming next. Card VI—the "Mother Card"—was "a poisonous cloud, growing larger, wanting to smother me." She pushed the remaining four cards away as sweat beaded on her brow and upper lip, though it was early December and the facility hadn't yet cranked up the heat. "I don't want to do this anymore. I'm seeing more than I want to."

And so had he. The hostility she saw all around her poured out at the worst times and in the worst ways, in overreaction, most infamously expressed by overkill to her victims, smashing those girls until they were unrecognizable. Suzanne felt herself a veteran victim, all too willing to jump at the chance to see herself as being exploited. It wouldn't amaze him to learn she had turned some other aggressor into hamburger meat.

His knuckles tightened as he recalled his own beatings when young, followed by emotional torment when he grew too strong and spirited to be smacked around. Suzanne was avenging herself against the mother who tortured her own child so long ago.

Even if it's hammered into you that you're worthless, you can still earn a scholarship and become the "Answer Man"—for a while. Eric learned to sublimate his fury and develop intellectual armor, but Suzanne, utterly alone, her sister sliced and punctured, had chosen another, imperfect release valve.

Abused children identify with victims or oppressors. If you go to Columbia, you can turn it inward, your sensitivity making you a therapist. If you lived in slums, you become a notorious avenger. "The Tigress Hunter," the *Post* dubbed her.

He recalled an early therapy session. While still sixteen, Suzanne had turned the tables one day and asked what scared *him*.

Caught off guard for once, Eric had blurted: "You do."

"Because of what I am, or what I did?" she had asked.

"No, not that," he'd said, trying to recover without appearing to. "Not physically. Mentally."

She arched her eyebrows, imitating Mr. Spock, knowing she'd scored big points in the perpetual staff-inmate game of "Gotcha."

He sought to salvage the session. "I meant all therapists worry they'll find a client they can't help. None want to admit they don't know all the answers."

She brought her knees to her chest, tossed her head back, and laughed. "You have a messiah complex, don't you?" she said. "I read about that in the library."

"More masochistic than messianic," he said.

When she chuckled over that, it sounded like cackling, the last straw. He had already suspected that in addition to seeing the devil within her, these sessions were becoming a mirror, and he didn't like what was reflected.

Irritated, he decided to regain control of the session. "It's time we talked about what happened that night."

" 'That night'?" She sprang up and paced the office. "Ah yes, the infamous night in question."

It had been a mistake to push, and it could have been the last error he ever made. She stood on tiptoe and looked down, sneering. "Counselor, the Court desires your client discuss in detail her 'Morris Avenue Massacre' before we allow ourselves to entertain her plea of guilty with an explanation so we can lock her bony butt up forever." She made for the door. "You know I don't want to talk about that. Christ, you can be such a Nazi."

She stopped, turned, and for a nanosecond Eric saw tears. Then she blinked them back. "Sorry. Low blow," she said. "I know you're sensitive about that, just as I am about that night."

"We need to talk about it."

"Do we, now?" She bit her lip, muttered, sighed, then dropped into her chair and leaned forward, far closer than ever before, invading his personal space, probing to see if she could share her discomfort. "What's to tell? It was the day I buried my sister. Those Tigresses came for me, broke down my apartment door to do to me what they'd done to Nancy, only I was still at her grave. That's what saved me—not your laws or your almighty police or the virtue of being righteous. No, just grief and pure dumb luck. It was the hottest night of the year, and that, plus an empty wine bottle in the street, gave me my inspiration and my salvation. I siphoned off a quart of high-test and . . ."

She pulled back, both physically and emotionally.

"Go on," he said.

"You're just a freaking voyeur, aren't you? Like that reporter from the *Post* who wanted to know what singed hair and burnt flesh smells like. Well, it turns your stomach. Especially when you hear the screams." Her eyes widened and glistened, as if reliving the moment gave her sexual release.

If she did that at the parole board, they wouldn't even let her out of prison to be buried.

"I yelled 'batter up' as they staggered out. The louder they cried the harder I swung, until they shut up and their faces looked like strawberry jam. When the bat split, I whipped out the tire iron and hit. And hit! And hit, yelling, 'That's for Nancy, and that's for Nancy!' until I was hoarse." She sat back. "The rest is history, available on the Internet. Happy now?"

"That couldn't have made for peaceful dreams," he said, admitting empathy.

"Sleep!" She jumped up again. "You try sleeping when your association with your pillow is terror, not comfort, because your mother threatened to kill you with it every night." Her eyes had flamed. "Think about that, Dr. Glass." This time she did storm out, not to return for two weeks. Four sessions.

Just enough time for her to be adopted by Karen Rainey.

Nearly three. Moreno wasn't calling. She had laughed off his report as psychobabble and figured him a "desk jockey," knowing only theory, not practice.

Yesterday's *Daily News* had a short paragraph about Suzanne, a filler on the bottom of page nine. "Honor Student/Teen Killer at Large," read the twelve-point headline above a grainy high school photo of her alongside a copy of last year's inmate ID, the before-and-after of a one-hundred-pound avenger. Neither picture showed her facial scars, her bushy left eyebrow bisected by that wide line or that white jagged one—like a lightning bolt—behind her left ear. The others remained unseen; she was always ready to pull up her shirt to show off the physical wounds, less eager to display her emotional ones.

The stolen auto recovered in White Plains proved she was back in New York searching for Marie, her personal white whale.

Almost time to meet the department's "Escapee and Absconder Unit" man in Suzanne's old neighborhood, Eric's old neighborhood. Even if they didn't find her, Eric might sense what she felt that evening when she turned the corner to see her blood-soaked sister convulsing on the pavement. Time for fieldwork, because everyone expected miracles from him, refusing to believe his therapeutic cupboard was bare. Phenomenal successes early in his career had everyone thinking he was the greatest thing since penicillin.

On his way out the dep for programs stopped him, uttering three of the most feared words in the English language. "Got a minute?" the dep said. Then he sat back, poised for trouble, the only sounds being the hum of fluorescent lights and the drone of his air conditioner, one of the few functional ones in the entire facility. "How's this Amerce thing going?" the dep asked.

"This Amerce thing"? Warning bells clanged. "I'm meeting someone from the Escapee and Absconder Unit to search for her in her old haunts," Eric said, tempted to cross his fingers.

"Albany is following this with interest."

"Oh?" Eric's chest tightened. "Because she escaped?"

"Because she's a killer, an arsonist. If she reverts to nasty habits, sets fires and kills innocent people, the press will jump on it like a wolf pack on a lamb. If in the process they learn she had a brilliant therapist treating her twice a week and it didn't do a thing for her . . . You can imagine."

Indeed he could. "I'm not that brilliant," Eric said, sensing where this was headed and dreading the arrival.

"You underestimate yourself. Until five years ago you were terrific, the Answer Man, the one we turned to for solutions."

Only now the Answer Man was highly questionable.

"With budget crises, tons of people would love to slash funding for programs and turn our prisons back into custodial dungeons," the dep said. "If they eliminate programs or cut them to pre-Attica levels, not only won't we 'correct' anybody, we'll have as many rapes, riots, escapes, and murders as other systems."

"I'm one man. That's a lot of responsibility on me."

"You're not just *any* guy. Before you wound up here, you interviewed and recommended the hiring of how many officers?"

"Hundreds. A thousand maybe."

"More like two thousand. If the media questions your competency in handling Amerce and then by extension wonders about your skill in screening so many officers . . .

The whole state budget is being held up by the Assembly trying to slash funding for prisons. You see the potential for embarrassment, or worse."

All too well. These past five years he had often imagined the weight of the world on his shoulders. Now the fate of the department's educational, vocational, and counseling programs were riding on judgment that often was not what it used to be. "I—"

The dep held up his hand. "Go. Do. Keep us off *Eyewitness News*. I still have five years until retirement."

Dismissed. Sent to accomplish what trained law enforcement professionals had not. Why let them jerk him around like this?

Because he had no choice, needing the job to provide for Veronica. And Debbie. Especially Debbie.

This trip was his first time back in his old neighborhood in fifteen years. He'd vowed never to return once he had moved, preferring to remember it the way it had been.

It was worse than he could have imagined.

Driving up Fordham Road toward the Concourse, he took in the flashes of spray-painted graffiti, the strewn garbage, the husks of stripped cars and derelict buildings of Suzanne's old haunts. Many abused kids like Suzanne folded in on themselves, becoming winos, predators, junkies, or schizophrenics. Others, luckier or grittier, control their psychic pain, using it as motivation or expressing it through art or music or sports.

Teenage girls lounged on stoops or cars, smoking pot or flirting with boys, their personal choice of escape. Suzanne, denied this outlet, too strong-spirited, was unwilling or unable to turn her anger inward and so spewed it against the world in general or some target in particular.

To compound the problem, research confirmed that trauma early in life contributed to "explosive personality syndrome." On top of all that, Suzanne had lost puddles of blood when she had sought to join her sister by slitting her wrists. A depleted oxygen supply may have damaged her brain enough to increase the likelihood of her going ballistic.

There, his old tenement and the stoop his mother had dragged him against when he was four, for some real or imagined sin, her voice ragged from screaming, from cursing . . .

A car honked, bringing Eric back to the present. He pulled up by the burned-out shell where Suzanne had earned her nickname and her sentence. 1972 Morris Avenue, a red pre-Depression apartment house built when the Grand Concourse was one of the fanciest neighborhoods in the most special city in the world.

On either side tenements stood shoulder-to-shoulder, giant brick sentinels, mute witnesses to decay and the death of dreams.

Eric strolled to the side of the building. Had Suzanne really understood what she was about to do on that sultry three A.M., as the assistant district attorney had claimed?

If so, had she cared?

No, not about those girls and not about herself. It was premeditated murder only in that she had taken the time and trouble to assemble the tools of vengeance. As Moreno had said, the judge may have wanted to make an example of her, or had been in a bad mood, or was hoping to earn an appointment with the Reagan law-and-order administration. Whatever his motive, her harsh sentence hadn't brought those girls back to life and, judging by the crime statistics, hadn't served as an example or a deterrent.

He took deep breaths, imagining the stink of charred flesh and the shrieks of agony and rage, visualizing those girls staggering out the smoky door while Suzanne waited, poised for a home-run swing on each of them in turn, howling as she pounded them until her arms ached, half torn from their delicate sockets.

He backed away, saddled with too many ghosts of his own.

Where was the Escapee Unit guy? Eric went to the old candy store, now a bodega, and dialed his office. As he waited to be connected, he saw the grocer staring at him. Eric smiled and nodded, then heard "Absconder Unit."

"This is Eric Glass of State Corrections. I'm to meet—"

"Glass? Oh, didn't they reach you? Guess not. Mo Stentor got food poisoning over lunch. He's getting his stomach pumped."

Great. Alone in the jungle.

With no clue as to Marie's identify, Eric couldn't look for her. Suzanne called her "the big, dark queen," but dark could have referred to Marie's soul rather than her complexion. Most women were larger than Suzanne, so "big" wasn't much of a clue.

He turned from the ruined tenement, this trip incomplete without a pilgrimage to where Nancy Amerce, aged twenty-one, had spent her last moments. 1969 Creston Avenue was also trashed, like the next block on the Concourse, where he had grown up when this was still a neighborhood and not a wasteland. He saw where he and his buddies had played stoop ball and Johnny-on-the-pony. The synagogue across the street where he had been bar mitzvahed and had married Debbie was now a Baptist church.

All the sites of great milestones in his life, gone forever.

The sidewalk looked ordinary. No bloodstain darkened its concrete, no yellow chalk marks outlined the killing ground on that warm evening, not unlike this one. Around him came the clank of pots and pans, the aroma of dinners being prepared, his cue to return to his daughter.

Turning the corner, Eric saw three teens leaning against

his car's door and hood. They watched, grinning, as he approached, key in hand. "Excuse me, fellas," he said.

"Okay," said the tallest. "Don't do it again."

"I need to get in."

"Go ahead. We're not stopping you." The tall kid, his cap on backward, extended his hand. "Provided you got fifty bucks."

The kid's arms had bare patches. "Knife fighter's mange," from dry-shaving the hair to test the sharpness of his blades.

He probably carried several.

Much as Eric longed to, hammering their heads in wasn't the answer. Assuming he could take on all three, the police took a dim view of citizens bashing children, even muscular ones with vulgar tattoos on their biceps and felonies on their minds.

His brain raced. Options? Few. Even if he made it to the bodega and called the cops, by the time they arrived his Corolla would have its windows shattered, its tires slashed.

Trapped. He didn't have enough for auto ransom, so they might attack out of frustration. If his mother were alive, she'd be screaming "Idiot!" and "Fool!" at him, her shrill voice rising octaves until it could shatter crystal.

One boy edged to Eric's left, his right hand drifting to his back pocket. Think smart. Try reasoning. "Listen, fellas, why don't we all just go home and have dinner?" His mouth was dry, his therapist's words too soft to command their respect. "I . . ."

The second kid moved to Eric's right, encircling him like Indians against a wagon train. Eric stepped from the filthy curb, wondering where to run, envisioning himself bleeding to death on the very spot where Nancy Amerce had.

Harder to breathe, to swallow.

He had no weapon other than his keys, protruding between splayed fingers, good only for blinding someone if he got the first shot in. If he hurt one, the others might back off. Smash the little bastard's face into the gutter where it belonged, then drag him by his scrotum until it pulled off . . .

Wrong! Don't! Think positive. Think logical. Think legal. "This doesn't have to happen," Eric said, his voice hoarse, his fingers trembling from the adrenaline rush, the boys probably mistaking it for terror.

Do something, anything, fast. He shifted his weight onto the balls of his feet, ready. . . .

The kids smirked, enjoying this as if it were foreplay.

"What you boys doing? Hector, Angel, you nuts? Get away from that car!" The stout storekeeper emerged from his bodega.

The tall boy got off the hood, hands in pockets. His friends stepped to the curb. "Damn, Uncle Jose," he muttered. They stood, rooted, uncertain whether to move in for the slaughter or not.

The man took another step. "Raphael, you want I should tell your mama? You boys hear me? Get! Time for supper."

Their sneakers scuffed at the curbstone as they moved off.

The storekeeper kept coming. "Mister, you want to die, do it on your own ground. You get messed up in front of my store, cops come, it screws up my business for the night. *Comprende?*"

Eric nodded, not trusting his voice. He tried to open his car door, but his shaking fingers couldn't fit the key into the lock. He asked the storekeeper in a croaking voice, "You knew Marie, leader of the Tigresses, eight years ago on Morris—"

"I don't know nobody. Just go." He gave Eric a nod, watching the sweat pour from him. "It's unhealthy for you here."

That was an understatement.

The storekeeper looked around, as if expecting those kids

to return in force. "So, you a welfare inspector?"

"I lived here once."

"Uh-huh. Thought so. Seen enough, Mr. Tourist? Listen, this neighborhood isn't like when you was growing up, you hear?"

No need to be cautioned twice. Eric's own journey to the edge of violence confirmed that Suzanne still bubbled with rage. As he drove off, it came to him—her battle plan. Her rage would be sated only if she killed Marie on the anniversary of her sister's death, June the twentieth, barely over two weeks from now.

Knowledge like that never comes cheap.

Chapter Eight

Sunday, June 2

The slow, steady rock of the D train was lulling Scorch to sleep, not the smartest move for a single woman on mass transit, even in an empty car. Yesterday she lived in a dungeon, where to relax was begging for punishment, and now . . . ?

The train left the station near Yankee Stadium to slip under the Harlem River, the air in the century-old tunnel stale from the exhalations of the billions who had ridden down here over the years. Her nose wrinkled as ozone wafted through open windows from sparks sizzling on the tracks. It compounded her fear of the tunnel's roof and walls crumbling, letting in millions of tons of water held off by only New York cement and concrete.

Dr. Glass always said "the child is the parent of the adult," making Scorch a better mother to herself than that sodden, drunken hag who glared at her, red-eyed and bitter, from over her bottle of cheap booze. Scorch squeezed her shopping bags and the plastic crackled, the burst of rage distracting her from fear of the place crushing her.

First agoraphobia in the mall, now claustrophobia down here. Irrational fears took a low priority during her years of therapy with Dr. Glass, her temper being a far more pressing concern.

The door at the end of the car slammed open, letting in cool air, the 130-decibel clatter of steel on steel and a guy who looked as if he'd been up all night, cruising for trouble without success. He sat across from her and leered as Scorch swayed to the rhythm of the subway car. Time to move.

He followed, his long legs letting him catch up to her without much effort. "Hey, pretty lady, where you headed?"

"Hell. Want to tag along?" She yanked on the door handle, but it didn't budge. Stuck in the corner, sealed like meat in a can with this depraved excuse for humanity.

He chuckled and planted those long legs wide for balance as the car made a sharp turn. He was too close. If she reached for her pocketed scissor to shove up his gut, he'd grab it easily. Besides, cops took a dim view of that, as she'd learned the hard way. "Anticipate consequences," Dr. Glass said. "Don't do what makes you happy for that moment but leaves you suffering later."

They wouldn't be at the next station for several minutes, and even then there was no guarantee someone would help her. Scorch smiled up at the guy while her left hand fumbled in her shopping bags for any makeshift weapon. She breathed harder, and not from the fear of closed-in places. No, it was just like when she was sixteen, gang-raped in that corner of the rec room.

The guy stroked the downy hair on her cheeks and arms. She thought of that brandy bottle, but why waste good liquor? She remembered how she had dealt with the rookie yesterday and then thought of the lighter fluid she'd bought last night for her snazzy new Zippo.

His hand roamed to her breast, giving it a squeeze.

She felt the smooth metal can, and her smile became genuine.

"I like you, pretty lady."

"I like me too," she said as she flicked open the can's nozzle and faked a kick at his splayed legs.

When his hands dropped to cover his groin, Scorch whipped out the fuel and squirted a long stream into his face.

He howled and staggered back, clawing at his eyes. She planted a real kick just below his zipper, Karen's favorite target. He grunted, and she booted him again as the train slowed, stopped, and the door opened. She held her lighter an inch from his face, ready to thumb its wheel and light him up. Do it, spare other women his sickness. Purify the world, one maggot at a time. Then the memory of crackling flame and sizzling flesh intruded, revolting her. Plus, news of a human torch so soon after her escape would be like taking out an ad in the *Times*—"Scorch is back in business."

So, as a new, improved model, she shoved his doubled-up body out onto the nearly empty platform, then ducked down, waiting.

No one boarding the train noticed, or cared.

Where else but New York?

Her car stayed empty, so Scorch sat, waiting for the shaking to stop as she took those deep breaths Dr. Glass advocated. The car reeked of lighter fluid and fear as she imagined herself on the filthy car floor, raped. Bloody. Dead.

She trembled all the way to Forty-ninth Street, but then anger replaced fear. Time to move. Dr. Glass said, "Terror comes from inaction. Do something, fight or flight. You can fall apart later." She dashed from the train and that dank, hundred-mile-long tomb, back to the earth's surface. The sun was higher, baking the streets, tempting her to hang a left to Grand Central or the Port Authority Bus Terminal, blocks away.

Greyhound advertised a presummer special, a one-way ticket to California. All she had to do was step up to the cashier, plunk down all her cash, and she would be off and away.

All she had to do was forget the past eight years.

Sure, like nightmares—just pretend they never happened.

The problem was this sidewalk was identical to the one back in the Bronx where Nancy twisted in her own blood, a dozen wet roses blooming all over her body as she screamed, "Sue . . . !"

Nancy, convulsing, gutted for thirty bucks and a Timex, her emotional agony worse than the physical; she knew she'd be dead in moments and nothing could save her.

Dying in her sister's arms, clutching at her as if holding on to life itself, until her arms dropped into that spreading red circle. Who knew the human body held so much blood?

All because freaking Marie, pumped on lines of coke, said "Slice her, girls!" just to show she had balls like a guy.

Sometimes crystal-clear memory is a bad thing. In this case, it aimed Scorch away from the bus and toward the homeless and hopeless on Eleventh and Forty-ninth, heart thumping faster than when the train had plunged under the river. Scorch slipped the scissors from their leatherette scabbard, keeping them against her thigh in case Marie popped up to visit her protégé, Tanya.

Scorch took the four flights two steps at a time, eager as a ghoul escaping from its tomb to terrorize its former village.

So Tanya was still alive—for now—unaware a wildfire was about to overtake her.

No bell, so Scorch banged on the scratched wooden door. No answer. Was the pathetic weasel out, visiting Marie?

Joel Ross

Hesitant steps. "Yeah?" asked the subdued voice of one beaten down by life. "Who's it?"

"Tanya, it's Marie." Scorch pocketed her scissors and prayed.

"Marie?" After a three-second pause to process this, a lock clanked, the door creaked open, and a scrawny, disheveled girl clad in ragged cutoffs and T-shirt looked down at her.

Tanya! Tanya, all right. Eight years hadn't changed her.

Scorch recognized the scars gouged into Tanya's cheeks and earlobes; she'd carved them there herself. She smiled, clapped her left hand over Tanya's mouth, and slammed her right fist into the young woman's breasts once, twice.

By the third shot, Tanya was slumped against the doorjamb.

Scorch slipped inside and kicked the door shut behind her. "You alone? Nod or shake."

Tanya, her eyes wide, tried to squirm away, so Scorch elbowed her in the stomach. "Answer!" she hissed. "You alone?"

Tanya's eyes refocused as she snorted air. She nodded.

"Good." Scorch pulled the scissors, held them in front of Tanya's face, and watched her eyes widen. Then Scorch placed its tip against the hollow of Tanya's neck. "Scream and die!" she said before yanking down Tanya's shorts and pulling her shirt up over her head and down her back, pinning her arms behind her.

It was a tiny studio apartment, stuffy, with an unmade bed in one corner. Nobody else here, unless they were hiding in the bathroom or under the mattress. Scorch dragged Tanya over to the bed, flung her onto it facedown, and straddled her.

"Remember me, maggot?" she said as she unhooked Tanya's brassiere and secured it over her wrists, tight as she dared without making it into a tourniquet.

As she was rolled over, Tanya yelled, "Who the hell . . . ?"

76

Scorch slapped her. "A simple 'yes' or 'no' will do. I killed your gang buddies eight years ago. Morris Avenue?"

"Help!"

Scorch slapped her again, then grabbed the lumpy pillow and held it inches from Tanya's face. "Scream again and it's over."

Although six inches taller than Scorch, Tanya was skinny, almost emaciated, as if she'd spent the past eight years burning up her body with coke and crack. After an abortive attempt to pitch Scorch off, she gave up, already spent. She had an acetic smell to her, as if she worked in a mortuary.

"Remember me, Tanya? You murdered my sister!"

The pale light of recognition switched on, then brightened.

"You! Scorch!"

"Me Scorch. You dead meat unless you talk."

For an instant, rage and hatred flashed in Tanya's eyes. Then her spirit flickered and died. "You scarred me up," she said. She looked away and bit her lip.

"You came out a lot better than the others, except Marie. Speaking of the devil, where is she?"

"Don't know. Get the hell off me."

Scorch smacked her again, shifted her weight, and rammed her knee twice into Tanya's midsection before jamming the pillow over Tanya's face. "One. Two. Three . . ."

The taller girl bucked and thrashed, but with her willowy limbs tied, her panicked squirming couldn't free her. Scorch leaned on the pillow with all her weight, all her hate. "Sixteen, seventeen . . ."

Tanya's struggles weakened. Scorch would hold it over her face just long enough to let Tanya feel the true terror of helplessness, of inevitable death. Scorch had been on the receiving end of this slow, silent horror far too often herself and feared she could enjoy it from the giving side. "Thirty-nine. Forty." Scorch risked becoming just like her mother.

She slid the pillow down a few inches, uncovering Tanya's eyes and nose. "Like it, Tanya? Want to try for fifty seconds?"

Tanya shook her head as best she could, while sucking in stale air.

"Ready to talk?" Scorch asked.

Tanya tried to nod.

"Good girl. Marie. Where?" She lifted the pillow an inch, uncovering Tanya's mouth.

"Please. Don't kill—"

Scorch stuffed the pillow over Tanya's mouth again, its edge just under her nose. "Wrong answer. Ready to go for fifty?"

Tanya's eyes screamed as she tried to throw Scorch off.

Bad move. Scorch shoved the pillow back over Tanya's nose, pushing with the same desperation as the young woman underneath her, escalating her efforts to match Tanya's.

This was dumb for them both. All the weasel had to do was answer. She was her lone link to Marie.

Scorch's rage stoked higher at that thought, and she hung on with her remaining energy, her arms quivering as they held down the pathetic girl under her.

Tanya's legs pulled out of her shorts, her arms threatening to tear free of the frayed T-shirt and bra. Fearing she'd get her eyes clawed, Scorch released one hand to punch Tanya in the temple once. Twice.

The scarred girl's struggles lessened. Ceased.

Scorch lifted the pillow. Was it too late?

Tanya, her chest heaving, fought for air. "Don't . . . I'll . . . tell . . . Please . . ."

"Marie? Where? Next time I won't stop. You got two seconds." She yanked Tanya's bikinis below her knees. "Then I cover your nose with your drawers. Want to die with the aroma of your own pussy juice in your nostrils, it's fine with me."

"Please . . ."

"You want sex with me? Maybe later. Talk."

"Last I . . . heard . . . Thirty-sixth Street."

"It's a big street. Be more precise."

"Five-thirty-eight . . . West . . . Couple years ago."

It was a start. She got off Tanya and leaned back, already feeling the strain in her arms. Her fist throbbed. "I find you lied, I'll come back and finish the job, and believe me, this will seem like lovemaking compared to what I'll do to you then."

Tanya's shoulders shook as she sobbed and curled into a fetal position. "You slashed up my face!"

"Why not? You were a Tigress, a vicious, stupid, stubborn chick who wouldn't give it up when I asked you nicely eight years ago. Besides, you came out of it better than your friends. Want to see scars?" Scorch yanked up her own T-shirt to show off her own mementos of rage. "Like these? And the ones you can't see are even worse." She covered her midriff and scanned the room, a pack rat's nest, with discarded furniture and junk. A vinyl purse lay on the dinette table, its contents dumped out. Scorch sifted through them. More crap and eighteen bucks. She swept them into her bag as she scanned the room.

"You ruined my life," Tanya croaked.

"Oh yeah?" Scorch ran over and kicked Tanya's butt twice, as hard as she had done to that bastard on the train. Then she grabbed Tanya's hair, ready to ruin her life further. "I was an honor student, ready for college, when your scum butchered my sister and left me homeless at fifteen. All you need is to wear a pound of makeup and you're okay. Whatever damage there is, you brought on yourself." Logic is wasted on children, or junkies. "What's Marie's last name?"

"Don't know. Something Italian or Spanish. Her street name was Sheena."

That narrowed it down. "What's she look like now?"

79

"Huh? Haven't seen her in a couple years."

"Still close, huh? What's she do to earn money?"

"She sold me dope sometimes. Coke. Pot. Don't kill me."

No need. Tanya had already killed herself, long ago. She just hadn't bothered to get buried yet. Scorch had spared her eight years ago because she had been just a Tigress cub, Scorch's age. Plus, the word on the street was she hadn't been involved in the slaughter. So all Scorch had done was use Tanya as a pincushion, a cutting board, until she learned all she needed to kill the others, the weak link dooming its chain.

What to do about Tanya? Killing her would be redundant, but Scorch couldn't have her free to warn Marie. Shaka Zulu said, "Never leave an enemy behind." Tanya probably sensed Scorch's ambivalence, and she cringed by the foot of her bed.

Scorch felt like grabbing Tanya by the hair and slamming her head against the wall until her empty skull cracked like an eggshell. How delicious. As she tied her to the bed with plastic trash bags, she thought about skinning off Tanya's nylon bikinis and stuffing them in her mouth. Hell, she could drown her in the tub or toilet, getting off on the futile twisting and flailing of those slender arms and legs. If she did that, she'd be as sick as those bitches who murdered Nancy or who had raped her that first nightmarish month in prison. Instead she gagged her with a pillowcase, to leave this pathetic creature to wriggle free, hide behind some drugs, and by the time she returned to earth it would be nightfall and perhaps Marie would be dead.

Scorch gathered her stuff. " 'Bye, Tanya. Nice seeing you."

All Scorch needed was a simple jab with the scissors, or an ounce of pressure to pinch Tanya's nostrils. No one would care. "I'm not going to kill you," she said. "I'll do something worse." She knelt beside the terrified girl. "I'm going to let you live with yourself."

Then she hurried out of that dump. Although her arms ached and her fist was already so swollen she could barely distinguish individual knuckles, Scorch felt good. It had been almost orgasmic up there, getting back Marie and company again.

So ended round one of the war between her psychic parents, Dr. Glass and Karen Rainey, as they battled for her soul.

She turned the corner and was halfway down the next block when she heard sirens. Had that pitiful junkie summoned enough courage to call the cops? Scorch clutched her bags under each arm to zigzag like a miniature O. J. Simpson between alleys. . . .

It was only an ambulance, racing back toward Forty-ninth.

Scorch kept walking. Halfway to Thirty-sixth Street she had to pause, her adrenaline finally petering out. Barely eight; what an incredible sixteen hours. No time to stop. Even if Tanya didn't warn her, Marie might learn of her escape. . . .

Finally, Marie's lair, a dump, with the smell of urine by the threshold and no buzzers or names by the front door. Palming her scissors, Scorch thumbed the building superintendent's bell.

Any moment . . . Scorch pictured Marie's eyes as wide with terror as Nancy's had been, as she saw the glint of steel, then felt seven inches of scissors pumped into her guts, over and over.

Would her blood smell like Nancy's?

No, the freaking bitch had ice water in her veins, just what you'd expect from a reptile who ordered up murder as casually as asking for a pizza.

A harried woman, Mrs. Super probably, answered. "Yeah?" She stared down at Scorch. "You selling?"

No, buying. "Hi. I'm a friend of Marie. . . . She's about

thirty. She lives here with her child." It wouldn't do to admit she didn't know the witch's last name.

The woman wrinkled her nose. "Marie? Yeah, she lived here last year."

"Lived?" Lost her. Scorch's shoulders sagged. "Moved?"

The woman nodded. "Yeah. She had, like, six or seven addresses before this one. I told the landlord a person like that don't stay long, wouldn't keep the place decent. He didn't listen."

"Did she leave a forwarding address?"

"Why?"

"I told you, she's a friend. Haven't seen her in a while."

The woman shrugged. "Don't think so. I could ask my husband if he wasn't still sleeping it off."

"Her deposits . . . They were sent somewhere."

The woman shrugged again, rolls of fat shimmering from the underside of her arms. "Landlord would have handled that."

Dead end. Get aggressive. "What name was she going under?"

"Thought she was your friend."

"She is. Er . . ." Look sheepish now. "I need to find her. She owes me money." Scorch pulled out a precious twenty. "If I got a forwarding address, I'd be grateful." The woman reached for it, and Scorch pulled it back. "If you tell me later this week, I could give you two of these."

The woman sneered. "I don't know. I'll try."

"I'd be really grateful." The woman couldn't imagine how much. Scorch ripped the twenty in two, handing her one half as an information deposit. "Will tomorrow be too soon?"

"Tomorrow. Tuesday. I'll ask next time I talk to him."

Scorch checked out the place. It was a dive, several steps down from the sort of building she herself had grown up in. Marie was on the run, changing houses every few years, living a nomadic existence just in case.... Or was Scorch giving herself too much credit, thinking this bitch lived in fear of her? No, what had been a loser as a teen remained a loser as an adult, scurrying from hole to hole, dragging her bastard kid with her.

Don't worry, Marie. If you're sick with misery, I'll cure you. Scorch moved down the street, a ship adrift without a home port or a destination.

She could wander Manhattan, hoping to see Marie, but she probably didn't look like she did back in '88. Scorch herself had added over five pounds of muscle and snipped off most of a healthy head of hair.

Scorch needed a place to lie low until the furor over her escape faded. Midtown, with its milling millions, was perfect.

Homeless shelters or the YWCA might be too obvious.... As she passed a grocery she absentmindedly plucked a plump orange. The citrus pyramid collapsed, so she took off, but she hadn't gone ten feet when she heard angry words behind her, the Asian proprietor sounding like he was barking. Cursing was the same in any language. Scorch kept walking, hoping the guy wasn't stupid enough to chase her for the sake of toppled fruit.

"He went that way," a tall, slender young woman said to the grocer, pointing in the opposite direction. She gave Scorch a wink and fell in beside her. "Pretty slick," she said.

"You too," said Scorch. "Would you like to share it?"

"Thanks, but I've got my own upstairs."

Upstairs? As in nearby? "You live around here?"

"Close by. It's convenient to the theater."

"You an actress?"

The girl laughed. "A wanna-be. I'm a dancer, an extra. I blend in with the scenery. Right now I'm a standby for *Cats*. I worked in *Les Mis*."

"*Les Miserables*?" About a fugitive. Talk about omens.

The girl nodded and smiled again, her eyes roaming over Scorch as had John's, the cop's, the bus driver's. Christ, was she giving out—what had Dr. Glass called it?—a pheromone, some subtle sexual signal, like ringing the lust dinner bell? Come and get her, she's fresh. Unused.

The young woman extended a warm, firm hand. "Name's Kelly. On stage I'm Candy."

Of course she was, with long legs that went on forever, leading to Wonderland. . . . "I'm Helen Glass. Of Troy."

Kelly giggled. "That's cute. You're cute."

"I have my moments. No, I'm from Troy. Upstate." An excuse covering a multitude of inconsistencies, explaining lots without forcing her to come up with a bunch of bull on the spot and blow her cover.

"So, you shopping?" Kelly pointed to Scorch's canvas and plastic shopping bags.

"Actually, I was looking up an old friend, but she's moved." Here goes. "I was hoping to spend the night with her. Now I'll just have to try to get a hotel room."

"Don't! The good ones are always booked this time of year, and the others are expensive but not always clean or safe." Kelly's blue eyes sparkled as she laid that warm hand on Scorch's. "I've got a couch. You could stay with me."

Too good to be true. "You don't know me. I could be an ax murderer." Or the next-closest thing. Actually, Scorch had once worked alongside one in the prison laundry, an upstate woman who had done in her husband with an L.L. Bean "Woodsman's Special."

"Lizzie Borden you're not. Let's do lunch."

Kelly guided her to a tiny Pakistani place.

She recalled Dr. Glass saying, "Go slow, because life first tests, then teaches. Be careful." She half expected him to kiss her on the top of her head after he said those things. It wasn't as if he didn't have a daughter of his own. No, it was more than a father-daughter thing they had, and definitely not sexual. She'd show up for his sessions with her skirt hiked way up or her pants pulled low; he'd never bat an eye, the archetype cool, detached therapist, desperate for her to have . . . what?

"Helen? Helen?"

"Huh? Sorry, my mind drifts sometimes." Got to keep track of the aliases. "What?"

"I asked, 'Have you given thought to spending the night?' "

"Sure. A lot. If it's not imposing . . ."

Kelly gave a mischievous smile. "No imposition. How did you hurt your hand?"

"Living an active life." And a dangerous one.

Sleeping with Kelly was light-years ahead of spending the night with John; she had more class and couldn't get her pregnant. Besides, Kelly was really cute, with curly red hair, those legs, those baby blues . . . Scorch could have a place to rest and plan while maintaining her technical virginity.

Was it virginity only if you hadn't done it with a member of the opposite sex? They'd discuss that strolling through Central Park now, or perhaps tonight, sipping that brandy.

Chapter Nine

The two corrections officers squirmed in their seats, the young woman once again seconds away from tears. Ironically, she had chosen the chair Suzanne always sat in. Suzanne . . . who had nearly cost this probationary trainee her job.

The chubby one, Fielder, lit up and blew smoke at the woman. "She shouldn't have been so careless, that's what done it."

Eric took a deep breath, despite the smoke, to avoid saying or doing something he'd regret. "A debriefing session isn't to lay blame, it's to sort out feelings concerning the incident."

"I'm feeling ticked off," Fielder said, his neck scarlet.

"You said take her to the bathroom, and I did," the rookie said, finally showing spunk and standing up for herself after just slumping in the chair and sniffling for fifteen minutes. "You shouldn't have left us alone for so long," she said.

"You was in there for two freaking—"

"Excuse me," Eric said, feeling like a cross between a

marriage counselor and a boxing referee. "We're here to vent feelings and describe reactions. The administration will do their own procedural postmortem later. Okay?"

The man snorted and stubbed out his cigarette. "Okay, I'm *royally* ticked off. I got nothing else to say."

"It's okay to feel anger," said Eric. "It's not good to act on it." It was a rule of life he'd given Suzanne so many times. She loved her rage, feeding it as one would a prized pet, to be trotted out and exhibited and sometimes—at inopportune moments—to be released, like lions upon Christians.

The two officers looked at each other. The pregnant pause.

The textbooks advised: "Let the silence work for you."

The man rose from his chair. "You got any other words of wisdom?" he asked as he headed for the door.

"None," said Eric, glad to be rid of him. If it weren't for his union, the guy would have been flipping burgers years ago.

"Then good-bye. I think you're a bleeding heart, a freaking 'inmate lover,' and you know what happens to them."

A hollow threat from a hollow head. Now that he was gone, the young woman allowed herself the luxury of really crying.

Eric offered her tissues and waited a moment. "It'll be okay," he said.

The rookie sniffed, daubed her eyes, and nodded. "Maybe I wasn't cut out for this. I flubbed my first real assignment."

"If you want it badly enough, you'll make a fine CO."

"I'm from upstate. These people from the city . . ." She shook her head. "I just don't know sometimes. Thanks, Doctor."

She left Eric alone to worry why he'd heard nothing further from Detective Moreno. Perhaps Suzanne was halfway to Florida or California, panhandling in bus stations, working in a laundry or a truck stop, doing something to get her life together.

Please, Suzie, don't look for Marie. Anger just gives ulcers or hypertension. He ran fingers through his hair, noting that fury also gives you gray where and when you don't need it.

The hall officer stuck his head in. "Doc, you free? Inmate wants a word with you."

Glass nodded. He often got "walk-ins," somebody upset because of a "Dear Jane" letter or a disastrous visit or a sick child or a failed appeal. Friday afternoons and major holidays were the worst, but crises came anytime, in any size and shape.

Karen Rainey came in, holding some sheets of paper, looking grim. "Hi, Dr. Glass." Her dark eyes darted around, sizing up an office Suzanne must have told her about many times over the years. She reinforced the impression of the Wicked Queen in "Snow White," with her sharp angular features. Her jailhouse name was Lucretia—or was it Arachne?

"I've been real upset since Scorch left," she said.

"You and Suzanne were close."

"Like sisters."

Interesting phrase. Rainey wore tight clothes, making him wonder where she concealed the inevitable weapon she must carry, probably a sharpened toothbrush handle or some other sliver honed to razor thinness. She was leaning forward, playing the seductress, but that could change in an instant if she grew frustrated or got ticked off because it suited her need to show power or status.

Did his portable alarm still work, and if so, could she lunge across his desk before he pushed himself out of range to pull it?

Maybe she was just groping for news. So how could he pick her brain without her knowing it and not give her anything she could use to her own advantage? "I'm sure Suzanne is okay."

"If she hasn't been caught yet, that means she'll stay in the clear, right?" she said.

Okay, Rainey was just foraging for current events. "I haven't heard anything." Which was true; the cops weren't treating him much better than the felons he dealt with.

"You think she'll make it?" she asked.

"She's bright, young, and resourceful. If she keeps her head and decides to, she could start a new life. What do you think?"

Rainey's eyes narrowed a millimeter. He had been too blunt and she suspected he was fishing, just as he figured she was, and they had tangled each other's lines.

"She can do whatever she sets her mind to," she said.

"You're right, Ms. Rainey." He decided to probe deeper, to see what nerve he tweaked. "Will she show good judgment?"

"Yeah, I think. Well, I don't want to hold you up. You probably got lots to do."

Did Rainey mean Suzanne was out there hunting? He had to be sure, so he tried for it. "You've known her a long time, and she was closer to you than me. Will she do the right thing?"

She shrugged, clammed up.

He had shown his hand and gotten nothing in return, other than confirming his suspicion that Suzanne was going for it. Rainey knew. She must have heard Suzanne recite her litany of hate far too many times over the years. Now he knew, and Rainey knew he knew. He leaned over to his desk calendar while keeping an eye on her. "Shall we get together next week?"

She weighed this for a moment, playing mental chess.

It was much easier to deal with younger inmates. They

didn't con you as well, and everything was up front with them. They thought they still had a future, dim as it might be.

"Sure. Monday morning?" she said.

He scribbled in her name as she stood.

"By the way, they cleaned out her cell today and the block officer gave me these." She held out two sheets of paper.

Drawings, done with colored pens, pencils, crayons, and Lord knew what else. The first showed a girl perched on a heap of skulls, pulling a small devil from between her legs to hand to a wizened man in a robe, with a long gray beard, a conical hat, the whole stereotypical nine yards. How flattering for her to think of him like that. So much for his words of wisdom.

The second was of a young woman clutching her head, screaming so loudly her open mouth took up nearly her whole face. Inside that mouth was a much smaller woman, screaming.

Peering into the second mouth, he saw a screaming little girl being swallowed up. In the lower right-hand corner of each drawing were curlicues, like tiny tornadoes, ending in the letters S.R.A. Suzanne's surreal period, no doubt.

"Interesting," he said as he tried to hand them back.

Karen shook her head. "You keep them. They're too creepy."

Indeed they were. "Thank you. I appreciate this."

A thin smile crossed her face as she nodded and left.

Well, that went poorly, with Rainey now suspecting he was trying to learn if Suzanne was still obsessed with Marie. It could get unhealthy if she spread the word he was rooting around for information. Or he might just be overly analytical, or just plain paranoid. Why shouldn't he be, as "Chiropractor of Hell's Anteroom"? Unable to focus, he couldn't work Thursday afternoons anymore, as he dreaded what was to come later in the day. Things were bad enough without him beating himself up like this.

He looked at the pictures again. The first, of the child on the skulls, was dated 1989, when Suzanne at seventeen had her first revelation in therapy. The second was from three years ago, when she finished recounting the horrors at the hands of her mom.

So to her Dr. Glass was an ancient shaman, a repository for her nightmares and emotional refuse. He had to get out of here and do his Thursday penance before the walls closed in on him.

When Lucy Moreno called the prison, she was told Eric Glass had left early. When she phoned his home, that West Indian woman said he was at the Children of Rachel Nursing Home in Mount Vernon and she could meet him there. Lucy decided to drive there, partly to apologize for having stormed into his home to pick his brain and partly to invite him to the precinct tomorrow to help her do a computer composite of Scorch's possible new appearance.

The Children of Rachel Nursing Home was large and silent, except for the hiss of lawn sprinklers and the hum of insects. The building was a chronic-care facility, with most of its inhabitants elderly or suffering from neurological problems. Its halls and lobby were quiet with subdued lighting; it housed people long past their ability to make much noise.

"Yes?" asked the receptionist.

"Uh . . . I was told Dr. Glass was here."

"If he's still around, he's in room 612."

As Lucy took the elevator, she figured Glass was moonlighting outside the prison. Why not? He probably did this to work with a more deserving and less demanding clientele. The sixth floor, antiseptic white, was the Long Term Care Unit.

Room 612 held two women, one in her seventies, the other half that age. Smith, Jennet and Glass, Debbie.

Debbie Glass lay hooked to machines that breathed for her, lived for her. Amber monitors bleeped and pulsed, bearing witness to her living death.

Eric Glass sat beside her, eyes closed, clasping her hands. His lips moved slightly, either whispering or praying.

Debbie Glass had long black hair that might have been lustrous when she was truly alive. Her eyes . . . ? Who knew? The pink lids were shut to the world. Looking closer, Lucy Moreno noticed Debbie should have been pretty but there was something not quite right about her. Her face was asymmetric, the left side indented . . . as if . . .

As if the skull had been smashed in and then not reconstructed perfectly, because what does a living corpse need with perfection, or care about its looks?

An aide came in, and Glass stood and talked with her for a moment before trying to press money into her hand.

The aide shook her head and backed off. On the way out, she smiled at Lucy. "Couple times a week he come and try to pay me for what I do anyway. Poor guy."

"How long . . . ?" asked Lucy, pointing to Debbie Glass.

"His wife? She was here when I come tree year ago. An auto wreck, maybe. He come and sit awhile like he do now, then try to give money away. Me, I don't take extra. Got to go. 'Bye."

Now Lucy suspected why Glass had not pursued licensure for private practice, nor had published gathered research.

His life was smashed into perpetual coma, confined to a bed, hooked up to life support.

He stood and kissed his wife's pale cheek, her skin probably cool to the touch. He strode from the room, past Lucy, as if she were invisible. She caught up to him by the elevator.

"Detective Moreno? Why . . . ?"

"I was told I could find you here. I'm sorry. Had I known, I wouldn't have intruded. . . ."

He held up a weary hand, as if most of his energy had been sucked out by those tubes that fed his wife. "It's okay. It would probably do me good to tell somebody. I mean, who does the therapist confide in? I used to be a jolly 'social' drinker." He pointed to Debbie's room. "The bastard who did this was your typical jackass, a forty-year-old adolescent with a couple previous DWAIs under his belt. That night he had been smoking crack. He still had a rock of the stuff and a pipe on the seat beside him when he plowed into us—caving in her side of the car. She was driving because I'd had four drinks at a party." He sighed as the elevator door whooshed open and he shambled in. "It could—should—have been me behind the wheel that night, but I was one over my limit, so she drove instead."

He touched that long scar on his forehead, another lasting reminder of that nightmarish night. He was silent on the way out, engaged in self-flagellation for having indulged in a harmless good time, with fate making him the sole survivor. "Let's walk," he said. "It's a pleasant afternoon, plus we shouldn't finish this in my home. My daughter readily latches on to adult females, even one as young as you."

She smiled at what he must have meant to be flattery. "Veronica looks on every woman as a surrogate mother since this happened, even Cassandra—she's our Jamaican neighbor—who took care of her after the accident and was—is—as different from her mother as yin from yang. You don't need to be next on her list. Still," he shrugged again, and almost gave way to a smile, "I guess it's less of a worry than having her sneak off with sixteen-year-old boys reeking of testosterone. On a more cheerful note, what's happening with Suzanne?"

Suzanne? Interesting he referred to her by her given, and

not jailhouse, name. Lucy filled him on what she had un-covered thus far, which wasn't much. "Come down to the precinct tomorrow afternoon and help me figure out what she may look like."

"If you'd like, but I have bad news for you," he said. "I spoke to her buddy today, and she confirmed my hunch: Suzanne wants Marie's hide and will risk it all to get it." He plucked a dandelion and handed it to Lucy.

"You think she will?" she asked as she stuck it in her hair.

"Oh yes. She may well succeed. She's highly intelligent, learned lots of bad tricks from experts, and has been through this before, eluding police for weeks as a raw, fright-ened fifteen-year-old. That's bound to give her the confi-dence to do it again now that she's seasoned. She'll probably try to hook up with a young woman, someone to be her surrogate sister. She's terrified of abandonment, but if she feels exploited or betrayed, it could look like her Mor-ris Avenue Massacre all over again."

"I guess her therapy hasn't made her a better person."

"It was to help her cope with the reality of living at least a quarter-century in that dungeon. We discussed sociology, philosophy, and human behavior, how people think and react, and how to deal with them. How to handle challenges and crises."

"By doing so, did you make her a more efficient preda-tor?"

He stopped and sighed. "Definitely. No doubt about it."

Chapter Ten

Thursday, June 6

Marie Balboa flicked the back of a damp hand across her forehead and blinked away sweat. She was long overdue for her break, but a bus accident at Times Square had dumped a bunch of possible fractures into Roosevelt Hospital's ER.

Timing is everything.

When she finished it was almost time for lunch, so she nodded to her supervisor. "Taking five, boss." She slouched in a molded plastic chair in the break room, ignoring the moans and cries from the ER down the hall. She had to earn big overtime this month. Her daughter Kala needed braces, or so the dentist had threatened. That secondhand air conditioner she was skimping for would have to wait until next summer. Hell, Marie had needed braces when she was a kid, hadn't gotten them, and had still managed to chew her cud through to adulthood, making it to twenty-eight without choking or biting her own lips.

As for beauty, who was able to smile these days, anyway?

Not much to read while she drank coffee with the taste

95

and texture of sludge, a muddy conglomeration that had been brewing since seven A.M. and probably could be eaten with a spoon. Just a few magazines she had already leafed through, and Tuesday's *Daily News*. Marie thumbed through it, noting the scandals and atrocities of Fun City. Would the Yankees dare move to Jersey? Hell, everyone else was leaving.

Nothing but crap in the paper.

She bolted upright. It couldn't be! She peered closer, hoping she had misread the name under the picture.

Amerce! Suzanne Amerce. "Scorch," they later called her.

The photos were grainy, but there was no mistaking those cold, dark eyes, like black holes. Seeing them once was enough.

Marie reread the story, eyes racing over the type. "Teen killer at large . . . anyone knowing whereabouts . . ."

The kid sister. Out! Marie looked at the date at the top of the page, then reread the filler article a third time. Tuesday's paper! Hell! She had been out since Saturday evening!

She could be here now!

Marie brushed limp hair from her eyes as she wondered if her appearance had changed enough from that evening when, wired on coke, she had told the other girls to puncture that woman, to teach the rest of the block a lesson, that the Tigresses weren't to be messed. If they told you to fork over your dough, you did it or you bled. Or bled even if you gave it up, because on their turf even the boys had better beware.

The pygmy psycho, with her gasoline bombs and her crowbar and her shrieking rage . . . The "Tigress Hunter," the papers had called her, making her into some kind of romantic avenging angel as she stalked them one by one, until only their leader, Marie, was left, the lone Tigress with the smarts to avoid the midget monster until the cops finally busted her.

Christ, she could be outside the door now, with another crowbar or rusted tire iron or broken bottle, waiting!

Marie slammed the door and scanned the break room for makeshift weapons, seeing only a coffeepot holding the tepid mud or cheap institutional chairs that couldn't stun a chipmunk. Yeah, Scorch Amerce could be outside or she could be in Miami now, lounging on the beach. They said she'd stolen a car, credit cards, cash. She could have moved on, stealing as she went.

Or Scorch was prowling the streets, seeking someone she had seen once at dusk eight years ago, while her sister lay gushing blood onto the hot pavement. Calm down.

Her thundering heart slowed and Marie took another gulp of coffee, though she was wound up enough. Think this through. Marie's lone advantage was that she knew, via the *Daily News* photo, what Amerce looked like, while Amerce had no notion of Marie's current appearance. That gave her some edge. Now, instead of braces for Kala, Marie needed to buy a thirty-eight or a nine-millimeter, anything compact enough to fit into a handbag or her waistband with a blouse over it. She had a knife, a good one, but the time for blades was past, dead as the Tigresses.

For that dwarf devil, she needed a gun, fast.

She pawed through her bag for her list of connections, wondering who could have a piece for her by dinnertime.

The rest of the day was a blur. She vaguely recalled getting bawled out by her supervisor for messing up X rays of twisted legs, dislocated shoulders. Let him try dealing with balky old machines when there was a maniac on the loose, waiting to slit her belly and strangle her with her own intestines. She thought of Lily and Minerva, unable to recall which friend had had her skull caved in, or who had been drowned in her own blood.

Marie couldn't very well go to the police. She'd be confessing to a killing and would be locked up as an accessory, at the very least. There was no statute of limitations on murder. But that had been in the past, and she had caused only one death, while Amerce had killed six! Six!

Marie, twenty then, had been strung out on coke and crack and amphetamines, unwilling to begin the morning without uppers or tolerate the day without grass, unable to sleep without barbiturates, or do anything without some chemical percolating in her nervous system. If the schools and Social Service and the church had done their job, nobody would have died and she wouldn't be looking over her shoulder every ten seconds, quaking at each corner in case a madwoman lunged to shove her in front of an oncoming bus or truck.

She stopped at the bank for all her cash and got to Kala's school late. She had sweated out a gallon of fluids as she trotted along the crap-covered sidewalks while wondering if her next step would be her last, if her picture would be alongside the little lunatic's in tomorrow's *Daily News,* front page:

"TIGRESS HUNTER CLAIMS FINAL VICTIM. Story on page 3."

The hall had no sounds of squealing kids. Sure, she was a few minutes late. . . . "Kala. Kala!" Christ, what if the pygmy psycho had tracked Kala down, found her alone, and . . . !

Would she take her hatred out on some innocent kid?

Marie had, eight years ago. What goes around comes around.

She ran down the hall, her sneakers squeaking on the freshly waxed floor. Nobody. She groaned, then yelled, "Kala!" Marie paused when she heard a sound. "Kala!" She envisioned her child in the center of a dark, wet circle spreading along the floor.

"What?" came a faint voice back the other way.

Marie ran to a classroom where another teacher, not

Kala's, was washing the blackboard while Kala watched. The woman looked up. "Are you Mrs. Balboa?"

"Huh? Yeah." She ran to Kala. "Didn't you hear me call you?" Marie scooped Kala up and shook her. "When Mommy calls, answer!" Kala's head snapped back and forth like one of those stupid dashboard dolls. Stop! Get a grip! She hugged her.

"Sorry," Kala said, her voice muffled against Marie's chest.

"Always listen to Mommy," Marie said. "You're all she has!" Though tempted to give her a smack for not answering at once, she recalled that there was a stranger looking on.

"Since you hadn't come yet," the woman said, "Kala's teacher asked me to watch her for you. I'm sorry if you were upset."

"Huh? Yeah, it's all right. Thanks." She took Kala's hand and moved her along. There was money to be scrounged or borrowed and pleaded for so she could have her gun by tonight.

Finally, after a tense five-minute walk home, after bolting all three locks, Marie turned over her handbag, pawing through the dumped contents for crushed bills, then rushing to all the secret hiding places for her drug dollars to add to the money she'd withdrawn earlier. Two hundred eighty-three bucks! That was it till payday, and she'd still need cash for food. She could walk to work, but Kala needed so much. While her daughter watched TV Marie took inventory of her possessions, wondering what could be hocked and for how much, but always coming up short.

Paulo had a used stainless-steel Smith & Wesson "Chief's Special" waiting for her, one with a shrouded hammer, for only four-fifty—nearly the same price as in a sporting goods store if you were eligible for a license, which Marie would never be.

She checked her oregano jar. Empty. She couldn't sell

pot even if she had it, and right now she could do with a few good tokes herself. Only one option left, revolting as it was.

She dialed Cal, half of her hoping he was home while the other half wished he didn't pick up. He did, sounding pleased to hear from her. She spilled her guts, telling him of the *Daily News* article, of the fear of reprisal from mad Scorch Amerce.

He listened and chuckled. "What do you need from me?"

She stared at the crumpled bills on her bed, disliking the option slightly less than the alternative of hanging up. "A gun."

He chuckled louder, the sound making her want to bash his face in with the receiver. "I don't have one. Even if I did, I wouldn't give it to you. We both know your temper."

"I can buy one. I'm just a little short of cash."

Silence on the line, with only a few phantom voices of a bad connection whispering ghost conversations. "Cal, for Kala's sake. I need to protect us." More silence. She was ready to explode and hang up when he asked, "How little is short?"

The bastard would come through after all. "Two hundred."

He laughed, that braying sound she hated so much, just like his smugness. What had she seen in him seven years ago? Whatever it was, it had been enough to make a beautiful child, even if she was bucktoothed.

"We could have dinner and see what develops," he said.

"I'm no whore! If I was, I could earn more on the street."

"Nobody's stopping you. Good night. Love to Kala."

"Wait! An hour, then."

Chuckling again, knowing, as always, that he held the upper hand. "An hour. Wear something nice, like only you know how."

Dial tone. Marie plopped onto the bed, the twenties and

tens crinkling underneath her. The bastard had her over a barrel, what he used to tease was his favorite position for her. Well, at least she'd get dinner from it. Cal knew how to cook and knew how to screw, in more ways than one. She couldn't take Kala to a ball-and-gun deal, although she had been brought as a baby more than once, cradled in sweaty arms, while Mama bought drugs.

"Kala, Mommy's going out." To visit your lousy father; he should rot after he gives us the money for a weapon. "Mommy will give you supper. Remember, don't open the door to anyone and don't touch the stove while she's out. Okay? Okay!"

Kala turned from the set, nodded solemnly, and went back to playing with the keys around her neck as she watched whatever the hell was on the screen. Marie made her a quick meal of soup and sandwich, showered, and threw on something fairly slinky, hoping to get it over with as fast as possible.

Amazing how losing all your friends and getting pregnant will change your outlook on life.

Marie lay back, soaked in her own perspiration, knowing she'd have a summer of sweating to look forward to. Maybe after she smoked the kid demon she'd resell the gun and still get that air conditioner. "Kala may need braces," she said.

Cal fumbled for his wallet and tossed crisp bills on the damp mattress. "Business isn't so good. You get four hundred a month child support. Don't the hospital have a health plan?"

She counted the cash. Twelve twenties. Maybe she *should* do some hooking. Then she looked at her soft midriff, counted the years, and knew she was stuck as an ER aide the rest of her life, unless that malignant midget crushed her skull with a crowbar. She winced as she finally recalled the wounds made by that nail-studded bat, how it had shredded Patty's face, gouged out Minerva's . . . She needed that gun!

Cal reached for his pants. His legs and stomach were still firm, still able to get her juicy and excited. "Want me to drive you to wherever it is you're getting your piece?" He grinned, *his* teeth looking so beautiful. Kala's orthodontia problems must come from her mother's end of the gene pool. "After all, I already got my piece tonight." He leaned forward to kiss her, but Marie pulled away, having had enough of his lips for one evening.

"If you want," she said. "It's Paulo, on Ninety-sixth."

He zipped up. "I'll wait outside, then take you home."

She would have argued, telling him she didn't want to chance having Kala glance out the window, see him and cry for her daddy, but Marie was drained, mentally and physically, and had to admit she *did* need him, at least for tonight.

They drove to Paulo's in silence, he mellow after humping her for an hour, she from contemplating what she had to do.

"You need more cash, you tell me," he said. "And don't let Paulo jerk you around. You tell him I'm waiting out here."

He'd be petrified to hear that. She slipped out.

Paulo was in T-shirt and cutoffs, watching the Yanks and swigging beer. "Want one?" he asked, holding up a bottle beaded with condensation. "Looks like you need it."

Cal had screwed her dry, so she took a gulp, then another. "Can't stay," she said. "Cal's waiting for me outside."

"Oh?" He got up and took a small bundle from a desk. "I didn't know you two were back together."

"We're not. He's helping me out with this."

Paulo grinned, and Marie wondered if he could smell the sour scent of lovemaking on her. Cal always could.

Paulo opened the bundle, revealing a snub-nosed revolver. "It's a beauty. Good value." He grinned again. This must be the guys' night for smiling. "The 'most bang for your buck.' "

She hefted it, noting its balance. With its shrouded hammer she could pull it from her purse in seconds without its snagging on an emery board or key ring, ready to aim and fire. "Got bullets?" she asked.

"You got an extra fifteen bucks? C'mon, Marie, store-bought ammo costs. Here," he took out a battered cardboard box, "these reloaded cartridges are free and dependable in a revolver." He took the gun back, flipped open its cylinder, and slipped in five cartridges. "Just don't get them wet and they'll be fine."

Sure, like she'd go swimming with them. She fumbled in her bag for the cash. Three-fifty, seventy-five, eighty-five . . .

He held up his hand. "Give me the rest next week. Only thing is, you shoot somebody with it, you wipe it clean and drop it into the nearest sewer, okay?"

She stuck it in her bag, noting that the damp waistband of her skirt couldn't accommodate a credit card, let alone a gun. Time to diet, and between skimping to save for Kala's needs and fear of Scorch she wouldn't be eating much for a while. "Thanks, Paulo."

"Don't thank me. Just pray you never need to use it."

Chapter Eleven

Tuesday, June 4

Dead ahead in the dimness Marie squatted like a toad, polluting the air with her breath. To stop that breathing and eliminate the last of them, Scorch tiptoed behind Marie, bottle sloshing with a high-octane blend siphoned from a truck, a bit of rag stuffed down its neck. Scorch thumbed her lighter and Marie spun around, her eyes wide in the flickering of the Zippo.

"No!" she screamed as she fumbled in her bag.

"Yes," yelled Scorch, lighting the rag, cocking her arm to heave the Molotov cocktail and send her to hell.

Marie stepped to the side and whipped out a knife, flinging it blindly, the blade flashing as it twirled end over end, mesmerizing Scorch, freezing her. It burrowed into her right breast, slicing through her lungs. She sagged against a wall, the firebomb dropping, shattering beside her, the deadly liquid igniting, spreading in a pool of heat.

Blades of flame shot up, searing skin, melting muscle, singeing eyes. . . . Excruciating agony, worsening, without end.

Through the curtain of fire Marie stood over her, looking like Satan Herself, grinning. "So how does it feel?" she asked.

Screaming, louder and louder, but no shriek could ease Scorch's agony as her eyeballs exploded from the heat and . . .

Scorch sat up, still hearing screams, realizing they came from her. She kicked off a damp sheet, her chest heaving.

Kelly ran in from the kitchen, skidding on the parquet floor. "What . . . ? Oh, another nightmare? Just relax."

Easy for her to say, but Scorch nodded anyway, struggling to get her breath, her bearings. She was still in Kelly's apartment and it was sunny, the start of another warm June day.

"It's okay. You're all right." Kelly tousled Scorch's shortened hair and kissed the sweaty nape of her neck. "I won't let anything happen to you." She gave Scorch a hug.

Scorch looked at the sodden sheets. Lord, she hadn't had this dream for years. . . . And she hadn't been this close to fulfilling her vengeance, with Marie almost within reach, out there. Somewhere. She lay facedown, hugging the pillow.

"Relax," Kelly said, rubbing Scorch's neck, kneading stiff muscles between her shoulder blades. "You're tight as piano wire," Kelly said as she lay and ran her hands along Scorch's neck, then sent her long lacquered nails zipping up and down Scorch's spine, setting her quivering. "You got such a great little body," Kelly said.

" 'Not too many scars. Some women got lots of scars.' "

"Huh?" Kelly laid a warm hand on Scorch's neck. "What's that mean?"

Scorch rolled over and opened her thighs. "A line from a movie, *After Hours*." She guided Kelly's hand to her favorite spots, an invitation for dreamy pleasures. Sex in prison was a sometime thing, hurried in the few minutes allowed you between regimented activities and lights out, if you were resourceful. Even that rape, when she was sixteen, had been quick, although at the time it seemed as long as root canal without anesthesia, her arms and legs pinned under slobbering bodies, a rag stuffed into her mouth to stifle her screams.

Kelly shook her head. "You *do* have scars." She pointed to faint rippling circles on Scorch's thighs, abdomen, breasts, visible close up in good light. "What caused those?"

"Lit cigarettes, cheap booze, no love, and constant frustration." She rolled back onto her tummy.

"Who did that? Your father?"

Dad was lucky—he died early. "My mother. She was allergic to happiness." She placed Kelly's hand on her hip and had her stroke her buns again, relaxing her. Kelly was sweet, knowing when to show concern and when to back off. Just like Dr. Glass.

And how was the good doctor? Did he even care she was on the run? What was he doing with all the free time her escape had given him? Did he think she had betrayed him by cutting out?

No, he understood. Maybe too well.

Kelly stood. "Much as I enjoy fondling you, I got to make a call." She tickled Scorch's ear, making her giggle. "Relax. Go back to sleep."

Scorch curled up, trying to avoid the wet part of the bed, trying to recoup her emotional strength after the stress of Saturday night and Sunday morning. In the next room she heard Kelly on the phone, her voice low and throaty, barely audible. "Yes, I'm sure. Incredible but true . . . Yes, worth lots. I know . . . see for yourself."

Scorch's eyes closed and she drifted off, the warmth of the late morning . . .

Two voices now from the next room, low, one Kelly's and the other, deeper . . . A man?

She sat up, wondering what man would be in Kelly's place.

Footsteps now, coming closer, to find her naked.

Scorch rolled off the bed and snatched her underwear from the floor. As she pulled up her bikinis a guy came in, tall, hard-looking, dressed in a silk suit with shirt to match.

She grabbed her jeans off the chair as he gave her a smile that nearly turned her to stone. She had blundered into a snake pit, eyes wide open, and the king cobra had just arrived.

"Well, now," he said. "Kelly's new friend, even more attractive than she said you were." His eyes roamed, examining every piece of her. Unlike John gawking at her three nights ago, or that bus driver, this was businesslike, an inventory of goods.

Her mouth got dry, and despite the warmth of the day, she felt cold, fighting not to shiver.

Behind him Kelly leaned on the doorjamb, looking bored. A setup. She'd heard about this stuff, bastards seducing teen runaways from Kansas, Nebraska, taking over their minds and bodies, then sending them out to hook. They must have assumed she was younger than she was, a common mistake all her life with her baby face and petite body.

Once again, she was about to pay the price.

What to do? They were between her and the door, both together weighing three times what she did.

If she ticked them off, didn't do what they wanted, they could smother her with a pillow or drown her in the tub, then slice her up to feed to mutant fish in the Hudson River.

No one would ever know.

Or care.

He ran his hands along her body, lingering on her nipples. "Smooth as a baby's bottom," he said over his shoulder to Kelly. "You were right."

"Listen, I was just leaving." Scorch tried to step into her

jeans, but her hands trembled so much her foot missed the opening.

"Not just yet," he said. He smelled of cologne, of fancy clothes, but nothing could mask the stink of sleaziness. "How about you and me party a bit. Kelly says you like partying." His smile wouldn't have looked out of place on a jackal. He snapped the elastic of her underwear. "You're dressed for it. Frederick's of Hollywood or Victoria's Secret? Real nice."

If she bolted past him, Kelly would slow her up and then . . . ?

"Helen," said Kelly, "this is a great opportunity for you."

Sure it was—to get syphilis, chlamydia, AIDS, or scarred up worse than she already was.

He slipped his hands inside her bikinis, probing her clitoris, caressing her butt. She wanted to scream, to claw his eyes out, to grind her heel into his windpipe. That would get her beaten and killed—if she was lucky.

Think! Her mind raced, and spun its wheels.

Pretending to give in and walk the streets for them, selling herself, wouldn't give her much of a head start.

They'd come after her, catch her . . .

She'd have to leave the city with only the whore's clothes they'd make her wear, forgetting about Marie.

NO! Only one way out, and a slim chance at best.

"I . . . I never did this before. With a guy."

He grinned, looking like the woodcut of Lucifer in the prison chapel. Hell, he had probably modeled for the artist.

"I know," he said. "And that's going to earn us lots of money your first time. Right, Kelly?"

"I guess," said Kelly, still bored.

"Now," the pimp said, his smile still there, like it was painted on, "I'm going to show you some tricks, something to help you earn us big bucks."

"I'll try," Scorch said as she watched Kelly enter the bedroom and wriggle into tight jeans and a snug T-shirt, her own bout of sex over for the moment.

"Good," the guy said as he started to peel off her bikinis. "You got solid calves and thighs. Must do a lot of running."

Yeah, away from creeps like him.

"Wait!" said Scorch, grasping at straws. "You first."

"Sure, whatever." He started to unbutton his silk shirt.

"And without an audience," Scorch said, pointing to Kelly.

"Of course. And Kelly, close the door."

Kelly grunted, left, and slammed it shut behind her.

Scorch unbuckled the guy's alligator belt and dropped his trousers to his ankles. She reached inside her jeans and clutched the scissors with her right hand while caressing his cheek with her left. He sighed with pleasure.

She thumbed his right eye and kneed his groin.

Snarling as he doubled up, he reached for her.

That's when she slashed at his throat with the scissors.

He ducked and the blade raked his left eye, zipped across the bridge of his nose, and gouged into something soft on the other side of his face. He howled.

Scorched kneed him again, brought both hands back, and swung, slamming the steel handle of the scissors into his jaw, knocking him sideways. His legs bound by his silk pants, he toppled over.

As he lay writhing, Scorch stomped his head, his neck.

Yelling from the next room, feet running toward her.

Tigresses!

Scorch grabbed the chair and ran to the door as it opened, expecting to smell smoke as singed Tigresses piled out from their burning basement. Scorch screamed, putting her whole being into the stroke, the chair nearly swinging her as it slammed into long legs, bringing down the redhead who burst into the bedroom.

Kelly! She pitched forward, and Scorch swung at her

again. Again. And again—until the pimp for the pimp sprawled, blood seeping from her coppery hair, trickling from her nose.

Don't! Don't kill them! The cops wouldn't lose a second's sleep over pimps getting slashed or battered, but a homicide is a homicide to the goody-goodies downtown. Otherwise they would have given her a medal for smoking those Tigresses.

Scorch spun in a circle, seeing a blur of furniture, clothes, those two scumbags laid out on the bedroom floor.

She dressed and grabbed her stuff. On the run again, needing money. She slit the pimp's silk pants, finding four hundred bucks in one pocket, two-fifty in another, plus a chromed gun, small enough to hide in her underwear. She'd figure out how to use it later. He had rings on his fingers, but she couldn't pry them off. Cut . . . ?

No! She was no cannibal. As she slid off his Rolex, she realized her fingerprints were all over this place. Oh hell, what if these two were dead, or had their brains turned to mush?

The cops would search the place, find her prints, do a dragnet, and scoop her up in a day.

No matter. She hadn't the time to grab a towel and wipe down everything she could possibly have touched, the faucets, the toilet, sinks, chairs, flatware . . . Impossible. This was like some Poe story about a murderer who flipped out after the killing and spent days polishing the house clean of proof until the cops came and nabbed him.

Just go! The hell with Marie. Dr. Glass said, "Living well is the best revenge."

A monster, its face a hideous mask of red streaks, contorted with rage and pain, roared from the bedroom.

The pimp—hands reaching—blundered out, lunging for her!

Scorch yelped and leaped aside as his bloody fingers

came within a millimeter of grazing her neck. Turning, groping, weeping blood and corneal fluids, his outstretched arms swept the air. Scorch kicked the back of his knee, sending him sprawling. She kicked him again and again, her foot finding hard spots on his body and making them soft and pulpy, until he lay still.

The neighbors had to have heard this tumult, unless Kelly was known for wild parties and thumping noises at noon.

Don't bother with anything else. Escaped murderesses travel light, with only fear, memories, and loneliness for heavy baggage.

Should she pour brandy on the bedding and set it on fire, incinerating these bastards and all evidence of her being here? Where were matches? As she looked, she recalled the stench of burnt flesh and her stomach turned. If she didn't roast them, if she let them be, they'd come for her, to teach her a lesson and keep their rep. Could she leave Prince Charmless and Princess Graceful to their comas? Not if she was smart. Besides, there might still be a few traces left of her existence with them.

There, the brandy bottle! Damn! How good life had been, if only for two days and nights. How long could it have lasted? She could have gotten used to Kelly's gentle hands, could have let herself be spoiled by affection and attention.

Forget it. Love and devotion were not in her horoscope. She must never forget she was nobody's child.

Chapter Twelve

Friday, June 7

Lucy hoped a bad connection from Boston or squad-room chatter accounted for her husband Tony's sounding annoyed.

"Working late again?" he said. "What's this excuse? Found Jimmy Hoffa's body or been invited to a party with Elvis?"

"Dr. Glass is coming by," she said, knowing it sounded lame.

"Oh?" asked Tony. "Is he making a house call?"

"I need him to locate Scorch. I need you for R and R."

"You'll have me for that again next week. Look, we both have to be glad I still can get electrician work, even if it means chasing out-of-town jobs. Just try to get to bed before midnight for a change. If that teenaged killer didn't murder nobody yet, she's not going to. See you Tuesday."

Yeah, if he was out of town just for work. Lucy hung up to find Eric Glass standing there. "Domestic affairs," she said, to explain. "Married six years. So, what's Scorch up to?"

"She's bound by a time frame—kill Marie by June twentieth."

Ask a silly question . . . "You know the hour as well?" she asked as she struggled to keep a straight face.

"Hear me out. June twentieth is the date her sister died. Killing Marie on that date gives her symbolic closure."

"Is that logical?" she asked.

"About as much as an eight-year grudge," said Glass. "But many people get very emotional on the anniversary of the death of a loved one. With Suzanne it could take the form of homicide."

"So we've got no more than thirteen days. If she doesn't find Marie by then, will she go ballistic? Lash out at strangers?"

"She might, if she feels threatened or betrayed, especially by a woman she trusts. Remember, she executed those killers for some orgasmic catharsis."

Finally, psychobabble. "Well, I appreciate you taking time to come down here," she said.

"I was glad to leave early," he said. "Fridays bring the depressed, the pseudosuicidal, and the hysterical out of the woodwork. They get their wounds bleeding and then come begging for my time, clawing at me like in the movie *Jesus Christ, Superstar,* when he was in the valley of the lepers. Well, from this I make a living. Oh, and I went to 'the scene of the crime' to get a feel for what Suzanne experienced that night. I'm sure now she'll never let her emotional wounds heal."

"The old neighborhood? You got a death wish, Doc?"

Glass gave her a sheepish look. Why would an educated guy take such a chance? What was Scorch's pull on him? Lucy wheeled herself through the cloud of late-afternoon cigarette smoke to a keyboard. "I think Scorch changed her appearance," she said, trying different computer images of

Scorch, based on her last ID photo. "They found a stolen pickup truck in Yonkers on Sunday night. Its owner says a small, cute, long-haired girl got him drunk and tied him up. Figure it was Scorch, considering the Corrections Department vehicle was found in the mall lot where he picked her up. If we get a hypothetical composite we can circulate it to every beauty parlor in the Metropolitan Area."

"No such luck," said Glass. "She worked four years as a beautician's assistant. She cut and restyled her own hair." When he leaned closer she smelled his aftershave. "Perhaps as a frost blonde. Curly or wavy, not her long straight look."

Lucy punched in permutations of Scorch's potential new appearance, then looked to him.

"I only knew her with long hair," he said.

"This is the look I would go for, but I'm no felon."

Glass smiled.

"What?" she asked. "I miss some in-joke? Oh, right. You think cops and criminals have similar personalities." She felt her face redden. "Is that true?"

"Except traits like impulsiveness, rebelliousness and risk-taking aren't as elevated for law enforcement personnel."

Her blush deepened. "You read that somewhere when you used to interview and hire officers, right?"

He nodded. "Sarge did her homework. Yes, I did that for several years, until budget cuts closed the Department's Psychological Screening Unit. My safety net was the job at Midland, which is why I'm a male psychologist in a women's prison. Oh, and Suzanne had a penchant for bright scarves so she might wear a kerchief. She was also partial to miniskirts to show off her shapely legs, her self-proclaimed best feature. Stuff like that."

Lucy grinned. "A wise therapist knows his patient. How's this?" She punched a key and the laser printer clicked and hummed, spewing out copies of a reconstructed "Scorch," like her yet totally different. An average Joe might not recognize her if she was sitting on his lap, which she might be doing while they dabbled with this electronic magic. "So is that her?" she asked.

Glass studied the printout from different angles, as if it were one of his Rorschach cards, to be scrutinized to death. He nodded. "Could well be. Now, instead of looking for half the women in New York, you've narrowed it down to one in twenty."

Lucy picked up the picture. "That elfin face, that thick hair, bangs, upturned nose. And those great long lashes . . . Boy, I'd practically kill for those. She looks so normal."

Glass nodded. "That's what makes her such a great hunter—she blends in, indistinguishable from her prey. She's not psychotic, just a kid made mad with grief. She lost all that mattered to her, reached her flash point while on the run, and finally exploded. From then on she couldn't turn back and start over, so she kept going, finished it, and lived with the damages."

Lucy tapped the Print button several more times. "NYPD has merged onto the information superhighway."

Now they had composites to distribute throughout the city, assuming Scorch was obsessed enough to hang around in the open. The bigger problem was locating Marie X, the unknown quantity. If alive, did Marie still live in New York?

DiGiorio ambled by as Lucy scooped up the composites. "Lieutenant DiGiorio, we have something to distribute on Scorch."

DiGiorio scowled. "On this you're screwing around on a Friday evening? Christ, Moreno, the captain's more concerned with solving new felonies than catching old felons." He snatched the composites, and they crackled in his hand. "Nobody's going to run out waving them, sounding the alarm like Paul Revere." He glared at Lucy. "Anything on the telex this week about young women in their late twenties murdered without a motive? No? Then I don't think

Scorch is still in the area." He noticed Glass. "You the shrink? Jesus, Doc, don't encourage her." He leaned on Lucy's desk. "Moreno, think. The odds are against it." He glanced at the composites before returning them. "Cute chick. Reminds me of my niece. Oh, by the way," he said, a glint in his eye. "The captain heard federal marshals can't spare anybody right now to help you out with this. Probably something to do with the Dark Paradise epidemic." He jabbed a nicotine-yellowed finger at the composites. "You can send these to all the precincts if it'll make you happy. Scorch already had her photo in the papers, so unless they put her on *America's Most Wanted* this is the most exposure she'll get. Take tomorrow off."

When he left, Glass shook his head. "Despite that, I'm sure she's in Manhattan, hiding in plain sight, mingling in crowds."

Lucy shrugged. "We've hit a stone wall looking for Marie, but we're not giving up. None of the girls arrested back then had that name, and whoever they are, they've dropped from sight." She shuffled off to dispatch the composite. DiGiorio, from the Stone Age, wouldn't expend effort on anything he didn't figure would win the admiration of the captain or the brass downtown. Maybe he was right, what with the Dark Paradise plague hitting the Northeast so hard. Lucy had caught Scorch once and nailed other killers, but it would be nice to do it one last time. She reached for her jacket. "Thanks again," she said. "Too bad we have no clues about Marie."

"I got the next-best thing. Suzanne may have visited a paroled buddy. Catherine Webster, in the Bronx."

Lucy sat back down at the computer, punching in another program. "Got vital statistics?"

He pulled out a paper with birth date, ID numbers, Social Security number, the works. Lucy tapped out the data.

"There, on Valentine Avenue in the Bronx. I'm paying her a visit."

Glass fell in beside her as she strode to her car.

"What?" she asked. "Don't tell me you want to come?"

"Not into her home. She violates parole and comes back saying I aided the police in catching Suzanne . . ."

"Want to sit in the car?"

He looked embarrassed. "Yes."

"Okay. I drive fast, so buckle up."

It was white knuckles for him as Lucy zipped in and out of Friday-afternoon traffic for the four miles to Webster's home. The car upholstery, baking all day, seared through her thin cotton skirt, and her air-conditioning was no match for an overpowering sun. When they pulled up opposite Catherine Webster's building, she left the keys in the ignition. "If cops hassle you, flip out this PBA card. If locals give you a hard time, cruise around the block."

He grinned. "I deserve this for asking to come."

"Yes." She got out and hitched her bag on her shoulder. Unlike most people, at least he accepted responsibility for his foolhardiness. As she hiked four flights, her blouse sticking to her back, Lucy half hoped Webster wasn't home so she could take off and head for her cool Queens apartment.

No such luck. Seconds after her third knock, a perplexed, disheveled woman answered. "Yeah?"

"Catherine Webster, Detective Moreno." Lucy shoved past without waiting for a response. It took the initiative away and let them feel they were in trouble—which most were, anyway. "I'm here regarding escaped convict Suzanne Amerce."

The flicker of concern would have escaped most people, but Lucy saw it and knew. Unless she botched it, she had Webster. "You've seen her, haven't you?" Lucy said. "Where and when?"

"Don't know what you're talking about." Webster looked out the window, as if hoping for the cavalry. "Ain't seen her."

"Try again, with sincerity and feeling this time."

"I don't got to talk to you," Webster said.

Time to bluff. "But you do, a condition of parole." Ease up, play good cop. "I don't care if you saw her. I just need to know where she went. Your part is all off the record."

"I want to call a lawyer."

"Everybody's got a lawyer now. Fine. Meantime, I get a warrant, search this place, and come up with pot, coke, another con, whatever. By Monday you'll be wearing green again at Midland."

"You don't care if I . . . ?"

Lucy pantomimed locking her lips and tossing away the key. "I want Scorch. I don't care how you live your life." She stared at Webster until she felt dizzy. "Shall I get a warrant?"

"She was here for a minute. I didn't know she was escaped. Honest. All she wanted was to find this Marie chick."

Ah! Sometimes life is good. "Uh-huh. And . . . ?"

"Didn't know about Marie. Told her about a friend of Marie, Tanya Smith, down on Forty-ninth and Tenth. That's all, I swear."

"Why wouldn't I believe you?" Dope user, check forger, and shoplifter that she was. "That's all you know?" Lucy asked.

"I swear. I don't know nothing about this Marie."

"This doesn't pan out, you can kiss your buns good-bye." Lucy chugged down to her car, where Glass looked forward, then glanced back into the rearview mirror, just in case. "She's a blank," she told him. "But she gave us a lead in the Sixty-first Precinct in Manhattan." Back at the station house, Lucy called the Six-One and was patched right to the watch commander, not a good sign. She listened for a moment, sighed, and hung up.

Glass was at her elbow, reading her face. "Bad news?"

"You bet," Lucy said. "Tanya Smith is dead. Drowned in her tub early Thursday."

"Accident, murder, or suicide?" he asked.

"You tell me. She had bruises on her temple, mouth, neck, and stomach, along with healing ligature marks on her wrists and ankles. Plus, fresh chafe marks below her knees matched the waistband of her underwear, as if she was trying to kick them off. They also found a load of semen in her vagina, and enough pot and beer in her system to put us both to sleep for a week."

"You think Suzanne . . . ?"

Lucy sighed, a sound she made often these past few months, then went to the computer and tapped out Smith's name. "Thought so. Tanya Smith, the only other Tigress to survive Scorch, was tortured by her eight years ago. Scorch goes back, torments the girl some more, gets what she needs, strips her, and holds her under." Lucy shook her head. "Although how a tiny woman could . . ."

"She worked out daily. Even keeplocked she did chins and pull-ups on the bars, push-ups and sit-ups on the floor. She added seven percent sheer muscle mass—not easy for most women to do."

Lucy nodded. "Obsessed. Right. Dead end, and it's Friday. We could check the numbers Tanya dialed in case she called Marie to warn her, except Tanya had no phone and the corner booth won't tell us much. So that's it." Outside, the sun was still fierce, early June invigorating everything with the promise of new life. She smiled. "Thanks for stopping by." If she listened to her instincts she'd head home, though with Tony on the road and her stepson away at school, all it offered was cool air. This evening, however, she felt adrift and uncertain. At least Glass had a daughter to return to. He even had cats; all she had was her job, with its frustrations.

He seemed to sense her ambivalence, and he struggled with his words. "On Fridays we have a traditional chicken dinner. Nothing fancy, but if you'd like to join Veronica and me . . . but I guess you've other plans."

All she had to do was say "no," but she found herself nodding. "Not tonight I don't." She computed options and found only one appealing. "If it's no inconvenience, it sounds nice."

"None. I'm sure Veronica will be happy."

"What about that Jamaican woman?"

"Cassandra? We're just friends." He fumbled for change, found a working phone, and spoke for a few moments. "Let's go," he said. What was she doing, going off with someone she was working a case with? Well, he wasn't a co-worker, just a collaborator, and this would be a working dinner, right? There be no wine flowing or drawers dropping by midnight. The man had sworn off alcohol, his daughter was home, and he had noticed her wedding band. Was *she* considering infidelity? No way.

As she followed his taillights up the highway, she kept asking herself if this was what she wanted, and was she a fool?

The answer was yes to both. She could always hang a U-turn and head for Kennedy's Bar, but tonight she wanted to spend time with someone who didn't just talk about crooks or guns or wiring.

When she came through the door, Veronica Glass eyed her and nodded hello. "You're the first woman we've had over since . . . the accident."

Eric busied himself with cutlery and crockery, as if he hadn't heard his daughter's remark. Now that he was home, he seemed more like a man being ground down before his time by a ton of frustrations and troubles, the sort of guy neighbors would describe to the media as always so quiet, calm, and friendly—until the day he exploded and went "postal."

The cats did figure eights around her legs, marking her, ignoring their master's command to stop rubbing and shedding.

Looking around, she saw that the apartment looked spacious and clean—probably at the hand of a housekeeper— but not neat, everything jumbled as if the effort to straighten things out would emphasize it was a home for two now, not three.

She wandered around, examining, speculating.

Three ceiling-to-floor bookshelves filled one wall. Among psychology and social work texts were volumes—both old and new—on philosophy, Jewish custom, and something called cabala.

"Cabala is the mystical interpretation of the Bible," Eric said from over her shoulder as he watched her peruse the titles. "It's supposed to help you in the search for universal truth."

"Has it?" Lucy asked.

"Not yet."

"My dad hopes there are miracles there, written between the lines," said Veronica. "He prays to God, but He doesn't answer."

"He answers," Eric said as he brought steaming plates to the dining-room table. "He says 'no.' "

An empty plate gleamed in front of the fourth, empty chair.

Veronica Glass lit three old bronze candlesticks, shut her eyes, and made waving gestures as she murmured a prayer.

"Why did you do that?" Lucy asked.

Veronica shrugged.

"I'll tell you why," said Eric. "As Tevya said in *Fiddler on the Roof*, 'You may ask why we do these traditional Sabbath things and I'll tell you: I don't know. But it's tradition.' "

Veronica rolled her eyes and groaned, a thirteen-year-old's response to what must be a stock joke by her father. She looked at Lucy while she helped herself to chicken and rice. "How come you're a cop?" she asked.

"Veronica, let officer Moreno eat before you grill her."

"It's okay," Lucy said. "When I was in college there were few jobs for people with B.A.s in sociology. I read how the department recruited women and minorities, so I signed up."

"My mom was a social worker when she was still with us."

"She *is* with us, in spirit," Eric said, his voice low. He looked as if he wanted to say more but returned to his meal.

Veronica put her fork down. "Dad says people become peace officers because they like excitement. And being in command."

"He also says young people should be polite," Eric added.

"Yes," Lucy said. "Your father and I had this discussion, sort of, earlier today. I guess in a way it's true."

"You're still married?" Veronica asked. "Dad says law-enforcement people get divorced a lot."

"Yes and yes," said Lucy, recalling when she and Tony had needed months of counseling years ago, her first exposure to a mental health professional, a Jewish social worker with her glasses on a gold chain around her neck. She knew her business, though. She and Tony remaining together was proof of that.

Eric poured a few drops of burgundy into a crystal goblet, murmured a prayer, and took a tiny sip. "For a sweet new week," he said, placing the goblet by the window, the setting sun glowing ruby through it, casting red light on her. "Elijah's Cup. Instead of leaving it for him only on the first night of Passover, I do it every Sabbath, just in case. You never know."

Then father and daughter ate in silence, like Trappist monks, as if in tribute to the empty chair at the table, the one that should have been occupied by Debbie Glass.

Eric coughed, as if the effort to keep quiet strained his vocal cords. "We leave a plate for Debbie every Friday night. Maybe the new week will give us a better time to come. On a lighter note, concerning our Ms. Amerce, whereas delinquent boys can't form normal relations, delinquent girls go overboard in their need for warmth and affection and are usually impulsive in their desire for immediate gratification."

Veronica started to grin, then caught herself, as if smiling were against the law in the Glass household. "Dad's always worrying I'll wind up like those wanton women where he works."

"And the inmates there are even worse," her father said.

"So what does Suzanne Amerce like?" Lucy asked.

"The usual," he said. "What we all crave. Affection. Security. Love. And Tom Cruise."

Veronica paused, her fork halfway to her mouth. "Oh?"

"I occasionally made 'house calls' and saw posters of him on her cell walls. Then one day they were gone. Her buddy Karen probably made her take them down."

"Maybe she did that because he's getting older," Veronica said. "So what did you two do today?" she asked.

"We used the wonderful world of computers to project what Suzanne might look like now." He got the folder holding the hypothetical composites. "Voilà. Suzanne Rene Amerce, living her new life as a blonde."

Veronica checked it out. "She's not bad-looking. Nice lashes." She turned to Lucy. "I was thinking about eyeliner and other makeup. Maybe you could give me advice. Cassandra says white women have different needs."

"Makeup?" Eric said. "When did this happen?"

Veronica rolled her eyes again. "My dad still thinks I'm a child. I just turned thirteen."

"Turned," he said. "As in milk spoiling?"

Veronica giggled. "What will you do with those pictures?"

"Well, we could roam Manhattan, asking everyone if they've seen her," Eric said. "It's as good a way as any to spend the weekend, considering we'll be in the City tomorrow."

Veronica finished her meal and scraped her plate clean over the disposal. She paused, then turned to Lucy as if inspired. "Tomorrow we're going to the Feast of St. Anthony down in the West Village, a family tradition from when . . ."

From when they were a complete family.

"If you come with us, you can keep an eye out for this unholy terror Dad is talking about. We can show her photo."

"Veronica, Detective Moreno probably has other plans."

"Ignore him, Lucy. Come. It'll be nice."

Now she was calling her by her first name. Should she go?

"Dad, tell her the weather's supposed to be nice this weekend and she'll have fun."

Eric smiled. "The weather's supposed to be nice this weekend. I can't predict if you'll enjoy yourself."

Lucy nodded. "I think I'd like that."

"Good," said Veronica. "It's settled, then. I'm going to Linda's for a while, Dad." She kissed his cheek. " 'Bye."

"Be careful how you go," he said. "Be home by ten."

"It's only down the block. Honestly." She shook her head and was gone, slamming the door behind her.

Eric looked to the heavens, whether for guidance or fortitude Lucy couldn't guess. "That's her, the fruit of my looms. Did you want wine? I'm used to not pouring for myself."

"No. It's okay. I should be leaving soon."

"Oh," he said, and seemed to sag slightly, as if he were an inflated doll and someone let the air out. "I understand."

"But I would like to attend this festival. We could stop on the way and ask people in Tanya Smith's neighborhood if they saw Scorch this week."

He brightened. "The festival is on Thompson Street, on perhaps the last mild weekend until Labor Day. More chicken?"

Lucy shook her head. Glass stuck the dishes into the washer and moved to the terrace. She followed him out to watch the sun glint gold on the river as the Jersey shoreline cast longer shadows on the Hudson and the setting sun kissed the lip of the Palisades. "Still thinking about Scorch?" she asked.

"Of course. You know, boys engage in predatory behavior, but rarely with personalized hostility to the victim. Girls commit crimes to fulfill direct needs or satisfy deep hostility.

Lucy felt warm wind on her face. "You understand her."

He gave a short, bitter laugh. "If she were my patient for another eight years, I wouldn't completely know her. No, it's the syndrome. That night Debbie got . . . hurt, I wanted to rip that driver to pieces." He looked away, as if embarrassed to admit to strong emotions. "Once I realized not all the blood on my face and chest was mine," he touched that scar on his forehead again, "I went berserk. I kicked in the guy's car doors, his windows. Anything surviving the initial crash got trashed by me, the only way I could avoid mayhem on *him*." His hazel eyes blazed and his fists tightened. "That's what happens: You learn anger early on and it taints your soul. You never forgive or forget. You ration hate, nurturing it on a low flame to make it last, so it can flare when someone tosses fuel on it, intentionally or otherwise. Sorry, sermon over."

Lucy noticed the long, thin parallel lines across his bare

125

forearms. Defensive wounds, a pathologist would say upon noticing them on an autopsy table.

He saw her looking at them. "A road map to hell," he said.

Did all shrinks speak in symbols?

"My mom," he said to her unasked question. "A 'survivor.' "

As if that explained everything. "Survivor?" she asked.

"Of a concentration camp. Her tolerance to pressure had been sucked out by the Nazis. I was a major stressor to her."

"What did you do to stress her so?"

"I lived." He watched the sun sink behind the Palisades, turning the river from aqua to indigo.

She had suspected that the link between Suzanne and Eric had been forged in hot rage. These two, nearly a generation apart and raised in different families and cultures, were bound together, Siamese twins joined at the psyche by fear and fury. Yes, to be effective a predator must fit in, nearly indistinguishable from its prey, as Scorch was to Marie. And Eric Glass to Scorch.

She edged closer, and he whirled around.

"Sorry. Another symptom of the abused child. Hypervigilance, alert to the slightest movement or sound, the sign that may mean you're about to 'get it.' Some say pain brings exquisite ecstasy, like the theme of a Clive Barker story, but it's only an enticement from the Devil to pass it on, like a hellish chain letter or an invitation to a party for the damned."

"This is how you understand Scorch? How and why she did what she did?" Lucy said.

"Empathy comes at an exorbitant price. I think she sensed it, although I never said anything, obviously. It helped me understand her when she talked about the 'fury.' "

He referred to it as if it were a living entity.

Maybe to them it was.

"We can meet at the precinct tomorrow and take my car," said Lucy, "though my PBA sticker doesn't always guarantee against tickets. We can spend a few hours in Tanya Smith's neighborhood, asking if anybody's seen her. That's a lot of what detective work is, wearing out shoe soles." Lucy picked at peeling paint on the rail. "She's already blended in somewhere, hasn't she?"

"Yes. Abused kids know how to be invisible. It's one of the ways they learn to survive." His eyes seemed more lively. "I'm helping because you swore to take her alive. If some street cop finds her first . . ." He shook his head. "She'd never come along quietly. Us abused kids 'don't take no crap from nobody. When in doubt, lash out.' It's what's been beaten into us, one of the first lessons we learn." He peered over the terrace. "And don't put her composite on the Internet. Some well-meaning citizen or deputy sheriff who tries to corner her would be in far more danger from her than she would be from them."

Chapter Thirteen

Thursday, June 6

It was twilight, the beige and red brick tenements taking on a softer hue as the sun dipped behind the Concourse, the day's heat still shimmering off the concrete. Scorch ran to head Nancy off, to stop her from the ambush, but Scorch's feet sank deep in coagulated blood, each step making her legs burn as she struggled forward, wasting time and energy. "Nancy, wait!" she screamed.

Rounding the corner, she saw Nancy, arms outstretched, sinking in a red pool spread over the Creston Avenue sidewalk.

"NO!" Scorch skidded on gore to grab her sister's blood-slick arms, but no matter how hard she squeezed, Nancy slowly, surely squirted from her grasp, to be lost forever.

"Help me!" Nancy shrieked, her eyes wide, blood leaking from all those holes, drooling from her mouth.

"NO!" Scorch screamed, clutching tighter. If sheer will-power could save a life, no one would ever die.

Nancy disappeared into the sticky wet pool . . . forever.

Scorch bolted upright, struggling to breathe in the dark

heat. Where was she? Right, in a crummy fire trap in Hell's Kitchen, off Tenth Avenue. Hard to breathe. Suffocating . . .

She fought for air, ordering her mind to calm her body. After a moment, her heart slowed and her breathing became normal.

This other nightmare, the one she had hoped to leave behind at Midland Knolls, was endured weekly, with her always trying different ways to save Nancy, always failing, even in dreams. Now she hid like a rat in a single-room-occupancy hotel a notch above a flophouse, its only virtue being that as long as you paid cash up front there were no questions asked or explanations expected.

The walls were so thin not only could you hear a TV in the next room, assuming the occupants could afford one, you could practically see its picture. At Midland she was secure, with brick walls and a steel gate to keep others out. And she had her own sink and toilet. Here, however, she had privacy and was free to do whatever she wished, within reason.

That was the world, always demanding a trade-off in the search for happiness, safety versus liberty, with life a constant struggle to find the right blend, because they wouldn't let you have one hundred percent of both.

She was smothering from the warmth and humidity, and it wasn't even noon, judging by the luminous dial of that pimp's fancy watch. Might as well hock it, find Marie, and force a Drāno cocktail down her throat. Some women dreamed of raising families, becoming doctors, the President, but Ms. Amerce's ambition was to hear Marie scream "No!" when she saw Scorch cock her arm to heave a firebomb at her.

Scorch recalled Kelly wriggling into tight jeans and a snug T-shirt, or dancing in her underwear, pretending to be "Candy." What a cruel, tantalizing glimpse of how good life could have been with two horny girls indulging each other.

The memory was a treasure, Kelly's soft, gentle hands all over her. Spoiling her with affection, readying her for exploitation, fattening her like a piglet for slaughter, to be served to perverse men unable or unwilling to make love to a woman who wanted them. Enough!

Karen would think her soft for even considering pleasure over revenge.

She slipped into jeans and a T-shirt, grabbed her scissors and a grubby towel, and scampered to one of the three bathrooms on the floor, the one with the sour-smelling shower, to scrub off last night's sweat. Funny how her world had flip-flopped in a week. Now she could eat and shower alone if she wished, and even sleep with someone, if she could ever trust them.

Someone rapped on the door as she toweled off. "Yeah," she said. "Two seconds. Keep your pants on." She looked to the scissors, lying on top of her jeans. Should she have taken it into the stall with her, or had she seen too many reruns of *Psycho*, one of Dr. Glass's favorites?

As she dashed back to her room she heard frantic words in Spanish slipping from behind a door, a woman's voice, her plea or argument punctuated by a slap. Scorch grabbed some cash and the pimp's tiny pistol—dressed to kill—gleeful her minivacation was over so she could comb Fun City for Marie.

First stop, Marie's old address to see if that dour, heavyset woman could tell her anything further. The sourpuss again answered the door, her man no doubt sleeping off another binge. "Yeah?" she asked, showing yellow teeth. "I know you?"

"Came Sunday, looking for Marie." Scorch held up her half of the torn twenty, a whole bill in her other hand. "Remember?"

"Yeah. Called the landlord, but he don't know her forwarding address. Sorry."

A lot more than you think, lady. She decided to hang in there. "You wouldn't, by any chance, know where she worked?"

"Nah. She came and went all hours." She turned to go, then paused. "Dressed in white, though."

That narrowed it down a little. "Waitress? Beautician? Nurse? Dental hygienist?"

"Don't know," said the woman. "She kept to herself. Didn't live here that long." She eyed the money in Scorch's hand.

"Thanks. If you or your husband remember anything, I'll be back." Just like *The Terminator*. Scorch gave the woman her half of the twenty, useless to her without its mate.

What now? Wander the streets to peer into every diner and beauty parlor, looking for a woman she had glimpsed only once, eight years ago, in twilight, as the most important thing in her world perished before her?

Why not? The weather was nice and she had no other purpose.

She marched to Eighth Avenue, as good a spot as any to start. Marie "came and went all hours," ruling out dentists' offices, which usually were daytime operations. Good, it would have been awkward traipsing up to each one, gabbing with the receptionist, just to sneak a peek into the treatment rooms.

Waitress? Glancing into every coffee shop and dive on the West Side would keep her legs toned and work up an appetite.

Nurse. Nurse's aide? Scorch came to the first phone booth still holding a tattered, moldy book and let her fingers walk the Yellow Pages. She tore out all listings for New York hospitals, figuring if Marie were still in Manhattan she'd work for a local one. Unless she was a private-duty nurse . . . ? Damn! She perched on a brass "Siamese" fire hydrant, wondering where to begin with tracking a woman who may

131

have changed her name and appearance with the seasons. She stood and stretched, wondering if the old bastard who had sentenced her was still alive. "Depraved indifference to life," he had said of her that day in court.

Depraved because she had been deprived. Should she have stripped in the courtroom to show her scars, at least those visible to the naked eye? Her Legal Aid lawyer should have gone to trial and shown the jury the autopsy photos of Nancy, her body slashed and gashed, the autopsy estimating it would have taken five hundred stitches to close the wounds. Then he could have asked them what they would have done in the same circumstance after having called the cops and been told they could do nothing.

No witnesses, no evidence. No case.

Too bad they smashed everything in your home, all those mementos of your sister. What a shame. Sorry, miss, tough luck.

Depraved? Maybe. Indifferent? No way. She had plenty of feelings, all of them powerful, few of them healthy.

She finished checking the hospital listings, then returned to the dog-eared Yellow Pages to rip out all listings for nursing services and nursing homes. Twenty bucks' worth of quarters was a start as she strode down the street. People moved slowly today, as if the humidity made the air harder to push through, everything steamy and damp as hot asphalt and concrete radiated the killer sunlight back up at them.

As she crossed the street, a cab ran the light and whistled past her. Jerk.

The cabby stuck his head out the window. "Careful, blondie. You looking to get some brains knocked into you? Dumb bimbo."

Yeah, right, jackass. Eat me. Houston, we have ignition. She snarled. "Yeah! And I'm going to do your mama!"

"You want me to get out?"

"Sure. Which door?"

The guy stuck a leg from the cab and Scorch reached for her scissors, ready to bury it between his ribs.

Again. And again and again, then to gouge out his eyes, carve his jugular . . . ! Whoa, down, girl. It's just the heat.

Yeah, to be followed by cuffs, fingerprints, and a free ride back to Midland Knolls, shackled to other losers while Marie laughed her butt off. Marie could be watching now, from the windows lining the street, the corner. Anywhere. Everywhere.

The guy stopped, perhaps seeing the homicide in Scorch's eyes. Smartest move he ever made. The first killing is the hardest, buddy. Take it from one who knows.

She saw a thin gold band on his ring finger. Some kid almost lost her father, some woman her husband. Probably no great loss if they did, but that shouldn't be her call. Stuff like that was left up to the courts and scum like Marie.

Scorch did an about-face, ready to "shank" the guy if he rushed her, but something in his face told her he was all bluff and bluster, and probably a bust in the sack as well.

She took deep breaths and counted to ten. And ten again. When she found herself up to seven hundred sixty she realized she was on Seventh Avenue, the other pedestrians—their "crazy radar" working overtime—stepping aside, parting for her as if she oozed blood from scores of abraded wounds.

Faces—white, brown, black—stared at her as she strode past, some of them silently screaming their own private insanities before turning away as she stormed by.

They'd better keep their lunacies to themselves.

She had enough of her own.

How long could she last like this? A guy up ahead with sandy hair and wide shoulders reminded her of Dr. Glass. She needed him now for advice and reassurance. She was twenty-three but unable to make decisions on her own. Not good ones, anyway.

She calmed down enough to think this through. Where did he live? Westchester somewhere, along with a couple million others. He got his doctorate at Yeshiva University—it was on his diploma on the wall—a no-brainer, and his only slipup so far as keeping his private life secure. He got smart or got warned, because he took it down after a week or two. Just enough time.

She fished out a few quarters and phoned Yeshiva, saying she was a classmate of a dozen years ago and was trying to find him.

They wouldn't give his address but said he was teaching at Fordham University last time they knew. How ecumenical of him.

She told the Fordham people she was a former colleague and asked if he still lived at a fictitious Yonkers address. They—more helpful or more naive—gave her a different street, but still in Yonkers. Warm and getting warmer. She called directory assistance, who didn't give out his unlisted number but didn't deny it was his address, a mere Amtrak ride away.

She went back to the Yellow Pages, to try the same ploy through the psychological associations and the State Education Licensing Bureau. Twenty minutes later, she had his address and number, decency once again proving no match for guile and deceit.

She held her breath, dialed, then hung up after two rings, more afraid of being rejected than of his calling the cops.

She headed downtown into the smog and noonday heat, with only homicidal dreams for company.

Chapter Fourteen

Thursday, June 6

Marie Balboa jabbed two fingers to part her blind's slats an inch as salsa music drifted in from across the street. Yeah, like Scorch was out there, staring up, ready to shoot.

Marie backed away as the sickly sweet stink of spilled garbage wafted up, turning her stomach. Shooting wasn't Scorch's style. Firebombs were her signature. That and a crowbar and a spiked bat. How could that demented dwarf have been strong enough to take out three girls at once, even if they were stoned, groggy, and half blind from smoke and fumes?

She must have been wired on coke or amphetamines herself. Yeah, a speed junkie, her nervous system all stoked up before taking on the Tigresses.

Marie went back to laying out lines of coke. Tigresses . . . The best. Toughest girl gang in the West Bronx. Hell, maybe the whole Bronx. Even guys gave them a wide berth.

What would that girl devil look like now, anyway? Marie glanced at the multiple copies of Scorch she had made from Tuesday's *Daily News* photo. She had doodled with them from every perspective, giving Scorch glasses, longer hair, shorter, curls, spikes . . . everything but a beard and mustache. What if she were masquerading as an old woman, stooped and gray?

Marie swept them aside. This was making her nuts! Was *that* Scorch's strategy, to make her crazy, to get revenge without lifting a finger? She was probably in Miami now, soaking up the rays, flirting with guys, while Marie sat in a darkened room, her clothes sticking to her as she waited for a Molotov cocktail to sail through the window or for lit gasoline to splash under her door, while the killer runt waited, another crowbar poised . . .

Jesus, she *was* going crazy, and Scorch had nothing to do with it. Making herself nuts inside these steamy walls . . .

"Mama!" cried Kala from the bedroom.

Marie grabbed her pistol, raced to her daughter, and clicked on the light. Kala sat up, sobbing.

Marie looked left, right, under the bed.

Nothing.

"What!?"

"Mama, a monster was after me! It . . ."

Christ, a nightmare, on this of all nights, while her mother was already stoned and paranoid, ready to shoot at shadows.

That would do it—busted for illegal possession of weapons, drugs, endangering the welfare of a child.

That's what Scorch wanted, for Marie to do time, too, and feel what it was like to be sealed away.

"It's only a dream," Marie said, sitting with Kala, hugging her, rocking with her, trembling with her, their hearts pounding in unison. Yes, there was a midget monster after them both, but that didn't mean she would get them, not if Marie could help it.

Worse came to worst, she'd return to Cal. He was big but

Marie knew his weak points, every one of them. If necessary . . .

She laid Kala down and stroked her hair until she returned to the anesthesia of sleep. Marie sat with her a moment more before returning to the living room, to inventory the stash of drugs Cal had given her, wondering if she dared cut the coke one last time before peddling it to coworkers. That would leave her enough to get high and avoid thinking of what the weekend might bring.

Christ, being like a hermit, or a fugitive, looking over her shoulder, peering into corners. This was no way to live.

Why should she be punished now for a sin committed when she was barely out of her teens and stoned, unable to think clearly?

Maybe the cops would find Scorch . . . ? Hell, if they could, they would have already done so. Marie was on her own.

She stared at the gate she had finally put up on the fire-escape window. It had taken two hours and three broken fingernails to install. She had never secured an apartment before, but who could blame her, being forced to move every year or so, fearing this very moment when Scorch got loose? Marie had turned into an urban nomad, a human turtle crawling along, dragging her home with her.

Who was she fooling? The gate would imprison her and Kala but couldn't keep out fuel and flame.

Move from New York? To where? There was no guarantee Scorch wouldn't find her no matter where she hid.

Trapped. Locked up in her own home, almost as effectively as Scorch had been up in Midland Knolls.

She brushed a wet lock of hair from her face as the floor fan squeaked, turning slowly, moving the stale air around, pushing her own wry scent back up in her face.

She paced the room, five steps, then an about-face, to

walk off another five. At this rate she'd be climbing the damp, dingy walls by Sunday night, with the weather forecast to be in the nineties and humid all weekend. She returned to the table and snorted the coke, to make the night pass easier.

There. Better. She sniffed and wiped her nose. Hey, what she needed was somebody else to help search for Scorch. But who?

Cal? Paulo? Those guys had neither the desire nor the balls. Tanya? Tanya! Yeah, the sniveling nymphomaniac was just the ticket! Even though she hadn't seen her in a couple of years, Marie figured the pathetic junkie would still do anything for a toke or a snort. Besides, as the last Tigress, she was bound by loyalty to help Marie. That, or guilt or fear. Besides, Tanya had nothing better to do. She didn't work, except on her back, and then only to earn enough to keep her in pot and coke.

Marie dialed her number, but a computer voice told her it "was no longer in service in area two-one-two." What could she do? Hell! Marie paced again. She might as well walk up there. Between the heat and the stress and the coke, she wouldn't get any sleep tonight anyway. Marie gathered some of her precious stash, checked her gun yet again to ensure it was loaded, then marched uptown to Tanya's, hoping little Kala slept while she was gone.

The streets were quiet, except for the whoosh of traffic on Ninth and Tenth Avenues, as she stared into every darkened alley or doorway for that malevolent midget, lying in wait for her.

The door to Tanya's building had had its lock broken, so anybody could get in. Great. Scorch could be crouched in shadows, ready to spring. Marie dragged herself up to Tanya's apartment and heard water running inside. She slapped on the door, harder and faster, until the water stopped and feet shuffled to the threshold. "Tanya, I know you're there. Let me in."

"I'm calling the cops."

"You don't have a phone no more. Open up. It's Marie."

Tanya fumbled with the lock for what seemed like minutes before she finally cracked open the door. "Marie! It *is* you!"

Marie pushed her way in. "Good to see you, too."

The place smelled sour. Tanya, her body glistening in the light of a dim naked bulb, slouched in pink nylon bikinis, the joint in her hand failing to mask the musky scent of recent sex. She must have just screwed a guy who had given her a few bucks and maybe a dose of the clap as well. A forty-ounce beer bottle lay on its side on a crummy table. In the bathroom a grimy tub was filled with brownish water. She'd interrupted the junkie in the process of scrubbing clean of her latest love.

"We need to stay in touch," Marie said. "Hang together. Look after each other."

"Dint think I'd see you again. Figured you was dead or gone," said Tanya as she weaved and struggled for balance.

"Why's that?"

"Huh? You know . . . Got dope on you?"

Marie fished out a vial of coke. "I know what?"

Tanya's eyes were riveted to the vial. Even in the poor light, Marie saw discoloration over Tanya's left eye.

"Huh?" Tanya said. "You know. Scorch."

So Tanya read the newspaper. "What about her?" Marie said.

"Thought maybe she found you."

Despite the temperature, Marie shivered. "Why would she?"

Tanya reached for the vial in slow motion, but the pot and beer made it mission impossible. "Can I . . . ?"

Marie held it away, but still in plain view. "I said, 'Why would Scorch have found me?' "

"Huh? She looking for you is why."

"How do you know?"

"She out." Tanya lunged for the vial, but Marie grabbed her wrist. Tanya winced, and Marie saw the bracelets of raw skin on both forearms. Maybe it wasn't from a "trick" tying her up.

"She was here, wasn't she? She bound you, threatened you. You talked, told her where I live?"

Tanya retreated to the only window in the room, an open one with a low, dirty sill. "She came last Saturday, Sunday, something like that. She beat me." Tanya pointed to her pillow. "Held that over my face, said she'd smother me if I dint talk. And I dint, the first time."

"But you gave me up, didn't you, you crummy junkie."

"She sat on me, dint let me breathe. My lungs burned. She counted while she smothered me, to see how long I'd last."

No great loss, but Marie needed the stoned-out wretch, at least for now.

"She be back, Marie. I know it."

"We'll find her and kill her. We'll be heroes, killing a killer. Otherwise, she'll get us. You said so yourself."

Tanya shook her head, as if to get her brain working. "She mad and don't care what she do. Let's go to the cops for help."

"And say what? We killed her sister?"

"Not me! I dint kill no sister. Look what she did to me." Tanya skinned her bikinis down to her knobby knees, exposing golf-ball-size bruises on her hips, the end product of a collision between her butt and Scorch's fist or foot.

"So you'll give me up to save your skinny ass, huh?" She grabbed Tanya's shoulders and shook so hard, she thought the scrawny junkie's neck might snap. "We got to hang together on this. Otherwise, if Scorch don't get us, the D.A. will."

"I wasn't there! I dint kill nobody!"

Her yelling wasn't the smartest move after midnight, even in Manhattan. Marie clamped her hand over Tanya's mouth. "We can't go to the cops," she hissed. "It's murder two for me, maybe manslaughter two for you. That's five-to-fifteen."

Tanya squirmed free. "I dint do nothing!"

Even a bubble-head like Tanya could figure she could get immunity and be safely stored away until the smoke cleared. "You're not getting off so easy. You give me up and I'll tell them you were there. I'll say you plunged the knife in first."

"No! Scorch knows! I'll tell . . . mmph!"

Marie spun her around, clapped her left hand over Tanya's mouth and her right arm over her bony wrists. "Right," Marie said, squeezing tighter when Tanya tried to wriggle loose. "Scorch will testify for you while I rot in Midland. No way."

What to do? Tanya was panicky; she'd get them both fried.

"Stop it!" said Marie, but Tanya kept struggling. Once her sweaty body slipped from Marie's grasp, she'd squeal and scream, everyone would hear, and the cops would come and bust them both.

Marie couldn't hold her forever. She remembered the tub. "Ready for a swim, Tanya?" She pulled the junkie toward the bathroom while she still had the strength to control her. With her bikinis around her knees, Tanya lost her balance and was dragged backward. When she realized what was in store for her, she nearly twisted free, her eyes wide in the mirror, pleading. "Just a moment more, Tanya," whispered Marie. "Be patient."

Marie got her to the tub, released her mouth, grabbed the back of her head, and dunked it, catching a glimpse of

Tanya's horrified face reflected in the water. There was a quick scream cut short, like the plug pulled from a blaring radio, followed by a splash. Then there was gurgling, the flailing of puny arms in the water, the air, against the tub, the scissoring of skinny legs as they tried to kick free of the tight nylon cloth.

With her other hand Marie pinned Tanya's clammy butt to the lip of the tub and held on, hard as she could.

Tanya clutched the top of the tub and pulled her head up, sputtering, coughing, gasping. Marie shoved her back in, recalling last winter when she carried Kala over icy streets to the doctor's. Reliving that desperation gave her the extra squirt of adrenaline now to control the drowning girl under her.

She had to do it, for Kala, so she wouldn't lose her mother to the cops. "Just a few more seconds, Tanya. That's it."

Tanya's struggles slowed.

"Good girl, Tanya."

They stopped. After the last few bubbles floated from Tanya's nose and mouth, Marie peeled off those scummy bikinis, dropped them on the floor, and flipped Tanya onto her back to make it look like she'd passed out while bathing and slipped under.

Then Marie was out the door, hoping nobody heard and was peeking out to see. At two A.M. the street was empty as she peered out the front door. No lights were on in apartments on this side or across the street, nobody seeing or hearing anything. New York, New York, it's a wonderful town.

She didn't slow up until she turned the corner. No siren. No cops. Safe, for now.

Scorch had claimed yet another one, the final one, without flexing a muscle, leaving Marie as truly the last Tigress.

Chapter Fifteen

Saturday, June 8

Three hours and forty diners, coffee shops, and beauty parlors later, Scorch hid from the aggressive sun in Bryant Park, in the shadow of the Forty-second Street Library. When she was eight, Nancy had brought her here to gawk at the lions and books by the millions, but the only thing making an impression on Scorch had been the sleaziness of Times Square. Even then she had realized this was the toilet of the world, and now not even Walt Disney had a hold on the area after midnight. When respectable people turned in fear, merchants vied to become the predominant species along with freaks, flashers, and transvestites. Joining them might be dealers, would-be prophets, wanna-be music stars, and girls eager to do time at Midland Knolls. Scorch used her last quarter to call Metropolitan Hospital, only to have yet another snooty toady snap at her, saying they couldn't divulge the names of employees over the phone.

Searching on foot put Scorch in danger of being recognized and shot while trying to escape, but it was a small risk for realizing the fantasy of stalking Marie, walking up and

Joel Ross

identifying herself just before slicing that tawny neck with
a jagged edge. Scorch pushed herself to her feet to trudge
uptown for Round Two, west toward the grungier part of
Midtown.

Again she thought of Kelly. Too bad the long-legged goddess hadn't been content to have Scorch around for a few
weeks, maybe the whole summer, but she'd been greedy,
selling her onetime "suck-bunny" to some jackass pimp.
Was Kelly dead, her brains squashed into guacamole? If she
and her pimp survived, was there anything to fear from
them? Scorch figured she had dealt out enough punishment
to keep them laid up for a while and the pimp might need
a tin cup, dark glasses, and an obedient dog hereafter.

If she couldn't kill Marie by the twentieth, then what? The
pimp's money wouldn't stretch far, and with no Social Security card or certificate of authenticity, she didn't exist. It
was suicidal to try for a job, and she knew from firsthand
experience that activity was no fun. Even dishwashers
needed . . .

A guy was handing out slips of paper. Behind him, in
garish letters, signs proclaimed:

GIRLS—LIVE GIRLS

Yes, live girls were preferable to dead ones. At the door,
a smaller sign read: "Dancers—Earn big bucks."

"This off the books?" she asked the guy with the handbills.

"Manager's inside," he said without taking his eyes from
men walking past, potential customers all.

Once inside, Scorch needed a moment to adjust from the
glare of noon to the cool dimness of an urban cave, with
heavy staccato bass rumbling from speakers the size of
small coffins. A few customers sat, trying to work up enthu-
siasm for a bored woman gyrating on a small stage.

The bartender eyed her. "Rest rooms for customers only."

She shook her head.

"Got to be twenty-one to drink," he said. "What'll it be?"

"Manager."

A yellowing Spuds McKenzie poster leered at her over his shoulder as he smirked and yelled, "Leo."

A thin guy came out, papers in hand. "What?" he said.

"Sign outside says you're looking for live girls," she said.

"And you're one, huh?" He looked her up and down, not unlike Kelly's pimp, before shaking his head. "Sorry, honey, but we want to *bring* customers *in*, not drive them off. Grow six, seven inches and we'll talk."

She toed off her sneakers. Time for that expensive lingerie to earn its keep. She wagged a forefinger before slipping it inside her jeans and sliding it around the waistband. Then she unsnapped them and wriggled them down her legs to the beat of the music. Kicking them off onto a chair, she started to lift her T-shirt, then lowered it before finally slipping it off, swinging it over her head and flipping it to Leo.

He sniffed it and nodded.

She undulated her torso, trying to recall the steps Kelly had shown her Sunday and Monday, moves Salome would have envied, foreplay through dance. They watched her shimmy her little butt and use her silk scarf to whip colored circles around her.

The manager looked at the bartender and something unspoken passed between them. "How old are you?" Leo asked.

"I'm legal."

"Okay. Twenty bucks a night, six to midnight, plus tips. Hey, it's off the books. We'll walk you to the subway."

Scorch retrieved her T-shirt, noting as she did that some patrons had turned to gawk at her.

"Okay, twenty-five," the manager said. "Two ten-minute breaks an hour. C'mon, honey, I got work to do." He waved his papers as proof. "You do good, build a clientele, you

145

can triple that in tips. That's like twenty dollars an hour, tax-free."

The best she'd ever done back at Midland was two bucks a day as a teacher's aide in a GED class for overage delinquents.

"Sold," she said as she squeezed back into her jeans.

"Start tomorrow night at six. Don't be late."

Nancy must be spinning in her grave. It was one thing to avenge a loved one, but another to sashay in a G-string in a dive like this, waving your raw meat before starving dogs. Still, the underground economy was her only option.

She waved to the bartender and skipped out into the blinding oven of the street. Real money! She could get a decent place and maybe meet . . . Whoa! Slow down. A life? A relationship? A home? These were not for her. At best she could look forward to pouring gasoline down Marie's throat and tossing in a lit match, but a normal life? Dr. Glass said his religion had a Day of Atonement when you prayed and it was decided who would be at peace for the year and who would roam in torment, who would find love and who would be an object of hatred. Right now her debit sheet didn't look too good. Being on Forty-ninth Street, she decided to pay Tanya another visit and see if she could squeeze more information from her. This time the skinny junkie would know Scorch meant business, eliminating the need to engage in behaviors that would appall Amnesty International.

She jogged up the four flights to Tanya's door and froze. A yellow banner, POLICE LINE—DO NOT CROSS, was taped across the door. Below it was a printed sign: CRIME SCENE—DO NOT DISTURB.

This wasn't a simple burglary. Had Tanya tried to do business with the wrong kind of pusher or an impotent customer? Damn! There went her only pipeline to Marie, weak as it was. She ripped the yellow plastic tape and balled it up in her fist. Damn it, Tanya! Couldn't you have stayed alive a little longer?

No! Why now? Maybe Marie had gotten to her. Sure, snitches get stitches. Scorch stuffed the tape into her bag, did an about-face, and headed back downstairs, glad for her sunglasses and scarf. As with Kelly's place four days ago, she wondered if she'd left prints. She had touched Tanya's body, her vinyl purse. Had they absorbed oils from her skin . . . ? Oh hell! She was about to be accused of the one atrocity she hadn't committed.

In the lobby two women stood at the mailbox, chatting about "the whore in 4B being drowned a couple days ago."

How had Tanya gone under? Scorch slipped past the women, then walked as fast as her little legs could carry her without breaking into a trot.

Had she so terrorized Tanya she tried to turn into a fish? Doubtful. She had been slashed up but good eight years ago, and compared to that, what was a partial suffocation? Tanya *had been* drowned, not *had* drowned. Not just semantics.

Intentional, not accidental.

Marie had visited and baptized her former protégé.

Well, she was clear of Tanya's, heading downtown again toward Greenwich Village. Dr. Glass would have been so proud of how she handled this.

Speaking of Glass, a guy across the street looked so like him, despite the jeans, sandals, and T-shirt, even more familiar than that guy she'd seen a couple of days ago. Sure, the sandy hair, looking lighter in the sunlight . . . Could it be? She had always seen him in jacket and tie, formal, a gentleman, not an aging hippie. Perhaps the sun had baked her brain into cottage cheese, causing her to misinterpret everything.

Females bookended him. His family? One was young, early teens. Daughter probably.

147

Scorch walked faster, angling behind them so she wouldn't be noticed unless someone called attention to her.

Yes, daughter. She had learned everything Dr. Glass could teach her on the nuances of body language. Yes, father and daughter. Even the vague memories of her own early childhood were enough to confirm the relationship.

That lucky little girl, to be with . . .

Why did the older woman also look familiar? She wasn't from Midland Knolls. Was she wife and mother? She was the right age for one, a little too young for the other, in her early thirties maybe. Another psychologist? No, even though they looked at each other as if conferring, comparing notes, occasionally stopped people, asking them things, showing them something.

Scorch's heart pounded, and it wasn't from the sunlight heating the asphalt to melting point. Glass—how she would hang on his every sentence, never knowing when he might utter the magic words to make life tolerable. He was a professional who had always treated her like an adult, a lady.

They passed behind a blue and white cruiser. Police. She was parading right into a nest of cops! Damn! She nearly smacked into a No Parking sign.

Careful. Anywhere else but New York and this would be wacky behavior, and then . . . ?

Scorch watched the trio stroll down the street, asking their questions. Much as she longed to run up and check them out to discover if this was Glass and family, she hung a right and headed down a side street to avoid the cops before they recognized her and pounced. Worse still, she feared if it was Eric Glass and she approached him, it would be like the final scene in *Body Snatchers* and he'd blow the whistle on her.

Better to keep her image of him as therapist and mentor than know him as a snitch and betrayer, his countless words of concern for her over the years proving false.

There was a rush of bodies, two burly men slammed into two others, then uniformed cops reinforced them, handcuffs flashing in the sun. Glassine packets dropped and were scooped up. Drug bust. More cops flooded the area.

Scorch stepped to the curb and an auto zipped by, leaving an afterimage of the passenger. Something about her . . . The sidewalk was crowded, and she couldn't see over their heads. By the time she peeked around them a cab had cut behind the car, screening the license plate.

Was it Marie? Beyond logic and all odds, could it be her?

People brushed past. Everything swirled around her, her brain overloaded by the past half hour's events. She turned to pursue Glass again, but if it was him, his party was gone.

Just a momentary lapse and it had all rushed away from her.

There! Another woman! Scorch hurried over, but no, it was just some female with her kid, too old to be Marie.

Between the nightmares, the fear, the frustration, she was losing it. Soon she'd think every face was Marie's and she'd crack up, to be taken first to Bellevue, then back to prison.

She couldn't last out here. She had no home but jail.

High above the other skyscrapers the Chrysler Building gleamed in the noonday sun. Could she sneak up to the top floor and hurl herself off, her final statement to a world that sucked?

ESCAPED CON FLATTENS TEN IN DEATH LEAP ONTO 42ND STREET

She leaned against a doorway, unable to stop the tears.

Chapter Sixteen

Saturday, June 8

Scorch heard a thump. Through a teary mist she saw a doorway and . . . Nancy? No, she was losing it. She blinked her eyes clear enough to see a young woman slumped to the ground. "Miss, you okay?" she asked.

The girl definitely was not Nancy, but with her long hair and longer legs, seen through a filter of stress and tears, it was an honest mistake, considering Scorch's state of mind.

She touched the girl's shoulder. "Lady, you all right?" Why should she care, this being New York, though humans were supposed to be compassionate, to reach out to one another. This was Dr. Glass's theme, offered in different forms and packages to his weekly violent-offender groups. Behind bars, though, it had been like preaching the Sermon on the Mount to sharks.

The girl's chest didn't seem to rise or fall. Scorch felt her neck. No pulse. She pressed harder. Still nothing. Scorch whirled. "Call an ambulance!" she said. "She's not breathing!"

A small knot of people stood behind her, stupid and stupefied, before one guy came to life and punched nine-one-one on his cell phone. "Anybody know CPR?" someone asked.

Nobody knew or dared admit it. Sorry, honey, it's not your day. As Scorch turned to go, she figured this girl was about Nancy's age when she had been killed. Maybe if someone had called an ambulance immediately back then, eight young women—seven of them Tigresses—would be alive today. Scorch turned to the bystanders. "Somebody help me," she said.

Help? She had to be kidding. The group began to fade into the Saturday-afternoon bustle, leaving Scorch to wrestle one hundred thirty pounds of deadweight. She tilted the girl's head back and covered her mouth with a handkerchief, a poor man's AIDS-prevention mask. Then she pinched the girl's nostrils and blew four times. Now what? Scorch straddled the girl and pushed on her chest as a long-ago CPR course came back into focus.

What if she messed it up? Hey, this chick was already halfway to the Other Side. What's to lose?

Nothing but her own consciousness. The humidity, the relentless heat, the exhausting repetition of giving your breath, your energy, your breath again made her light-headed. She had to stop, to get out of the killer sun, if only for a moment, but if she did, this girl was dead. Scorch Amerce had taken enough life. Maybe it was time to give one back.

She puffed more breaths into the damp cotton handkerchief, then got back on the girl. "C'mon, honey, breathe. Live. Don't give up on yourself." Scorch's sweat dripped onto the girl's face and neck as her own chest, shoulders, and arms screamed with pain from each push and retraction.

Then someone in white eased her into the scant shade of the apartment entrance's awning. A second EMT wheeled their gurney over. "How long has she been out?" he asked her.

"Don't know," Scorch said. "Couple minutes maybe."

"Five minutes," said someone from the crowd. "She collapsed, and this girl gave her mouth-to-mouth and chest massage."

Five . . . ? Jesus. The EMTs got the girl onto their gurney. "You her friend?" the cuter one asked Scorch.

"Me? No. I happened by and saw her fall. Sunstroke maybe?"

He shook his head. "Looks like a heroin overdose. Dark Paradise strikes again, twentieth one this week." His partner nodded. "You coming with us?" he asked Scorch.

Before she answered, a deeper voice asked, "Who saw what happened here?" The crowd parted for a navy-blue uniform, brass buttons, and a badge as a cop shouldered through the crowd.

Scorch smiled up at the EMTs. "Where you taking her?"

"Roosevelt Hospital."

Roosevelt was on her list of places to check for Marie. "Yeah, I'll come. The Chinese say if you save someone you're responsible for them." She moved alongside the gurney, clutching the girl's hand, looking down at her and away from the cop. She climbed into a stuffy ambulance stinking of alcohol, antiseptic, disinfectant. Fear. The perfume of New York.

The ambulance took off, pinning Scorch to the wall like a butterfly on a collector's board. She grabbed a strap, ignoring the slice of pain through her shoulder. The cute EMT was doing his stuff with IVs, oxygen, all the magic that was a miracle when it worked and garbage when it failed. "Yeah," he said to himself. "OD." He pointed to the track marks on the girl's arms. "Probably a hooker to support her habit."

That explained her hot pants/gauzy blouse/no underwear look.

He opened that blouse and a nice set of boobs spilled out. He applied the paddles and jolted her. Nothing on the EKG. He upped the voltage and zapped her again. The EKG bleeped for a moment. Before he could give her another round, the ambulance stopped and his partner helped roll the gurney into the hospital.

The ER had junkies vomiting, kids crying, and battered mates cringing. Hieronymus Bosch would have loved it.

They wheeled her to a manic medical team, who rolled her onto a table, drew translucent curtains, and yelled jargon at one another. Someone shouted "Clear" and they zapped her again. Scorch saw the girl's back arc and her leg twitch.

The EKG remained flat and silent.

"C'mon," Scorch whispered, "don't give up now." Fight for your life, honey. It may suck, but it beats the alternative. They upped the voltage and zapped her, then again, with enough juice this time to power Cincinnati for a week. She flatlined anyway, successful in her goal of wasting a voluptuous young body.

Scorch wandered to a water cooler and drank long and deep, trying to forget she had spent five minutes in lip-lock with a dead girl. As she finished she saw today's ER duty board. This might not be a total loss. She ran an index finger down the list. Near the bottom, X-ray tech for the day shift: M. BALBOA.

"Marie's last name is something Italian or Spanish," Tanya had said before she had failed in her imitation of a submarine.

"She wore white and came and went at all hours," said the super's wife.

Scorch crumbled the paper cup and picked up a phone,

dialing X Ray. "Like to speak to Marie, please," she said.

"Marie Balboa? She's working now. Should be off at three."

Scorch hung up and followed the arrows toward X Ray. Too good to be true, or just hard work and sick obsession paying off? She waited, patient as a vulture, nobody noticing her as they scurried to or from the latest calamity. After an hour a woman in white trudged across the hall, brushing thick bangs from her tawny face. A bit older, a little heavier, but with the same ticked-off expression Scorch had seen once, when she was still Suzanne, when she still had a life, a family, and a future.

Her! Scorch ducked around the corner, knees like Jell-O. Now what? She retreated to the waiting room, pulled a wad of gum off a chair in the corner, plopped down, and took a deep breath. After a moment, her fingers stopped quivering. Found her! Next step? Steal a bottle of ether or rubbing alcohol, toss it into the witch's face, and light a match? What a headline tomorrow:

ESCAPED CON TORCHES FINAL KILLER BEFORE HORRIFIED PATIENTS

The *Daily News* would love her for it, but Karen would say, "Be a ninja, not a kamikaze. Survive this." Now what? Follow Marie home? Yes, find her lair, meet her spawn, set her up.

Beautiful. An exquisite torture is in your cards, Marie.

"You okay, miss?"

She looked up to find the cute EMT standing over her, showing more concern for her than for the dead junkie in hot pants. "You look pale," he said. "Are you upset?"

More than he could know. "Never been near a dead girl before," she said. Not in eight years, anyway.

"Yeah, it's freaky the first time," he said. "Someone is a

person one moment, just a body the next. Can I buy you a coke?"

Another one! Was he also a pimp, thinking her sixteen, a refugee from a corn state in need of a "manager"? He looked more like a twerp than a white slaver, slightly over-weight, late twenties with nice blue eyes and wavy blond hair. She caught herself saying "Why not?" Why was another one attracted to her? She wasn't *that* pretty, even on her best day, and this was not one of them. "It's been a really intense week," she said.

He nodded his understanding, as if he were a surrogate sent by Dr. Glass to comfort her while she was beyond his influence. "I'm on break," he said as he pumped change into a soda machine.

She nodded but didn't take her eyes off the X Ray Department as a couple of cans clanked down the chute. Marie's shift would end soon and she'd come down this corridor again.

"What's your name?" he asked as he handed Scorch a cold one.

"Helen." It came out so naturally now, that alias.

"I'm Mike. I say something funny?"

She must have been smiling at her own warped humor. Not good. Where was Dr. Glass now that she really needed him? "It's just rare to meet nice people in New York." As if she ever had.

She angled herself to monitor intersecting hallways, look-ing not just for Marie but for Kelly and her pimp. If they survived their beatings they could be getting discharged from here in a moment, bent on revenge, just as she was. The huntress might become the prey, but the pimp's pistol in her bag gave her a fighting chance, if only she wasn't too tired of battling.

Mike turned to see what she was looking for. "Something wrong?" he asked.

"Nah, just stressed." She started to twirl her hair, her nervous mannerism, but there was little hair to twirl these days.

Mike nodded, as Dr. Glass often did, that gesture indicating he didn't understand her latest problem but was willing to go along. She'd have to be careful not to drop her guard with him. He didn't look like a predator, but neither had Kelly. Kelly . . .

On Monday, Scorch didn't think she deserved Kelly's long, firm thighs. On Tuesday, she knew she didn't deserve her deceit.

"Yeah," he said to fill the silence. "Dark Paradise heroin came from Jamaica or the Greater Antilles a few months ago. Very potent. For its powerful rush you have to inject a near-lethal dosage. In addition to its great high, the danger factor also makes it so popular. Most junkies are high risk takers."

She nodded. "Like eating that deadly Japanese blowfish, huh? The thrill of living on the edge?" She thought of the addicted and compulsive types back at Midland, all eager for that one-way ticket to a tight death spiral.

"You okay?" he asked. "It's just you seem . . . haunted."

Haunted. Hunted. Whatever. She nodded. "Bad week, bad few years. Life isn't all it's cracked up to be." As she peered at the crowds shuffling past, she noticed him checking her out, ogling like a teenager, not a flesh merchant. If she thrust out her chest in her damp T-shirt, he would be seconds away from an erection. As if reading her mind, he asked, "What do you do?" diverting the conversation to something safe and dull.

"Little of everything. Beautician." A little white lie. "Laundry." The honest truth. "Kitchen and bakery." She'd had dishpan hands to prove it. "Now?" She leaned back and stretched, trying to release today's tension. "I'm between jobs." She could make guys drool by dancing in pasties and a thong, or extinguish the object of her hatred just down the hall. All she had to do was decide to dare stay in New York until she got Marie. It would have helped had she torched Kelly's apartment and eliminated both evidence and felon, but it wasn't in her nature. Plus, forensics people were smart and might figure it was to hide a murder and realize fire was her MO.

A cop came in, looking for a gunshot victim, so Scorch leaned close to Mike, shielding her face. The cop strode past, perhaps figuring anyone who consorted with an EMT was too respectable for mayhem. She drained her can. "Thanks for the drink and the concern." Nearly three. At this time on Saturdays back at Midland Knolls, she would be lounging in her cell, stroking herself while daydreaming of Tom Cruise, or down in the rec room hearing the latest gossip and talking the vilest trash.

Walking with Kelly in Central Park on Monday as heat shimmered off asphalt, plastering T-shirts to the backs of bikers, joggers, and skaters, she'd considered a new life. Today the park would be filled with squealing kids, hormonal teens, blooming flowers, rustling trees. Life. Foreign stuff to her as she waited to tail a lizard to its den. It was dangerous to have Cinderella fantasies today, of all days, and yearn for what she would never have.

"How did you hurt your hand?" he asked.

That? She'd forgotten her desperation when terrorizing Tanya. "Accident. Stupidity." Cleansing the hive of losers and bastards for those who wouldn't appreciate it.

"Where do you live, Helen?"

"With a friend." Yeah, her weapons.

He smiled at her. She could ask for his number. . . . Christ, a date? Last one she had was when she was fifteen, with Nancy telling her to be home by eleven. It had been so good, they had rolled on her bed two evenings later, Scorch letting him get to "third base," promising they'd go all the way that weekend.

157

But then Nancy was murdered, followed by her killers.

While a dinner date beat eating out of a can warmed over a hot plate, it wasn't worth the risk. She always made the wrong move. She hesitated, and then it was too late to get his number.

Babbled conversation grew louder as the hospital's day shift clocked out and streamed past to the exit.

There, Marie-the-monster in their midst! Show time.

"Got to run," she said, tousling his blond hair, enjoying the feel of the yellow silk. "Something important just came up."

She turned away before she saw disappointment or indifference in his face. The departing staff divided at the hospital exit, half heading uptown. Scorch slipped among them to keep Marie in view, but it wasn't hard—she was the one turning left and right, scanning everyone, looking for Scorch.

Marie stopped for beer at a corner grocery before heading to a basement apartment. Her home? Almost too easy. Scorch slipped in for cigarettes herself, but the storekeeper demanded ID first. Christ, even on the streets the government controlled her life.

She stepped back outside just as Marie emerged with a small child in tow, a girl in pigtails with a too-serious expression.

Scorch did an about-face, slipped back inside, and watched them trudge on, Marie spending more time studying the streets than talking to the little girl. Then mother and child turned onto Eleventh Avenue and entered the crummiest building on a block whose sidewalk was clotted with uncollected garbage. So the snake and her spawn lived in a hovel worse than the Tigresses's hole back on Morris Avenue.

Scorch ducked into a putrid alleyway, holding her breath

as much as possible while consulting the pimp's fancy watch. When Marie didn't emerge after an hour, Scorch knew she'd found Marie's lair. Perfect.

Like Tanya, Marie had succeeded in making her own hell.

Chapter Seventeen

Monday, June 10

When the hall officer nodded "good morning," Eric Glass reflected that for the first time in years it was for him.

Saturday had been delightful, with beautiful weather, Veronica enjoying herself and Lucy an interesting companion. It had been wonderful, even though he'd had this bizarre feeling of being watched, being tailed. As if . . .

A fat envelope lay on his office floor, just past the threshold. Departmental correspondence? Not likely to be slipped under the door over the weekend. A love letter? After all these years, he still got a few. Suzanne had probably sent most of them, along with unsigned valentines. He had no proof, but she was the prime suspect.

This envelope smelled funny. Earthy. He was about to toss it onto his desk when he thought about how it bulged, with something crinkly or dried inside.

It couldn't be.

He slipped a nail inside the flap, ripped, and tilted. What spilled out looked like oregano but smelled like pot. Sure it was. He hadn't smoked since way before Veronica was born, but he remembered his college days all too well.

A setup! Who . . . ?

Should he show it to the administration? No way; everyone here had been the recipient of injustice at least once.

He replaced the pot, folded the envelope carefully despite trembling fingers, stuck it in his pocket, and headed for the bathroom, scanning every face, whether in inmate green or security blue, wondering if they were the culprit. Halfway to the men's room he saw the captain coming down the hall, a sergeant in tow. Eric rushed into the men's room and found a vacant stall. Good; in this "two-holer" both were often occupied. He slipped inside and latched the door before emptying the envelope over the toilet. He tapped it several times before flushing, then shredded the envelope and flushed again.

The bathroom door opened.

"Dr. Glass?" It was the captain, not his favorite person under the best of circumstance. "You in there? We need to talk to you."

Eric sat on the toilet seat so his shoes were facing outward. "I don't feel so good," he said. That was no fib; his insides were cooking. Who had done this to him?

"We need to speak with you," the captain said.

"We," as in the inspector general's boys and girls? Sure, this would make a juicy scandal, all right. Who wanted to set him up, to roast him over a slow flame? "I'll be out in a few minutes. I'll come to your office."

"We'll wait here and go to *your* office."

No privacy, even in the john.

What could happen . . . ? Cuffs, prints, county lockup, lawyers. Veronica would be virtually an orphan, both parents alive but sealed away. His gorge rose.

He flushed for effect, jingled his belt buckle and started out, then turned and vomited into the bowl, hard.

When he emerged from the stall the captain was there,

watching, while Eric rinsed out his mouth. "You okay?" the captain asked, his lack of concern surpassed only by his lack of effort to conceal his apathy.

"I think so," Eric said. They walked to his office, joined by the sergeant and one of those guys in polyester suits, both of them looking appropriately grim.

"Dr. Glass, I'm John Sears of the Inspector General's Office," Polyester said. "I'd like to look at your stuff."

His "stuff"? Like what, his manual typewriter—not much newer than Gutenberg's original printing press? His scarred oak desk, bought when a Roosevelt was governor, nobody quite sure if it was Teddy or Franklin?

"Sure." Eric stepped aside for them to enter. Be obsequious and deferential and maybe they'd go easy on him. He clasped his hands behind him so they couldn't see them shaking.

They snooped around, like ferrets ready to squirm into a hole searching out whatever it was ferrets ferreted. The captain turned to him. "Can we look in your file cabinets?" he asked.

It was a private place, but as he had been told last Monday, when things got tight nobody wanted to know from patient–therapist confidentiality. Eric fumbled, unable to get the key into what had suddenly become a tiny lock. They were watching, no doubt already assuming his guilt and devising punishment.

There—open.

"You okay, Doc?" asked Inspector Sears.

Eric shook his head. "Happens every time I have sausage for breakfast. That's what I get for not eating kosher."

The captain and IG man exchanged glances. Sears flipped through the files, occasionally lifting one, sticking stubby fingers through the papers.

"Looking for D. B. Cooper, or Judge Crater?" Eric asked.

"Actually," said Sears without lifting his eyes, "we got an

anonymous tip you were bringing drugs into the facility."

"Drugs? Who the hell said that? I don't even take aspirin!" He looked to the captain. "Who said that?"

"We have to protect our source. Pot and coke were smuggled in recently. You're not the only one we've checked out."

No, huh? Eric sat, his legs no longer to be trusted. "Guilty until proven innocent, huh?" He emptied his pockets. "Want to do a cavity search?"

Sears looked up and almost smiled, then caught himself.

Who . . . ? Fielder, the chubby CO who had screwed up on Suzanne's funeral escort, had made that veiled threat Thursday. Not much in the way of proof, but who else would want to?

Anybody. Everybody. Fielder was just the most recent.

So there was motive. What about opportunity? On weekends people swept and mopped the halls. All it took was a flick of the wrist to slip that envelope underneath and . . . bingo.

The sergeant started opening Eric's hardcover texts and peering into the gap behind the bindings. When he got bored with that, he pulled out plants by their roots and sifted through the soil in their clay pots.

There were a thousand places to hide a dusting of drugs if someone was resourceful, motivated, and had the time and the key. The bottom of the chair or desk, seat cushion, radiator cover . . .

His office was a smuggler's dream, a patsy's nightmare.

After ten minutes, Sears came up for air and looked at the sergeant. Eric's texts were dumped on his desk, its drawers removed, their contents emptied. It would take hours to return everything into even a semblance of order.

Finally, anger overcame anxiety. "I'm ticked off," Eric said. Inspiration replaced helplessness. "Don't I get someone from the union to come down?"

"Sure," said the IG. "If you're charged, and right now," he shut the cabinet, "I'd say this was a false alarm. Be careful." He leaned closer. "Whoever tried to set you up has got a real hard-on for you. Watch your back."

Chapter Eighteen

Monday, June 10

The Midtown West station house was one of Manhattan's old ones, cleaner and less depressing than Lucy's first posting at the Four-One, the South Bronx's "Fort Apache," but with fewer amenities than her current base. Like any other New York precinct there were people milling about, yelling, complaining, or cursing in a half-dozen languages.

A handmade Day-glo poster towered behind the desk sergeant, showing a syringe dripping black blood over a map of New York.

In bold letters it proclaimed:

DARK PARADISE

Below it were numbers pasted over one another, surrounded by text:

AS OF THIS MORNING IT HAS KILLED 59 PEOPLE. ANOTHER 217 ARE STILL IN COMAS. BE SMART. DON'T DO IT.

165

Sure. Just say no. The sergeant arched an eyebrow when Lucy showed her composite of Scorch. "Yeah, this is . . . ?" he said.

"Suzanne 'Scorch' Amerce." Lucy flashed her gold detective shield before continuing. "She escaped from Midland Knolls last Saturday. We suspect she's down here, looking to kill the last member of the gang that murdered her sister eight years ago."

"And who would that be?"

"First name is Marie."

He sighed and flipped the composite onto a pile of papers, which fluttered whenever wheezing floor fans rotated toward him. "Uh-huh. And you want us to do what?"

"Circulate it at lineup for the next seventy-two hours. Post it on your bulletin boards. Have your plainclothes people ask their snitches about her. Usual SOP."

He frowned and tapped the poster behind him. "I don't know how it is up by you, but we've had over two dozen overdoses this month so far from Dark Paradise. Right now that's all the captain and the watch commanders are concerned about." He went back to whatever he had been doing. "We'll do our best," he said without looking back up, without doing much to assure her he'd do anything but leave here as close to three P.M. as possible.

Lucy snapped shut her shield case, dropped more composites onto his desk, and backed off. At a coffee machine in the corner a man watched her, grinning or leering; she couldn't tell in the dinginess of the precinct. He nodded to her and started over.

Another hidden admirer? He held up both hands. "Hey, Moreno, you forgot me after only ten years. I'm hurt."

The gravelly voice, the product of several packs of unfiltered every day, was more recognizable than the face.

"Reaumur?" she said. "Doug Reaumur. Didn't know you were here." She and Reaumur had been in uniform together at Fort Apache. Then Lucy passed her detective's exam and moved up to the Five-One, leaving Reaumur still a street cop.

Apparently he was working Anticrime now, patrolling in plainclothes. His bull neck had thickened from another decade of pumping iron. His hair remained blond over lifeless dark eyes, like those of the mechanical shark in *Jaws*. He either had broken his nose again or hadn't bothered to fix it right the first time.

"So," he said. "I hear you're detective sergeant now."

She nodded. He was still tracking her career. He had resented her rapid rise, claiming it was the result of affirmative action rather than talent. For his own part, he blamed reverse discrimination rather than lack of brains and perseverance for holding him back. Being sloppy and lazy never entered what there was of his mind. Still, he drank and mingled, always back doors up the ladder.

"And what do we have here?" he asked as he snatched one of Lucy's composites with nicotine-yellowed fingers. He moved back, but the smell of black coffee and smoke lingered.

"Scorch Amerce," she said. "You wouldn't be interested. It's a 'cold case,' not high profile. Not important."

"It was for you. Got you promoted pretty fast."

There he went again. In his case, time didn't heal wounds. He grinned and nodded to his watch commander walking past. "Lieutenant, this is Detective Sergeant Moreno, out of the Five-One in the Bronx." He showed him the mock-up of Scorch. "She's looking for this escaped con who might be in our neighborhood. I don't mind keeping an eye out for her while we're closing in on those Dark Paradise pushers."

The watch commander hardly broke stride. "Good," he said as he nodded to Lucy. "Get her number in case something breaks."

The man must have gone to the DiGiorio school of supervision: Follow the book, don't make waves, and call me in the morning. When he was gone, Reaumur turned to Lucy. "So," he said. "What's the value of a quick recapture? The truth."

"Told you. Not much."

He nodded. "So why do you think she's here, of all places?"

She shook her head. "I've also been to the Midtown South and Central Park precincts with these composites. Manhattan is a good place for a fugitive to blend in."

"Assuming she's still in town," he said as he studied the picture. "This is a composite. You think she changed her appearance? What do you have to go on?"

"Not much." She doubted he could do much with the information, but the goal was to catch Scorch and it didn't matter by whom. "We think she's after a woman in her late twenties, name of Marie. No, we don't have a last name or anything else."

"We?"

"I'm working with the Corrections Department," she said.

He smirked. "Oh, really? Well, it sounds interesting, and a well-aimed bullet could save the state lots of money. Thanks."

As she got to her car, she saw unpleasant consequences of talking to him. She'd promised Eric they would try to take Scorch alive, an idea Reaumur wouldn't even consider. If Reaumur messed up, it would alert Scorch, alienate Eric, and put Lucy onto a bull's-eye.

Chapter Nineteen

Wednesday, June 12

As Eric's friend Cassandra dealt out ten tarot cards in a T
shape and flipped over each in turn, her forehead furrowed.
When she chewed on a knuckle, Eric knew it was bad.
"Rick, you got an interesting future looking at you." She
shook her head, and her long silver earrings tinkled. "You
got Queen of Swords." A stern woman glared up at him. "A
grieving female of perplexing intellect, subtle, devious, and
cruel." She tried to grin as she flicked over another card.
"Rick, lots of women in your life now, and none bringing
you happiness."

He nodded. "Tell me something new, Sandy."

"But dis one here." Her long, lacquered nail tapped at the
Queen of Cups—a regal woman with a golden chalice on
her knees. "She going to push you hard, I tink. A practical
woman, fair, honest, and devoted. One you should listen
to." She cocked her head. "It makes sense to you?"

All too well. "Yeah."

Cassandra stopped with the next card halfway turned.
"Sounds like dat police lady. Veronica says she's nice, huh?"

Joel Ross

"She's okay." Sandy was joining Veronica as social director, to make him like nice women, even if they were married.

"I seen her last week. She got a nice bottom, not too big, and I know you like longer hair."

True, he had been attracted to Debbie's long, shiny black hair when they'd met, but he would have loved Debbie if she were bald, or had a mustache like her grandmother. Even now, lying like a corpse, her skin cool and dry to the touch in that twilight sleep linking life and death, he loved her so much.

The next card was Page of Swords, a girl brandishing a sword, point downward, from a throne set in the middle of storm clouds. Cassandra shook her head. "Dis one I don't get. It's a younger woman, wild, dark, with baffling and conflicting emotions. Is it de lady con de cops looking for?"

Who else? "Sure, why not?"

"So why you giving all de leads? What if she realize you de only one who know her, understand all her moods, her moves?" She reached over and touched his hand. "Rick, maybe you shouldn't get involved too deep."

"A little late for that now. I'm hoping if I help them find her, she won't get shot down by some street cop."

"You rather she get killed by somebody she already know?"

Cassandra, always questioning everything. If she had gone to law school, she'd be arguing cases before the Supreme Court. She next laid out the Nine of Swords—a woman sitting up in bed, weeping. Then came the Ten of Swords—a body with ten sabers jabbed into its back. Devil! The Devil, with the Hebrew letter Aye-in, the all-seeing eye sensing potential violence or paralytic fear. Then the Moon—symbolizing treachery and betrayal—followed by the Chariot—strife. The last card was Death. Death! The end of some long-term situation. Taken all together, the layout meant despair, martyrdom, and desolation.

Cassandra sat back and sighed, trying to put a good spin on it, but even if she had kissed the Blarney Stone, she couldn't make this one sound good.

"You've been reading my cards long enough for me to know this one looks bleak," he said.

"Death can mean change. You got changes coming?"

He'd be forty all too soon, but he suspected she saw a lot more than that. All those women, each demanding a piece of him.

"What else?" he asked.

"Be careful for a while. People around you got it in for you." She looked over the layout again. "It's not personal, but . . ." She got up, holding his hand as he walked her to the door. "It's dangerous for you the next few weeks, at least. Watch your back." She hugged him, her neck smelling of herbs and flowers. "I invested too much time in you to have you get hurt on me." She pecked his cheek. "Love to Veronica. See you next week."

He walked her down and out into the fading twilight, watching as she went down the block to her shop. He ambled around the street for a while, enjoying the warmth of the river breezes while wondering who had the knife poised to plunge into his back, and when they would decide to stab. People at work were never to be trusted. Look up *treachery* in the dictionary and it should show a picture of a prison.

His personal life . . . There was no personal life anymore, not since the accident. He never went to concerts, conferences, lectures, anything that reminded him of time spent with Debbie, hence anything that gave pleasure. He didn't attend Tai Chi classes anymore, at a time when he most needed defensive skills.

171

Nearly all his activities now revolved around Veronica, and driving her to and from soccer games or Hebrew school didn't constitute a well-rounded social life. As he walked upstairs, he wondered what he would do if he were Suzanne. He wasn't, although he had the same simmering rage.

Veronica was home now, in the living room, headphones on. She flicked off the stereo and spun around on the ottoman, her brow knitted, her most common expression the past few years, far too serious for someone barely thirteen. "Dad, we need to talk."

Eric sighed and plopped onto the couch. No rest for the weary. Whenever women prepared to give him a hard time, they prefaced it by saying, "We need to talk," and it never came out good. "What?" he asked.

The phone rang, and he reached for it. "Hello? Hello!" Nothing. Veronica stood when he hung up.

"Not even heavy breathing," he said.

"Uh-huh. It's happened a couple of times."

"Really? When?" The hairs on the back of his neck stood at attention.

"This week. And late last week."

"Not before?" he asked. He tried to swallow, but his mouth was suddenly dry.

"Maybe. Don't remember. Could be telemarketing. If they don't get a response, their automated machine just rings up somebody else. Linda's dad told me about them." Veronica walked to the terrace door. "Dad, this isn't easy to say."

What? She was pregnant? An alien abductee? Got a pierced navel? How bad could it be? "You know you can talk to me."

Her face tensed. "Are you going to pull the plug on Mom?"

Whoa! Totally out of left field. If she had slammed him in the gut with his Louisville Slugger, she couldn't have stunned him more. A decade of counseling cons made him think nothing could throw him, but this had. He sagged onto the couch, his chest hurting. Maybe he was finally getting a coronary, a family tradition for centuries. "What do you mean?" He knew perfectly well but had to play for time. How do you respond when your kid wonders if you're ready to sign a "Do Not Resuscitate" order so you can throw the switch on your best friend?

"I saw something about that the other day on *Oprah*. Dad, she's not getting any better."

"Yes, but . . ."

"At least this way we'll have a funeral, say 'Kaddish,' and go on with our lives."

Kaddish? Why was she eager to recite the prayer for the dead? "You've been speaking to your grandmother again?"

Debbie's mother, living alone with her grief down in Miami, was unselfish about sharing it. It was okay when she bugged Eric, but Veronica was too young to be saddled with such guilt. There was plenty of time for that when she got older.

"Grandma says so. The school guidance counselor. Sandy."

He was outnumbered. "What did Cassandra say?"

Veronica shrugged. "Some voodoo mumbo jumbo about the soul being immortal and Mom always being with us, no matter what."

Sounds like Cassandra. "Makes sense. What about Grandma?"

"She wants . . . 'an end to it,' whatever that means."

Kaddish, mourning, a finality to this living death. Legally Debbie was alive, medically she wasn't really, and morally . . . ? There was a logic to it, with Debbie in that limbo from which the only release was a cheap pine casket and six feet of dirt.

"Mrs. Kennedy the guidance counselor talked about closure."

Social worker talk. No matter—three women from different backgrounds and cultures all suggested the same thing.

Well, let *them* push the button on *their* loved ones, but as long as she still breathed, even if she needed a machine to pump her blood, Eric wasn't punching Debbie's time card.

Last year he'd stood by her bed, feeling the rubber tubes in his hand, as if it were her life pulsing through them, wondering if he had the guts to rip them out, or flick the switch.

"When your mother and I took marriage vows fifteen years ago . . ." Had it been that long? The ceremony seemed like it had occurred last month—the accident last week. "They were 'in sickness and in health.' It didn't say end the relationship without a fight." Did he love her enough to let her go?

"Grandma wonders if you'll want to 'get on with your life.' "

That sounded like good old Grandma. "Is this about Saturday? You, Lucy, and I shared a few nice hours together, most of which was spent discussing Suzanne Amerce." He stood, as if guilt and indignation had energized him. "I'm not about to lower your mother into a hole just because of that. Lucy's nice, and she's married. You and your mother are my life."

Life was imploding, crushing him. Vacation wasn't until late July, not soon enough.

Veronica's shoulders shook as she sobbed. Damn, he knew the right words for hardened cons, but not for his own child.

Whenever life got too tough for Suzanne and she cried, he longed to hug her, to give her comfort—a luxury denied prison shrinks. Not so here so he walked over and wrapped his arms around Veronica. "I can't do it," he said. Could he end Debbie's life without a battle, without exhausting all hopes of a miracle, remote as that might be?

He caught himself squeezing harder when he realized this might be damaging Veronica's young psyche even more than it was messing up his. It's hard to scar a scar.

"I know," Veronica said, her words muffled as she spoke them into his chest. "I just . . . I want something to happen! It's been the same for so long! Why?"

Why indeed? Maybe love, like pain, was just another way for life to hurt us. "I don't know, bunny, I don't know."

She pushed away. "You're supposed to have all the answers!"

Ah, yes. The Answer Man.

"Only the Almighty does," he said, "and my pipeline to Him doesn't work anymore." Disconnected, perhaps because of a failure to pay the bill when it came due. Eric had gone over this so many times the past few years, wondering if only he had done this, hadn't done that, been more religious, less hypocritical, given more time or money to charity, laid on the hands more to cure the sick, raise the dead . . . "I've used up my answers. All I've got left are questions."

"I know." She blotted at her tears with the palm of her hand. "This isn't your fault."

No? Then whose?

Veronica scooped up the cats and went to her room, to listen to her CDs and try to make sense of a senseless world.

Eric wandered to the terrace to gaze at sunlight flashing off the river. Bad move. It reminded him of Debbie's accident, of the blare of horns followed by the glare of headlights that awful night, the screech of brakes, the sickening impact and crunch of metal and glass, their car spinning a hundred eighty degrees, the intersection whirling past their windshield after they were broadsided.

Then Eric recalled that nauseating pain along with the warm, metallic taste of blood—his and Debbie's—the stink of gas, and worst of all, the feel of Debbie's head lolling on his chest, her blue eyes staring at him. Wide. Unseeing.

Then the phone rang again, just once.

Chapter Twenty

Tuesday, June 11

Lucy again scanned those old mug shots from Bronx precincts and Riker's Island. She tapped a ragged fingernail on a glossy photo of a swarthy girl with thick dark hair. When booked she had given her name as "Sheena Eastern, with a phony address. She had to be Marie, though it was only instinct that led her to think so, and instinct needed to be backed up by evidence. She had to laugh. NYPD at its finest. Can't come up with a last name, can't even find a hundred-pound escaped con, a strange little critter, hot-blooded and cold-blooded at the same time, her shrink saying it was a characteristic of abused kids.

They douse themselves in oil, then dance near a flame.

How far could Scorch get on a credit card and ninety bucks? Why hadn't she charged up a storm that first night? Lucy stared at Scorch's photos, at large, dark eyes that seemed to follow you like a trick painting. She was feeding them false clues. At Tanya's place forensics came up with a partial thumbprint that might be Scorch's but were really smudged. Among a bunch of others were several clean sets of palm and fingerprints from the alias Sheena Eastern. Lucy sat back, disgusted with the meagerness of a lone clue. Why wouldn't Marie meet with Tanya for mutual protection from Scorch. Once a gang member . . .

DeGiorio came by with Paul Sanders and gave her his patented stare.

"When you going to retire, Lieutenant?" she asked.

"A week after you, so I can know a little peace on the job again before quitting."

He stomped off, leaving Lucy to sift through reports from homeless shelters, local YWCAs, church basements, Salvation Army, anyplace a small woman with a baby face could get herself a bed. Wasted energy, since Glass felt she'd hook up with a guy, or gal, setting up light housekeeping in Midtown, blending in.

Paul Sanders returned and gave Lucy a wink. "So how you and Tony getting along these days?" he asked.

"Okay."

"Okay?" He seemed about to say more but didn't, perhaps watching DiGiorio in action having showed him that tact and good manners can't hurt. "Here are the Manhattan precinct reports."

Lucy riffled through them, run-of-the-mill purse snatchings, robberies, drug busts, rapes, the epidemic of Dark Paradise overdoses . . . and last Tuesday, a twenty-eight-year-old woman mauled in a West Side apartment, along with a blinded pimp suffering from internal injuries. Was Marie now a whore, Scorch found her and . . . ? Jesus, the guy's injuries were worse than something inflicted over a half-dozen Super Bowls: fractured ribs, injury to spleen, liver, crushed testicle. Ouch! One of his eyes sliced beyond repair, the other with its sclera torn so badly . . . But why wasn't the woman killed? This happened last Tuesday and she was only getting the word now? Reaumur! Why was he sabotaging . . . ? Of course! He was hoping to nail Scorch himself and achieve his long-delayed moment of glory while depriving Lucy of the arrest. She pulled up the location of the two messed-up pimps on her computer.

"Paul," she said. "You done good. I think I'm going to visit these two at Roosevelt Hospital."

"Why, you want to bring them flowers?"

"Rumor in Midtown is this guy was a 'kiddies pimp,' scouting for young runaways fresh out of the Port Authority Bus Terminal, scooping them up, sending them out to whore for him." She consulted scribbled notes. "The woman was either a prostitute from his stable or the one who trolled the streets, luring young girls to him."

The woman had suffered a busted skull, with fractures of the shin, collarbone, and shoulder blades. Could a hundred-pound girl inflict all this damage? Sure, at fifteen, Scorch had fricasseed three Tigresses at once, then pounded their skulls into granulated sugar. Amazing what maniacal strength can accomplish. She copied the pimp's name. "Worth checking out. Lucy dialed the precinct and learned the investigating detective was out on a homicide case. With the murder rate climbing faster than the temperature, a couple of maimed slimeballs wouldn't command much priority. If she wanted to find who had mutilated them, she'd have to do it herself. Besides, this jived with Glass's prediction of Scorch going ballistic if betrayed. It was a slender lead, but despite Reaumur blocking her access to information she could not resist checking it out? "I'm off on a case, if DiGiorio should ask," Lucy said.

As she drove to Roosevelt Hospital, she noted all the young women out in Midtown, a quarter of whom could fit the description of Scorch, or Marie.

Lucy needed to cut her wheel to avoid an ambulance racing into the emergency-room entrance and slipped around it to the front entrance. There she flashed her shield at the reception desk and nurses' station, ignoring first their exasperated looks as she pawed through files and then their orders to stop searching. Third floor. She hustled upstairs, fueled by hope.

The woman was a "veg," stuck so full of tubes she looked like a porcupine. According to her chart, she was conscious at times, but this wasn't one of them. She bore little resemblance to any of the girls from those eight-year-old mug shots, but with her face bruised and swollen, her head bandaged, that wasn't surprising. Jesus, the terror she must have felt, poor woman.

Poor woman? She exploited and abused children. Was Lucy's compassion wasted on the wrong people? Rather than wait for Jane Doe's return from La-La Land, Lucy visited her boss, "Luscious" Louis Johnson. His rap sheet was probably as long as Scorch's, except he had never been accused of killing people's bodies, just their souls and spirit. His eyes were bandaged, and it was obvious he was on painkillers. The room smelled antiseptic, sterile, like Johnson must now be.

"I'm Detective Sergeant Moreno." She started to flash her shield, then shrugged and slipped it back into her pocket.

Johnson zeroed in on her voice. "I'm glad for you."

"Who ripped you up? A competitor?"

"Screw off. I'll handle it later."

"Oh yeah?" Lucy glanced at the medical chart dangling at the foot of the bed. "Only thing you'll be handling is a white stick and a tin cup. You want whoever did this to get nailed, you talk to me. I've already spoken to your partner."

"Nurse, this cop's hassling me."

"Have a nice life," Lucy said. The woman was her last hope, if she ever returned to Planet Earth and was more cooperative than her buddy, who thought he was tough as nails.

"Hey, cop, wait." Nails sometimes bent and broke.

"Yeah, what?"

Johnson tried for a more comfortable position, but after a couple decades of taking drugs the hospital's analgesics were inadequate for him. "You really going to look for her?"

Her? Lucy felt the adrenaline surge. "Yeah, it's my job. Who was she and where can I find her?"

"Name was Helen, fresh off the bus, staying with Kelly. How is Kelly? Every time I ask, they give me mumbo jumbo."

"She's stable. What did this Helen look like?"

"Real short, real cute, great little butt."

"Eyes?"

"Two."

More than this guy still had. "Color and size?"

"Color? Dunno. Brown, I think, but real large. Bedroom eyes. Soft, smooth olive skin. Firm thighs."

Sure they were. "Hair?"

"Short. Blond."

Blonde and short. Their work with the composites was on track. What other identifying . . . ? Lucy recalled Scorch's purchases at Victoria's Secret. "How big were her breasts?"

Johnson smiled. Being blinded and neutered hadn't erased his sense of humor. "Not too big. She had nice proportions."

"Thirty-four B? Weighed maybe a hundred pounds? One-oh-five? Size two?"

"Yeah, That's her! Catch her for me and burn her, hear?"

Lucy heard. That's what she was here for.

Chapter Twenty-one

Tuesday, June 11

Rainey's file, while not as thick as Suzanne's, was filled with nearly as much mayhem. Eric scanned her crime history.

"Karen Rainey began her felonious spree by robbing other prostitutes while at the same time having several abortions."

Eric pinched the corners of his eyes. Rainey must have been voted "the most likely to conceive" by her classmates, assuming she even attended high school. He read on.

"Then, as she either became jaded or in need of ever-increasing amounts of money to support her drug habit, she and her female accomplice would beat these fellow prostitutes before stripping them of jewelry and clothing. This escalated to brutalization, torture, and, ultimately, at least three murders she admits to. This started in 1977 and continued up to her incarceration in 1982. It is felt that . . ."

This was whom Suzanne had turned to for protection? Maybe her surrogate big sister hadn't revealed her entire biography. Speaking of sisters, he wondered if by June twentieth . . .

A stocky, middle-aged woman clicked her nails on the steel door frame. "Got a second?" she asked.

He covered the file and gestured to a vacant chair.

She plopped and grinned. "Hi, I'm Barbara White."

Suzanne's archenemy, come to gloat, or do damage? This was why he arranged his office chairs so he was between them and the door and not vice versa. "Pleased to meet you, Ms. White." The faded number on her shirt showed she'd been incarcerated more than fifteen years ago, so she must have killed somebody.

Or somebodies, just like Suzanne.

"There's something you should know, Dr. Glass."

Yes, when working around here there's never a dull moment.

"Somebody's trying to set you up," she said.

Ah yes, the danger Cassandra has predicted. He acted nonchalant but felt his heart trip. "Who?"

"Don't know." Her grin widened. "But the word is out."

He didn't doubt that. Prisons had a communications system that rivaled ITT and could put the CIA to shame. "It's nice of you to come tell me." Sure, she'd done him a favor and would expect one in kind. "How come?"

"You helped a friend of mine a few years back." She stood, probably unused to spending so much time this close to a man. "If I was you, I'd be careful who I trusted from now on. Things aren't what they seem, and not everybody's a friend."

"For example?"

She shook her head.

He tried another angle. "I appreciate this," he said. "Especially since you and Suzanne Amerce didn't get along."

She paused near the door. "She tell you that?"

"No, but I read reports. You two fought a lot."

"Yeah." She fumbled in a pocket for smokes and lit one. "Scorch was like a little jackrabbit, never staying put long enough to cast a shadow, getting into everyone's business, helping people who didn't want or need help." She blew smoke rings, savoring each puff. "She a friend of yours?"

Careful. "We saw a lot of each other over the years."

"Don't doubt it. Girl's crazy." White tapped her lumpy forehead, suggesting plenty of cerebral scar tissue, gifts from mates poorly chosen, ones who found her a convenient punching bag. She probably had killed him, or her, and was consequently doing a lengthy "bid" like Suzanne, except Suzanne had probably surpassed her, killing a half dozen, an extraordinary feat even in a place like this. Or not. If he looked at Barb's "jacket" sometime, he might find she was even more infamous than Suzanne.

White paused to take another drag. "Yeah, be careful. Watch your back. Don't trust nobody." She moved off, leaving his office stinking of Lucky Strikes.

Veronica and Debbie knew that whenever he'd counseled Suzanne he'd come home reeking of Camels. She was the only one he'd allow to smoke in his presence, his one concession to get her comfortable enough to open up. If she smoked as much the rest of the day as she did during their sessions, her lungs must resemble a lump of coal.

Almost four, quitting time. He double-locked everything, a wasted precaution in a place where petty thievery was a reflex and he was one of the few who didn't know how to pick a lock.

In his mailbox was a message from Lucy Moreno. Christ, he'd forgotten to call her and say how much he enjoyed her company Saturday. What with the planted drug in his office yesterday morning, and everything else . . .

Some excuse. If he'd thought about her that much, he'd have phoned Sunday or last night. Who was he kidding? Attractive as Lucy was, they were both married, in every legal and moral sense. If Debbie was dead, or he and she were separated, his life would be better defined, but with his wife in that shadow world without consciousness or the ability to live without artificial aids, who knew what his obligations were?

It had just been nice to be with a woman who talked, who laughed, who thought and walked. Who lived.

He phoned Lucy at the precinct, and she chuckled when she heard his voice. "I got news," she said, "about West Side male-female pimp team who got demolished by a small woman last week. She did a job on them that would put a Green Beret team to shame."

"Suzanne?"

"The pimp didn't know from names and didn't want to cooperate, but he'll only be half a man from now on. The woman might be Marie, though he called her Kelly. She had no ID and like most comatose people was a crummy conversationalist."

Eric winced, imagining another woman—like Debbie—with pumps and motors living for her. "It might have been Suzanne," he said, "getting revenge against a mother-surrogate who betrayed her."

She chuckled again. "If so, she's on the loose and at this rate could clean up this town in six months if we gave her an Uzi, a bulletproof vest, and carte blanche, but we got bleeding hearts running this city. Moreno's sermon for the month. I'm heading up to Yonkers for a sale in Cross County Shopping Center. I can give you details there."

"I don't want to monopolize your time."

"Don't worry about that. We leave now, we'll meet in half an hour. When guys are down they drink, but women go shopping."

Oh? "Are you depressed?"

"No. Concerned. This Scorch thing, from your revelation about her giving herself up, and . . ." she lowered her voice, "as you saw Friday, our lieutenant isn't the easiest guy to work with. He's getting old and crotchety. Half hour?"

"Where will you be?"

"Macy's. See you there."

The shopping center was on the way home. Was this a smart move? Why not? He arrived at four-thirty, parking near Lucy's red Prelude. Eric wandered inside, noticing young women in tight shorts or short skirts, recalling how great Debbie looked in what he called her "slut outfits," enjoying her blush, then feigned annoyance when he teased her. She embarrassed so easily.

The girls made him think of Suzanne. He didn't know whether to be relieved or concerned that Lucy believed Suzanne had pulped those two Manhattan pimps.

"Eric, good timing." Lucy came out of a shoe store, arms full, dressed in a blouse and skirt that made her look even sexier than her jeans and T-shirt of Saturday. "Have you given more thought about those two people mauled by a petite woman? Might it have been Scorch's handiwork?"

Eric shrugged, sensing potential embarrassment no matter how he answered. It had been five years since he had studied forensic psychology, and he was rusty on the older theories and unaware of any new ones. Maybe he could talk his way out of answering. "The Talmud says a virtue of angels is their short memory for unpleasant things." He took a package from her. "I had some bad days at work and have had trouble concentrating. That's why I didn't call to say what a nice time we had Saturday." He told her of the planted drug, the search and the warning from Suzanne's archenemy, and that fat officer Fielder.

Lucy stopped short. "Those were practically threats!"

He shrugged. "It's prison. Everybody threatens everybody else. It's expected." As he walked beside her, the random contact of her soft, bare arms made him relish her body heat, the smoothness of her skin, the firmness of her flesh on each casual touch. It had been so long since he had been so close to a woman whose blood coursed through her veins under its own power. He was getting excited at the worst time.

Besides, they were both married.

Lucy matched his stride with her own, her long thighs in occasional contact with his, her warmth enlivening him.

"Oh, there was something important I needed to tell you about Suzanne and the twentieth, but . . ." He rolled his eyes. "My mind is like that 'Magic Slate' we had as kids—you wrote on it, but once you lifted it, the message was gone." He was forgetting too many important things these days, dwelling instead on those that upset him. He needed to concentrate on living. "Let's have dinner. Fish or steak?"

"How about Veronica?" she asked.

"I don't eat Veronica."

Her dark eyes flashed. "She's vulnerable now. She needs you to pay attention to her. I have a fifteen-year-old stepson. I know how teens can be."

"You're right, I should call."

"She's a sweet girl."

He nodded. "Takes after her mother for her positive traits."

"And from her father . . . ?"

"She gets her temper. Her judgmental nature. Her desire to see the right thing gets done. Her impatience with unfairness."

"Sounds good to me."

He nodded. "Usually. How about Japanese?"

She hesitated. Probably not first on her list, eating raw fish or stir-fried beef. "Oh," she said. "We got a partial print that might be Scorch's, from Tanya Smith's apartment. Since Tanya was a Tigress, there's motive for Scorch to hold her under. Other prints matched a young woman's, aged twenty, picked up just before Suzanne's capture eight years ago. She called herself 'Sheena Eastern,' a bastardization of the singer's name."

He shook his head. "She only spoke of her as Marie. Wait," he snapped his fingers, "Suzanne sometimes referred to Marie as 'Queen of the Jungle.' I thought she was speaking in metaphors, but Sheena . . . ? Could be. Where can those prints lead us?"

"Nowhere. It was a fictitious name and address. Anything else you can think of?"

"Not really." Once again, the Answer Man came up short. Time to change the subject to something pleasant. "So maybe Italian?" he said. "There's a nice place a mile from here."

Teenagers burst from a video arcade. One blundered into Lucy and knocked a package from her grasp.

The boy, perhaps seventeen, looked at them and smirked.

"Good manners have gone the way of the buffalo," Eric said to Lucy as he stooped to pick it up.

The kid sneered. "Got a problem, pop?" He grinned at his friends.

Eric stood, handed the bag back to Lucy, and walked her toward the exit.

The kid grabbed Eric's arm. "I asked if you had a problem!"

Eric yanked away.

The kid, a pimply loser with a gerbil's brain, assumed a stance. "Don't screw with me. I said if you got a problem."

Eric turned back to Lucy, and the kid seized his arm again.

Eric spun, jerked free, dropped the packages, and clutched the front of the kid's collar, shoving him across the marble floor, slamming him against a wall. Eric pushed his hands upward, twisting his knuckles against the boy's throat. A few pounds of pressure against the carotid, a few more against the jugular . . .

"You're crazy!" the kid gasped, his eyes widening.

187

Yeah, and your point is . . . ? Eric saw him through a thickening red haze, the boy changing, becoming one of those punks last week in the Bronx, the ones dying for trouble to begin.

His face inches from the kid's, Eric felt his fingers pulsing with adrenaline, with power, his brain filling with visions of blood. Did he want to do this?

Almost as badly as he wanted to avoid it.

The kid turned pale, finally realizing he had chosen to dive headlong toward a spinning propeller.

He looked to his friends, then back to Eric.

Eric saw the punk sweat, felt himself sweat. They were both seconds from something that would change their lives forever.

He thought he heard Lucy say something.

It was overpowering, the temptation to teach him a lesson, to show him what it would be like for someone to call his bluff. Eric didn't care about his own pain; he was anesthetized by rage.

His knuckles dug deeper into the kid's neck.

The boy's eyes widened even more as he muttered something.

"Eric!" Lucy tugged on his arm. "Eric, don't!"

No. Veronica was expecting him home tonight and not in jail or alongside her mother, his brain also homogenized. Eric let go and swallowed the first taunts that came to mind, knowing they'd be wasted on this clueless kid and his imbecile friends.

Despite the mall's air-conditioning, his shirt was glued to his body. So close to committing the ultimate stupidity.

The kid ran to his friends, who stood to one side, open-mouthed, before heading for the exit. A few passersby waited, saw nothing else happening, and drifted off.

"Right, let's go." He escorted her to her car, hearing only their footsteps. Shame competed with anger, robbing him of the words to apologize to her. Blown it, for the minor satisfaction of letting himself go. So many years spent holding it in, and now, of all times, to let it spew out.

She opened her car door.

Maybe he could still salvage the evening. "So what about that unpretentious little place where the eggplant parmigiana is superb and scented candles mounted in chianti bottles grace authentic plaid tablecloths?"

She shook her head. "You need to cool off. Maybe a rain check."

"Oh, that? It's nothing. I wouldn't have hurt him."

"He was just a kid."

"Teens younger than him commit murder every day. You of all people should appreciate that."

She nodded. "It's just that seeing you like that . . ." She shook her head. "I shouldn't make comparisons, but my husband gets upset by things like that. I wouldn't enjoy the meal." She looked at her feet. "Maybe some other time."

"Was he abused?" A personal question, but she had brought it up, and that's what shrinks did, ask stuff like that.

"I don't know. Maybe. He and his father didn't get along." She put her stuff in her car, then paused, hand on the door, back in cop mode. "So who planted the grass? The officer?"

Eric shook his head. "Flatline? I doubt it. He doesn't have the brains to direct a one-car parade. It might be Suzanne's friend Karen trying to sidetrack me so I can't help find her. She did ask for an appointment that Monday morning, so she knew I'd be in my office in time for the captain to come by. Or it might have been Suzanne's worst enemy, Barb, somehow thinking I helped her escape. The list of usual suspects is endless."

"How did the drugs come in?"

"Visitors, most likely, though sometimes staff get coerced into aiding and abetting smuggling. So how about that rain check?"

"Sure." She handed him a business card with her home number on the back. "As long as you promise to stay cool." They looked at each other for a long five seconds, neither of them able to break the spell.

She nodded and drove off, leaving him alone with his flaws.

Chapter Twenty-two

Stops at The Pleasure Trove for sequined G-strings, pasties, and thongs, and to Salvation Army and secondhand stores for vinyl miniskirts and other accoutrements, and Scorch was in business. The Pleasure Trove salesman leered as she purchased the "toys," but cash was cash. Perhaps the dog leash, rubber phallus, and other stuff was a bit much, but she was eager to make an impact her first night. She'd peeked into a few clubs to see what the girls on parade were doing to drive the boys wild.

It wouldn't hurt to have this stuff on hand, but could she drive them too wild? Doubtful, but they kept beefy guys near the stage—their biceps bulging out of their muscle shirts.

Almost five. This was her first job, unless she counted working in the prison beauty shop at a quarter an hour, or her two years as a teacher's aide.

At Grand Central Station she paused, debating whether to split with what was left of the pimp's money and start a new life or hang out until June twentieth and end Marie's miserable life.

Tomorrow she'd go to a cemetery, jot down the birth date of some poor stillborn kid from eighteen years ago, and with a birth certificate in that name get a Social Security card, driver's license, all those validations of existence. It could be a passport to a real life, but if only she turned her back on her first dream, butchering Marie. She headed to the Crystal Grotto, and the doorman of the strip club sneered. "You lost, kid?"

Her throat got dry. Was this a mistake, making herself the center of attention in a place like this? Was it worse than what she had? "I go on at six," she said, holding up the bag of goodies as proof she was about to become a professional tease.

"We got a liquor license. You got to be twenty-one to work," he said.

"I already cleared that with Leo." She slipped on past, the place looking dimmer today, with the pulsing jungle beat of a sound system with so much bass it reverberated through her skeleton, tickling her organs. Everything seemed wilder this evening, and the women writhing on stage seemed more focused.

Could she compete? What if she got booed off? It wasn't too late to turn around, get a refund on the facial and body makeup she'd bought, and get that bus or train ticket.

Guys were nursing drinks at tiny tables, the bar, or against the wall, their libidos fertilized by the gyrating girls. A few checked Scorch out, stripping her with their eyes as if comparing their fantasies with what they might see in the flesh.

Did she want to go on with this? Could she? It was this or rolling drunks or scrounging for empty beer bottles in garbage cans.

She strode past and tapped on the manager's door. "I'm here," she said, belaboring the obvious to the oblivious.

Leo looked up. "That's nice. Who are you?"

"You said work six to midnight. Helen?"

He shuffled crumpled papers. "I did?" His forehead creased.

Damn!

He'd forgotten. So much for earning a legitimate living.

Then he nodded. "Right, the little one who stripped to her skivvies for free. Okay, dressing room is third door on the left. Tell Mona to show you the ropes."

Mona? Oh boy, she'd need a stage name, something so sluttish she'd have to keep from cracking up when she said it. "Jezebel" or "Remora." Maybe even "Candy."

She opened the door and was hit with the stink of pot. Three young women—long, lean, and leggy—sat in a narrow room taken up with clothes hooks, three-sided mirrors, and tiny desks holding makeup kits. The tallest, lounging naked on a table, glanced down at her. "Sorry, kid. Adults only. Take a hike."

"I'm working. Leo said Mona would show me the ropes."

The other two giggled. One, black, not much older than Scorch and with skin the color of honey, but with eyes that had seen far too much way too soon, nudged her companion. "Ropes? Yeah, he tried to get me up to his place once. I asked if he had cable and he said, 'No, but the cords should be strong enough.' "

They giggled again. The black one came over and batted her mascara as she lifted Scorch's chin. "I'm Mona, and this minx is Sheila. Yeah, you'll do." She hefted Scorch's bag. "That your stuff? Let's see." She dumped the contents onto one of the few uncluttered spaces in the room and sorted through them. "Yeah, this is good, this is okay. This," she held up feathers and giggled again, "is definitely out. That your makeup? You got that and body stuff, but no lipstick."

Couldn't think of everything.

"I'd give you some of mine," said Sheila as she applied

eye shadow, "but I don't know where your mouth has been."

Nor would she want to. Scorch accepted the favors and did herself up, watching the others watch her out of the corner of her eye. In the poor lighting would her scars be noticeable, despite the body makeup?

"You done this before?" asked Mona.

"Not really, except for my tryout yesterday."

More giggling. "You're the one who stripped in the back? All right, my girl." Sheila gave her a high five. "So what did you do before this?"

"Stuff, laundry, bake shop, beautician. I'm between gigs."

More giggling. They started smoking more homegrown, and Sheila handed Scorch a joint.

She shook her head. "Maybe later." She'd never done marijuana, and now was not the time to experiment and risk mental and physical coordination. As it was, her stomach was twisted up with the anticipation of what was to come.

"What's your name?" asked Sheila.

"Sue . . . I mean Jezebel."

"I'll tell Leo."

Great. She had to calm down, cool her jets. She squeezed into the red vinyl miniskirt, silently begging Nancy to forgive her for what she was about to do. The skirt fit like plastic skin, making her wonder if this was what Saran-wrapped meat on a deli counter felt like, just before it was sliced and served.

Then she slipped on her disguise, a gaudy Mardi Gras mask she hoped would distract them from noticing her large eyes. Copper bangles on her wrists should cover her scars from eight years ago, and what cops would expect her to hide in plain sight?

Beside, eyes and wrists were the last places these guys would gawk at.

On stage Leo announced that "Jezebel from New Orleans, 'Queen of the Crescent City' " was the rare treat they were about to enjoy.

Oh Lord. It got harder to breathe, to move. To think.

Do it. Show time. She took a deep breath and coughed up a lungful of pot-scented air. Once her head cleared, she strutted onto the stage. By her sixth step, with those hungry faces turned on her, sweat bubbled from every gland, and it wasn't from the pair of red and blue lights focused on her. Dull faces raised toward her and dozens of pairs of eyes zeroed in, screwing her physically. One in particular, a husky guy with a shiny face and a cheap suit, seemed fascinated by her.

It was happening again! Her whole life she'd been treated like a thing—somebody's object—one of abuse by her mother, of hate and fear by the Tigresses, of scorn by the COs, of desire first by Karen and now by these testosterone factories whistling and howling out there.

What now? The moves she'd rehearsed in her head were erased. They stared at her while the music pounded through the speakers.

Think provocative and manipulative. Think Salome.

She pointed to her groin, then curled her index fingers under the hem of the miniskirt. They hooted, easily pleased.

She lifted the hem an inch, two, three, her fingers walking up her thigh. There wasn't much more material to play with, and she had nineteen minutes to go. They shifted in their seats.

To the beat, she raised the hem, bent, and kissed it. Wolf whistles. These guys were really hard up.

She undid the catch, let the skirt drop, then caught it, mock horror on her face. She let it fall and kicked it away.

A few more leaned forward.

Cigarette smoke billowed across the lights, making the place resemble the set of a bad vampire movie. What a life this was, one step above prostitution and two up from grave robbing.

Her anxiety burned away, replaced by contempt. They were perverts, titillated because they thought she was in her midteens. But she was in charge. Whatever happened now would be of her making. Control, at last. Make them pay.

Out of the corner of her eye she noticed that the stocky, oily guy had a bulge under his left armpit. When he reached inside his jacket, she saw the poorly concealed shoulder holster.

Cop!

Made! Busted, cuffed, shackled, dragged back to Midland, letting Marie off the hook. Better to break a bottle, carve his carotid, and get the death penalty, rather than rot away. . . .

Where was the rear exit? Play for time. Maybe he didn't want to make a scene. Maybe he hadn't recognized her. The show must go on. If she ran off, she'd arouse suspicion when there might be another way. She sashayed to the other part of the tiny stage, where another patron plunked down an empty beer bottle and weaved over to clutch at her ankle. She tap-danced away, forced back to the husky guy, who leaned forward, reached out, and . . .

Reached out to hand her a dollar bill. She thrust her pelvis forward and he tucked it into her G-string, leering at her, all but licking his chops. His fingers lingered, eager to caress, a tempting target for her to snap off.

Repulsive and cheap. What a combination.

She gyrated away before she sweated off the makeup and he saw her tiny scars. She wrapped herself around a pole and swung until she felt dizzy. She paused and let the room settle down while relishing the feel of their eyes on her, feasting on her every move. The sleaziness was contagious, driving her to indecency. She squatted over the empty bottle, wriggled lower, wiped the bottle's mouth, then shifted her thong. Then, using muscles previously reserved for more private pursuits, she sucked it up by its neck with her labia.

They howled louder when she lifted it a foot into the air.

Those private moments with Karen had finally paid off.

Time telescoped and her shift was over, leaving her both energized and exhausted, for twelve dollars in tips.

Sheila gave her an approving look. "Nice effect, picking up that bottle with your pussy. What you do, rub oil on yourself?" She pointed to the sheen coating Scorch's legs, chest, and belly.

"Sweat. And it wasn't all from the exertion."

"You that nervous, girlfriend?" asked Mona. "You did okay." She handed Scorch a towel.

Leo popped his head in the door and beckoned to Scorch. "Nice gig, toots. Now, if you go among the customers and have them buy you drinks, that would be appreciated."

Mona tossed the damp towel at him. "Leave the girl alone. She needs to recuperate."

"I don't drink," said Scorch as she picked through her stuff for another outfit to put on, only to peel off later.

"So what? Let them buy you club soda, at five bucks a pop. C'mon, people, this is a high-rent district. No point getting these guys hot and bothered and then not let them cool down by guzzling beer." He tossed the towel back at Mona. "Drink something, Jezebel. We don't want no dehydrated ladies here. And all of you, shake your tails. The sign says '*Live* Girls.'"

Sheila blew him a raspberry, and they all laughed.

All except Scorch, who wondered if she had picked up any diseases along with that bottle.

Leo peeled off those bills as if they were layers of his own skin. "You coming back tomorrow?" he asked Scorch.

"I guess." Why not? Fifty-six bucks in tips on top of his twenty-five, plus all that exercise meant she'd sleep fine tonight. Tomorrow she'd find a furnished room in a decent place where the singing of drunks and the curses of junkies didn't jolt her awake at four A.M.

Sheila and Mona paused outside the door. Mona must be a favorite; she earned at least a hundred in tips tonight. "You coming for a drink down at Reno's?" she asked.

Scorch hesitated. It was late, she needed rest, there were plans to make and enemies to kill . . . She had never gone out to a bar. She hadn't done anything with a friend in eight years.

There was catching up to do. "Lead the way," she said.

On the way out the oily guy leered at her, licking his lips. She scooted off before he got too close and tried to adopt her.

Reno's was a step above a dive, but no one was passed out on the floor and it didn't reek of sweat or vomit.

Mona ordered a round of beers, so they wouldn't dehydrate, but Scorch asked for Chablis, having read in *Cosmo* it was a "ladies' drink." Nancy had impressed on her kid sister that college, class, and style were a mark of decent people, the "right kind." Sluts, whores, and inmates were the opposite end of the spectrum, and guess what . . . Dr. Glass had her read *Lord Jim* five years ago, to see what the road to hell was paved with.

He'd have a stroke if he were here tonight.

Reno gave her a dirty look. "Got ID?" he asked.

"She with us," Mona said, as if that alone made her an adult and worthy of trust. Her peer group had risen from felons to stripteasers. Nancy, wherever you are, sorry.

"So why you here, Jezebel?" asked Sheila. "You're not the sort of girl to work bars. You doing a term paper on hustling?"

"I got a degree," Scorch said. "Two years ago." She hid

behind her wineglass in case she blushed. "Need a job, is all."

"I know what that's like. Got knocked up at sixteen."

Not long after Scorch was sentenced, only Sheila had imprisoned herself voluntarily—by love, not hate and rage.

Mona nodded. "Me too, at eighteen. Boyfriend died in a drive-by, leaving me with a kid. For somebody who didn't go past tenth grade, this isn't bad." She smiled, showing beautiful teeth, as she leaned forward and whispered, "No taxes."

Scorch grinned and drained her glass, with Reno pouring another before she could refuse. One of the patrons sidled up and started murmuring to Sheila, who laughed, pushed him away, and then laughed again. Mona crossed her legs, and long ones they were indeed, worthy of Scorch's envy. More guys came up, shirts unbuttoned to show gold chains and chest hair as they offered drinks. Scorch shook her head but eyed one man's cigarettes. Despite the week's excitement, she had cut back and fought the withdrawal symptoms. He flicked the pack, holding one out. She declined again. In prison a favor accepted was a favor owed, and he wasn't a guy to be obligated to. Plus, no point getting close to someone who might have a badge. The wine hit her, and she grasped the end of the table to prevent the world from spinning away. Not good, getting tipsy. Which way was home? That could make anyone suicidal, having to consider that flophouse "home."

Once home had been three spacious rooms with . . . forget it, that was ancient history, not long after when dinosaurs walked the earth. Then home became an eight-by-ten hole in a dungeon with unreliable plumbing. Now it had graduated to a firetrap with roaches the size of mice and rats the size of cats. The only people who cared about her now were pot-smoking strippers.

She was maudlin. One more chablis and she'd be in tears,

and there was way too much to do. "Got to go," she said, dropping bills on the bar and smiling at her newfound buddies as she steadied herself. "At least I'm leaving you in 'good spirits.'" She winked at Sheila, who squeezed her shoulder.

Mona gave her a wink. "You be back tomorrow, Jezebel? Don't worry, you'll get used to it."

"Yeah," Scorch said, but hoped not. What a dismal future, to spend her best years parading before salivating men, wearing only buttons on her nipples and a thong wedged between her buns.

Across the street a man leaned on a bus pole, face in shadows. He watched her weave, then regain her balance as she headed to her niche in that cave masquerading as a hotel. At a quarter past one, was he waiting for a bus? Dope dealer or rapist? Both?

He continued to stare, as if studying her face.

The hell with him. She was on Eleventh Avenue, a few blocks from Marie's home. Maybe she'd be coming home herself about now after finishing a hard shift, exhausted and not expecting Scorch to walk up and slice her jugular. No such luck. The street was deserted except for that guy. Marie slept soundly.

He walked after her, ten strides to the rear. She quickened her stride, but he kept pace. She groped in her bag for the first weapon she touched, the scissors. Good, with silence and surprise in its favor. The man either decided she wasn't worth keeping up with or was indeed waiting for the bus and hung back.

Cooler breezes off the Hudson brought the promise of tomorrow. Her footsteps echoed off the darkened tenements and the dull bass of rap music reverberated in the distance, then faded as she strode up the block, finding home.

Why should Marie sleep well? Dr. Glass said use all the

talents and tools at her disposal. Her paternal grandfather was from Haiti. . . . Sure! Thanks to the *Daily News*, Marie knew Scorch was out, so surprise wasn't in her favor but anticipation could be. Psychological warfare was the key. She had to disrupt Marie's days and ruin her nights to even the odds.

Under torture Tanya had revealed how superstitious some of the Tigresses were, especially Marie. There was her edge, if only she figured how to exploit it.

A few people, drunker than she was, lounged in the lobby, devouring her with their eyes. She brushed past them to her room, ready to fall out. She stripped again, for good, and curled up in the lumpy bed to plot Marie's future nightmares.

Chapter Twenty-three

Tuesday, June 11

Marie's head swiveled around so much, even Kala was uneasy.

"Daddy, what's Mama looking for?" she asked Cal.

He smiled and tousled her hair as he negotiated the West Side's evening traffic. "Sometimes Mommy gets nervous," he said. "We have to be patient with her when she does."

Marie ignored the self-righteous bastard. How calm and self-assured would he be with a mad dog poised to go for *his* throat? He hadn't seen the bodies of Lily and the others after Scorch had finished with them. He didn't know the fear of being hunted by a creature both more and less than human, one that did anything to get what she craved—to see Marie as dead as her friends. Marie saw Cal's eyes in the rearview mirror, taking note of how she was doing, but he hadn't said anything since taking her to Paulo's last week to get the gun. Its weight felt good in her bag, like an anchor securing a boat in choppy seas. With a few seconds' warning, she could defend herself. But how much warning had the others had? The last three Tigresses had little, the first three none, and that made all the difference.

"Who wants ice cream?" asked Cal as he pulled over.

"Me," said Kala, turning to her mother to second the motion.

"Sure," said Marie. "Why not? It's warm out." That was an understatement. It was ninety today, the same tomorrow. Their tiny apartment was so stuffy and humid you could grow orchids. When Cal had been over last night, he had noted the discomfort and offered to buy an air conditioner this week or next. Until then, a spin in his car and ice cream was the best they could hope for.

Kala skipped ahead down the street.

"Kala, be careful!" said Cal. He touched Marie's arm and drew her closer. "I talked to Paulo again last night. He's trying to help."

"By doing what? Kala, wait up."

"He's put the word out about this girl and has people looking for her. Maybe she's forgotten about you."

"Ha!" Marie snatched Kala's wrist, steering her clear of two skateboard riders balancing boom boxes on their shoulders. "She hasn't forgotten." Why should she? Marie wouldn't.

Scorch hadn't roughed up Tanya just for recreation.

He shrugged as he bought three strawberry cones, the one thing this disjointed little family had in common. "Just the same," he said as he handed them out, "he's looking out for you. If he wasn't, you'd bitch that nobody was helping."

She licked in silence, sulking. The man knew how to push her buttons. A petite, long-haired girl walked by, freezing Marie's blood. No, it wasn't her, the dwarf demon.

He stroked the damp crook of her elbow. "It's your temper," he whispered, barely audible above the noise of people moving past in the Manhattan twilight. "You get angry over nothing."

It wasn't nothing. Being whacked with an electrical cord or a belt—for being around when her father decided to whale on her mother—left you with a sour attitude. Then there were those nights when he was so drunk the devil inside him came out and he poked and prodded her, treating her like an inflatable party doll, preferring her body to her mother's. Even now, many years later, there were times when the thought of a man's fingers on her, or in her, made her want to throw up or strike out.

She stared into the face of every young woman walking past.

What did Cal know about growing up where parents screamed and swung at each other as routinely as he brushed his own teeth?

The three of them stood under an awning, finishing their cones as hundreds strode by, none worrying about a murderess stalking them. Instead they admired this evening's pink and rose sunset—a gift of today's pollution—creating a beautiful backdrop for what could be her last night on earth.

"If it wasn't for that temper, we'd still be together," Cal said, his fingers encircling her arm. "Most people get older, they mellow, they learn to overlook stuff." He caressed the tender flesh of her elbow, making her tingle despite herself. It was like her clothes were melting into her flesh, and it had nothing to do with the temperature. She stopped licking her cone, ignoring the pink cream dripping down her fingers. "That a criticism, a suggestion, or a proposal, Calvin Jones?"

"Think about it. When this is over, we could start over." He knelt to clean the ice cream dribbling down Kala's chin.

There was a lot to put behind; she had a long memory, mostly for the bad stuff. Still, he was gentle with Kala, he earned a living, and he was still good in bed, as he proved last week. She could do a lot worst. She had done a lot worse.

She'd been with men who abused her as often as her own father had done. One guy even bound her with her stockings when she lost her cool one night and smacked him. Then, when she kept screaming, he had gagged her with her slip and left her like that for an hour, watching her squirm and rage at him, helpless and furious, her bare legs kicking futilely as he sat grinning just beyond reach. It was a wonder she hadn't had a stroke.

And that dumb social worker from high school, her glasses dangling from a chain, had no idea why Marie Balboa was a tramp, a delinquent, the leader of her own gang. The woman hadn't a clue why she had been such a bad girl.

Marie bet Scorch Amerce understood and was probably a fellow member of that not-so-exclusive sorority of the damned.

Cal drove them to their apartment, but as they walked up the stench of rotting stuff hit them. Marie froze on the landing. On her threshold yellow chicken feet stood in a circle around a large fish head, its mouth open as if it were gasping for air. Like Tanya in her tub as Marie held her under. Brown water, tinged like blood in the dingy hall, puddled around the head.

"Look at that mess," Cal said. "What a stink. Crummy neighbors, leaving their crap. C'mon, stay at my place tonight."

Yeah, for tonight they'd be okay, but for how long could she relax with a devil roaming free, eager to have her join Tanya?

Chapter Twenty-four

Wednesday, June 12

Eric was caught up in a mob, a human leaf in a river of screeching people, the torrent dragging him deeper into a huge grotto that led to a gigantic hall, gray and somber, its stupendous walls supported by gargantuan pillars.

The arched ceiling rose beyond his sight, towering over thousands of alcoves and niches holding stained-glass windows.

Far beyond came the sound of moaning. Standing on tiptoe, he saw women on stage, writhing, arching their backs, twisting.

Being tortured? Having orgasms? Both?

Others around him wept, tore their clothes, ripped their flesh.

Next to him a man in a slate-gray uniform cradled an infant.

"Is this hell?" Eric asked.

"It's heaven!" shrieked the man as he swung the baby, smashing it against Eric's head.

Eric staggered across the chamber as blues and yellows

and reds whirled about him. A barbed-wire noose looped itself around his arm as a crowd of emaciated women pushed him forward. "You're going to The Father," they screamed.

The others wailed when they heard this, their keening shattering windows into millions of shards.

He was prodded up a quartz stairway that spiraled so high it hurt to draw breath. The women ushering Eric wept as they delivered him to The Father!

Up ahead stooped a haggard woman in a torn white robe, blue numbers tattooed on her arm. . . . His mother!

Her splotchy skin dried and withered, peeling away to show the chalky skeleton underneath.

As he was dragged past, her bones crumbled to dust.

His female escort goose-stepped forward, leaving him to peer over a great ledge, onto a vast plain where numbers and symbols flashed past. They were important, these numbers. Dates? Whatever they were, they needed to be remembered, accounted for.

He recalled only one-nine-seven-two.

Then it came, not so much a voice as a thought, flowing through his brain. "What you do is right. It is good. Continue. Do not worry about what is said."

He bolted awake, hearing screams from the next room.

Veronica!

He sprang from the bed, nearly tripping over furry bodies as the cats scrambled out of his way.

Veronica was sitting up, sobbing. He clasped her to him, feeling the heat radiate from her. "Mommy's dying," she said.

"It's all right," he said. Mommy was already dead, only her husband and daughter were too stubborn to admit it, so they kept her hooked up like some Frankenstein creation in a museum of living death, so they could visit and feel sorry for themselves. "She's okay," he said. No longer content to lie to himself, now he was doing it to his own flesh and blood. "It'll be okay."

Yes, it was okay. "The Father," whoever that was, had told him so. Whatever he had been put on this earth to do was right and should be continued.

He kissed Veronica's sweaty brow, laid her down, and after a moment her breathing became regular. Children were resilient as long as their traumas were infrequent and not lethal.

He stumbled to the bed he and Debbie had shared for ten years, to contemplate that nightmare.

Nineteen-seventy-two . . . The year he started college and began martial-arts training in jujitsu.

The year Suzanne Rene Amerce was born.

He lay awake until dawn, replaying the nightmare over and over, wondering if Satan—and not God—had sent it to him.

The purple sky turned maroon, then orange. Time to rise and face both poisoned souls and the ones who kept them at bay. He showered and went onto the balcony to watch the shadows fade from the Palisades, burned away by the rising sun. He moved in slow, tight circles for the Short Tai Chi form, but nothing went right, as if the nightmare had infected his body as well as his sleep. The maneuvers refused to flow, his movements jerky as an epileptic in full seizure. Finally, he gave up and headed to the kitchen, where Veronica sat, crunching on cereal, stroking cats. She made no mention of *her* nightmare, nor he of his, and so they ate in silence, the only sounds being the scraping of flatware on porcelain and the blissful purring of imbecile felines.

As she swept up her books, ready to go, he touched her arm.

"You okay, honey?" he asked.

A long hug and a short kiss were her unspoken reply.

Some psychologist, unable to connect with his own daughter, but then his father had once said the cobbler's children were the last to wear good shoes.

As he locked the front door, the phone rang. When he went back to answer, they hung up after the third ring, so he left to drive to work on autopilot, trees and cars flashing by, barely noted and avoided. That dream—was it a portent or a reminder?

Who was "The Father"?

As his shoes squeaked on freshly waxed floors, Eric heard a clank near his office. Fielder, the chubby, slovenly escort officer who had contributed to Suzanne's escape, slouched on the wall, tapping his hickory baton against the brick.

When he saw Eric, Fielder sneered.

Same to you, buddy. Eric plopped in his chair, still reeling from the shock of that nightmare, of having an infant's skull slammed against his temple, still feeling the hot bite of barbed wire into his flesh. He rolled up his sleeve, half expecting to see bloody holes, or at least fresh scars, but the only marks were old ones inflicted by a mother consumed with unhealthy passion three decades ago.

Where was she now, heaven or hell? Probably neither, with Satan unwilling to stand the competition. Wherever she was, she had probably arrived with her own personal flock of demons. If his nightmare was any indication, the dream Nazis had gotten her after all.

The quartz clock ticked loudly, echoing off the brick walls as always when there was awkward silence in this office. Its crystal was dirty. As he went to clean it, Eric recalled Suzanne's reflecting on his name.

"Glass is interesting," she'd said. "It's hard but delicate. Fragile. And clear. You can see right through it."

"Can you see through me?" he'd asked.

"Uh-huh. Sometimes. Glass is good, because it can help you see things so much clearer, both the very tiny and the very distant. Stars and microbes . . . Humans really are at the center of the universe, aren't they? They can see the extremes."

"I guess." That image—two people back-to-back peering through a microscope and a telescope—was the symbol of the Bronx High School of Science, their mutual alma mater.

"Glass can help heal and it can kill." Then she peeled back her sleeve to expose the jagged scar on her wrist, legacy of that window shard in the shape of a dagger she'd ripped across her tender flesh the first time despair got the better of her.

He couldn't blame her, barely sixteen, with nothing to live for except the same perpetual, numbing routine, broken only by the occasional dangerous encounter. He had visited her daily in the hospital back then and had counseled her three times a week for months after her return to the prison. Debbie had teased that he had come to know Suzanne better than his own wife.

And maybe he had.

Raised voices came from outside his door, one of them shrill, that clank of wood again, followed by the thump of something large and soft.

He opened up to see Fielder standing over an inmate sprawled near the wall. Karen Rainey, her blouse torn and blood streaming down her forehead, pulled herself to her feet. When she saw Eric, she pointed to Fielder. "He hit me," she said.

Fielder looked at Eric. "Bull! She must have belted herself, crazy bitch, then ripped her shirt!"

Another inmate stood halfway around the corner. When she saw Eric look at her, she ducked away.

"He hit me," Rainey said to Eric. "What are you gonna do about it?"

Other inmates came from around that corner, clustering

near the wall, looking from Fielder to Rainey.

The officer started to sweat.

"Want me to call somebody?" Eric asked.

"Huh? No. Just go inside." Fielder plucked his walkie-talkie from his belt and requested assistance.

For a moment Eric thought the officer would "pull the pin," the panic call summoning a flood of blue-shirted officers.

Christ, everything was falling apart on him—the job, his personal life, even his dreams were conspiring against him.

Eric returned to his office and closed his eyes, but that nightmare infested his brain. His phone rang, and he flinched. The last time he had experienced a startle reflex was just before his mother had slapped him for ten minutes for no particular reason other than that her demons had urged her to.

Eric picked up to hear the captain say, "Glass, I hear you saw what happened outside your office a half hour ago. I need a statement."

Had thirty minutes elapsed already? "I didn't see anything," Eric said.

"Whatever. Put it in writing, my office, ten minutes."

Eric slammed down the phone and hurried to the captain, his shirt sticking to him. Word about the incident must have already gotten out, because inmates and staff alike stared as he strode past. Maybe it was just that nobody had seen him move this fast since Debbie had been hurt.

The captain was scanning papers on his desk. "Glass, nice of you to come. Got your statement?"

"I told you, I didn't see anything. This is a no-win situation. Either I lie to protect Fielder and face an inmate grievance and a formal investigation, or I incriminate him, become known as an 'inmate lover,' and make enemies of everyone here."

The captain lowered the papers and sighed. "I'd say you summed it up nicely." He stood, face-to-face with Eric. "That's what makes it prison."

"This was a setup," Eric said. "Like when somebody accused me of bringing in drugs."

"Uh-huh. The book isn't closed on that one either. Right now I got an inmate claiming assault by an officer, and with the IG's people down here every other day as it is, you can bet they're going to want to see us dot every *I* and cross every *T*. You got a statement?"

"Yes. I saw nothing. I was already warned someone would try to set me up. This could be it."

"Warned? By who?"

"Another inmate."

The captain threw up his hands. "And round and round we go. Fine, put that down if you want. This place needs a good laugh. Meanwhile, the IG is on my case, so now I'm on yours."

"It rolls downhill, huh?"

"Precisely." The captain scribbled something on a pad. "I'm expecting something, and I will get it. Understand?"

"All too well," Eric said. He stormed out, knowing he was nailed as effectively as if the planted drugs had been found. As Cassandra had foreseen, people were laying traps for him. Already perched on the razor's edge, he'd either topple or get sliced in two. Rainey had put him out of action, rendering him useless to the police. Though it was only Wednesday, he visited Debbie this afternoon to tell her the latest, even if he got no feedback.

At the home Debbie lay, as always, eyes shut. Was she still alive, even in the clinical sense? If it wasn't for the screens bleeping at him, he'd figure she was dead, the home faking it to bilk the insurance company. Maybe the monitors deliberately gave false readings, lying to everyone.

This was his life, a deathwatch. He'd give anything to do it over, to get it right. He had messed up everything, and now he was on course to screw up Veronica too. He leaned closer, searching for a sign, any sign, that she lived.

He couldn't even see her chest rise and fall.

Had she passed away today, between visits by the nurse's aides? Dead, with no one knowing, not even her neighbor Jennet Smith, who also dwelled in the dusk of "predeath."

He removed the oxygen tube from her nose and placed his palm against her face. Nothing! She *had* died! He was about to run to the nursing station when he felt a faint tickle of air against his skin. Technically, she was still here, still with him.

All he had to do was stay like this a moment, his hand where it was, and he'd end this parody of living. Veronica would mourn, get over it, then get on with her life.

Could *he* live with it? He was living with it now, had been for years. Once before he had contemplated yanking plugs from outlets, letting her go. Could that be worse than this? At least there would be closure. The closure of a pine box so he could never see or touch her again. So selfish, prolonging this living death, just to hold her hand a few times a week.

Just a few more seconds, a few ounces of pressure . . .

Could she feel this? The monitors bleeped faster.

Her arm twitched, her mouth opened, trying to vacuum in a few more molecules of air, a few more seconds of life. She fought still, just as she had hung on all these years, as well as she could, with whatever power and resources she had. Her spirit, her emotional energy, kept her body alive.

But had her soul fled, leaving a husk without that spark, that piece of God that distinguishes humans from animals? Machines pumping air into her and sloshing blood through her were unnatural. What was before him might not be a thing of God but a temptation from Lucifer.

He uncovered her nose and mouth and she sucked in oxygen, the reflex that had kept her going.

Who was he fooling? He was no murderer. Would Suzanne, who had killed half a dozen, coldly execute her beloved sister if she lived in such a coma? Perhaps.

He replaced the oxygen tube and hurried out, ashamed to be sharing space with Debbie after this.

Now he was reduced to using Suzanne as a role model. She could be killing Marie even now, savoring every millisecond of it as deeply as he was torturing himself. It was like sucking snake venom out of a bitten friend's wound; he had swallowed a bit of poison himself. Too many years of linking minds and psyches with Suzanne may have finally contaminated him, putting him on the brink of murder himself.

Chapter Twenty-five

Wednesday, June 12

Lucy had a choice: gobble lunch or call Roosevelt on the off chance Jane Doe had regained consciousness and could be questioned. She dialed, and after ten minutes of being bounced around learned the young woman was lucid for the time being.

She grabbed her bag. "I'm off to Roosevelt Hospital," she said to Paul Sanders across the room.

"Midtown Manhattan's a little out of our jurisdiction."

"NYPD never sleeps. I'm on Scorch's case, but don't tell DiGiorio." She stopped. "Scorch shattered two pimps by herself."

"So be careful. Speaking of care, shouldn't you tell . . . ?"

"No way." She put a finger to her lips, smiled, and headed down the back steps to the parking lot. She could grab a hot dog for the ride down if it meant a half hour later she'd learn where to find a hundred-pound woman who had savaged two healthy adults. Maybe Scorch was slowing up. Eight years ago, she had killed three at once. Glancing in the rearview mirror, Lucy saw her sober look, the one that crossed her face when she saw a corpse, or a bloody gurney, or a grieving family.

Time to get into aggressive mode, ready to honk and yell at cabbies and pedestrians in crosstown traffic. She had moonlighted as a taxi driver to work her way through school, one more thing to give her father, a first-generation traditionalist, apoplexy. That memory vanished, replaced by that of Scorch marching out of her lair like the queen of the West Bronx. That image stayed with Lucy longer than the photos of Scorch's victims, or were they the objects of her justice?

A truck's horn blared, returning Lucy to the present. As she swerved back into her lane, she hoped never to live long enough to know what hurt and fury could drag a girl down to the depths to do what Scorch had done, and be ready to do it yet again.

She thought of Eric's explanation on his terrace last Friday. What could a parent do to a child to turn them into human nitroglycerin? She swung around the truck and flipped the driver the bird. Her father always told her to pick her fights, but did she listen?

As she ran into Roosevelt, she hoped being a woman detective might make Jane Doe more cooperative. Lucy flashed her shield at the receptionist. "You admitted a Jane Doe with a fractured skull and collarbone last Tuesday the fourth," she said. "If she's still conscious, I need five minutes with her."

The receptionist ran a lacquered nail down a list. "She's in serious condition . . ."

"Upgraded from critical and now conscious," Lucy read upside down, seeing that Jane Doe was in the same room as last week. "Five minutes is all I need. Thanks," she said, ignoring the receptionist's muttering.

The young woman's head was bandaged, her shoulder in a sling. Unlike her blinded buddy last week, Lucy's gold shield could be flashed for effect. Jane Doe pretended to be unimpressed, but Lucy saw concern in her eyes.

"So," Ms. Doe said. "What's it to me?" She attempted to shrug and winced. She was a muscular young woman, yet Scorch had pulped both her and her hundred-eighty-pound pimp.

"We want to find who did this. Thanks to them, the only female your buddy's going to be close with is Lassie. Was it a gang? A struggle over drug turf? Rivals in the skin trade?"

Ms. Doe closed her eyes. "Slipped in the shower."

"With your clothes on? In the bedroom?" Lucy leaned forward, switching to "good cop." The pimp had said her name was Kelly. "Kelly, what did she look like?"

"She?" Kelly opened her eyes and sighed. "All right. She was small and young, maybe sixteen. Adorable, with big, dark eyes, great lashes, short wavy blond hair, and the cutest little butt." She cupped her hands and smiled. Sounded like Kelly had a crush on her would-be killer. "And a virgin, too," she added.

Virgin? Maybe. Scorch was busted at fifteen, a good girl until her rampage.

"What was her name?" Lucy asked.

"Name? Yeah, Helen. Helen . . . Glazer? No, Glass."

Glass? Glass! Thank you, Lord. Sometimes the pieces still fit, the puzzle still made sense. Lucy felt the electricity that coursed through her whenever she got close to a breakthrough, the lone thing still making the job worthwhile.

Kelly closed her eyes and winced again, only this time Lucy didn't think it was from physical pain. "She's real short, maybe five foot, but solid. Couldn't have weighed more than one hundred, one-oh-five. Who would have thought . . . ?"

"Thought what?" urged Lucy, touching the woman's hand, a surrogate sister empathizing with distress.

"Sweet and soft-spoken, until . . ."

"Until what?" Lucy prompted, now on a roll.

Kelly shuddered. "Until she started killing us! Jesus, it was hideous, that really cute face twisted up with hate, screaming like a banshee. Damn!" Tears slipped from the sealed lids. She opened them and looked to Lucy, as if only another woman could understand. "I've never seen a face so wild. Mad."

High praise indeed. This woman had been around.

"The hate . . . God!" Kelly said as a prayer or an oath. She shuddered again. "I figured she'd kill me once she had me down. She kept pounding me with that chair, shrieking, 'Nina! Nina!' "

"Nancy?" suggested Lucy.

"Nancy? Maybe. You can't believe what it was like."

Lucy could. She'd seen photos of those Tigresses, the damage done to them long after they were obviously dead. Dynamite, small and compact, did terrible stuff when ignited. That was Scorch, Little Miss Nitro. Eric Glass knew his stuff.

Ready for the pièce de résistance. Lucy removed composites of Scorch from her jacket pocket, took a deep breath, and considered uttering a prayer. Sacrilege, wasn't it, to ask for help to indict a human, but could a mere human do such damage?

Lucy held it out. "Kelly, you recognize this person?"

Kelly gasped, her face turning as pale as her sheets and hospital gown.

"Thanks." Lucy nodded and walked to where pimp Luscious Johnson lay, his eyes still bandaged. Scorch's other victim.

She had shattered two together.

Maybe Paul and her husband Tony were right. The smart thing would be to let Scorch go on her way, but after so many years on The Force, who could claim they were smart?

Chapter Twenty-six

Wednesday, June 12

The Bronx train ride brought back old memories for Scorch, most of them unpleasant, as she took the "Mugger's Express," the Woodlawn Jerome number 4. Almost all the faces were black or brown now, swaying to the motion of the car as they traveled far to jobs probably reserved for the desperate. The adult passengers thinned, leaving bored kids going to DeWitt Clinton or Walton High, plus a few scared nerds heading to the Bronx High School of Science. Scorch had passed the stiff entrance exam to Science, something else she had in common with Eric Glass. She had just finished her junior year before life got in the way, so instead of being a medical student learning to treat illness or a researcher seeking cures, her claim to fame was her picture in sleazy tabloids until the next atrocity caught the public fancy.

Woodlawn Road, end of the line, literally and figuratively.

Trotting from the station to the cemetery, Scorch marveled at how the neighborhood had disintegrated in eight years, with its boarded-up shops, mounds of garbage, graffiti on brick and plywood, husks of stripped cars lining the filthy gutters. The decay and despair of her old neighborhood had oozed up here like a toxic spill. She found a discarded lock cylinder in a pile of rubbish and scooped it up. Karen had shared her secrets of lock picking, so Scorch tucked it into her bag for later amusement.

Inside the cemetery she was tempted to visit Nancy's grave. She had never seen its tombstone; once she was on her warpath, she had been afraid to come in case cops had it under surveillance.

Nancy Amerce's grave, facing the Bronx River, gave her a nicer view than any she'd had when she was alive. Were the cops staking it out now? Doubtful. They had limited manpower and limited imaginations, but a man and woman stood nearby, seemingly lost in thought but perhaps waiting for her to get within range.

She slunk away, easy to do when you're small.

The graves were laid out in neat rows, orderly, precise. A pity the people buried in them hadn't found this perfection while still alive. After ten minutes Scorch found the ideal tombstone, Joan Perter, born October first, died October third, eighteen years ago, the dates leaving Scorch legal and younger. If people asked where she had been all these years, she'd say she'd been a schoolmate of Chelsea Clinton back in Little Rock.

Yes—Joan of Arkansas, her new stage name. She jotted down the date to bring to the Borough Hall for a new birth certificate. Joan's death would give birth to a new person, and if given a second chance Scorch wouldn't dishonor this name.

That middle-aged couple was gone, either returning to their lives or lying in wait for her to show herself. Scorch ambled over to Nancy's grave as if sight-seeing, pausing at older, sunken headstones before standing by her sister's. "Sorry, Nancy. Didn't mean to shame you. Like I promised the day they laid you down there, I would think of you constantly and love you always. I didn't want to be bad, but . . . oh, hell!"

She threw herself on the ground, her arms around the tombstone, her forehead against the cool marble, wondering if her tears could seep through the dirt onto her sister's bones.

Instead of being a lady, a college grad, someone to look up to, little sister was respected only by convicts and went by a name that inspired dread. The family that had once gone out for Sunday dinner together had dwindled down to one short murderess who might not live to her twenty-fifth birthday.

"I screwed up bad! My life's crap! I killed them, and what good did it do? Lord, Nancy, I am sorry. So sorry!"

She knelt as the long shadows of morning shrank to almost nothing, waiting for lightning or inspiration to strike. Was there room in her heart for repentance, for forgiveness? "Nancy, you can't imagine that nightmarish place." Gazing into the polished surface of the headstone, she saw a tortured face staring back, a reminder of that first month in prison, the second time she dared leave her cell for recreation. She had gone to the gym and sat in the corner with a novel, trying to be invisible. Then their shadows fell on the page, four of them grinning down at her, then their hands, one over her mouth, the others grabbing her squirming limbs, lifting her, dumping her behind the benches, stripping her, groping her, their tongues and fingers all over her like it was buffet time and she was the food. The officers broke it up immediately, but not soon enough.

She slammed her fists into the warm, hard dirt, cratering it. "I wanted to die after that." She held out her wrists, the jagged white scars bisecting them proof of her despair. "Every Christmas and Thanksgiving, everyone else getting visits . . ."

221

She finally found the strength to rise and get the hell away from this city of the dead. As she rode back on the train, the thought ate at her like acid. She'd lost her resolve, thinking of a future, of a new life, a better one. She needed to refuel, to visit the former neighborhood, to stoke up. Seeing the site of Nancy's murder could get the old hatred flaring again.

She got off at Tremont and took the bus to Arthur Avenue. The line for documents, manned by apathetic clerks, was long and slow, and it was early afternoon before she headed west to Fordham Road. She was midway between the Social Security office and the old neighborhood, and like a psychic magnet it pulled her back to the ruined tenement on 1972 Morris Avenue. It still stood, bare and skeletal, its windows boarded up, their frames blackened to highlight the basement apartment of the Tigresses.

Yes, her masterpiece. Some artists work in watercolor or oils or clay, but Scorch Amerce preferred "performance art" using gasoline and matches.

Nobody paid attention to her, not something to be proud of.

She strolled one block to Creston Avenue, where she had grown up, where Nancy had bled to death. The bodega was still on the corner, still the focal point of the block.

There, where Nancy had writhed on the filthy pavement, both of them knowing she was dying with no power on earth able to save her. When she killed Marie, would Satan dare take her?

Time to go before someone in the harsh daylight recognized her before she got what she came for. She marched down Jerome Avenue to the Social Security Administration, vicious sunlight streaming between the rails and ties of the elevated train tracks and making the street seem like the floor of a tropical rain forest.

This office was the bureaucratic version of hell, with snaking lines of desperate people, enough to fill a football field. It took ninety minutes to get to the window, with everybody glancing at one another at least once, but unlike post offices her picture wasn't on display. Still, the security guards checked her out, increasing the chance of being recognized. Were there hidden cameras recording everyone, the old, the lame, the ones who obviously had come from other countries, other continents? She held her paperback up, pretending to read, wondering if she was hiding her face or just calling undue attention to herself as she inched forward.

When she finally got to a clerk, she figured she was in business, Joan Perter of Valentine Avenue. "Joan of Arkansas."

The clerk took the birth certificate, pulled out a sheaf of forms, and asked, "You got proof of address?"

"Huh?"

"We need to verify residence. Driver's license?"

"I don't drive." Unless she was escaping from the law.

"Anything," the clerk said. "Library card. High school transcript. Mail addressed to you?"

"Uh, nothing on me. I thought all you needed—"

"New regulations. Too many illegal aliens. Blame George Bush and Bob Dole." The clerk frowned and ripped up the applications. "Come back when you got something, honey. Next."

A day wasted. She could have been out hunting instead of stumbling through an administrative maze with no exit. No wonder the country was falling apart. She headed downtown for her stuff for tonight's performance, stuck as Jezebel, Joan Perter having died a second death only hours after her rebirth.

Halfway to the club, a guy followed her with his eyes, or seemed to. Was he the creep who had tailed her Sunday night? She'd find out soon enough; he crossed the street after her. As a bus rolled past, Scorch used it as cover to duck into a grocery. The guy strolled past. Scorch counted to ten and peeked out to see him moving down the street. Cop? Perhaps. Was he too obvious and unpolished, or had she honed her police radar to perfection? Maybe all he wanted was to catch the bus.

She forgot about him as she pondered whether to leave or stay, to dance or kill. Eric Glass would say live a constructive life, while Karen would advise her to continue seeking vengeance.

Neither one was here now, leaving Scorch alone to make her biggest decision.

Chapter Twenty-seven

Wednesday, June 12

Lucy chose to walk from Roosevelt Hospital to Midtown West Precinct, partly to think things out and partly in hopes of spotting Scorch. She was fracturing a dozen rules, official and unwritten, on this jaunt out of her jurisdiction. If DiGiorio caught her, he'd turn her into food, publicly. Armed with Kelly's ID of Scorch, she presented them to the same desk sergeant, who didn't even pretend interest this time.

"Where's the detective on this case?" she asked him.

He flicked an ink-stained thumb toward the door. "Out trying to stem the Dark Paradise epidemic, like you should be," he said. "Why would she still be here?" he asked like a DiGiorio clone. "If she messed these people up and she's smart as you say, she'd be out of here by now. I already had the watch commanders show this at lineups." He shrugged, as if pitying a cop with so little to do she went to another precinct fifteen miles away hoping to catch somebody she had no business looking for. "We had two homicides, ten rapes, and ninety armed robberies since last time you were here, not to mention twenty more ODs." He pointed to the poster keeping score of death and brain damage. "I'll call if we got news." He looked at Scorch's composite again, as if incredulous this large-eyed girl could be guilty of anything except lots of sex. Mistaken identity. Must be.

"Doug Reaumur here?" she asked.

"Yeah, getting chewed out by the watch commander. Should be out soon." Sarge grinned, suggesting Reaumur wasn't his favorite guy either. When Lucy didn't ask why, he volunteered. "Yeah, Doug's conducting his own private pussy posse, concentrating on women users rather than male pushers. Not playing the percentages won't get this poison off the streets anytime soon."

Lucy nodded and smiled. Sarge had confirmed her suspicion of Reaumur targeting Scorch as an easier path to a gold detective shield than busting one of the many pushers who had sprung up like mushrooms after a thunderstorm.

She went to the bulletin board to pin Scorch's composite on again. As she turned, she smelled nicotine. Reaumur stood over her, his face the color of a Santa suit. Behind him the watch commander sneered, no doubt having enjoyed roasting Reaumur over a low flame.

"Hi, Doug," she said. "Just visiting."

"Reaumur," said the sarge. "She thinks we're holding out on her on this Scorch who she thinks hospitalized a pair of pimps."

Thanks, Sarge. Tell your whole precinct, why don't you?

Reaumur stopped. "Huh?" he said, forehead furrowed.

She had given him too much credit, if that was possible. Reaumur hadn't bothered to follow up leads on Scorch, preferring to stroll the streets and rely on luck over planning. He glanced past her and saw Scorch's composite fluttering on the board.

"So she is around here, huh?" he said, attempting to think. He plucked the composite off and stared at it like he'd just discovered the cure for AIDS. "Good work, Moreno."

Yeah, right, her work for his good.

He leered as he pinned it back on the board. "That's good to know. Looks like it pays to walk the streets, huh, Sarge?"

The desk sergeant rolled his eyes and went back to trying to catch a breeze as the floor fan groaned back his way.

As she left the station house she took a deep breath, as if to track Scorch by smell. She was around. Lucy sensed her like she felt the wind on her skin. There were shabby brown tenements all around, the ones that trapped the summer heat, soaking up the sun's rays while blocking off the river breezes. Lucy knew these tenements and the communities they formed—and stifled. If Scorch had chosen to live here, she was punishing herself.

Lucy should meet Eric Glass to download what she had learned from Kelly and see if he could figure what was on Scorch's social calendar for the next week. Ordinarily, a guy like Glass was a godsend, someone who knew Scorch as well as she knew herself, maybe better. Lucy couldn't afford to waste a resource like this, but the good doctor was off in the ozone, worrying about the world's troubles when his mind should be focused on Scorch. Perhaps he wanted her to escape, his subconscious way of getting back at a system he detested.

To top it off, Lucy knew he liked her, wedding band and all—"liked her as a person," even though she caught him ogling her legs, her breasts, and areas in between when he thought she wasn't looking, even though he was so wrapped up in his concerns. And how would she know unless she'd taken a peek into Eric Glass's head, just as he'd installed a microscope into Scorch's?

As she headed to the West Side Highway, Lucy wondered yet again what she'd do if she survived her own twenty years of service and was forced to decide on the rest of her life. Some choice, to wind up like DiGiorio, getting older but refusing to admit it and give it up, or to cash in her chips like her old partner Acinar and be reduced to spying on people for their jealous spouses.

Before getting on the highway, Lucy turned off to follow up on the last of the twenty-year-old girls busted eight years ago in the Bronx just before Scorch had surrendered to her. This one, on Thirty-fifth and Tenth, was a rubble-strewn lot now with a blue and white sign announcing it would be an urban-renewal project someday. So much for chasing old, cold leads.

Once back at her precinct, Lucy phoned Eric. This might be a good evening for that rain check dinner, as long as she kept focused. Until an hour ago, when she'd seen terror in Kelly's eyes, she felt she could handle Scorch.

His answering machine kicked in before someone picked up and mumbled. It sounded like Eric and yet didn't.

"Eric, you okay?" Lucy asked. She shook the phone in case wires were loose, but his voice was low, raspy. Was he sick or having a reaction to some medication? She suspected the answer but chose to ignore it. "Eric, is Veronica home with you?"

"No. At Sandy's."

"I'll be there in a half hour. Don't do anything."

His response might have been a laugh, but it sounded more like a bark.

Lucy got there in twenty minutes. Beneath his terrace lay a pile of lipstick-stained cigarette butts. Had Veronica not only made good on her threat to experiment with the mysteries of makeup but was also copping smokes when Dad wasn't looking, then tossing the evidence onto the sidewalk?

Lucy rang the downstairs bell five times before she got buzzed in. She jogged up to find the loft door open, the smell of incense wafting out at her. A bottle of kosher wine lay on the coffee table with Eric staring at it, as if communing with it. All that alcohol in a man who hadn't drunk in five years.

Eric lay sprawled on the couch, shirt open, a glass in his hand. "I tried to kill Debbie today." He dropped the glass and held up his hand, staring at his palm. "I covered her nose and mouth." He looked to her like she was a juror deciding his fate. "I felt it was for the best." He snatched the empty bottle, yelled, and flung it across the room, scattering the cats who had sat, loyal companions, one on each side of him.

The bottle shattered, scores of shards flying through the air, spraying a shower of rainbows against the evening sun streaming through the terrace windows.

"I can see why you're upset," she said as she rummaged in the kitchen for a broom and dustpan.

He sagged back, as if all his remaining energy had gone into the throw. "That what they taught you in the Academy, to reflect the psycho's feelings back to them? Not bad."

They hadn't taught her how to respond to that one, so she started sweeping up the glass. The routed cats regrouped; one peeked out from another room, the other from under the sofa.

"Leave it," he said. "There'll be more. In Russia they say broken Glass is good luck. Well, at last Glass is broken."

"The cats will get it in their pads, and you walk in sandals a lot. And then there's Veronica."

"Veronica has shoes, and a father who's only good for euthanasia now. First he killed her mother partway, now he almost found the guts to finish the job."

The cats crept out to supervise.

She put the broom aside and gave him her undivided attention. "You didn't kill Debbie," she said.

"No? Then she must still be alive. You know, I couldn't tell if she was breathing today." He stood carefully, like a man trying to get out of a canoe. "Couldn't even see her chest rise and fall. Know how I found out?" He knelt beside her, his eyes wild, as he held his hand an inch from her nose and mouth. "Like this," he said. "It would have been so easy!"

Lucy imagined Eric going berserk right now and clamping his hand over *her* face, she trying to squirm away, trying to shake her head "no" but being unable to. Trying to scream "STOP!" but managing only a pathetic whine before blacking out.

"I was angry at her for just hanging on, not either returning to us or ending it by just going away for good," he said. "I'm furious at myself for letting her linger."

Even if she got him into a cold shower and poured hot coffee into him, all she'd have would be an alert, wet drunk. He wasn't her responsibility, but how could she leave him like this? She stood and took his wrist. "You need to lie down," she said, leading him to the bedroom.

"You're a good woman," he said. "Your husband is a fool if he doesn't worship you as a goddess."

"That's what I tell him," she said as she sat him on his bed and untied his laces.

He grabbed her wrist, his hand strong as a vise. "Stealing shoes is a misdemeanor," he said as his eyes strained to focus. "I could do a citizen's arrest."

"I want you to lie down."

He leaned back, caressing the downy hairs of her arms until they stood up. Great—first she was afraid he'd smother her with his hand and now she wondered if he would do it with kisses.

As she got his other shoe off he pulled her close, kissing her cheek, her forehead, her hair. "You smell interesting."

"Interesting?" That was different.

"Yes," he said. "Like Obsession. And L and M's."

"Precinct cigarettes," she said, trying to straighten up.

"Debbie always said I smelled like Camels whenever Suzanne was in my office." He moved his thigh against hers, unbalancing her as he tugged again to draw her onto the bed beside him. He wrapped his arms around her, as if afraid she'd fly off. "Debbie was jealous of Suzanne. Once I brought home a photo, to show her Suzanne was just a petite angry kid." He shook his head, and Lucy smelled the wine on his breath. "Didn't help." He looked at her, his eyes bloodshot. "I mean—Debbie knew it wasn't sexual or anything, but she envied the connection Suzanne and I had, different than husband and wife, or father and daughter." He gazed at the ceiling. "Almost like brother and sister, except deeper, because it wasn't from an accident of birth but something much more sinister. Satan's stepchildren, except without the horns or tail."

He stroked her arms, her neck, her back, her shoulders.

She had this irrational image of Tony barging in, pliers and wire cutters in hand, shouting. She tried to rise, but Eric held her closer; you couldn't slide a sheet of paper between them.

"You're warm. It's been so long since I held a warm woman." His hands quit roaming and instead encircled her in a tight hug.

There was no polite or easy way to break this spell. "I should be going," she said. "I have to . . ."

His hand slipped over her mouth, gently. "Shush," he said. "Let me enjoy this a moment longer before you take me in."

"Mmph?" She hummed into his hand until she could wriggle her mouth free. "Huh?"

"I confessed I tried to kill my wife. At least thirty, forty seconds I had her covered up. Euthanasia, attempted murder, whatever, I came within seconds of it." He sat up. "You've seen her. She lies there like something out of a bad science fiction movie, or a soap opera." He tried to rise, but

231

gravity got the best of him and he plopped back down. "Put me in protective custody. There are too many guys in jail whose wives, girlfriends, and mothers were my patients. They'll fight to line up hoping to become my proctologist."

Lucy slid off the other side of the bed. "Eric, listen to me. I came to tell you we have proof Suzanne was in Midtown Manhattan. Do you know what she'll do next?"

"Probably."

She came around to his side. "What?" she asked.

He snored softly. She covered him up, debating whether to stay the night as she found Cassandra's number and called.

"He's asleep now," Lucy said.

"Good. He'll get up tomorrow wit a hangover. I already fed Veronica. She'll be over in a few hours to keep watch on him."

"I could stay," Lucy said.

"It's okay. Between Veronica and me, we can handle one drunk head doctor. Tanks but don't worry."

After watching awhile to make sure he was okay, Lucy headed home, figuring they could brainstorm tomorrow, provided Eric's brain was no longer pickled and today's traumas were just a memory, and assuming he could subdue his troubling demons.

Chapter Twenty-eight

Thursday, June 13

The alarm went off, sounding like hornets disturbed at whatever it was hornets did for a living. Eric had been unconscious for eleven hours, the most sleep he'd had since Debbie's accident. When he rolled over, he was struck with wave upon wave of nausea. He vaulted from the bed and staggered to the toilet just in time to heave his guts out. When he stood, his head hurt worse than his chest, but at least all the poisons were out now, both the alcoholic and spiritual ones, though there had to be better ways to cleanse oneself. He weaved to his bed to let the room spin past without sweeping him along with it.

Why had he drunk . . . ? Right, Debbie. And that sickly sweet excuse for wine, and then . . . Christ! Lucy! He saw his shoes in the corner and realized it had been neither a dream nor a hallucination. That poor woman had seen him at his worst, twice within a week. What must she think?

That he was human. Well, if she had any respect for therapists before this, it must have evaporated by now. After all, "if gold will rust, what will iron do?"

Cassandra left him a note on the sink. She had come last night, surveyed the wreckage and repaired it, then chosen to keep Veronica for the night. Just as well. He showered but decided against shaving lest he slice his throat, either accidentally or yielding to an impulse to end it all. Like a thrown rider, he had to get up and return to the dungeon; otherwise he might never be able to psyche himself up to return.

All through his morning commute he kept telling himself his headache was a mere hangover and not mallets wielded by gremlins trying to escape from his skull. Despite the pain, he had to go to work, which next to hell was the place he least wanted to be.

Come to think of it, was there a difference?

Sure, Midland Knolls was cooler, but only in winter.

The only advantage to being late today was that columns of inmates were already trudging to various programs or work assignments. A desperate man could slink among them unseen.

Once in his office, he had no further place to hide. Well, maybe like most addicts, he had finally hit bottom and could only go up from here. A guilt junkie, that's what he was.

At ten his supervisor phoned. "Eric, the word from the captain is you saw inmate Rainey get hurt. That true?"

"When I came out, she was already sprawled on the floor, her blouse torn. Anything could have happened."

"We're not talking 'anything.' We're talking possible abuse. The inspector general's people are down here again, third time in two weeks. The superintendent is upset, and need I remind you that isn't a pretty sight."

"We have no proof of any—"

"Rainey got a lump on her head the size and density of a golf ball, and she's complaining of headaches, double vision, voices, the whole nine yards. We've gone years without such an incident and we're spoiled."

"That doesn't mean Fielder did it."

"I need *something* from you. The doctor says the injury was 'blunt trauma' from a rounded object striking her temple. Round, as in a hickory baton. You think it was self-inflicted?"

Oh hell, here was the trouble Sandy had foreseen in her tarot reading a few days ago, the treachery, the strife and contention. Forewarned was not necessarily forearmed.

Then Eric's brain, still marinated from yesterday's alcohol, came painfully back to life. "The corner of the wall is round, the same approximate diameter as a baton. What if . . . ?"

"She slipped on the newly waxed floor, had a litigious inspiration, and decided to scream foul?" said the dep. There was a moment of silence, as if paying tribute to a long shot. "Yeah, it might work. I'll talk to the doctor again."

"I needn't remind you he's neither Albert Einstein nor Albert Schweitzer, and forensic medicine is not his specialty. Still," said Eric, "it's enough of a possibility to suggest it to the IG's people. It might take the pressure off."

"Good. You're starting to be valuable to us again. You still may need to talk to IG anyway. Don't leave town."

Eric's headache increased despite an aspirin breakfast, but perhaps because of it his neurons kicked in. Why was Karen Rainey outside his office? Did her morning program allow her to be there during that time? As he cradled his aching head, he recalled how Sears of the inspector general's staff had picked through his stuff searching for contraband, which had appeared magically in time for Monday morning's search, just about the time he was to be in his office waiting for Rainey.

He had been too eager, too open with Rainey last Thursday, asking what she thought Suzanne would do. Were these two incidents part of a plan to get him out of the way, or at least so tied up mentally he couldn't think of Suzanne's next moves and thus be unable to advise on her recapture?

Was that too convoluted a plot, even for here? Was it the end of the line? Had he become too paranoid even for New York? What other motive could there be, other than a malicious need to cause hurt? Then again, it was prison. He could talk to Rainey, show concern, see how she was doing, offer his help . . . He checked this week's "Cell Book," found where she locked and dialed her cell block, only to be told she had a visitor today.

Who? A compensation attorney, to discuss the size of the lawsuit? Suzanne maybe? Eric strolled to the visitors' room. The last time he had been down here, several years ago, he had witnessed a drag-out brawl when an inmate had unexpected company in the form of both husband and girlfriend. So much hair littered the floor afterward the place resembled a beauty parlor at closing time.

Karen Rainey sat in the back with her forehead bandaged, talking to a woman with her casted arm in a sling. What was there about their body language, the way they looked around . . . ?

Eric moved to the side, so as not to be noticed by them should they look his way; they were scanning everywhere else.

Yes, now they watched the visiting room officer. As soon as the officer's attention was diverted, Eric saw furtive movements, subtle shifts in posture, their hands groping under the table, and it wasn't for sex. One didn't have to be a Ph.D. to know a transfer was taking place. Pot. Pills? Coke probably, more concentrated and thus more worth the risk.

Eric ambled over to the officer and nodded hello. "Is that a clumsy family back in the corner, or are they just unlucky?"

The officer consulted the visitors log. "She was here last week, too, with that cast," she said.

"Maybe they like to walk under ladders," Eric said, feeling the inspiration bloom. "Yeah, I remember her now. Say, wasn't that cast on her other arm then?" Having planted the seed, he smiled and did an about-face, content to wait to hear how it grew. With luck the officer would search both Karen and friend.

Being caught smuggling should remove Ms. Rainey from the equation, at least until the twentieth. By then . . . ?

Who knew what other plots would be hatched, where and when he least expected them?

Chapter Twenty-nine

Friday, June 14

Carol Amerce slammed six-year-old Suzanne against the wall. "Look what you did, you worthless little puke!" The spilled milk ran to the edge of the table and dripped off into a white puddle. "Clean it up, you ugly little shrimp. Jesus! If it wasn't for you, your father would still be alive!" The veins on her mother's forehead bulged and her face turned red, like that of some alien being, as it usually did when she drank and raged.

"Not true," Suzanne said, trying to blot up the milk.

"It's *my* fault, you little bastard!" Carol Amerce grabbed Suzanne by her hair and dragged her to the bedroom. "See that, you puny imp? I sleep alone now because you gave him the stroke! Alone!" She threw her onto the bed. "Stop crying!"

Suzanne couldn't, knowing what was coming. She tried to run, but her mother grabbed a pillow, stuffed it over her, and screamed, "Shut up! The neighbors will call the cops again. Shut up!"

Everything dark, the soft foam molding to her face, her

chest tightening, burning. No air. Pushing at the pillow, but stronger hands holding it over her, flattening her nose, crushing her face. Hurting so. Muffled sound weakening until the screams were only in her head. Helpless. Petrified. Waiting to die. Why? When? Please! No! Sorry! Won't do it again! Suzanne's legs kicking futilely at the mattress, the mother, the air.

Slower, everything dimmer, like a covered votive candle.

Scorch bolted upright, gasping. So real. A nightmare? A memory of things long buried? She clawed at her pillow, wanting to shred it as if it were her mother's face and she were six again. Christ. Sleep was no longer an escape. It was four P.M., with people arguing in three different languages from as many directions, making Scorch awake and irritable.

Then she saw the cup of melted ice cream by her bed. That's what did it! She recalled Eric Glass saying sometimes an odor, a sound, was enough to trigger a flashback of a trauma. Ice cream, milk, all the same when it came to dredging up those times.

Carol Amerce resented life for imposing on her, resented her second pregnancy—living for two when she could barely survive herself. Then her husband—her lifeline— died working overtime to support their second, unplanned daughter, leaving cheap booze as mother's only solace. Suzanne was reduced to being a constant reminder of life taking more than it could give.

Lying on her damp sheet, staring at the cracked ceiling, Scorch balked at haunting Marie today, and with no friends, she had no one to ventilate to. How she missed Eric Glass now. She thought of Michael, that EMT she met at Roosevelt Hospital.

What a great call that would be if she asked him for a date. Their social life would be a limited one. "Hi, honey, we can go out, but I've got a narrow window of free time—

like before six, after which I have to parade around showing ninety-eight percent of my flesh before schnooks, or past midnight, after they've already seen me nearly naked. Still interested?"

She dressed and left for her job, passing young women leaving work to race to subways or bus stops for home or dates. Still, stripping was a living. She would never disparage working girls as long as she lived, for as long as that might be.

At the Crystal Grotto her six hours of dancing was spent gyrating and spinning harder than ever. After that she headed with her new girlfriends to Reno's, to split a couple of pitchers of beer, to prevent dehydration. It was a fair substitute therapy to overcome the nightmare legacy of her afternoon nap.

"Hey, Jezebel," said Sheila. "Come back to Planet Earth."

"Huh?" Scorch found herself staring at bubbles floating to the surface of her beer and forgetting her newest alias. Who was she anymore? "Sorry, Sheila. Just tired. See you later." She dropped cash on the table and left Reno's, the humid air slamming into her like a sodden blanket. As she turned the corner, a husky blond guy cut her off. He had a bull neck and a nose looking like it had collided with a Mike Tyson right.

He was also about to have her kick a field goal with his scrotum if he didn't move—and soon. He reached into his pocket, and she got ready to bolt. Damn! Mugger! Rapist!

"Hold up," he said, and flipped out a badge. She would have been better off with a rapist. Did she have her scissors, her pistol? She backed up, ready to run. Let him shoot and put her out of their misery. A second guy, younger, leaner but with eyes hard enough to sharpen a razor with, blocked her retreat.

"You got ID?" the stocky guy asked, holding out his hand.

"Yeah, do you?"

Without a word he showed a laminated card. Officer Reaumur.

Okay. She dug into her bag, feeling their eyes on her. "So," she said. "What's up? You mistake me for a Broadway actress?"

"We're looking for peddlers of Dark Paradise," Reaumur said.

"Not me. I love life too much," Scorch said, holding her bag open for them to see she wasn't holding heroin.

"We need to check," Reaumur said.

All she had was her birth certificate, not the usual thing people carried, but she had no choice. As she handed it to Reaumur, she smiled up at his partner, but he was scanning the streets as he checked a paper.

They were prowling, looking for what? Her? Yeah, right. How could they know? What were the odds?

"You a hooker?" Reaumur asked as his eyes roamed over her, making her feel dirtier than she had back at the Crystal Grotto.

"I'm a dancer," she said, mustering all the indignation she could, considering that her heart was pumping hard enough to rattle her bones. She showed her costumes, fighting to keep her hand from shaking.

They ignored her, instead consulting that paper. She stood on tiptoe and peered at it. It was a portrait of a cute female, real familiar, with short but straight blond hair. In his other hand was a photo of the same girl with longer, darker locks.

HER PRISON PHOTO! Her breath froze in her lungs. She was sandwiched between them. No way out! They'd jump her! She looked again. The first picture was a composite, done by an artist or one of those computers. It wasn't exact, but close enough.

How did they know? Who could have . . . ?

Forget that. Talk. Try. Don't give up. Say what? Think. She

snorted and flicked the composite. "Her again," she said. "Third time today I've been mistaken for this chick. I'll be glad when she's off the streets." How did they figure her new look?

They checked her closer. "Third time, you say?" Reaumur said.

Scorch nodded and gave them her hundred-dollar smile. "Yeah, first time was downtown coming out of NYU after I registered for class. Second time was on the way to this scuzzy gig I need to pay for summer school tuition."

They stared at her long enough to bore holes into her with their cold, sharp eyes, but she had been eyeballed by killers of their own children. These guys were nothing compared to that. Soft sodium vapor streetlights and the red neon of bar signs cast shadows on her. "How much do you weigh?" asked Reaumur.

"One fifteen," she said, and flexed her calf and thigh. "That chick there looks anorexic. What did she do, steal food?"

The cops exchanged glances, reminding her of the silent consultation Leo had with his bartender before they hired her.

So what is it, boys? Thumbs up or thumbs down?

"Why are you carrying this around?" Reaumur asked as he shook her birth certificate at her.

"Told you," she said. "I was registering for class. Needed it for the registrar." Neither of these guys looked bright enough to even spell college, let alone attend one.

"So where's your college ID?" the partner asked.

"Get it after my check clears and before classes start."

They noted the sheen of sweat all over her. Hey, she had just finished dancing and it was still ninety out here. Then Reaumur sighed and handed back her birth certificate. "Head home before some junkie mugs you for the price of a fix of Dark Paradise."

"No problem. Thanks loads, Officers." She sauntered down the block, trying to maintain a casual pace when she really wanted to sprint for the Port Authority bus terminal.

When she turned the corner, the cops were trolling for fresh meat. That was her cue, and she took off, running through a night thick with humidity, each footfall sounding like "How? How?" She got to her room, panting, drenched, throwing herself onto her lumpy bed to lie in darkness as she fought to calm her brain and body. Was she compromised? Was Marie saved? No, she had just bluffed a pair of cops, and the easiest way to hide something was in plain sight. They might move on to other neighborhoods once they realized their fugitive wasn't around, or if the heroin epidemic worsened, forcing a shift of limited manpower.

So how were street cops able to make such a good guess about her now, picturing her new hairstyle? She sat up, trembling, unable to move for a moment. Only two people knew both her ability as a beautician and the undying hate holding her here when any sane person would have left long ago. One was Karen, who despite her protestations of love might roll over on her in exchange for considerations. But Karen, like Scorch, was doing life. There wasn't much they could bribe her with. If she got a color TV and VCR for her cell, everyone would know she snitched and her life sentence would become hard time, with inmates and officers alike tormenting her.

That left her buddy Eric Glass. Glass, who had come in that weekend when she'd slashed her wrists, who sat with her, later bringing her books, helping her appreciate poetry, art, music. Who had treated her like an adult, a lady. A person.

Dr. Glass!

Why, Eric? Because he worked with police, because when push came to shove, it was society versus the cons, and despite his platitudes, she was a murderess, deserving of sympathy only so long as she was safely locked up. Glass! Betrayed by the one who knew her best, like having your favorite uncle turn you in for smoking pot. How could she enjoy a decent sleep knowing the cops after her were guided by her shrink? Glass . . . who lived in Yonkers, only a thirty-minute, air-conditioned Amtrak ride away.

Chapter Thirty

Thursday, June 13

Marie slipped her head from Cal's arm and tiptoed to the window to watch clouds of moths flutter around the streetlight, like snowflakes from last winter's blizzard. From uptown came the whoosh of late-night traffic, from downtown the flash of sparks from the train tracks of the Williamsburg Bridge.

What was she doing, reigniting her own sparks with Cal while a wildcat prowled the streets, craving the chance to cave in her skull? Cal said Paulo had people checking out the whereabouts of Scorch. That was well-intentioned, but what were the odds? The cops would have already found her if she was to be found, and the chances of her having left the city were slender.

Scorch was driven by hate, an emotion Marie herself knew all too well, and it was doubtful she had mellowed with age while festering in prison with other evil spirits.

No, she was out there, stalking.

A *Daily News* survey found that two-thirds of New Yorkers favored vigilante behavior by victims or their families if the legal system denied them justice. Great, now Scorch had most of the city on her side.

Home was no longer a refuge, not with Tanya's ghost invading her dreams and after dropping by to leave mementos.

The floor creaked beside her and a hand touched her waist.

She flinched.

"Whoa. Jumpy, aren't we?" Cal said before kissing the nape of her neck, his lips warm against her clammy skin.

"You'd be, too, if you had a maniac after you."

"So let's stand by the window, facing the street, giving her a clear shot." He pulled her back onto the bed and his lips went to work at her nipples again.

She fended him off. "That's the point. Long range wasn't her style. She liked to do it in close, so she could feel your last breath leave your body." She jabbed him in the ribs with a chewed fingernail.

"I told you, don't worry. Paulo . . ."

"Yeah, right, he and the boys. A lot of good they're doing, looking for a runt who can't be found." She sat up and faced away. "Maybe they'll come to my funeral."

He laid a hand on her shoulder. "If it bothers you that bad, get away for a few weeks, take time off from work, and—"

"And who'll watch Kala? You? Hah!"

"I can take care of her for a while. Maybe the three of us could go off together, like in the beginning."

She bent down, searching for her underwear.

"Why are you so sure she's after you?" he asked.

"I just know."

"Specifics, after so long."

She spun around, her brassiere half on. "Because when I was fourteen I roamed the streets, letting guys screw me for a meal or two or a T-shirt. Then I made a few bucks, bought some drugs, cut and sold them for a profit—"

"Lots of kids do that."

"Let me finish!" He was ticking her off again with his holier-than-thou attitude. His older brother and uncle looked out for him, took him into their grocery business, gave him a chance at life. What the hell did he know? "Then I got into the Tigresses, moved up, took over as older girls got busted or died." She caught herself twisting her shorts into a knot.

"You don't have to go on," he whispered.

But she did. She'd never told the story before, and now that the spigot was open there was no closing it. "One evening this girl walked past without paying the 'toll'—just a couple bucks." She stared out the window at the clusters of moths. "Two freaking bucks. It had been a hot day, a real scorcher." She laughed at that. "I was ticked off at her, this snobby girl who thought she was hot stuff because she had a job downtown. I'd been doing lines of coke since two in the afternoon, so . . . so I told the others to teach her a lesson."

He held up his hand. "Okay, you don't have to—"

Too late. "Lily, Minerva, and Choana got a little too enthused. They pulled blades, and the others . . . Christ, it was like wolves on a calf—they all joined in. I could have stopped them. I *should* have stopped them, but I just stood there, yelling, 'Yeah! Yeah!' Then, when there wasn't much left, they backed off, leaving her twitching, pumping out her life on the hot concrete. That's when her little sister came around the corner and saw her in this spreading red puddle." Marie turned from the window. "She ran to her, tried to stop the bleeding with her tiny hands, but the blood kept spurting through her fingers. Then she saw me." Marie turned to Cal. "Those big, dark, pain-filled eyes, focused on me, narrowed like arrowheads. When Satan gets enraged, he has an expression like that. I knew the way she glared at each of us, one after the other, she'd come for us. We threatened the neighborhood so nobody testified against us. After the sister's funeral, she got her justice. She went to the cops to keep the case open, so we broke into her place to shut her up for good. She wasn't there, so we trashed everything."

She closed her eyes, the "kill site" intruding after having been buried for so long.

"Much later that night, I went with three others to score some coke, and that's what saved me. She came with her firebomb and her spiked bat and tire iron and pounded on Choana, Lily, and Minerva until you couldn't tell one from the other."

It was Cal's turn to go to the window, but he didn't face her. "So she still carries the grudge?"

"Grudge? You stay mad at somebody awhile, that's a grudge. This is vendetta. She'll never stop. I didn't know her, but I know her kind. If it takes a dozen years, twenty, she'll kill me if she can." As she dressed she thought of Tanya's scarred face, her life bubbling out of her. "I'm the last."

He was still staring out the window. Well, maybe men will listen to stories about their partners' infidelities, committed with other men—or women—or all kinds of other sins, but apparently they drew the line at murder.

Big surprise. She should have kept her mouth shut, but then, there were a lot of things she should have done. Besides, this thing just spilled out, like the blood from Scorch's sister. "I'm taking Kala now. Thanks for the ice cream and the screw."

"I'll drive you home."

"Don't put yourself out." She went into his living room to shake Kala awake. "C'mon, honey, we're going home."

"I wanna stay here," her daughter said, rubbing the sleep from her eyes.

Yeah, here, where big, strong Daddy had air-conditioning and nice furniture and strong muscles while Mommy takes you to a flea trap so a dwarf with a crowbar and a firebomb can broil you both.

Someday, if she lived, she'd tell her daughter what to avoid with men—and women.

Cal, dressed and keys in hand, opened the door for them, but all the way down and all the way home he said nothing, just stared at the road, as if there were nothing but him and his car.

Once again Marie had a tough choice and made the wrong one.

So much died that evening on that filthy sidewalk.

If only she had been thirty then, instead of twenty.

Chapter Thirty-one

Friday, June 14

Eric saw Suzanne float toward him on a carpet of clouds, arms outstretched. "Run," bellowed a voice from far away and deep within himself. Why? He was her friend, her lone island of stability in a sea of corrosive passion. He waited, anticipating.

Suzanne's face metamorphosed into that of his mother, filled with rage, loathing. A gorgon would be beautiful compared to this grotesque travesty of a woman, with long crooked nose, stringy hair, and rotted teeth. It reached for him, grabbed him, its long splintered nails burning him with their touch as they tore at his arms, his flesh, to gouge at his eyes, his groin. . . .

He sat up, panting, glad to see the sun rise. The phone next to his bed—its receiver probably knocked off during this nightmare—bleeped at him. Yeah, same to you.

He got up and stretched, then looked between his legs. Yes, just that old hideous nightmare again. Since Veronica was undoubtedly his daughter, whatever his mother may have done to him as a child hadn't prevented him from having one of his own. Except for the scars on his hands and arms, all the damage was on the inside, in places only a psychiatrist or a deep-seated dream could reach.

To purge this latest nightmare, he went onto the terrace to perform the Tai Chi Form in intricate detail as the orange glow of sunrise warmed him. Then he did it again, trading precision for speed and power, violating the philosophy of the art for much-needed therapy for the therapist, sacrificing serenity for sublimation of the pent-up anger that triggered the nightmare.

There, better, good enough to face the world. He rapped on Veronica's door as he moved to the bathroom to shower and shave. "Let's go, Nick. Reveille. Up and at 'em."

The hot needle spray relaxed his taut muscles but didn't do much for his spirit. A brisker workout this evening might get him back on track. He made them both an omelet, one of his few specialties. Why learn to cook when your wife was a whiz in the kitchen, the bedroom, and the workplace? Why? Because someday the dream sours, reality seeps in, and you have to fend for yourself, becoming mother and father to a sensitive, spirited child about to become a woman herself.

"How's your science project?" he asked, trying to make early-morning small talk, a highly recommended family activity.

"Okay."

His daughter, a female of few words. Most of the time.

The buzzer rang.

"Friends of yours?" Eric asked.

Veronica rolled her eyes. The buzzer again, then pounding.

"Hope the building's not on fire," he said as he hustled to the door. Through the peephole he saw Cassandra Lewis banging.

He opened up, and she stormed in.

"Rick, don go to work today. Bad stuff happen if you do."

"You ran two blocks at seven A.M. to issue some dire prediction? I prescribe a quick vacation for you, Sandy."

"I'm serious as a coronary. I tried calling, but your phone off. I had a dream, read cards, and saw evil today. Stay home."

He sighed. It was bound to happen. The whole world was going nuts, one soul at a time, just when he was least able to help them deal with it. "What did you see?" he asked, hoping if he humored her she'd calm down.

"Cards show dat Page of Swords come to cause havoc. I seen it, Rick. You got to be careful."

"I'm always full of care," he said as his chest tightened. Yes, that card, with the young, impetuous women galloping in, wreaking havoc unintentionally. Humoring them might control his own fear. "Want some juice?" he asked, but he was afraid to pour in case his hand shook so much he spilled it. Seeing that might really freak them out. "If gold rusts, what will iron do?"

"Dad, if Sandy saw something bad, you're in trouble."

So much for your child's loyalty. "If, even once, I yield to the temptation not to return to that dungeon, I'm through. I'll never get the strength to go back, which is how I earn the money for the mortgage which keeps us from being homeless."

Veronica snorted, and Sandy shook her head.

He looked from one to the other as if he were at a tennis match. "Both of you, get a grip. If every time Cassandra saw something bad in her cards or her ouija or her tea leaves, we'd be in straitjackets. That or hiding under our beds."

"I'm not going to school," proclaimed Veronica.

Snotty little twerp, just like the ones at work. If he were his mother he'd slap her lopsided, Mom's way of handling even minor insurrection. But he was not his mother, and he recalled the sting of a wire hanger whipped against his head or nearest vulnerable body part, his forearms burning just from the memory. Instead he contented himself with crumpling a napkin. "You're going to school, I'm heading to work, and tonight we'll laugh about this. Sandy, you mean well, but I have to go in today."

"Rick!" Cassandra touched him, and her hand, normally warm, was cool and clammy. "Please tink about it."

He patted her shoulder, needing to reassure her even if she was scaring the hell out of him. "You're sweet to be concerned. If you go home and cast the runes or spin the bottle, I'm sure you'll be able to conjure up a better interpretation to put these dark thoughts to rest. Everything will turn out fine."

She pulled her hand away and stormed to the door. "Eric David Glass," she called over her shoulder. "You're a stubborn intellectual too smart for his own good." She pointed to Veronica. "At least let Nick stay wit me today."

"Oh no! She needs to go to school."

"I could work on my science project with Sandy," Veronica said between bites of egg and cheese.

"What the two of you will do is waste the day picking flowers, communing with butterflies, and conning each other into thinking you see fairies dancing across the Hudson River."

"Veronica Glass, you want and I'll adopt you."

"Wonderful. She'll spend the rest of her life working in your herb shop, telling gullible people that if they smell jasmine or orange blossoms their troubles will—"

Cassandra's slamming of the door shook the house.

"Nice going, Dad. Sandy comes to warn us, and you bust her chops." She grabbed for her books.

"Brush your teeth. I'm driving you to school today."

"No way. I'm not going to school in your geek car."

"Yes, you will. You want your picture on a milk carton, do it when you're living on your own." Get a grip. She's thirteen. He tousled her hair. "Besides, a Corolla is not geeky. I had a Mustang when I dated your mother." But Corollas now have side airbags, to protect the most precious of cargo.

When Eric got to work, things were too quiet. Perhaps Sandy had foreseen something after all. There were rumors of a pending "lockdown," with all inmates confined to their cells while everybody searched for contraband, perhaps fallout from Rainey's bust for smuggling. It wasn't Eric's first choice for a day at work; civilians filled in doing inmate jobs, meaning he'd toil in the kitchen or sweat in the laundry. The other rumor was that Karen Rainey got a "Tier III" sanction—the toughest—Eric being on target about her friend bringing in coke in her cast.

He reclined in his chair, about to pat himself on the back for that maneuver, when his door swung open. Officer Fielder barged in and planted his sizable girth over Eric's desk, his knuckles inches from Eric's hands.

"You know, Fielder, a couple of years ago I hoisted a guy about your size onto my back in a fireman's carry and body-slammed him. I think I could still do it. What's bugging you?"

"The abuse charge against me still stands."

"Rainey may drop it now. She's got other things on her mind these days."

"One thing has nothing to do with the other. You know these people, these lifers. They live to cause trouble." Fielder straightened as sweat beaded on his forehead and upper lip. Maybe he wasn't such a tough guy after all, or such a bad one. "I need you to say I didn't grab her and belt her," he said.

Eric held up his hands. "Much as I'd like to, I can only state I saw her down, after the fact, and while I personally believe it was a setup, that may not hold water with the IG."

Fielder slammed his palms on the desk. Eric understood

his being upset, since his work record was marginal at best.

"Fielder, I'm sorry you're angry, but realize this, I—"

Fielder raised his hands and balled them into large fists. "You realize this! This is my job. I don't tolerate inmate lovers screwing it for decent people, and neither do my co-workers." He stormed out, another threat in his wake. Perhaps Cassandra was as good a fortune-teller as she claimed to be.

Chapter Thirty-two

Friday, June 14

Derelicts, alcoholics, and "danger junkies" lounging by Penn Station checked Scorch out as she left the Amtrak train. Wild-eyed millennial prophets approached her, but she declined; she had spent most of this afternoon spreading "the word."

Today's showers had only made the city more humid. Wisps of steam writhed from hot asphalt and concrete like vaporous snakes, making people move with effort, as if underwater. Scorch zipped past them to the Crystal Grotto to tell Leo his Jezebel would dance past midnight this time, lifting enough beer bottles with her vagina to stock a grocery.

No point telling him she was killing time until three A.M., when Marie should be asleep. Dancing, stripping, teasing, sweating were just foreplay for her tonight. Six hours later, she strode to Marie's house despite Glass's quote, "Living well is the best revenge." Glass was in the running for Hypocrite of the Year, despite knowing all the best proverbs.

Marie's apartment had three locks, including a pick-proof Medico and a tubular cylinder that could be jimmied only with special tools and lots of noise. Only the most desperate and/or paranoid would shield them with thick brass plates. They'd be dealt with before June twentieth, and if Marie showed before then, Scorch would gleefully make her face look like Swiss cheese.

She fished in her bag for one of her remaining souvenirs of Tanya to push under Marie's door. Last week she'd strung up the Police Line tape and left a snapshot of Tanya in a bikini on Orchard Beach, a photo taken before she became a scrawny junkie who failed to break the underwater breathing record. Now Scorch would leave mail addressed to the dear departed Tanya. Only a visit by Tanya's corpse could rattle the soulless Marie more.

Just a few more such setups and Marie would be tenderized, ready for cooking. Scorch stifled the urge to cackle.

A guy sidled up from an alley. "Hey, honey, want to go out?"

Sure, just what she needed. Scorch accelerated, but he fell into step beside her. "You look hot," he said.

Yeah, inflammable. If he only knew how much . . . She groped in her bag for her scissors, couldn't feel it. Go to plan B. Run. Her heels clicked, echoing off the dark brick canyon of Eleventh.

He matched her pace. "You look good in short hair," he said.

And a shorter skirt, skimpy enough to be a hazard to health. She sucked in moist, heavy air and prepared to sprint, though there was nowhere to run to.

She might die in a moment, still a virgin.

A blur out of the corner of her eye. She sidestepped and swung her bag of costumes. It caught the creep as he lunged for her, deflecting his arm. She turned to flee, but he caught her hair, grasped her collar, pulled her against him. She tried to scream, and he clapped a grimy hand over her mouth. Don't bite.

His blood may carry diseases they didn't have names for yet.

She retched from his foul stench of tobacco, sweat, and beer as she struggled to squirm free. When he clutched tighter she smashed her heel into his instep, against his ankle, slammed a bony elbow into his gut. He let go, and she pulled free. He seized her arm and spun her around. She dug her heels in, tugging with all her spirit. He lost hold of her sweaty wrist and she sprawled on her butt, legs wide, skirt up by her crotch.

He towered over her, leering, salivating. "Pretty puss you got," he said. "I'll bet it's nice and juicy."

She braced her palms on the hot, gravelly concrete. Her last hope was to kick his groin or face as he leaned over to grab her.

No point yelling. No one who might hear would care.

Besides, she needed her breath for fighting.

Brakes squealed. Car doors opened.

The creep stopped, looked up, and straightened. Flashing red lights made him look like a demon in heat.

Scorch scooted back, ready to jump up and run.

Racing cops dashed from a police car alongside. The bastard took off down the block, one cop in pursuit. Scorch pushed herself up, set to bolt.

The second cop looked at her. "You okay?" he asked.

"Yeah." As well as could be expected.

"Wait here," he said.

Sure. Just what she needed.

She heard a grunt down the block. The would-be rapist slipped in a puddle and pitched forward, the first cop catching him, jumping on him, whipping out cuffs, snarling, "Shut up."

As Scorch scooped up her stuff scattered all over the sidewalk, the second cop—"Morgan," read his nameplate—came over. "You okay?" he asked, pointing to the blood oozing from her scraped palms.

"I'm fine. Honest." She blotted at her hands with a handkerchief. "I can make it home okay." She turned to go.

"Hey, honey," Morgan said. "Hold up a minute. C'mere."

She ambled over as her handkerchief turned red and sticky from stinging abrasions. "Thanks for grabbing him," she said. "He's sweating, in withdrawal. Probably from Dark Paradise."

"You didn't proposition him?" Officer Morgan asked.

They, like Reaumur earlier this week, assumed she was a hooker. "No way," she said as she smiled. The other cop hauled the molester against the cruiser and recited the Miranda warning.

"Well, thanks again," she said as she started to turn.

"Hey, not so fast," said Morgan.

Her smile stayed frozen on her face. "I forget something?"

"Yeah," he said. "We need your statement."

Statement? Oh boy, law and order strikes again. "You guys were on the ball and caught him. Why do you need me?" she said.

"Why don't you want to make one?" the partner asked.

Trapped. If they thought the lady protested too much, it would arouse more suspicion.

"We'll take you to the precinct to fill out your statement," Morgan said as he opened the passenger-side door, ending debate. She got in, bookended between him and his partner as the stink from the degenerate in back filled the car, nauseating her. She fought to keep from shaking, but the sweat poured from her. "Sure is hot in here, huh?" she said. Morgan rolled down the window.

Two minutes later they were at the precinct, the partner yanking the perp from the back as Morgan scanned her thighs, with her skirt up past midthigh. She walked in on autopilot and drew a sharp breath, as if she were about to plunge into icy water.

"It's okay now," Morgan said. "He can't hurt you in here."

The pervert was the least of her worries. This station house, only the second she had ever been in, was an older, more depressing version of the one in the Bronx. The lighting was harsh, the people harried, the conversations mumbled. A bald sergeant sat at a desk, repiling papers blown off when a whirring fan swung his way. Behind him a garish poster warned of Dark Paradise heroin, announcing it had claimed a hundred victims so far, the hot-pants, see-through-blouse hooker from last week among them.

"We got assault, attempted rape, attempted robbery, and drunk and disorderly," one cop said as he shoved the creep forward. "He grabbed and knocked down this little lady here."

Little lady. She was short, is all, and there hadn't been much ladylike about her these last eight years. If he only knew.

Maybe he did. A computer composite of her likeness was among the papers on the sarge's desk, with another flapping on a bulletin board covered with a hundred other items. Morgan jolted her back to reality by flicking a carbonless form with multiple copies, one for the watch commander, the District Attorney's Office—half the criminal justice system in Manhattan.

She shook her head.

"What's the matter?" he said. "You forgot what happened?"

"No, it's just . . . What if this guy gets out with a grudge and comes for me?" she said. "I mean . . ."

"No way. You watch too much TV," he said. "Let's do it."

The fan turned toward her, rearranging her damp hair. "I'm not feeling too well," she said to the sergeant, "and your men caught him in the act. Isn't that enough?"

The sarge wiped his pate with a handkerchief and scowled. "Yeah, enough to charge him with attempted assault and attempted robbery, which a smart Legal Aid lawyer can use to reduce bail to maybe a couple thousand dollars and then get him to plead to drunk and disorderly, a misdemeanor which will let him molest some other girl." His watery blue eyes narrowed. "I got a daughter your age, and I don't want this piece of crap back out there doing to her what he almost did to you." Those blue eyes hardened. "Most women would jump at the chance to put this scum away for a while. You know what they do to rapists in jail?"

She knew and didn't care. She tapped the forms. "I've been on my feet for sixteen hours." No lie and no joke. "Can't I go home now and do it in the morning?"

"It *is* morning. If he's to be arraigned today, we need all the paperwork in. Now. My experience is if we don't get it right away, we don't get it at all, and then another scum bucket walks." He pointed to an ancient manual typewriter. "We need you to go over there with Officer Morgan."

She sat on a rickety chair, legs crossed, skirt hem almost high enough to get her booked for soliciting.

"Got ID?" Morgan asked her.

"Guess I lost my wallet in the skirmish."

He frowned as he typed her statement, doing a two-finger dance for so long on the aged machine that her butt started to fall asleep. As he rested his fingers, he ogled her thighs. "You sure you didn't do anything to encourage him?" he said.

"He just came up to me. Trust me, he's not my type."

He stared at her, and she maintained eye contact for so long her eyes burned. He resumed typing. "Where do you live?"

"Live?"

"Your address," he said. He stopped to stare again, longer

this time. "You nervous? You're sweating and shaking."

"I've been groped, choked, pushed, and now I'm getting the third degree in a place with less air than the Black Hole of Calcutta, so sure I shake and sweat. Who wouldn't? I don't know how you guys stand this, night after night."

Sarge and Morgan's partner stopped processing the pervert and watched the show. Morgan asked again, "Where do you live?"

She blurted out an address near Tanya's house. Morgan mulled it over for a while. "How long you been there?" he said.

"About a month. It's cheap."

He and the sarge exchanged looks. "Crummy neighborhood," Morgan said. "So what were you doing over on Eleventh at this hour?"

"Getting off from work at the Macumba Lounge. I'm a cocktail waitress when I'm not a part-time student."

"Macumba? That's a black bar," Morgan said.

"Yeah? So?" Her olive skin had tanned beautifully the past two weeks as she had prowled the streets. She was about to add that her paternal grandfather was Haitian, but Glass always counseled not to give up too much information if it wasn't asked for. Her black-and-white prison ID photo, taken in winter, showed a pale chick, obviously white.

Morgan looked primed to say more when the drunken degenerate gagged, retched, and vomited near his partner's shoes. The other officer cursed, steadied the man, and asked for a mop and pail.

The spell broken, Morgan went back to typing her statement, made some more errors, corrected them, and rolled the form out of the typewriter for her signature. She pretended to peruse it and signed "Helen Glass" in a fourth-grade-style penmanship to avoid telltale handwriting clues. As she did, she felt a stare from Morgan. She looked and saw her composite on the bulletin board billowing like a banner as the floor fan turned toward it.

"Remember the Four Ds," Glass had advised. ReDirect and Distract to Diffuse Dangerous situations. She smiled at Morgan. "I know you," she said. "You helped my father a couple years ago. He was in a taxi accident over on Eighth."

Morgan shrugged. "Couple years ago? Yeah, right. How is he?"

"Died," she said. "A stroke." He'd had one when she was six. Tears for him came, finally, hot and salty, as she recalled Dad gasping, falling over, dead before he touched the ground from that massive blowout. She sniffled, tried to hold it in, but coupled with the delayed reaction from that jackass grabbing her, too many emotions ganged up and she let them run their course.

She blotted her eyes dry and saw Morgan's partner glancing at her computer composite. Not again. Take the initiative. "I'll bet you got that from Officer Reaumur," she said. "You haven't found her yet? She must be in Aspen or L.A. by now."

"Doug Reaumur showed you this?" the sergeant said.

She nodded. "Yeah, he and his partner were stopping every blonde in the theater district earlier this week."

The sarge didn't look convinced. "This week, you say?"

She nodded, sniffled, and took a tissue from a soggy box as her mascara ran, probably making her look like a racoon.

"Reaumur's due back in a while," Sarge said. "Stick around in case he wants to talk to you some more."

In better light, after being a reluctant complainant. Cops were like guards. Men get freaked by women's intimate concerns. She leaned forward, pushed her legs together, and looked uncomfortable. "Are any policewomen here, or female clerks?"

Morgan arched an eyebrow. "No. Why? What's wrong?"

"Uh." She leaned closer and lowered her voice. "Is there a tampon dispenser in the ladies' room? I'm starting to—you know."

"Your period?" He squirmed and looked to the sarge, who rolled his eyes with a put-upon look. "Well . . . I don't think so."

Keep pushing it. "Can I look in the desks of female detectives?" she said. "They may keep some for emergencies."

Morgan shook his head. "Those are kept locked."

"Could you loan me five bucks for the all-night drugstore?"

Sarge sighed, and the fan came his way again and sent another paper cascade down his desk. He muttered as he got them into a semblance of order. "Okay, we got a statement to make the case." He tapped them straight. "I doubt it will go to trial. Legal Aid will plead him out to attempted assault, a class E felony, and he'll get credit for time served at county lockup."

"Can I have five bucks?" she asked. "I'll pay you back."

"You can go," Morgan said. "And be more careful out there."

"You bet. Thanks." She gathered her stuff and ambled out, fighting the impulse to streak like a meteor through the stale early-morning air. She headed to her room, propelled by a belated adrenaline surge. She'd survived again, winning the privilege of spending yet another night in a steamy coffin, still without her first soul-nourishing sleep in nearly a decade.

Chapter Thirty-three

Friday, June 14

The note was to the point. "Inmate Rainey, Karen, 83 G 0941, requests Dr. Eric Glass assist in her defense of her recent Tier III sanction for contraband and smuggling."

The fox asking to meet with the chickens. She was up to something, but he was bound by regulation to help. His head still swimming from this morning's nightmare and Cassandra's wild warning, Eric entered the keeplock cell block, hoping to finish this so he could go home and pick up the pieces.

Unlike the general population, this cell block was dingy, damp, and smelling of sweat and musk, with hygiene and pride taking a back seat to self-pity and apathy. The block officer glanced at Eric's note and yelled, "Rainey, company. You decent?"

"Go screw yourself," said a raspy voice from down the hall.

The officer nodded to Eric. "At least she's awake. Give her a minute to get something on. The girls like to lounge around naked this time of year."

Something to look forward to. Eric ambled down the center of the steamy hallway, watching each cell he passed in case someone decided to share their bodily wastes with him.

"You a counselor?" asked a woman from her cell.

"No, a psychologist. A lower life-form."

"Yeah? Psyche this." She raised her skirt. No underwear.

"If that was mine, I wouldn't show it off so often."

"Screw you," she said, plopping onto her bunk.

No, thanks, honey. Across the way another woman lay on her back, legs spread, enjoying herself. Literally.

Welcome to Hell's Waiting Room.

"Karen Rainey, you dressed?"

She sat facing the wall, smoking, a towel covering her hips and torso. "Who wants to know?" she said. Suzanne's Tom Cruise posters decorated her walls. Did she want Suzanne back as well? Was that what this tête-à-tête was all about, her giving up Sue?

"Your friend and admirer. C'mon, I don't have all day."

She spun around. "Glass. Glad you came."

"The pleasure's all mine. What's up?"

"Tier assistance. I could have anyone, and I chose you."

"I'm honored."

"So how did they know I was 'holding'?" she asked.

"They know everything. It's post-1984. Big Brother is everywhere."

She took another puff as she considered this. The ceiling above her formed a charcoal-gray Rorschach from generations of nicotine addicts, making an odd pattern on the otherwise sickly yellow paint. "I think somebody tipped them off."

"They're smarter than you think. They can be trained, like bears. Your problem was you underestimate authority and society in all its forms."

She nodded. "You're smart. Scorch said you were."

"Flattery will get you nowhere."

She ground out her cigarette and toyed with a Styrofoam cup on the sink, its contents currently a mystery. He should stand to the side, but he relished the chance to match wits with someone who had probably tried to victimize him.

"I was set up," she said. "That's my story."

"And a fine one it is, too. I imagine you've had lots of experience with setups. You're saying your visitor did not bring in thirty grams of coke in her phony arm cast? I heard she's facing a possession charge and the Westchester County D.A. *will* prosecute." He placed both palms on her gate in case he needed to make himself scarce in a hurry.

Her eyes narrowed. "Some SOB squealed on me. You know what they say about that?"

"A snitch in time saves nine?"

"Jackass!" She grabbed the cup and flung it at the gate.

Though braced for it, Eric hadn't anticipated her quickness and barely missed getting a golden shower. The arc of urine splashed against and between the bars to splatter on the hallway floor. Other inmates went to their gates and howled.

"That's enough!" The block officer banged her baton twice on her desk. "Keep it down on the noise!"

"Or else what?" asked the woman who had flashed Eric.

"Or whatever keeplock time you're already getting, I'm sure we can double it."

Eric shrugged at Rainey. "You must do something about your temper. Next time you come off Keeplock, we can discuss it."

Rainey dropped her towel, turned around, and bent over.

"A rather full moon in yonder cell has risen," he said. "Get lots of exercise over the next six months or the only clothing that'll fit you will be that towel." He paused, though a prudent man would have already been out of the block. "And tossing bodily wastes is now a class E felony. Even if you're doing life, there's no reason for it to be hard time. Have a nice day."

He strode past the officer. "You'll need a mop down there. Ms. Rainey lost control of her bladder. I'll return next week."

"Rainey," said the officer. "Need a diaper?"

"Up yours! Both of you," she screamed from her cell.

When other inmates took up the chant, the officer slammed her baton on the desk again and silence returned. It was an old desk and had hundreds of dents.

When all else fails, percussion therapy succeeded.

Eric stopped by his supervisor's office on his way out the front gate. The deputy superintendent for programs was hunched over his desk, columns of paper surrounding him. "Glass, glad you're here. I need you to rewrite the incident report between Officer Fielder and Inmate Rainey."

"I just came from Rainey." Eric gave a thirty-second summary of the abortive tier assistance. "What's to write?"

"Just because she's scum doesn't mean he didn't smack her."

"I don't like Fielder, but . . ."

"I know, there's lots of him, but little of him to like. Nevertheless, we investigate. If he knocked her down or copped a feel, he's going up on charges."

"And then I'm known as an 'inmate lover' who turned in an officer. You afraid I'll live too long? That sort of action makes for very unhappy tenure in a place like this."

"You know the rules," the dep said. "No creative writing, but try to give more details if possible, okay?" He started scribbling. "By the way, what's new on the Amerce case?"

"The police brass don't consider it a priority."

The dep paused in midstroke. "Pardon?"

Eric sighed. "A 'cold case' doesn't advance a career." He saluted and left, understanding now why the average correctional worker died at fifty-nine, most often on a Monday.

He pulled up across from his home. As he got out he saw a mound of cigarette butts, their tips stained purple. Why did people dump their cars' ashtrays on the curb? Crossing over, he found a similar pile under the terrace. He stooped to look.

Camels? Camels! No, it couldn't be. He knew only one woman who favored purple lipstick. He ran upstairs to find Veronica brushing the cats and drinking milk, probably swallowing an occasional hair in the process.

"You were mean to Sandy this morning, Dad. She was trying to help."

"She was spreading hysteria in the household." Speaking of hysteria, religious tracts and dire warnings of Armageddon lay on the coffee table, publications worthy of a psychiatric center or the bowels of Times Square during a full moon. He held one up. "You thinking of becoming a fanatic?"

"Found them in front of the door a while ago," she said.

From who, a Jehovah's Witness, come to harass him? No friend would leave this. Something here didn't compute.

"Oh," said Veronica. "Lucy called. You seeing her again?"

Only if she had a high tolerance for masochistic men. None of his friends were "born again" or had children who were. Who? He scanned the pamphlets. One proclaimed in bold red letters:

HE WHO BETRAYS HIS TRUST SHALL BE SMITTEN AND SUFFER

Another's front page announced:

THE SINS OF THE FATHERS SHALL BE VISITED UPON THEIR CHILDREN

Then he saw the other thing on the table, the compact disc with excerpts from all the great classical pieces. He jumped up.

He had brought Suzanne the cassette version of this album when she was recovering from her slashed wrists. She especially loved *Bolero*, immediately grasping its significance, relishing the crescendo, the innuendo. She beamed whenever she played it.

"Where did this come from?" he demanded of Veronica as he felt his heart slamming against his ribs.

"It was on the front steps too. Why?"

She'd been here! Was she still around? Had anyone seen her? Should he call the cops? Why bother? She had changed her appearance. She probably still looked fifteen.

Chapter Thirty-four

Veronica stared wide-eyed, unused to seeing her father react like this. The cats' ears twitched. "What's wrong?" she asked.

Wrong? A murderess had found them. "When you came home, did you see a short, cute girl with really large dark eyes? A wide scar behind her left ear? Another over her left eyebrow?"

The brush dropped. "Uh, I saw a girl like that, yeah, the big eyes. I didn't notice scars. Dad, what happened?"

Her! How had she . . . ? What did he expect. She had an IQ of 147, four points above his own.

No matter how, she'd done it. Why search for Suzanne when all he had to do was sit tight and let her find him?

"Get your shoes on," he said as he fished out the Yellow Pages and riffled through to the section on security systems.

"Why? What's the matter?"

"We're going to Central Avenue to get a burglar alarm."

"Who's putting it in? You? You can't program the VCR."

He jotted down the addresses of several stores. "You

271

sound like your late, diabolical grandmother." After five. Places might be closing. . . . Veronica was right—when it came to electronics, even simple stuff, his mind was all thumbs.

He dialed the precinct. Lucy was still there.

"We have a problem," he said. "Suzanne was here today."

Out of the corner of his eye he saw his daughter's face turn the same color as the milk she was drinking.

"How do you know?" Lucy asked.

"A bunch of clues." He told her of the cigarette butts, the tracts, the compact disc. "Also Veronica described her." He cupped his hand over the mouthpiece. "Did she look like those composites we showed around last week?" he asked Veronica.

She shrugged. "Uh . . . maybe. All I noticed was her walking down the block toward the Amtrak station. Her hair was shorter, I think, but she had long lashes. They curled upward."

His daughter the detective, the Nancy Drew of the suburbs.

"We have a positive ID." He raised his hand to silence Veronica's protest. "You know anything about home alarms?"

"Why did she come?" Lucy asked. "What makes you think she'll return?"

"She's sending me a message, letting me know she's found me. What do we do?"

"Let me put you on hold," Lucy said.

Eric pawed through his address book. He couldn't ask any friends, his or Debbie's, to house them as a homicidal fugitive roamed the streets, looking to do Lord knew what. Debbie's mother lived in Miami, which next to prison was the place Eric would least like to be in late June. "Veronica, how would you like to spend a week with your aunt and cousins in Brooklyn?"

She pretended to stick her finger down her throat and gag.

"Veronica, we can't stay here, not without protection. What about Cassandra's house?"

Veronica brightened. "Sure! Sandy would love that."

Sure she would. By the time he got his daughter back, she'd either be a Rastafarian-in-training or a guru to the adolescents.

Lucy came back on the line. "Eric, the only one I could find who would come over on short notice to install an alarm is my ex-partner Bryan Acinar on Broadway. He said he'd be over in a hour. I'm on the way. Stay put. You have any weapons?"

"A kung-fu staff, a ginsu knife, and a Louisville Slugger from when I played right field for Columbia's junior varsity."

"Well-armed. Don't go near any windows or open up to anybody but us."

They had become prisoners, while Suzanne remained at large.

He latched the terrace door, though you'd have to be a circus performer or Olympic gymnast to shinny up without a ladder. Over Veronica's objection he locked the fire-escape window.

"Why worry about her coming to get us?" she said. "We'll just suffocate up here. It's still in the eighties outside."

"Tomorrow you can call Child Protective Services and have them remove you to a group home stocked with rapists and murderers. Tonight we seal ourselves in." That said, he went into the spare room to rummage for his staff and bat.

Lucy showed up at six-thirty bearing Chinese takeout. "What did Scorch want with you?" she asked.

"To scare us," Eric said. "I'm just thankful she didn't try to come in." He tousled his daughter's hair. "This is why I told you never to open the door for strangers." He sifted through the day's mail. "Our mailbox is not locked. Christ!" He held up a letter from the nursing home. "She could find out plenty just by looking at the return addresses on this stuff."

Lucy looked at Eric. "Think she's armed?" she asked.

He grimaced. "Suzanne fashioned weapons from stolen spoons, old toothbrushes, even a cigarette filter. . . . She could do more with common household items than a terrorist."

Bryan Acinar arrived, huffing, schlepping a carton and a toolbox. Considering his nicotine habit, Eric was surprised the man made it up the steps. He started measuring, drilling, and shooing Athena and Achilles away as he set up on the stairway. "These damn rodents are screwing up the sensors." He coughed between puffs. "I can't make the setting too sensitive or you'll pick up their movements and get false alarms. Can't you give them away?"

"No!" said Veronica, scooping up Athena. "They've been with us for years."

Five years, bought to comfort her after Debbie's accident.

"Then lock them up or I'll have to set the sensors higher."

"Do it," said Lucy. "The odds are she won't return."

Acinar tightened something with pliers that slipped, causing him to curse and suck on a finger yellowed by a two-pack-a-day habit. "Damn, I'm getting too old for this stuff. Next thing you do, Doc, is buy yourself a twelve-gauge pump, Remington or Winchester. Get a pistol permit and a Colt Python .357 Magnum shooting safety slugs. Low penetration potential, but they chew up a target. That should handle your problem."

Now he had to get firearms.

Why the hell hadn't Suzanne headed for California?

"Would it be safer to relocate?" Eric asked Lucy.

Acinar snorted and lit a fresh cigarette from the stub of

his last one. "Move? Hell." He stood to his full six feet two
and clasped a fraternal hand on Eric's shoulder. "This is
your home. Why live in fear? That's the trouble with this
country: too many liberals making criminals into damn heroes and treating victims as deserving it. We need another
guy like Reagan."

Archie Bunker had come to do home improvements for
them.

Acinar smiled at Veronica. "Sorry about the language,
little lady."

"I'm no lady. I hear worse at school."

"Oh?" Eric said. Cassandra had indeed foreseen evil.

Acinar finished his final adjustments. "This should do."

Eric pulled out all his cash. Forty bucks short. Acinar held
up a hand. "Lucy says you're on the wagon. I saw bottles
of Jim Beam, Johnny Walker Black, Wild Turkey. I'll take
them off your hands and we'll call it even."

"For an alarm like that?"

"Yeah—got it off a friend for nothing. The camera outside
the door is a dummy to scare them off before they try anything. Yeah, this booze is worth plenty." He pinched Veronica's cheek, loaded the bottles into the carton, and left.

A dummy camera, sensors on the stairs, and a terrace
twenty feet off the ground, safe from all but champion pole
vaulters.

"I was thinking of calling the state police or the Yonkers
P.D.," Eric said to Lucy.

"And say what, somebody left you religious stuff?" Lucy
lifted the CD box with a handkerchief and held it to the
light. "Looks wiped clean except for Veronica handling it.
I could have it dusted for prints, but it's Friday evening, so
we won't get the results before Tuesday, the earliest."

"Can I hire someone to stake the place out?" Eric asked.

"Stake it out? You watch too much TV. She won't return."

275

"With Suzanne there was no wasted energy. She wouldn't have come unless she was overwhelmed and afraid she was losing it."

Lucy shook her head. "No way I could get DiGiorio to arrange for protection from another city. At best we could ask the Yonkers P.D. for regular 'drive-bys.' "

"That wouldn't stop her. She's a felonious genius."

"But now she knows you're alerted and prepared, she'll . . ."

Eric put his arm around Veronica. "She came because she's disturbed now, mired in an unstable situation. You're thinking logically, figuring her to be cool and rational. Look at her from the perspective of someone becoming more impulsive and angry. Anything can happen."

Chapter Thirty-five

Sunday, June 16

Shattering. Wailing. Cursing. Screaming.

Eric tossed aside the damp sheet and sat up in bed.

The wailing continued. His car alarm?

He blinked the sleep from his eyes and peered out the window across the street. The car behind his had its window smashed, with bits of glass scattered on the asphalt, gleaming like rhinestones in the streetlight. A kid kneeled nearby, wearing what looked like a tasseled red nylon jacket. In this heat?

A siren wailed, closer, louder.

The kid tried to get up and run, but a Yonkers Police cruiser cut him off and he sat back onto pebbles of plate glass as the cops came over.

It wasn't a red nylon jacket the kid had on. His back glistened with bloody strips of flesh hanging from his arms and back like satin ribbons. The boy, sixteen or seventeen, rocked as the cops questioned him, but all he did was shake his head.

Eric pulled on pants and a shirt and ran downstairs as an

ambulance pulled up, its siren adding to the chorus of the police cruiser and the vandalized car's alarm.

The cops were looking through the kid's bag, finding screwdrivers, pliers, a wrench. "Doing a tune-up at three A.M.?" one asked. "Or maybe cut yourself shaving?"

The boy shook his head again as the paramedics came out. "I wasn't doing nothin'," he said to the cops. "Just tripped."

Just like they say in prison. He was all set for the three-to-five for grand-theft auto he would get the next time he tried to steal a car, or the time after that, assuming he lived awhile.

"Who cut you? The ticked-off owner? Your partner?"

"Nobody. Told you. Fell."

The cops smirked. "Right. And sliced your shirt off."

On a hunch, Eric leaned forward. "How old was the girl who did this to you?" he asked the boy.

The cops snickered, but the kid's eyes widened.

"You were stealing stereos, right?" Eric said. "And when you were about to get into the next one," he pointed to his Corolla, "a girl jumped you, cut you up?"

The kid looked down. Lucky she hadn't gutted him or turned him into London broil. As they whisked him to Yonkers General Hospital, the kid looked at Eric with an expression of disbelief.

Sure, it happens to everybody once. They run into somebody meaner, wilder, fiercer. Nobody expects it to be a woman, though.

"Lover's quarrel, huh?" said the cop. "That your car?"

Eric shook his head. "The next one."

"Lucky his girlfriend picked that moment to lose her cool," said the cop as he pulled the cable on the battery, ending the keening of the alarm's hundred decibels. "Otherwise it would be your insurance company getting a call right about now."

Yeah, real lucky.

Three A.M. and she had been out here, waiting, keeping watch on his home, his car.

He considered telling the cops, but Lucy was right. It was all circumstantial, and without proof or eyewitnesses there was no way anybody would take him seriously. The kid she'd cut would die rather than corroborate his story. No male in his right state of testosterone would admit being outfought by a tiny girl.

Still, they could sweep the area. . . . He went back to ask the cops if they would look for the kid's assailant, but then their radio squawked about a burglary down Broadway and off they went. By the time he called the precinct, Suzanne would be long gone.

Hopefully.

As he walked back home, he imagined her eyes on him. That was how she had lived the past third of her life, scrutinized all the time. He'd never experienced that sensation before. Was this what it was like to suspect your every move is watched, to never know if or when you're under surveillance?

He checked the burglar alarm before walking upstairs. As he saw where Acinar's tool had slipped, he recalled a violent-offender group years ago, when one woman described her sexually abusive husband. That had got the band playing, and they all chimed in, one after another, about what they'd do if their man got rough or tried to rape them. It got louder, more boisterous as each tried to outdo the other with war stories and tall tales.

Suzanne just sat, staring straight ahead as everyone talked themselves out. When she finally spoke it was almost a murmur, her face angelic but her eyes smoldering. The clamor faded and died. "Lorena Bobbitt let her man off way too easy," Suzanne had said. "What she should have done was renovate his plumbing with an ice pick and pliers." She pantomimed inserting, clamping, twisting, yanking until Eric found it was all he could do to keep from crossing his legs or running from the room.

The eeriest part was the way all those others, most of them old enough to be her mother, listened to this petite nineteen-year-old virgin. Their looks bordered on awe. If they ever considered rioting, it was obvious who their leader would be.

Eric lay in bed, his aluminum bat resting against the right nightstand, the oak kung-fu staff on the left, just in case.

At ten A.M. Lucy showed up to hear Eric's latest theory about Suzanne. At eleven Cassandra Lewis flounced in, her dress a riot of tropical colors. "Veronica Glass, you ready to come with me?"

Veronica giggled as she gathered up a suitcase and the cats pleaded pitifully from within their carrier.

Lucy shook her head. "I still think you're overreacting. Now that you've got the alarm, you should reconsider. The fact the Yonkers P.D. responded so quickly should make Scorch think twice about returning, assuming it was her."

"Forget that, Lucy," said Cassandra. "If Eric Glass don't behave, Veronica can stay with me until she's able to vote."

Eric paused with the loaded cat carrier in hand. "Unless we get somebody to watch this place twenty-four-seven, I'll feel safer with Veronica staying with you."

Lucy shook her head. "Well, maybe we'll find her, or locate Marie, warn her, and then grab Scorch before she adds another notch on her lighter."

Eric snapped his fingers. Veronica and the cats flinched. "Remember at the mall I said I had something important to tell you but forgot? In keeping with Suzanne's warped sense of ceremony, not only would she want to kill Marie on the same date as when her sister was murdered, she'd want to do it in the same place, Creston Avenue. It's logical in a perverse sort of way."

"How would she do that?" asked Veronica.

"The same way she wiped out the gang, survived in prison, and escaped." Eric stuck his finger in the carrier's airhole, and the cats sniffed and licked it. "I could check out Manhattan, find her, and try to convince her to give up the hunt."

"Uh-uh," said Lucy. "You find her, you're compelled to—"

Cassandra cleared her throat. "Sorry," she said. "We should go before you change your mind or get weepy."

Eric nodded. "As poorly as I may sleep with Veronica gone, I'll get none if she's still here." He shrugged. "Hey, I'm Jewish. I've honed worrying to an art form." He hugged Cassandra. "Sorry about the other day. I was a schmuck, but what else is new?" He looked at Lucy and Veronica. "It's one of my talents, what I do best. Cassandra, I'll forgive me if you do."

"Nothing to forgive. I'll return your child when you need her." She paused halfway out the door. "Lucy, my cards this morning say a man give you advice you need to follow. Den dere's two women, dark wit anger, gonna cause you bad trouble."

Eric sighed. "As if there's good trouble."

Cassandra took Lucy's hand. "Promise you'll be careful."

Eric stepped to the window and looked skyward. "Jesus! She did it again!"

"Dad!"

"Right. Sorry. Sandy, go spread gloom and doom. Your parents named you well."

Cassandra moved to the door. "I repeat what the cards tell me. Eric, you of all people should know what I say will soon be. Lucy, follow your instinct."

After she and Veronica left, Eric muttered about lunacy. "I'm sure you think I'm nuts, but . . ."

"So bring her back," Lucy said.

Easier said than done. "Often violence is a reaction to betrayal. If Suzanne is royally ticked off at me, there's no telling what she might do, and if so I don't want there to be any collateral damage." He sighed, frustrated at his inability to explain in words what could only be felt.

Pain cannot be described, only experienced.

Chapter Thirty-six

Sunday, June 16

When her phone rang, Marie flinched as if she'd been nipped. She dropped the joint she'd been rolling and lunged to answer it before it woke Kala. Who would call near midnight on a Sunday? "Hello?" she said. The line had a hollow sound. "Hello?"

Nobody there, the third time this week. Was it Scorch? Finding Marie's unlisted number wasn't beyond the ability of the dwarf demon. Marie hung up, and as she went back to her joint it rang again. She drew the curtains, shutting off even the slight hot breeze that puffed through occasionally. Then she grabbed her gun, switched off the light, and wondered if Scorch was across the street with her firebombs and spiked bats. The phone kept ringing. Not telemarketing, not at this hour. She snatched the receiver. "Yeah?" she asked, her voice husky with tension.

"Marie? It's Paulo. I just talked with Jose Colon."

"The creep? So?"

"Those pictures of that girl you gave me . . . He says the word is the cops have given up looking for her, the pressure from City Hall to cut off the 'Dark Paradise' traffic. Sorry."

"Yeah." Sure they were. She was on her own, as usual. She stuck her pistol into the damp waistband of her jeans. "You tell this to Cal?" she asked.

"No way. Didn't want to worry him, but figured I'd warn you. Listen, if that girl hasn't found you by now, she must be gone."

Yeah, if she was sane. Paulo hung up, leaving Marie alone with the biggest problem of her life. One A.M. If she went to bed now, she'd get three or four hours of sleep, the most she'd had this week. Great, just what she needed to be alert.

At least Kala got her rest.

Marie lit her joint and sucked in a lungful of smoke while adjusting her headphones. Soft smooth jazz, something Cal had introduced her to, floated in from one of the easy-listening stations. She took another toke and let her eyelids shut.

Tanya, naked, dripping, stood before her, pointing a bony finger at her. Tanya's eyes were sunken in, her lips pulled back in rigor mortis, making it seem she was smiling—or snarling?

Sorry, Tanya. Didn't mean to drown you in that scummy water. I was scared. You were scared. Scorch is to blame.

Tanya shook her head. Something cracked, and that head with its scraggly hair tipped and fell, thudding to the ground. Tanya's scrawny body collapsed as if a hangman had just cut her down. Beige water gushed from her mouth, covering the floor, rising higher, faster, slopping into Marie's face.

Marie snapped awake, ripped the earphones off, and gasped for air as she thought of what skinny Tanya's body must be like now, dead ten days. Worse than that nightmare vision she'd had. Was it a dream? Three times someone or something had left voodoo stuff by her door, all reminding her of Tanya. Coincidence? Scorch? If she believed in ghosts, she'd think it was Tanya's doing. Why shouldn't she believe in ghosts? She believed in demons. If not Tanya, then who? Scorch! Sure, she knew where Tanya lived, had nearly smothered her. But how would Scorch have that stuff? Because she craved the last Tigress dead, that's how. Something—a shadow maybe—darkened the bar of light leaking under Marie's threshold. Someone at the front door?

She reached for the light switch but froze. No, don't show them anyone's awake and don't give them a target. Instead Marie pulled her gun, tiptoed to the door, and listened. Her breathing and the thudding of her heart made it hard to hear all but the loudest sounds. She couldn't stand here all night.

She turned each lock slowly, then yanked the door wide.

Nothing. The landing was empty. Was that a footstep on the stairs? She inched forward to the banister and peaked over. She glimpsed something, a shadow maybe, flit away. Gone.

Eric Glass flicked the switches of his new alarm system and checked the locks. Safe. Had he overreacted by calling Lucy and allowing his home to become a fortress? Maybe they hadn't been visited by Suzanne—or had he become too stupid for his own good, praying they were safe here from a mass murderer?

He leaned on the railing of his balcony, hoping for a midnight breeze to cool him enough so he'd sleep refreshed to start the workweek. How had it come to this, becoming a prisoner in his own home, jumping at conclusion and shadows?

How? Because he'd tried to help Suzanne rid herself of her personal demons. He had wasted all that energy, when he should have concentrated on freeing himself of his own.

285

Monday, June 17

Marie woke on her sofa in her underwear. Last time she had slept on this couch, years ago, she and Cal had made love for what had seemed like hours, far longer than the time she had slept on it this morning. She zipped into the bedroom, roused Kala, and got them both into the shower. As the water stroked her, she thought about the last time she and Cal had made love, his hands on her, fingers in her, bringing her to climax three times. She caressed herself for a moment, trying to relive that evening.

No good. Nothing good was happening anymore. She got out, and she and Kala got dried and dressed.

While Kala munched cereal, Marie considered taking her gun.

No, this was no time to be caught with it and maybe get suspended, if not fired. She hid it behind the refrigerator, slurped scalding coffee, rinsed dishes, and got Kala up and out.

She turned to lock the door, but the key wouldn't go in. She blinked bleary eyes and tried again. No go.

She lit a match and saw why. Someone had squirted epoxy glue into two of the cylinders, the Medico and the tubular one, the two that couldn't be picked.

Chapter Thirty-seven

Monday, June 17

A deputy superintendent on the line early in the morning is never a good thing. "Eric, were you born under a bad sign?"

"Under a ladder more likely. What now?"

"Your troubles continue. Inmate Rainey accuses you of both refusing her tier assistance and also not accurately reporting what you saw regarding her and Fielder. In essence, a cover-up."

"She's lies."

"Probably, but the regulations require that we respond."

"We should give that fiction the attention it deserves. She threw a yellow liquid at me Friday, and it wasn't orange juice."

"You file a report?"

"Not yet. She missed. The block officer and I had a good laugh about it. I was going to do it this morning."

"Do it now, as soon as you give her tier assistance."

"I didn't bring my raincoat. Should I wear a garbage bag? A bathing suit? My birthday suit?" Eric grabbed a clipboard, preferring it were an umbrella, and headed back to keep-lock.

The block officer saw him coming and smiled. "Back for round two, Doc? Rainey, get ready."

"I'd prefer seeing her out of the cell this time, with no liquids that aren't still in her body."

"Got it. Wait here." The officer walked down the corridor, clanking her baron against each cell's gate in turn.

Not even nine and already the walls were slick with the humidity of a day forecast to be muggy and unpleasant everywhere, but doubly so here. Rainey came out wearing a short skirt and a T-shirt trimmed to show off her flat midriff. Not bad for a woman who didn't remember how many times she'd been pregnant.

They sat in a small room near the officer's desk, where they could be monitored without being overheard.

Eric decided on a preemptive strike, to see how Rainey reacted. "So, Karen, what will it be today, trick-or-treat?"

She brushed damp hair from bleary eyes. "Back to harass me?"

"Strange the way memory plays tricks. I recall it was the other way around. Before we go into the abuse complaint against Fielder, I wondered if you'd heard the news yet?"

"What news?" For a tired woman, she suddenly looked perky.

"Somebody will say you banged your head against the wall that day. The doctor confirmed there's no way to in-validate that theory. Besides, even if Fielder is fat—mentally and physically—he's never been accused of abuse before."

"There's always a first time."

True, but there was less certainty in her voice now. He had to maintain momentum. "Why are you trying to set me up?" he said.

"Am I?" She looked blasé but fidgeted. "Got smokes?"

"Don't change the subject. This phony abuse thing . . ."

"It's not phony."

"Right. Of course not. Then there's the drug thing."

"Drugs?"

"Somebody tried to plant pot on me."

"Pot?" Her face yielded a sly smile. "I don't bother with pot. Too much bulk, too much risk for too little gain." Her smile widened. "Barb White and Iris Valentine smoke. And sell."

"Why would they want to set me up?"

"Maybe they think you helped Scorch get away."

"That's crazy."

"They're crazy." Her smile grew. "Besides, there's history behind this. Iris was a Tigress twelve years ago."

So that was it! Barb and Iris were Karen's pusher rivals! Needing muscle to fight them, Rainey must have sucked Suzanne in, using her like a tool. Suzanne thought she was fighting for her life in here, but she'd been duped into being Rainey's enforcer, protecting her drug trade! Rainey was a viper with legs, taking advantage of a terrified sixteen-year-old who had already lost her sister, her home, her freedom, and was desperate for anyone who would take her in. At least Iris's reason was personal and Barb White's cauliflower ears and lumpy temples, the receiving end of so many shots, would leave anyone with bizarre judgment.

How had he missed this? Since Debbie's accident he had functioned much of the time as if in a coma himself, needing to smack bottom last week for his mental faculties to regain fighting trim. "What were you doing outside my office?"

"Going to commissary."

"That's the long way around."

Rainey squirmed. "I needed the exercise."

"Drop the charge against Fielder," he said. "Screwing with him won't make your life any easier."

"No?" She stood, interview over. "But I'll sleep better."

"Sharks don't sleep. Drop the charge and I'll do my best to see your penalty for smuggling is lighter than you deserve."

She stopped. "You'd do that? Why?"

"We have a mutual friend. I'll also conveniently forget to charge you with throwing urine at me, that class E felony."

She sneered but nodded. Even the antisocial had limits and knew when to give up. "See you around, Eric."

"Let's hope not."

Eric strolled out to the locator desk to check the "Alpha List" for inmate work assignments. Barb White was cell block janitor, but Iris Valentine, the other coconspirator, mopped the floor outside his office on weekends. The last two weekends. He ambled over to the area sergeant. "You know my poster you admire so, the one of the Rangers winning the Stanley Cup? It's yours."

The sarge nodded as his eyes lit up. "How big are the alligators I'll have to wrestle for it?"

"No strings attached. Of course, I've found that on weekends when Iris Valentine is hall porter doing the floors around here, they don't seem to sparkle as much."

"Don't worry. We could assign her to clean toilets."

Eric could always get another poster, and in this place, if someone wanted something badly enough, they had no trouble taking it. He phoned his boss. "Rainey will come to her senses, provided she still has any. I need the rest of the day off for other business, a bloodless resolution of the Amerce case."

"Central Office wants an end to it. Do what you have to."

Eric took the West Side Highway to Manhattan, hoping to find Suzanne and persuade her to give up her vendetta. He parked in a garage near where those pimps had been bludgeoned. Using that as a focus point, he'd fanned out to where Tanya Smith had died. The news reported a young woman's death early this morning, but Suzanne wouldn't kill Marie until the twentieth, giving him three days to check these sunbaked streets until he passed out. Not much of a plan, but his expertise as hunter was limited to searching for clean and unwrinkled clothes in the morning.

Eleven A.M. was the wrong time to prowl, with sidewalks crowded with young females. Many of Midtown's secretaries and their bosses went out early for lunch before it got so hot their spiked heels stuck in softened asphalt that stank like the LaBrea tar pits. Hustlers hawking baubles or jugglers working crowds for change made it resemble a cross between a Renaissance fair and the postmillennial version of Saigon, 1969. Gamblers with phony three-card-monte games took up part of the sidewalks, cramming pedestrians into choke points between them while guys gave out cards advertising seminaked dancing girls.

He roamed for three hours. The torrid air reeked of bus exhaust, excrement—both animal and human—and tension, with everyone poised, expecting something to happen.

Suzanne would do what he was doing, search for Marie, watching all these faces. He paused on Forty-fifth Street and Broadway, scanning the matinee crowds for a tiny woman in shorts or miniskirt. To compound the problem, school was out and high school girls roamed Midtown. The malevolent sun, three days from its brightest, glared down like the clichéd spotlight in a police interrogation room, boiling his cerebral juices. It reflected off the gutters and sidewalks, the heat shimmering, making things appear as if under water. He certainly felt wet enough.

He leaned against the wall of a strip joint to indulge in the six inches of shade it provided while a man giving out flyers boasted of the "live girls" working inside. Yeah, see Mona, Sheila, and Jezebel all hot and sweaty. Would Mona moan?

A guy sidled up to him. "Want reefer? Got coke."

As Eric moved away, the man grabbed his elbow.

Eric whirled, throwing the guy off balance.

"Easy, man," the pusher said. "Didn't mean nothing." He held up his hands, grinned, and vanished in the sweaty throng.

The next felon could go for his thirty-eight or switchblade.

The thermometer on the building across the street read ninety-two, that unholy temperature at which the largest number of homicides occurred, when tolerance and patience evaporated but people retained enough energy to be murderous.

Who was he kidding? If he found Suzanne, he was bound by law to turn her in. Besides, he had a biological daughter and a home to protect, on the off chance Suzanne returned there. Much as he was linked to Suzanne by forces and energies he could not begin to fathom, she was out of luck.

She wouldn't go peaceably, and at the moment of truth he might not have the guts to call the cops. He was putting himself in a no-win situation, either being a snitch or aiding and abetting a fugitive, both likely to make Veronica an orphan.

Sorry, Suzie. Much as he cared for her, she was on her own.

He hung a U-turn and headed for his car, and home.

The loft was deserted, Veronica and the cats still with Cassandra. Eric wandered around, checking wires and window locks. Then he plopped onto the sofa, trying to read but being unable to in the unaccustomed quiet and emptiness, the loft seeming to echo with each footfall, each breath.

Was it worth it, hiding up here without Veronica, jumping at faint or imagined noises? He rose and paced. His paranoia had carried over from work, making him so dysfunctional that all he was protecting was his loneliness.

The phone rang, and he jumped. "Eric, it's Cassandra. I

got to go to New Jersey tomorrow. Can Veronica stay by herself?"

"No, I'd rather have her here at night than alone until you return. Besides, this place is for living, for being with what is left of my family. Veronica is coming home."

Chapter Thirty-eight

Tuesday, June 18

Even with the terrace door and all other windows open wide, the air in Eric's loft remained still and sultry. He went out to lean over the railing to gaze at ships' lights shimmering on the dark, oily waters of the Hudson. How would it all end? Debbie's condition, the job, Suzanne, life. It had all gotten away from him. He'd lost his touch. He was no longer the Answer Man.

The smart thing would be to quit the prison and land another college teaching position, though that meant relocating, uprooting Veronica when she could least afford to be pulled away from her social supports.

On the Day of Atonement, Life was likened to time in a celestial park, until Death, the Lord's Nurse, came to summon home the soul. For some it was a summer's day, for others a winter's morning. For Eric Glass, it was an autumn picnic, gobbled alone.

Where were the cats? They usually draped themselves all over him once Veronica turned in. As he shuffled to the bathroom, a breeze tickled him. If state workers got their first raise in four years, he'd install central air. Despite the heat he took a hot shower to relax his tense body, luxuriating in the steamy needle spray until the water cooled. As he toweled off, the bathroom door opened. "Veronica, wait! I'm not dressed."

"That's what I was counting on."

His hair was clutched, his head yanked back to expose his throat. He started to pivot, to go with it, to spin and smash their nose into their brain, but a bony forearm encircled his neck and something sharp jabbed against his windpipe.

"Eric! Stop unless you want to die. And you deserve it."

He froze in midpunch, as if turned to stone. No! How . . . ?

He'd locked the door, set the alarm!

The pain in his neck let up a trifle.

"Give me your word of honor you won't yell or struggle, and I won't hurt you."

"Suzanne!"

"Suzanne died eight years ago. The name's Scorch."

"Suzanne, I—"

"Promise!"

The pressure and pain increased. He saw his life ebb away.

"Yes," he whispered. "I promise. My daughter . . . ?"

"Never mind her!" The pain in his neck got worse.

"Don't hurt her."

"What the hell you think I am, a child killer?"

More pain, like a savage insect bite. He heard a drop hit the bathroom tile. Then another. His blood!

The blade's pressure eased. "Eric, don't act stupid and I won't hurt you."

He swallowed hard. "Okay, Suzanne. I promise."

"And promise not to call the cops."

"I'm bound by law to—"

"Cut the crap! You always said your word was the most important thing in the world, next to your family. If you don't promise . . . Hell, I won't be responsible! Now swear!"

"Yes. I swear it. What about Veronica?"

"Shut up. Let's go to your bedroom. Now!"

Lucy nodded to DiGiorio as he ambled by. Here goes. "Lieutenant, I suspect last week's shootings near Fordham Road are part of the drug war over Dark Paradise. They seem to center around Saint James Park. If I stake it out . . ."

"Yeah, whatever." He waved her off, his mind clouded by thoughts other than what one of his detectives was cooking up.

"I'd like to be around there most of Thursday."

DiGiorio ripped sheets off the telex. "Just be sure all your paperwork . . ." Then he straightened up, a veteran of so many interrogations. He stared at her until she sweated. "You're up to something, and it isn't a turf war in the park, is it? Don't tell me." He put a hand to his forehead, as if he were a psychic contemplating a cosmic question. "It's a moldy oldie, eight years old and getting older and moldier." He put out his other hand, thumb down. "Scorch Amerce is history, and unless you want to be too, you'll work on unsolved cases like the city expects you to."

"But I'll be in the neighborhood . . ."

"Good. Drop me a line." He walked off, his damage done.

Lucy plopped into her chair and sighed. Nice move, Moreno, forgetting how in this precinct upsetting the mentally constipated caused frustration and static. She brushed damp hair from her face as she filled out a personal-leave form to spend Thursday staking out Creston Avenue with Eric Glass on the off chance he knew what he was doing.

Yes, he did. Despite his messed-up personal life, he knew psychopaths in general and Scorch in particular.

Rather than try to mollify DiGiorio, Lucy dialed Eric again but got yet another busy signal. Who could he be talking to all night? Maybe he was online. She dialed the phone company, asking if they could check if there was trouble on the line.

"We don't ordinarily do this. Is there an emergency?"

She caught herself twisting the phone cord. Should she abuse her authority? "I'm a police officer. I need to speak with this party regarding an investigation." Just a tiny bending of the truth, and she really did want to speak with him.

Fifteen seconds stretched to thirty, then sixty.

"Officer, there doesn't seem to be any damage with the external lines. If might be something as simple as the phone being off the hook at the customer's end. We can check for you."

Why would he disconnect his phone? He had an answering machine if he didn't want to be disturbed. "Yes, please do. My precinct number is 555-7328. Ask for Detective Lucy Moreno."

Eric walked with bent knees as she forced his head back. Options? Few, none good. If he botched an escape move, he'd be dead and so might Veronica. Few people had ever taken as many lives as Suzanne Amerce, and he doubted she'd lose sleep by killing one or two more.

She ushered him to his bedroom, where four red candles flickered on the nightstands. "On the bed." She pointed with a long scissors that tapered to a wicked point. Lucky it hadn't punctured his carotid. "Now take off your towel. I want to see what a circumcised prick looks like." She laughed. "Not a bad pun." Her baby face grew hard. "I want it off!" She ripped the towel from him and shoved him hard, toppling him onto the bed.

He lay on his back, facing her with his arms and legs bent.

She stood at the door, her hair short and wavy now, blond, not much different from Lucy's theoretical composite of her.

His towel lay out of reach even as minimal padding to fend off a frenzied attack. If he survived, he'd never watch reruns of *Fatal Attraction* or *Play Misty for Me* ever again.

"You made friends with cops, Eric. I know! Don't deny it." The point of her scissors, glistening red, waved back and forth like a maestro's baton. "You went to the cops."

"No, they came—"

"Bull! I trusted you like I trusted nobody since Nancy."

What words could delay the inevitable if she was set on violence? "I don't want you to die out there," he said.

"You'd rather see me rot forever in that brothel for the Devil's daughters! What a pal!"

"I want to see you live."

"I'd die before I go back."

She was fixated on death. Keep her talking. Maybe she'd get distracted, or someone would call the cops. Grasp at straws but keep her talking. "Why are you still in New York?" he asked.

With a blur of flesh and steel, the scissors shot half an inch into his oak desk. "Why do you think?" she said.

"Marie?" he said, gambling that wouldn't throw her into a total frenzy of stabbing and slashing. He scooted to the head of the bed to give himself six feet of breathing room.

She sneered "Marie," like it was the ultimate profanity.

"Leave. Forget Marie. Make a life."

"Know what sort of life I've got now?" She flicked on the stereo and fiddled with the knobs until she found a station with a heavy pulsing beat. At no time did her eyes leave him.

She was as close to the door as he was, maybe closer.

Escape was a poor alternative, and then what about Veronica?

"This is my living now." She wriggled out of her miniskirt, tossed it onto the bed, then raised her T-shirt over her head.

His chance, with her vision blocked, her arms encumbered.

If he was quick and silent, he could spring off and plant a side kick into her firm, flat stomach and push her back, maybe even slam the breath from her.

"Uh-uh, Eric. I know what you're thinking." She lowered the shirt and wagged a finger at him. Then she whipped off the shirt, fast as a cobra striking, and danced for him in underwear so sheer he could see her nipples and pubic hair, even in the rippling light of the candles. "Like it, Eric?"

"Not at all," he said. "You're acting like a slut."

The flickering illumination cast multiple shadows against the walls, off the mirror, making him wonder if he was in hell. Perhaps she *had* plunged the scissors into his jugular and he was dead now, with this his hereafter. Tiny scars decorated her stomach and chest, mementos of a mother gone mad with grief.

She stopped shimmying. "Oh, but I am one now, dancing nearly naked every night, but the tips are good and I get plenty of exercise." Her tone had softened. Maybe this was the avenue to explore, the hope of a real future.

"It's a start," he said.

She pursed her lips. "Sure, the start of a great career. A great life. Something I look forward to, like our sessions twice a week." She grabbed the scissors, pushing and pulling until it broke free. She brandished it. "Back when I still thought I had a chance to learn how to live. Back when I believed you."

"I was always sincere. You ready to move on with your life?"

"Maybe." She toyed with the scissors. "Now I don't know anything anymore. Three weeks ago I thought I knew my path, and now I don't know what I'll do tomorrow, or in the next minute."

"Winning involves risk. Ships in the harbor are safe, but that's not what ships are for."

"Whoa, a new platitude, just when I thought you'd given me all of them." She grimaced.

"I thought you believed in what I said."

"I did." She leaned against the desk, stroking the hole she'd made with the scissors. "Back when I believed in you. When I believed in justice." She came closer again. "Why, Eric?"

"The detective—she promised to take you alive."

"She?" Even in the dim light he saw those large dark eyes flash. "Brother, what a line."

They couldn't all be winners. "I believe her. Moreno. She busted you eight years ago."

"Moreno? Moreno! Yeah, I remember her." She sneered. "But all cops and guards are pigs." She came nearer still, so close he could see sweat beading on her body. If he moved quickly . . .

"I won't let her take me. I'd die first. Is that crazy?"

Death again. "I . . . I don't know, Suzanne. I'm not you."

"You'd die for your daughter?"

Still with death. Wrong turn. "Why do you . . . ?"

"Damn, I hate when you answer a question with a question." She paced the room. "You drove me nuts when you did that."

He couldn't help grinning, and then neither could she.

"Yes, I remember you storming out more than once."

She giggled as she peeled off her underwear. "Yeah, and afterward I'd tell Karen you were a jackass and she'd say, 'But aren't they all?' "

Here they were, just a couple of friends, naked, reminiscing about old times. At least she was out of the murderous mode.

"Suzanne, why did you really come?"

She drew herself up to her full height, but she seemed smaller without clothes. "To find out why you worked with the cops."

She wouldn't risk her freedom just for that. "What else?"

She seemed to shrink and, for an instant, in the guttering candlelight, become a child again. "I'm scared." She sat on the edge of the bed, shoulders hunched. "I don't know what to do."

"Escape. I'll give you all the money I have lying around so you can get away." Yeah, right, the Glass millions, all donated to aiding and abetting a fugitive. A killer. Only, she didn't look like a killer now but more like the frightened girl she claimed to be, on the run and afraid to stop and rest.

She ripped the sheet with the scissors. "Marie has to die."

Still harping on death. "She will someday," he said. "And God will judge her."

"There is no God. You should know that better than anyone."

That he should, if only he dared. "In 1946, they found something written in blood on a cellar wall in Cologne, Germany.

"'I believe in the sun, even when it doesn't shine.
I believe in love, even when I am alone.
And I believe in God, even when He is silent.'"

She crawled across the bed, making him want to wriggle into the headboard, but he could only wait for her. She wrapped her arms around him, but even though her body was hot, she shivered. "Eric, make love to me." Her scissors poked his kidney.

"Huh?" he said as he tried to untangle himself, but she clung tighter, as if fearful of drowning.

"Don't you want to?" Her breath tickled his ear as she whispered, "I always wanted to. I know you did, too."

He had, a couple of times, when caught up in her conscious or subconscious seductions, feeling dirty and lecherous afterward, then going home and humping Debbie until they were both near exhaustion. "No," he lied. "I love you like a father, and I'd crawl through razor wire for you, but you . . ."

Despite himself he was aroused by her firm breasts, her warm solid thighs, the scent of her. After all this time the dam of his resolve was splitting, letting repressed and profane desires pour out. In the end, raw passion is so overpowering.

Her hands were roaming now, stroking a sudden erection that was so stiff it hurt. "Your words lie," she said. "Karen said this is the only part of a man that tells the truth."

Her hot, moist mouth sucked at him like a leech, vacuuming up his will. If he gave in to her it would be the final betrayal of his profession, his marriage, whatever he still held sacred.

She pushed him against the pillows and straddled him.

"No," he said, hands on her waist, ready to pitch her off.

"Yes." She pressed the scissors' point into the hollow between his ribs, and he winced. "I've been pushed around enough. Now I take charge." She raised the scissors and studied its point while planting her free hand—warm and damp—against his chest, leaning with all her weight.

Clicking the scissors open, closed, open, its blades glinting in the candlelight, she stared at his erection. As he braced for escape she reached behind her, pulled a foil packet from a skirt pocket, and snipped. A condom. When he shifted his weight to rise, she again poked him with the scissors. "Uh-uh. Play time with this 'Coney Island Whitefish.' Let's see if it fits like a glove." She unrolled it onto his erection, balancing herself with the palm of her hand, the

302

scissors warm on his chest. She lowered herself, working him into her. She perched, her grin mischievous in the candlelight. "Now, don't go soft on me."

"My daughter . . ."

"Yes, I wanted to be. Oh, you mean little Veronica? Don't worry, I won't tell her. Shush. No noise. Cover my mouth." She grabbed his palm with her free hand and clapped it to her lips as she pumped her pelvis, faster and faster.

In the flickering candlelight it seemed like the Gates of Hell had shattered to release a plague of succubi.

She started to moan, then scream. She clamped his hand tighter over her mouth. Her nostrils flared and closed, snorting faster. Faster. Her hips shot back and forth as if on pistons, her small muscular thighs flexing, squeezing his ribs.

In her frenzy the scissors dug deeper. He grabbed it with his free hand but could barely push it back a millimeter as she bucked and gyrated, her weight coming forward, holding that pointed steel in place.

Then a last muffled scream and shudder.

He lost his fight for control and joined her in climax, the danger of the moment adding too much to the excitement.

His first true orgasm these last five years.

She uncovered her mouth and looked down on him with the first real smile he'd ever seen from her. "Whew, what . . . a ride." She rolled off and lay beside him, panting. "Don't suppose . . . you have . . . cigarettes?"

"Smoking is bad for you." As was sex with someone holding a weapon against your heart. He eased the scissors from her, its tip covered with a quarter inch of his blood. "You have to go."

He flipped the scissors across the bed.

"In a . . . minute . . . Got to . . . catch my breath."

He could smother her with a pillow while she gasped for air. No jury would convict him. Who was he kidding? He couldn't do it to Debbie, and neither would he suffocate

Suzanne. Which of these two women loved him less, or drained him more?

"No," he said. "I mean away from here. New York. Marie."

She nestled against him, her heart thumping. "I need you."

Christ! Still? "You're a grown woman now, Suzanne. You can make it on your own."

"I told you, I'm frightened. It's scary out there." She sounded like a child again, like Veronica those first few years as Debbie lay comatose.

"So? Join the club."

"You too?" she murmured, caressing his chest, drawing circles in his sweat with her finger.

"Especially me."

She glanced at the middle of the sheets, grabbed the towel, and blotted at a dark wet spot. "Ugh, sorry about the mess," she said. "Gross. I remember you saying how Orthodox Jews display the stained sheet to the wedding guests to show both families they postponed their ultimate pleasure so they could make a trophy of it. No offense, but I think that's nuts." She grinned. "Yes, deflowered, finally, like a cherry bush, saving myself for my first love." She giggled, wadded up the towel, and crawled back into his arms. Her breathing slowed, became normal. He could wait until she dozed, tie her wrists, and call the cops.

Then they'd cart her back to prison, where word would get out he'd turned her in and his life there would become more hellish than it already was. And Suzanne would be successful in her next suicide attempt. He became a healer to help people, but often that path was obscure and winding, with few signposts.

She had done her minimum eight and a third years for manslaughter one, the valid sentence. She had paid her debt.

"Suzie, wake up, shower, grab some money, and go."

He scooped her up and carried her to the bathroom. This time the hand around his neck was tender, stroking him until he got chills. He quivered despite himself.

"You like my body?" she whispered.

Yes, as revolted as he was by that admission. He turned the faucets and placed her in the tub. She lifted her arms.

"Her Majesty wishes I soap her?"

"That's what Karen always did," she said.

Talk about gross. "Do it yourself. It'll wake you up."

While she washed, he considered calling Lucy. Christ, what had he just done? And what should he do now? Once again they'd brought out the best and worst in each other. As he vacillated she came out, dried off, and rummaged through the clean laundry basket. She pulled out a pair of Veronica's pink cotton hipsters. "See, your daughter's underwear fits me. We could be twins."

The only resemblance was physical. "Suzanne, you've got to go now! Quickly!"

"Yeah, always giving orders. Maybe I want seconds."

So did he, but second chances happen only in Hollywood. She watched him scoop her red satin bikinis off the bedroom carpet. He could imagine Veronica's questions in the morning.

"Save those as a souvenir," she said as she finished dressing. "You won't call the cops?" she asked.

She'd read his mind once again. "I promised. Now go. Quick." He fumbled in his wallet for whatever bills he had.

She pushed his hand away. "If I take money, I graduate from tramp to whore." She stood on tiptoe to kiss him. "I'm sorry I brutalized you before, but you know what I can be like."

Indeed he did. In eight years she had mutated from angel to demon. He'd be safer juggling nitroglycerine.

"Eric, I needed to see you, to get answers, but I lost control as usual. You mean so much to me."

Joel Ross

And she to him. What could he do—hide her in the spare bedroom, claiming she was his distant cousin? No, he needed her to leave as badly as he wanted her to stay. Besides, one night he might wake to find her standing over him clutching a lethal weapon, ticked off by some real or imagined slight from earlier that day, that week.

"I circumvented your alarm by snipping an exposed wire and creeping up the stairs below the sensors. And get new locks on your door. I picked them in three minutes using a small slotted screwdriver and tweezers. I've become a woman of many talents."

"The best talent is to be selective in love. Be careful. Be safe. Learn to trust, but use good judgment."

"Okay." She squirmed. "Enough already."

He held her face, committing her features to a final memory. "What will you do?" he asked. "Will you forget about Marie?"

She pried his hands off, kissed him one last time, long and hard, and looked away. "Probably. See ya." She skipped away.

Had he talked her out of vengeance? Maybe.

He stood naked on the terrace to watch her walk out the building and around the corner. "Good-bye, Suzanne," he whispered.

Once again, she was out of his life, out on her own, for good or evil.

He went back to the bed and lifted the phone. A man bound by ethics must obey the law, but sometimes ethics supersede man's law. And sometimes he must honor his word above all else, because in the end, what else is there?

He replaced the receiver, snuffed out the candles, and lay in darkness, remembering, inhaling her scent until it faded.

Gone.

Chapter Thirty-nine

Scorch smiled as a wilted Marie, her damp street clothes clinging to her, trudged four blocks to the grocery. What kind of mother leaves a six-year-old alone? For that reason alone, Marie deserved to die before she made her child into her own twisted image. Bearing a child isn't the same as raising one, and Marie must figure her function as a mother ended until she had another bun baking in her oven.

Scorch figured she had forty minutes for her plan to lure Marie to the old neighborhood on the eighth anniversary. The only problem was if Marie wasn't food shopping but merely getting beer and cigarettes; but having watched Marie's routine for two days, Scorch figured she had enough time. Once satisfied that Marie was gone, Scorch headed across the street and slipped inside, the downstairs lock still broken from when she had jimmied it with her screwdriver. "Learn lock picking in your spare time at our cramped correctional facility," Midland Knoll's color brochure could read. The flathead screwdriver, the scissors, and a pair of pliers should get her past the lone remaining apartment lock.

How had dumb Marie managed to live this long? Probably fate, saving her for Scorch, but if fate were that kind, it would have killed them both long ago and spared everyone what was about to happen. Marie hadn't yet replaced the two glued locks on her door, something Scorch anticipated. The remaining one wasn't a formidable dead bolt, and while she had tools to pick it or yank it out with a screwdriver and wrench, six P.M. meant she didn't have a whole lot of time to work unnoticed or undisturbed.

As she wriggled the screwdriver in the cylinder, she tried for Plan B. Would the kid open for her? What was her name? From across the street it had sounded like Calli. Scorch rapped on the door. Nothing. Pressing her ear against the warm metal, Scorch heard a TV. I know you're in there, little piggy, and I'll get you out. Scorch leaned on the buzzer until small feet scuffled closer, the kid tearing herself away from cartoons.

What kind of mother leaves her child . . . ?

"Who's there?" demanded a small voice.

"Calli," Scorch said in her most authoritarian yet motherly voice. "I . . ."

"Kala."

Right. "Kala, I'm a friend of your mommy, Marie. She's been hurt. She needs you to come to her."

Silence. The kid was processing this or had fallen asleep.

"Kala?"

"Mama says never open the door to strangers."

"I'm not a stranger. How could I be a friend if I was a stranger?" Irrefutable logic at any age. "Kala, Mommy needs you."

Something scraped against the floor inside. A barricade? Scorch couldn't kick this in. Think of something else. A lock turned. The kid had pushed a chair to the door to reach it.

Scorch pushed, hitting a chair. "Kala, move the chair back so I can come in."

"What's your name?"

"Sue."

The chair scraped against the floor again. If she knew her name, then it was all right. Amazing how a child's brain works.

Scorch came into a stuffy apartment, one sealed off from the world. Kala wore only clean but torn underwear. What sort of mother . . . ? "Hi," Scorch said. She held out the note she'd written on orange paper. "We'll leave this on your refrigerator in case the super comes, looking for Mommy."

Scorch could wait here, surprise the bitch, and slit her throat before she knew who killed her, but where was the pleasure in that? Besides, she didn't want the child to see it and then carry that horror for the rest of her life, to spread more poison to others like her mother had.

If she lured Marie to the Bronx, would she come alone? The only friends Marie had had died in the Bronx eight years ago, and anyone she was close to now was, like the late Tanya, bound by fear or intimidation. If Marie came with a group? So what?

Let them learn what a witch they hung with and why she deserved to die. And if Scorch died too . . . ?

The odds on her staying free were poor. At some point a cop visiting the Crystal Cavern would recognize her or see her photo in the post office or on *America's Most Wanted*.

At least this way she'd take Marie with her.

More important, Marie would suffer as she hurried to the Bronx while tasting the dread of knowing the only one she loved was dead or in danger of becoming so.

That pain alone would make it all worthwhile.

Scorch took Kala's hand and escorted her into the kitchen, where she stuck the message on the refrigerator with a magnet.

MARIE YOU LOUSY BITCH. IF YOU WANT TO SEE YOUR LITTLE PIGLET ALIVE AND STILL RECOGNIZABLE AS A LIVING CHILD—LET ALONE YOUR CHILD—COME TO 1972 MORRIS AVENUE, ALONE, ASAP.

REMEMBER THAT ADDRESS? REMEMBER EIGHT YEARS AGO? COME ALONE. REMEMBER MY NEW NAME. SCORCH! DON'T BE LATE. SEE YA.

Kala stared, wide-eyed, as Scorch rifled through drawers for decent underwear and clothes to dress her for the turning point of her life.

"Ready?" Scorch asked, smiling but hating the fact that she wasn't hating herself for doing this to an innocent child. Still, if Kala were raised much longer by Marie, she would lose that innocence, and probably her humanity as well.

"Uh-huh," said Kala, holding out the key dangling from a cord around her neck.

"Good idea," said Scorch. She took the key, did a quick inventory of the apartment, grabbed duct tape, and headed out, clutching Kala's hand. "Want to go in a taxi?" Scorch asked.

The kid better say "yes," because she had no choice.

Once outside, Scorch prayed they didn't run into anybody who knew Marie, but that was a long shot. If anybody had fewer friends than Scorch, it was Marie. A greater concern was if the kid started crying or yelling or tried to run away.

If that happened Scorch would have to brazen it out, hustle Kala away from the tenement, and dump her somewhere before she ran back and waited to execute her mommy.

The child stayed passive, ready to be herded uptown. Great. No matter what Marie had done, vengeance should not be extended to this child, who might someday grow up warped like her mother but was now still innocent.

For an instant Scorch thought of poor Eric, probably home with his daughter, concluding that he had talked her out of revenge.

Sorry, Eric. Karen won the battle of wills and spirit.

She smiled down at Kala. "This will be fun."

That it will be. Scorch flagged a cab and ushered Kala inside. "Metropolitan Hospital," she said. "Ninety-sixth."

"Why are your hands shaking?" Kala asked.

Scorch looked down. Yes, she was trembling. "I'm nervous about seeing your mommy again," she said. And that was no lie.

Up ahead a sea of red taillights shone back at them, but the driver seemed unconcerned with his meter running. They slowed, and Kala fidgeted. Scorch wrapped her arm around the child, gave her a lollipop, and pointed out tugs on the river, birds in the air, everything out there that might amuse a six-year-old. That killed a good five minutes. "Let's sing," suggested Scorch.

What songs did they learn in kindergarten?

The kid shrugged her ignorance. What irony if Scorch was so delayed by traffic that Marie got to the Bronx ahead of her.

"I get off here," the driver said, as if expecting applause as he pulled off onto York Avenue and shot uptown. Scorch rolled up the window when she got a whiff of hydrogen sulfide.

"Ugh," said Kala. "Bad eggs." She held her nose.

Scorch tousled Kala's hair, wishing the next few hours were over with. It wasn't too late to turn around and head for Vegas.

Was she a murderess or an executioner? Would she slaughter someone in cold blood or hot?

Which was more likely to leave her like Marie?

"Where's Mama?" Kala asked, craning her neck, as if her

311

mother were on the streets that whizzed past.

"Soon." Not soon enough. Scorch patted Kala's hand.

"I want to see Mama!"

"Me too, Kala. Just a few minutes more. Driver?"

The cabbie held up his hands in mute surrender. "Stadium traffic, maybe," he said. Just her luck the Yankees were in town this evening. Who would have thought she needed to consult the baseball schedule before planning an execution?

"Stop here," Scorch said. She slipped him a ten and marched Kala toward the emergency room.

Chapter Forty

Marie trudged up the steps, drained and sticky, wishing for the millionth time that she lived in an elevator building. She was getting too old for this. "Kala, Mommy's home."

The television was on, Road Runner or some other cartoon.

"Kala. I'm home." She dumped the groceries on the kitchen table and looked around the room. "Kala, you on the toilet?"

She peeked through the open bathroom door. Empty. She went into the bedroom. Kala wasn't on her bed, or under it.

"Kala, if you're hiding in the closet, you got two seconds to come out before I tan your little buns. Kala!"

This was no time for hide-and-seek. Marie yanked open the door, expecting to see her daughter jump out. "Kala!"

Marie switched off the TV, hoping that would get the kid to pop out of whatever hole she had found to hide in. Back in the kitchen, she saw the note on orange paper stuck on the fridge. She tore it off, the magnet clanking to the floor.

Morris Avenue! Scorch, alive! She had Kala!

The dwarf demon, here in her home, stealing her child!

Marie reached into her bag for the revolver, yanking combs, lipsticks, and loose change out with it. What could she do with it now? The damage had been done. She stuck the gun into the damp waistband of her jeans and draped her soggy shirt over it.

Come alone . . .

Like hell.

Marie dialed Cal, got his answering machine. Who else? None of her few friends would dare help. She phoned Paulo, but he was also out, no doubt enjoying the longest evening.

Some evening . . . Her daughter was kidnapped, threatened with mutilation. Dismemberment.

The gun hung heavy against her sweaty skin. They had all been so sure Scorch was gone, but Marie knew. She'd known from day one who had left those little voodoo reminders of Tanya those nights, who had gummed up her locks, had been watching, waiting just for this moment. Damn!

She slapped the refrigerator, then swept the kitchen table clear of napkins, mail, whatever. She longed for a joint, but this was one time when she really needed a clear head. Think.

She poured herself a glass of cola, wishing it were bourbon.

Options? None. She couldn't go to the police.

Let us get this straight, Miss Balboa. You ordered the murder of this girl's sister, and now you got the nerve to ask us to help you when she comes looking for payback? You have the right to an attorney. If you cannot afford one . . .

What if she didn't show?

Would Scorch wait until midnight, then go away?

Would she leave a dead six-year-old when she did?

No way Marie could chance that. The only positive thing she had ever done was give birth to an illegitimate child. Not much of an accomplishment, but if she walked away from this now Scorch might as well have killed her.

No, she had to go up there. She had been a fair mother at best for Kala, but she could always get better, couldn't she?

She flipped back her pillow and got her knife, the one she'd carried for five years as a Tigress, before AIDS, turf wars, jail, and finally Scorch, wiped the gang out.

Would Scorch hurt Kala? Marie remembered the damage done to Lily, to Minerva, their skulls fractured in a dozen places.

Sure she would. Scorch herself had been hurt too badly, first by the Tigresses, then by those jackals in prison, feasting on a cute, tiny girl. So should she go into Scorch's trap, gun blazing, or slink up there with her knife? She knew the area, having prowled it all those years as a feral child in a jungle partly of her own making.

What the hell should she have done instead, flipped patties in Burger King? Washed dishes? Worked in a sweatshop sewing cheap skirts at a buck an hour? She had been fifteen when she had joined the Tigresses, just . . .

Just the same age as Scorch the Slaughterer.

What goes around comes around.

She went back to dialing up anybody she had ever known, hoping someone, anyone, might come through for her so she didn't have to face this alone.

Chapter Forty-one

Thursday, June 20

Scorch ducked into the alley leading to the doorway of the Tigresses' burnt-out apartment where she had lost her innocence and they their lives eight years ago. Though the blood had long since washed away, she still heard their screams and coughs, still saw the blur of naked flesh as they piled out, going down under her frenzied flailing. She smelled the sickening stench of singed hair and flesh and heard herself screaming, "That's for Nancy! That's for Nancy!" Sorry, Nancy.

She touched the doorknob, then pulled back as if it were electrified. Get in before someone saw her or she lost her nerve. Was this ruin now a nest for junkies to snort, shoot, or deal? No, the blackened door remained locked. On either side, faded gold-leaf tigers glinted through slitted lids— arrogant predators. She slammed her hip against the warped door two, three times.

The frame split and she slipped inside, out of the light.

Squeals. The rustle of junk. The tap of claws on wood as something scurried past. Her eyes grew accustomed to darkness that made her feel she was wrapped in a wet blanket. She must be the first human to set foot in here in nearly a decade. Accessible yet secluded, the apartment had been given a wide berth by both local kids and addicts, as if haunted.

Or cursed. So this was what it looked like on the inside, this place where she had earned her jailhouse name and her notoriety, where three heartless girls spent their last night before waking to flames and smoke, groping, arms outstretched, choking, shrieking, falling, writhing, crying. Dying.

For what? A hovel? A snake den?

A few bars of light leaked through cracks in the warped plywood boards over windows facing Morris Avenue, enabling her to see a rotting sofa where they must have rutted and snorted. That freaking armchair must have been where Marie sat while plotting to shake down the block for cash for drugs, boys, and booze. On that table, dark with soot-covered dust and smoke-blackened plaster, they must have done their coke and smack.

The humid air reeked of mildew, rot. Animal droppings. A charred door led to the bedroom where she'd lobbed her firebomb. She stepped toward it. No! The sight and stink might send her out screaming, into Marie's knife. The early-summer heat and humidity was almost too heavy to breathe, but she sucked in fungi and mold that had festered here since that nightmarish three A.M.

She angled the couch to monitor both the door and window, flipped over a funky cushion on the smoke-cured sofa, and settled in before easing the pimp's pistol from her waistband. She retracted its slide an inch. Loaded and chambered. Next she drew the scissors. She'd like to do the deed noiselessly, but getting close enough to puncture so small and hard a target as Marie's heart would challenge even an experienced knife fighter.

The twenty-five-caliber pistol should be almost as quiet.

What if Marie called the cops? If so, she'd have to explain why an escaped con kidnapped her child. That could only lead to more explanations, the last of which should earn her shiny handcuffs and a recitation of Miranda rights.

Scorch's stomach tightened at the thought of cops busting in, but quitting now meant returning to a flophouse room and a career as a stripper. Better to finish what she had started.

Marie would come. She had to. Even the lowest life-form protects its young, sacrificing all for them.

Maybe Scorch had discovered a new species of mother, one that would rather abandon her offspring than risk her own life.

The heat of the longest day drenched her, weighing down her eyelids. She stretched, stood, and paced. If she wasn't alert like at Midland Knolls, she'd wind up back there or alongside Nancy in Woodlawn Cemetery. This sucked. She had to remain sharp indefinitely in this stultifying, moldy air, while Marie could pick and choose her moment to attack, maybe hours from now.

Outside something stirred, scratched at the burned wood. She thumbed off the gun's safety and clutched the scissors for a thrust to the spleen or liver, depending on the opening after her first feint. If she missed or the pistol misfired, she'd rush Marie, her whole being focused on the tawny throat for a death slash, no matter where Marie's blade pierced her.

Dr. Glass said that was the samurai's secret, to be so bent on killing their killer with focused spirit, pure psychic energy.

As she crouched, ready to spring, a rat peeked in, nose and whiskers quivering. It stared with beady eyes.

"Scram," Scorch whispered. "I'm waiting for your big sister." The rat glared, bared its teeth, then backed away.

Scorch let out the breath she didn't know she'd been holding and leaned against the wall, feeling the scratchiness of heat-curled paint through her damp T-shirt. What was the point? If Marie didn't get her, the cops would. She'd never live to have her own child, see the Pyramids, or leave any mark other than as an angel of death.

Something squealed in the alley. Someone stomped. A kid taking a shortcut home, or had her invited guest arrived? Scorch wiped her palm on her miniskirt and left a damp smudge. Don't punk out. Keep sharp. Finish what you came to do. She tried to swallow, but the saliva didn't come, and it had nothing to do with the temperature.

Another footstep, like that a two-legged rodent would make if sneaking up on someone. Scorch counted to one hundred, then two hundred. The new silence was thicker than the dead air in this apartment. Was it just imagination? Hallucination? The heat?

The door moved a millimeter, as if a hot draft had zipped through the alley. Scorch breathed through her mouth to avoid even a telltale whistle of air through her nose. Nothing. One minute became two, three. The door creaked again as it opened another millimeter. Her pistol's handle grew slippery in her palm as she leveled it at the entrance. No doubt about it. Scorch's next breath failed to relax the tightness in her chest.

The tip of a blade shone from dim light filtering in from the alley, followed by the rest of the knife. The door swung wide and there she was, fear diluting the hate in her eyes, but still the same witch from eight years ago. She looked left. Right. Saw Scorch's gun aimed at her breast.

"Hi, Marie. Remember me?"

Marie froze, eyes widening. Her hands, large for a woman's, weren't big enough to hide the knife in her hand, but Scorch had the pistol. "Drop the blade or bleed out all over," she said.

319

"Where is she?" Marie cried. "Where's Kala?" She shifted her grip on the knife handle as if preparing to fling it.

Scorch aimed between Marie's breasts. Even with a short barrel, at this range she couldn't help but hit some vital organ.

They held each other's gaze, sweat running down their faces. Then Marie nodded, as if she had known Scorch all her life. The dagger clattered to the charred floorboards, handle toward her, as the last Tigress surrendered her claw.

The years had made Marie hard without making her strong.

"Good. Back away. Good. Now, down on your knees. Now!"

Marie knelt, palms on the floor, and eyed her dagger, a tempting foot away, worth a desperate lunge.

"Smart move," Scorch said. "Now, lace your fingers together and clamp both hands over your mouth. Do it!"

Marie started to stand, then, glaring, knelt, hands clenched, staring alternately at Scorch and her knife.

Scorch pointed the gun at Marie's belly and thumbed back its hammer. "All right, we'll do it this way. They say it's a real painful, lingering death."

"No, wait!" Marie said. Her eyes flicked around the dump before settling on the bedroom door. "My baby! Where's Kala?"

"Do as I say and maybe I'll tell you."

"Please!" Marie said before clasping hands over her face.

"Why are those least deserving of mercy the first to demand it?" Scorch said as she circled Marie like a mongoose meeting its first cobra. She kicked the knife away, nudged the door closed, and watched Marie's chest heave. Was the viper really scared? Good, now *she* knew the feeling. Scorch sneered. "Last time I saw little Kala, she was in Metropolitan Hospital's emergency room," she said.

Marie's eyes flamed. Hah, her little darling was probably

getting more attention now than at any time since her birth.

Marie hummed "please" again.

"I'll bet Nancy begged." Scorch pointed the gun again. "I fought hard not to be a monster like you. I never killed in *cold* blood." She scratched an insect bite on her arm with the pistol's sight. "I resemble you too much as it is." So to kill, or not? After all this time, to still have second thoughts. Maybe just kneecap Marie, leave her crippled, hobbling for forty years, every pain-racked day a reminder of her sins?

As Scorch edged closer, her pistol still beyond Marie's reach, the door creaked, then slammed open.

Chapter Forty-two

Thursday, June 20

Bits of ice rattled inside the paper cup as Lucy slurped the melted remains of her soda. "Three hours wasted on a useless stakeout on Creston Avenue," she said as she brushed aside a lock of hair plastered to her forehead. "Maybe we should pack it in." She crunched the ice. "Scorch won't show."

"She'll come," Eric said. "I could tell two days ago. She avoided eye contact when I asked what she'd do, and her voice got lower. You don't collect that much rage and hate and let it just evaporate. We have to be as patient as she."

"I'm going for another drink." Lucy shielded her eyes from the baleful glow of a setting sun that had cooked them but good in her navy-blue car. Her damp blouse clung, showing her nipples all too well, but Eric, gentleman that he was, had pretended not to notice. She headed for the corner bodega for a bottle of Mavi, its leaves freshly fermented in Puerto Rico. How could she have let Eric sell her on his prediction that Scorch would lure Marie up here to kill her?

It sounded good at the time and gave her a place to set up and wait. In this heat it beat wandering Midtown, clueless as to the whereabouts or appearance of either woman.

Someone squawked down the block. A tall kid with a backward baseball cap grabbed a woman's bag and took off down an alley. Gray things scattered as he ran past, favoring one leg. Eric saw the purse-snatching and piled out of the car toward her.

"That's the kid who spit on me two weeks ago," Lucy said. That day when she hadn't worn her bulletproof vest because it was so hot, though not as torrid as today. "I'm going after him. Dial 911, say 'Officer—Shield 8759—needs assistance on 1969 Creston Avenue.' Wait for them. Don't budge from here." She moved without discussion, unsnapping her holster before going to the side of the building as she had two weeks ago. If she were paired with somebody like Sanders this evening, *he* would be the one playing middle-aged cowboy, but she was alone, officially off duty, to do it herself, the hard way. Dark things—cats or rats—shifted in the shadows, stirring up the stench of things lying around too long in this weather. Rap and Spanish music floated and bounced off the hot brick.

Things rattled and banged from within the warren of alleys separating these graffiti-scrawled tenements. Knowing that meant trouble, tenants slammed their windows shut above Lucy as she followed the kid. The alley ended in a T. She paused, partly to calm her racing heart, partly to listen for the telltale sound of heavy breathing, but despite his twisted ankle of two weeks ago the kid's desperation had probably helped him escape.

Which way? Faced with decisions, she always made the wrong choice. Wrong man, wrong career, wrong moves every one.

She turned left, both hands steadying her pistol in front of her. The sun had passed this alley a while ago, but the shadows still steamed. Another step. Another. Dead end. An air shaft.

A garbage can clattered behind her, and she whirled to see a huge brown rat scamper off. Sweat coursing down her did little to cool her from the ninety-plus temperature.

False alarm. Her knees shook. Stop. Control. She inched back to the main alleyway, about to holster her Glock when she heard voices from farther down. She looked away, knowing vision was more acute out of the corner of her eye.

Nothing there. Taking a deep breath, she eased the Glock forward again, waiting for the piercing pain, the shock of a hollow-point bullet expanding inside her, shredding her organs.

Maybe she'd be lucky and get it in the head, never hearing or feeling the shot that murdered her. That was her, Lucky Lucy.

She advanced, Glock in the "Weaver stance," arms extended to form a triangle of her body.

Muffled voices echoed between eighty-year-old walls as her arms trembled from the strain of holding them straight.

A charred basement apartment was to her left. Was the "perp" there, boasting to buddies? Maybe it was a TV program. She'd give anything to see Eric Glass run up right now. Lucy took a breath, letting the adrenaline run its course through her body.

Windows shut moments ago during her dash into the alley, sealing in the summer heat, opened again, letting out cooking scents, conversations, arguments, and heavy Latino beats.

From the burnt-out apartment door, slightly ajar, came those voices again, high-pitched. Women's voices.

Lucy tiptoed up and peeked in. Nothing. False alarm. As she turned to leave, she heard a female voice, intense, stressed.

Lucy peered. In the dimness a small blonde in a miniskirt pointed a pistol at a woman who knelt, hands over her mouth.

Scorch! With Marie or an innocent bystander? Here? Of course, the site of the Morris Avenue Massacre! Eric had the right date and neighborhood, but the wrong street and crime.

Scorch was no kamikaze. She'd want to give herself a chance to escape by killing Marie in a secluded place, a private act.

Storming in and screaming might precipitate the slaughter. Even if Eric had called in the purse-snatching, backup might not be here yet or, arriving and not seeing her or another cop, would conclude it was a crank call and leave. No time to go back and wait. She moved the door another few inches. Just a slight creak. The larger woman, on her knees, resembled mug shots from eight years ago. It was Marie! Scorch *had* found her!

Scorch shook her head. "Why are the people who most demand justice and mercy the ones least ready to grant it themselves?"

"Mmph?" The kneeling woman hummed her fear.

Scorch glared down at her as she rubbed her arm with the pistol. She shook her head, as if debating an unspoken question. Then she sighed. "I fought so hard not to be a monster like you. I never killed in *cold* blood, but I resemble you too much as it is." She glared at Marie and seemed about to aim her gun again.

Lucy's cue. She shouldered the door aside and yelled, "Stop! Police! Freeze, Scorch!"

Scorch tensed, twisted, then relaxed. "Hey, if it isn't Detective Moreno, Eric's buddy, to the rescue, like the cavalry. This doesn't concern you, Moreno. It's between us killers."

"Scorch, put down your pistol. Down. Now!"

"Do-gooders, for the wrong side. If you'd waited a few

seconds, the world would have been a better place. But there's a difference between being merciless and pitiless." Scorch laid her automatic on a blackened table. "Law and order! What a crock!"

The woman reached into her sweaty waistband, pulled out a chromed, snub-nosed revolver, and leveled it at Scorch.

"I said freeze!" yelled Lucy, her extended Glock now with the woman in its front sight.

Marie aimed at Scorch, then Lucy, and then back at Scorch.

"You don't have to do this," Lucy said, ignoring Scorch while aiming at the woman. "Just drop the gun, get out of here, and I'll handle Scorch."

"Cop, get real," Scorch said. "This is Marie the Tigress, a cold-blooded bitch who'd shoot you too. To her, killing is as pleasurable as sex." She grinned eerily. "Maybe for her it *is* sex. Leave while you got the chance."

Marie aimed at Lucy's chest, her eyes wide. Lucy kept her own gun up, unsure how long she could maintain a stand-off. In the dimness the sweat glistened on Marie.

"Go while you can, Moreno," said Scorch. "Quick. Her time bomb is ticking fast. Take it from one who's done her own personal countdown for far too long."

"We're all walking out together," Lucy said.

"I'm tired of walking," Scorch said. "Tired of running, of hating. The whole nine yards." She collapsed onto a burnt, moldy chair, as if gravity had finally claimed her. "Christ!"

"Let's go, both of you," said Lucy, looking from Scorch to Marie. "C'mon, Marie, for your own sake."

Marie aimed at Scorch, her arm tensing as she pulled the trigger. Just a dull click. She fired again. Another dud.

"No!" yelled Lucy, lining Marie up in her sights. Marie's eyes widened even more as she turned toward Lucy, who saw the muzzle flash from Marie's gun, felt a hot punch as lead burrowed into her chest, felt her legs turn to water, refusing to support her. Lucy returned fire as the pain, sizzling, fanned out to steal her breath before turning cold, so cold. Unable to move, to scream, Lucy collapsed like a pile of old cloths and coughed out a thick, red foamy clot. Breathing became torture.

Lung shot.

Marie yelped and hobbled off.

Scorch, off the couch, grabbed a soggy cushion and lifted Lucy's head. Lucy, unable to move, feared she'd suffer the fate Debbie Glass had escaped last week, smothered while helpless. She tried to shake her head "no," but nothing worked, her body unable to obey as wave upon wave of frigid pain rolled through her.

Scorch bunched up the cushion and placed it under Lucy's head, then snatched Marie's knife to slice Lucy's skirt into strips to bind the pumping wound. Scorch tried to secure the cloth with duct tape, but the spurting blood soaked through the cotton, staining it dark red, making her blouse and flesh too slippery for the tape to hold.

Scorch tore off more tape, trying to stanch the flow. "Oh God, Nancy, you're bleeding so bad! I'm trying, Nancy! I can't stop it!" She shook her head, and a tear leaked from the corner of one eye. "Sorry. Never mind. You blew that one, Moreno. Was it worth it, one good girl for one bitch?" She placed two fingers to Lucy's throat as she consulted a fancy watch. "Christ, so much blood . . . ! I'm trying! Don't you die too!"

Lucy heard Eric's voice out on the street and opened her mouth to scream, but only whimpered. Frothy blood spilled out.

Scorch peeled off more tape. "I should gag you," she said, winding more strips on the wound before getting them to stick and hold the skirt scraps in place. She held more tape near Lucy's mouth, as if measuring it for size or color, before binding the wound. "I think the bleeding is slowing. You have to get to the hospital. Sorry, Moreno, but I got to run. Can you talk?"

Lucy shook her head, her mouth and throat again filling with thick, salty blood.

Scorch turned Lucy's head to the side. "There, now the gunk can drool out without you choking on it. Learned that in first-aid class. Don't go anywhere." She snatched up her gun and gazed at Lucy. "Give Eric my love, Moreno." She shook her head. "Tell him he won, I think." Scorch dashed to the end of the alley and screamed "Fire!" before taking off in the opposite direction.

In the sudden quiet, things moved from the shadows; gray scurrying creatures scuttled across the apartment floor.

The rats had come to reclaim their home!

Lucy tried to move, but everything grew dim, a dark, damp fog rolling in, shrouding her. More scrabbling behind her.

From far beyond she saw a pinpoint of light.

She drifted toward it, spiraling closer, faster and faster.

As the light became as large as a new dime held at arm's length, she felt sharp pains in her back, her legs.

From very far away . . . a man's voice. Eric? Shouting . . .

The light was larger now, closer as she swirled toward it.

As big as a nickel at arm's length. Now a quarter.

The pain in her legs got worse. There wouldn't even be much of Lucy Moreno left for them to find and bury if the rats had their way. Despite that, she had to fight!

Where the hell was the backup?

She heard more yelling, farther away, as cold fog thickened. She floated again, the light now larger than a silver dollar, so warm and inviting. Fight! The light contracted a bit.

She couldn't move. Did she want to spend the next forty

years as a quadriplegic, trapped in a wasted body?

The light shrank and faded. She sank into a warm velvety darkness, like a July night, or freshly poured tar.

Scorch sprinted out of the alley, glad to be alive. She froze when she saw the red splotches glistening on the hot concrete. A second chance, after blowing it by letting Marie live a few extra moments. Like any wounded animal, Marie would be doubly dangerous now, but like Hansel and Gretel's bread crumbs, the blood would lead Scorch to her. Shot in the thigh, Marie couldn't run fast or far. With luck, the cop's slug had nicked her femoral artery and the bitch would die in minutes, cheap justice for once.

The drops grew smaller and more widely spaced.

Damn!

Scorch tiptoed closer, wary of ambush. Did the last Tigress still have her gun? Who paid attention to such details when hot lead was zipping all around? Scorch came to the junction of two alleys on Creston, near where she had holed up eight years ago when Tigress-hunting. Up ahead, toward the mouth of the alley, garbage cans stood waiting for tomorrow's pickup.

Among them was something blue.

Denim? Jeans?

Marie! Found her!

Now, how to get her? Tiptoeing, Scorch moved slowly, so slowly she felt her joints creak. Ten yards away. She pulled her pistol in case Marie saw or heard her and tried to run or shoot. Otherwise, Scorch would use her scissors. Delicious irony if the last Tigress, priding herself on cold steel, died from a lowly pair of shears.

Yes, it was Marie. Even in the purple of late twilight, Scorch knew it was her. And they were still alone. The shots of a few moments ago had driven people—even the homeless—from the streets, from their windows, giving her a few minutes of privacy for this most intimate act. From far away she heard a siren.

She had only a minute or two to do it, or leave and forget it forever.

She crept closer, careful as a cat stalking a bird.

She heard sobbing, grunting. Not-quite-human sounds from a not-quite-human creature. Only five yards away. Four. Two.

Had to be careful. Scorch recalled that dream with Marie shooting her in the chest and belly, the final injustice.

Marie, bent over and doing something to her leg, heard or sensed Scorch and started to turn, to raise her arm.

Scorch planted a kick in Marie's kidney, followed by another to the back of her neck. Marie's head shot forward, cracking on the pavement, as something shiny and metallic clattered across the concrete. Her gun!

Scorch booted her again. And again.

Then she grabbed Marie's hair and yanked her head back—as she had done with Eric, except this time Scorch meant business. Exposing the tawny throat, Scorch placed her scissors' tip on a bulging jugular vein—quick death if punctured. "Hey, Marie, remember me? Got any last words for your adoring public?"

"No . . . !"

"Eloquent to the last! Jackass that you are, you even shot the nice policewoman who tried to save your life, which isn't even worth the price of a bullet." Scorch increased the scissors' pressure, waiting to feel it pierce flesh and then the rubbery tube of blood vessel. "I'd let you say a prayer, but what demon would listen to yours? Look at the bright side—not only am I ridding the earth of vermin, I'm saving a child. I left little Kala with the triage nurse at the hospital, who's probably got her to Social Services by now."

Marie tried to claw free, so Scorch slammed her head

once, twice, against the ground. What beautiful music a hollow skull can make. She kept thrashing, so Scorch banged her temple against the concrete a third time and Marie lay still. Great! Where was the fun in slitting the throat of an unconscious person? Marie was cheating her even of this. Like Nancy, Marie should be aware of her life spurting from her.

Scorch cocked her arm, waiting. . . .

"Suzanne! Don't!"

Cops! Not now! Hell!

Eric, ten feet away, more scared than when she'd raped him.

"Go away, Eric. This is a private moment. My life's work."

He inched forward, sweaty, nervous. "You're *my* life's work."

"Brother, you never give up."

"Suzanne, you do this and you're a murderer, just like her."

"Got news for you. I already am, or have you forgotten?"

"No! You're not. Please. For the sake of your soul."

Soul? He lived in a dreamworld. "I have no soul anymore." She jabbed the scissors at Marie's breast and a red pinpoint glistened on the unconscious woman's white T-shirt, blossoming into a wet rose. "This monster took it. She and those others."

"No. They can't take your soul. You have to surrender it."

"Eric, shut up. Babbling all the time about fairy-tale stuff." She raised the scissors and waved it around her at the filthy alley. "THIS is the real world."

"Babbling? So why haven't you already murdered her?"

"Temporary insanity."

"You always said you wanted Marie punished, imprisoned. Hear that?" Sirens again. Closer. "She will be now. Why are your hands and arms so bloody?"

331

She wiped them on Marie's jeans. "Moreno . . . is she dead?"

"Lucy! What happened?"

"What do you think? This bitch shot her. I taped her up for now, but she needs a hospital, quick."

Eric looked behind him. "She's down that alley?"

"Hey, if she dies, it's murder one. How's that for justice? Otherwise, Marie goes to Midland Knolls and makes your life miserable until you retire or get a coronary. Meanwhile . . . Moreno becomes worm food. That's your society, your justice." She raised the scissors again, psyching herself for the plunge.

Eric ran partway to Moreno, then turned, paused, his hands out to her. "I have to help Lucy. Suzanne, for your own sake, leave. There will be justice. You believe in justice."

"I did once, when I still believed in God."

"For Nancy's sake. Killing Marie won't bring her back, but her soul's in heaven, watching. What would she want you to do?"

"Huh?" Scorch froze. He was ruining it for her. "Who knows? Everybody always says 'What would the dead person want?' News flash. They're dead. They don't want anything anymore."

"You're twenty-three, free for three weeks. You've escaped. Use your second chance. It's what Nancy would have wanted."

True. Nancy would disapprove if she were here now. Nancy never held a grudge, and if anyone was in heaven, it was she.

Nancy and Eric, the two people she couldn't say "no" to.

Nancy versus Marie. Eric versus Karen. Some choice.

Damn! She released Marie's hair and stood. "Damn you, Eric! Every time, with your Talmudic quotes and proverbs.

You're got an answer for every occasion, don't you? Dr. Hallmark."

"No, but I'm glad I had the right one this time. If I never have another, I'll die happy."

"You stick around here much longer, you may get your wish all too soon." Even with his lady friend bleeding, he had stayed to keep alive whatever he saw in her still worth saving. Maybe she did deserve a second chance. He won, after all.

"We'll try it your way. 'Bye, Eric. Thanks." When he ran to help Moreno, Scorch took off down to Fordham Road. She flagged a cab, grateful there was no more blood on her hands.

"Where to, lady?" asked the driver.

"Manhattan." Got to give an address. Why not? "St. Patrick's Cathedral. I need to give thanks."

Lucy saw that light again, hot, huge, now taking up half the sky. Lots of scuffling. Was heaven crowded? Maybe it was hell?

"We're getting a solid pulse." It was a woman's voice. Mrs. Saint Peter? "She's no longer defibrillating. No more epinephrine. What's her blood pressure now?"

"Eighty-five over fifty."

"ALL RIGHT! Beth Goodman does it again! Tying off that punctured artery brought her back. This is the greatest emergency-room team in the universe!"

"Dr. Goodman, I think she'll make it."

"Of course she will. Lucy, you hear that?"

"She's still out, Doctor."

"Hearing is the one sense that always functions. Asleep, unconscious, comatose—they all hear. Right, Lucy? Let's stitch her up. Between the gunshot wound and those chunks the rats chewed out of her, she won't be wearing any more bikinis on the beach, but at least she'll live another thirty, forty years."

Lucy squinted against the blazing sun, discovering it to be an overhead light, thousands of candlepower of incandescence illuminating a hospital ER.

The doctor's voice again, above her, her head eclipsing the overhead lamp for an instant. "Tell the cops and the shrink waiting outside that she'll recover." A hand clutched Lucy's, securing her to Planet Earth. "You're a lucky lady, Lucy Moreno."

Epilogue

The only sounds were the murmuring of old women, the clink of their glass rosary beads, and the hiss of guttering candle wicks. Scorch lit a taper and held it to another candle on the altar. It flared before settling into a steady flame, filling the air with the scent of beeswax. Scorch watched the wick dance, recalling that Lucifer was once the Bearer of Light, so fire was His true and loyal friend. Fire helped Man learn and thus rise above other animals, so Lucifer must be the Lord of Knowledge.

So those who worshiped it must worship Him. Of course.

She muttered prayers for the souls of all who had died in this affair, and of course for Eric, her spiritual stepfather, even if he still spent all his time these past few weeks visiting those damaged by life, especially the convalescing policewoman.

Ah, Eric, what are we to do with you?

Satisfied with her religious bit, Scorch left the church, the gnarled women huddled in the pews barely glancing at her.

335

What would they have done had they known the Devil's daughter had just passed among them?

Probably nothing.

Scorch stepped out onto the road paved with good intentions.

THE CRIMINALIST

WILLIAM RELLING JR.

Detective Rachel Siegel is a twelve-year veteran of the San Patricio Sheriff's Department. But she's never seen anything like the handiwork of the Pied Piper, the vicious serial killer who's been terrifying that part of California for months. Because she's the best at what she does, it's now her job to catch this maniac—but she has very personal reasons, too, for wanting him stopped

Kenneth Bennett works for the Department of Neuropsychiatry at St. Louis's Washington University. There's something special about the Pied Piper case that draws Bennett almost against his will to the west coast. He has no choice but to help Siegel in her frantic search—even if it gets both of them killed in the process.

BODY PARTS
VICKI STIEFEL

They call it the Grief Shop. It's the Office of the Chief Medical Examiner for Massachusetts, and Tally Whyte is the director of its Grief Assistance Program. She lives with death every day, counseling families of homicide victims. But now death is striking close to home. In fact, the next death Tally deals with may be her own.

Boston is in the grip of a serial killer known as the Harvester, due to his fondness for keeping bloody souvenirs of his victims. But many of those victims are people that Tally knew, through her work or as friends. Tally realizes there's a connection, a link that only she can find. But she'd better find it fast. The Harvester is getting closer.

- -

ANDREW HARPER
RED ANGEL

The Darden State Hospital for the Criminally Insane holds hundreds of dangerous criminals. Trey Campbell works in the psych wing of Ward D, home to the most violent murderers, where he finds a young man who is in communication with a serial killer who has just begun terrorizing Southern California—a killer known only as the Red Angel.

Campbell has 24 hours to find the Red Angel and face the terror at the heart of a human monster. To do so, he must trust the only one who can provide information—Michael Scoleri, a psychotic murderer himself, who may be the only link to the elusive and cunning Red Angel. Will it take a killer to catch a killer?

ISOLATION
CHRISTOPHER BELTON

It was specially designed to kill. It's a biologically engineered bacterium that at its onset produces symptoms similar to the flu. But this is no flu. This bacterium spreads a form of meningitis that is particularly contagious—and over 80% fatal within four days. Now the disease is spreading like wildfire. There is no known cure. Only death.

Peter Bryant is an American working at the Tokyo-based pharmaceutical company that developed the deadly bacterium. Bryant becomes caught between two governments and enmeshed in a web of secrecy and murder. With the Japanese government teetering on the brink of collapse and the lives of millions hanging in the balance, only Bryant can uncover the truth. But can he do it in time?

RAGE
STEVE GERLACH

In some ways Ben is just like a lot of other guys in his college. He is a little awkward around girls, but he keeps trying and hoping that someday soon he will find the love of his life.

But in one very important way Ben isn't like other guys at all. Lately he's been thinking a lot about some pretty awful things . . . and he's bought a gun. His loneliness has become bitterness, and his resentment has turned to hatred. It is all boiling up inside him and it's only a matter of time before he explodes. Then it will be just a question of who will be the first to die.

CHINA CARD

THOMAS BLOOD

With the Russian economy in a shambles, and the hard-line leaders in power, renegade KGB operatives an ultra-secret document detailing the exact location of over one hundred tactical nuclear weapons secretly placed in the U.S. during the height of the Cold War. Thousands of miles away, in Washington, D. C., a young prostitute is found brutally murdered in a luxury hotel. The only clue—a single cufflink bearing the seal of the President. These seemingly unrelated events will soon reveal a twisting trail of conspiracy and espionage, power-brokers and assassins. It's a trail that leads from mainland China to the seamy underbelly of the Washington power-structure . . . to the Oval Office itself.

___4782-9 $6.99 US/$8.99 CAN

Dorchester Publishing Co., Inc.
P.O. Box 6640
Wayne, PA 19087-8640

Please add $2.50 for shipping and handling for the first book and $.75 for each book thereafter. NY, NYC, and PA residents, please add appropriate sales tax. No cash, stamps, or C.O.D.s. All orders shipped within 6 weeks via postal service book rate. Canadian orders require $2.50 extra postage and must be paid in U.S. dollars through a U.S. banking facility.

Name _____
Address_____
City_____ State _____ Zip _____
I have enclosed $ _____ in payment for the checked book(s).
ayment __must__ accompany all orders. ❏ Please send a free catalog.
CHECK OUT OUR WEBSITE! www.dorchesterpub.com

An Execution of Honor

Thomas L. Muldoon

They were a Marine Force Recon unit under the CIA's control, directed to maintain the power of a Latin American dictator, despite his involvement in the drug trade and a partnership with Fidel Castro. When rebel forces drove the dictator into the jungles, the unit led the holding action while his army was evacuated. But before he left, he tortured and killed two of the Marines. Now the unit wants justice—but Washington wants to return the dictator to power. So the surviving Force Recon unit members set out on their own to make the dictator pay. Both the United States and Cuba want the surviving unit members stopped at all costs. But who will be able to stop an elite group of Marines trained to be the most effective warriors alive?
